No Men of God

Dwight Mathieu

ISBN: 099141201X

ISBN-13: 978-0-9914120-1-3

For Christopher

I gotta get away from this day-to-day runnin around,
everybody knows this is nowhere.

-Neil Young

1

The Rabbit

To: reese.becker@ncis.us.gov

Dear Dad,

Sorry it's been awhile since I've emailed. You know how that goes. I've been really busy here without much down time, but I've finally completed advanced training. Thought I would let you know I was 2nd in classroom instruction and 1st in field exercises. I did especially well in something called Approach and Apprehend, where I earned 17 shells and 1 takeout. You might know about this, it's sort of like graduating Summa Cum Laude. Because of the takeout I'll get my choice of assignments, but they haven't told me the choices yet.

I was supposed to go to a closed commencement ceremony tomorrow, but they ordered me to attend a special meeting with a Navy Admiral instead. His name is Keeler. I was thinking you might have heard of him.

The other agents in my group received their station assignments already and they got to take a 10-day leave. Marshall Dudek told me that I probably won't get a leave.

Anyway, that's all I know right now, but I'll contact you as soon as they let me and when I receive any news that I can share. Maybe I'll be able to call you from wherever I end up. I love you Dad.

Your son,

Marty

Thirty-hours earlier…

The windowless cabin of the helicopter wouldn't allow Martin Ian Becker, who was soon to graduate from FLETC-the Federal Law Enforcement Training Center in Brunswick Georgia, to watch the sun come up over the horizon, nor did it give him a preview of the surface as they set down in the Georgia marsh. When the door slid open and his feet hit the ground, he scanned the landscape and quickly determined that the solid earth where he stood was one small sandy island amongst several others, scattered across a sea of reeds carved up by a zigzagging stream of shallow tidewater. The reeds around him were waving furiously in the wind from the rotor blades.

Straight across the expanse of the marsh, out toward the horizon, he saw the mouth of the crooked stream where it meets the Altamaha River. To the far left he saw a larger island, maybe five hundred meters in diameter, rising up out of the marsh and bearing a stand of tall green pines. To the far right was a darker place, a swamp area lined with river oaks dripping strands of gray Spanish moss. Behind the oaks, he saw the tops of spindly pines, half dead from constant immersion in the brackish water, yet rising up from the dark. The whole of this low-lying area appeared solemn and evil; most mammals probably wouldn't go in there willingly.

Marty wore a small waterproof pack belted onto his back. It contained a can of chigger spray, a snakebite kit, a seven-inch folding Buck knife, a monocular infrared night vision lens, a GPS based Emergency Locator Transmitter, a spool of 50 lb test fishing line, a Bic lighter, a bottle of water, and an apple. At his waist, in the back, hung his 9mm Walther pistol; a remarkably resilient weapon, issued that day in case of a confrontation with a non-human *element*. His black leather boots were laced tightly around the legs of his camouflage fatigues. A black half-sleeve spandex shirt gripped his upper body and was tucked in tightly. What little exposed flesh remained was covered with shoe black.

Marty and the other five trainees who jumped from the helicopter were beginning their last mission before becoming U.S. Marshals Service Special Operations Group Agents. After graduation they would, technically, remain deputies, but this special group had come into existence after the advent of terrorism on U.S. soil. The outcome of this, their final exercise in Approach and Apprehend training, or A&A as it was called in camp, would one way or another ordain them; they would be SOG Agents regardless of the results. But their work today would also determine the quality of their assignment after graduation. Mission success would give them a choice between postings. Failure would leave their destiny in the hands of someone else. The pressure was an upside down pyramid with the weight of their career possibilities bearing down on a single exercise.

The trainees knew all about the man they would pursue that day, the so-called *Rabbit*. His name was John Christian and he had a perfect record three years running. He had not been 'apprehended' or 'taken out' in fifteen previous exercises. All of the prior trainees had been painted by his CO2-fired paint gun long before they could pin him down. Marty was determined not to repeat history. He was going to get this guy and anything short of a takeout would be unacceptable. Certainly Christian was equally determined; he had a hell of a streak going and would surely do anything necessary to keep it alive. This Rabbit would not make a foolish error. 'If I were him,' Marty told himself, 'I'd be ruthless.'

In a strategy meeting the day before, the trainees had carefully selected a sequence of standard textbook maneuvers designed to flush out a perpetrator in a swamp. Afterward Marty studied again the mission notes from previous A & A exercises with this Rabbit and found that all of the tactics the earlier groups had deployed hadn't brought him down.

"Coach, this strategy won't work on Christian," Marty told his training instructor after dinner that night. "He's too good."

"Just stick with the plan Becker," the instructor said irritably. "If you guys execute properly, you'll have the advantage." Marty didn't agree and was certain the instructor only wanted to avoid convening another tactical meeting. 'Lazy fuck,' he thought.

Now, standing on the sandy island, Marty had arrived at decision time. His teammates scurried for cover with their hands over their eyes, fighting off the sand whipped around by the helicopter as it lifted off again. They're good guys, he thought, and in the end they'll make good agents. But today, in this case, he was certain he'd be better off alone.

As the helicopter departed and the group leader went down on one knee to read his map, Marty carefully stepped away toward the reeds, dropped low behind a mound of pampas grass, crab walked across the muddy sand to the edge of the tidal stream and slid into the water on his belly. For the next twelve hours, he wouldn't be seen again.

By mid-afternoon, he'd been floating on his belly most of the day, pulling himself along by his hands aided by the flow of the stream. The water was a tepid 80 degrees, but being immersed in it for so long had caused his body temperature to drop. His lower jaw and cheeks were trembling uncontrollably and he was making more noise than prudent in his struggle to advance. He would pause occasionally to survey the area over top of the reeds and confirm his position, which helped temporarily, but he would need to get out of the water completely very soon. When he floated near an outgrowth of tall fescue on a small sand bar he pulled himself onto it and sat in the midst of the grass, stripped himself naked, and flattened his clothes to warm them. As long as he didn't make any commotion, the tall grass would conceal him there, shaking pitifully as the sun began to warm his wilted skin. Struggling to find the apple in his pack, he finally retrieved it and bit it in half with one chomp, then put the rest back for later. The juice stung his raw fingers. Examining himself, he saw how the hours in the water had affected his feet and penis. 'Jesus,' he whispered, 'talk about friggin prunies.'

The sun began to restore him as he lay on his back, basking in its warmth. For nearly an hour, he drifted in and out of shallow slumber, then awoke with a start as sobriety gripped him, suddenly becoming aware of his naked vulnerability. He brought himself into a crouch position and peered through the reeds for a look around.

Approximately one hundred meters in the distance, the winding stream began to spread out. Another few hundred meters further, he saw it converge with the Altamaha. In the distance, a shrimp boat was making its way along the river to the ocean. Over his left shoulder, to the northwest, was the high ground he noted when they touched down, and to his immediate right, the moss-draped oaks framed the much darker place, the swamp he still couldn't see into, hidden as it was in the shadows underneath.

He sat down to pull his pants on. The process was arduous because everything was saturated and caked with muddy sand. His socks and boots were particularly troublesome and his impatience only added to the problem. After finally tying his bootlaces, he reached for his shirt and fanny pack, but froze as a minor commotion alerted him. He rose slowly in a half crouch and looked through the grass toward the high ground. Initially, he saw a group of noisy crows taking flight from the pines on the south side of the high ground. 'Couldn't be Christian,' he thought, 'no way would he would be that careless.' Then five humans appeared at the edge, stepping into the marsh, seemingly unconcerned that they were out in the open and visible. He pulled the monocular out of his pack, switched it to daylight and brought his teammates into view. A splattering of fluorescent pink paint became obvious on the hip of one of them. Pink was this Rabbit's color. Apparently Christian had painted all of them and it wasn't even dark yet.

Marty scanned the area around his position with the monocular, being methodical, making two compete revolutions. At one point he noticed an irregular movement in the reeds, a slight flash of the stalks shifting unnaturally, then nothing further. He sat down again and calculated his next move. It was likely, he thought, that Christian would have painted the others maybe an hour or so before they found each other and made their way out of the woods. After dispatching the five, he would have moved out, knowing that the sixth man was not with the group and further work remained. That could have been him in the grass a minute ago, or, 'shit,' Marty thought, 'it could have been a fuckin gator.' As he slid back into the water, a chill swept through his mid-section once again. But it was only fleeting; his heart was pumping strongly, and adrenaline now fended off the cold.

Marty's gut told him Christian would head for the swamp. Reports from earlier missions had mentioned it. The disturbance in the reeds might confirm this, though he also knew it could be unrelated. He decided to trust his intuition. Putting himself in the Rabbit's shoes, he would certainly try to hide in a place where no one else would want to go. Marty chose to make his way toward the area where the stream met the river, then head south along the riverbank and enter the dark swamp from the rear.

At the edge of the river the fescue grass receded, requiring him to crawl between patches of scrub pines and vegetation. The sun was disappearing behind the pines that stood tall over the high ground. Under the dense vegetation, the swamp was enveloped in early gloaming. With his face close to the earth as he crawled along in relative darkness, the soil took on a different smell: that of decaying organic matter. The sphagnum compressed under the weight of his elbows, bringing to mind the fresh prospect of coming face to face with a non-human element as mentioned in the mission briefing. He reached behind his back and pulled out the 9mm, then elbowed his way to the edge of the swamp, gun first.

Darkness was setting in quickly and with it, an increased urgency to find a place to stake out, as the swamp surface would soon become unmanageable without light. He needed a place that afforded him both good cover and good visibility, enabling him to observe any movement by Christian without exposing himself. When the soft soil finally turned to mud and his elbows began to sink in, Marty got to his feet and stepped into ankle deep black water. Then he made his way toward an island situated about thirty feet off the point of a peninsula, thinking the island would be suitable as a strategic hideout.

En-route, shrouded in the semi-darkness of the forest swamp and trudging through knee-deep water, he stumbled and almost fell over an old stump just below the surface. If Christian was in the area he had surely heard the commotion. He gathered himself and within twenty feet of the island, the bottom began rise up as he approached it. He quickened his pace, feeling vulnerable out in the open. With mere steps to go, he heard the unmistakable dull thump rendered by the discharge of a paint gun. He didn't need to turn to find out what it was; he'd recognize the sound anywhere. A plumping splash in the brackish water to his left followed immediately and he instinctively broke into a run, weaving left and right, then dove into the nearest cover. Crashing head first, he shielded his eyes and face, leaving his shoulders and forearms to take the brunt of the damage. The hard branches of a dead pine tree scraped across his upper body. As he landed against the trunk of another tree, the spiny limb protrusions tore into his flesh. He let out a groan, but then gritted his teeth and managed to keep from groaning again.

Everything hurt. His hands, face, arms and shoulders were scratched and bleeding. Blood dripped down his side from a small puncture wound just below his ribs. Then, coming to grips with the fact that none of the injuries were serious, he rolled over onto his stomach and got up on his hands and knees. After pulling out the infra-red monocular, he slowly did a full 360 degree turn to examine his location. He was in the midst of intertwined tree limbs that he had dived into, making it very difficult to move quietly. To his left, just beyond a slight thinning in the branches, he saw an opportunity. A stump perhaps three feet in diameter and a fallen tree next to it provided the cover he sought. Moving quickly, he tucked the lens in his left hand and rolled toward the opening in the brush. Up on all fours, he frog-hopped toward the stump, landing behind it with little grace, but feeling protected, at least for the moment. He checked himself thoroughly and found no sign of paint.

"I think I missed the little fucker," Christian whispered to himself. He had been in this swamp so many times he knew every square inch of it and thought he had seen every possible move by a trainee, but this was the first who had tried to come in from that direction. One fool had even tried to wait in ambush by digging a foxhole in the mud. Every scoop of dirt the kid took out of the hole was replaced by swamp water. Christian had sneaked up on that one and painted him squarely in the buttocks as he was bent over digging.

Christian was conflicted now, though, concerned that Marty might be hurt. He knew the lay of the land and the danger of moving in the dark. He could visualize the trainee skewered on a tree limb. On the other hand, he could be just fine; banged up a little maybe, but breathing, conscious, and able. He realized time had become an enemy. Hurrying to get to the trainee could result in the end of his streak. He finally decided that the kid wouldn't die in the ten minutes it would take to reach him cautiously. Listening without so much as a breath, he heard nothing further past the first groan.

He knew it was useless to follow Marty's path to the island. It simply wasn't safe to enter from that direction, as the kid had just learned. The only way to enter tactically was to turn back toward the oaks, cross over from the point of the peninsula and go in from the other side. The going was much easier over that route and he'd be able to keep the entire area in his sights. He would also have a clear shot, even if the kid had started to move off the island in retreat. He flipped down his infrared goggles, gave the switch a push and waited briefly as the headpiece produced a faint whirr. The lenses illuminated his surroundings.

By this time, Marty had collected himself. The stump and the heavy brush to the rear provided decent cover. He had some pain from the gouges and bruises, but didn't feel it as much at the moment as he would in the days to come. Looking through the monocular, he could see there was no sign of Christian on his side of the fallen tree. He also knew it was nearly impossible to gain access to the island from the direction he had come. The tree limbs were so dense that even a small dog couldn't slip through unscathed, assuring him that if the Rabbit were in pursuit, which he surely was, he would have to find another route. Marty turned himself around staying low and slid the monocular over the crotch of a tree limb, putting his eye to the lens.

"Son of a bitch," he whispered. About one hundred meters away a figure was gliding through the trees and around the forest debris. The adrenaline had Marty's heart beating in his throat; he took a slow deep breath to regain control. He couldn't make out specific details except for the paint gun pointed straight in the air and the fact that Christian was having absolutely no difficulty navigating. In fact, he easily slid around trees without making a sound. 'He must have goggles,' Marty realized, 'of course, shit, he's got goggles.' When comparing the Rabbit's superior technology to his own outdated little infrared monocular, Marty became painfully aware of his disadvantage. But a chink in the armor was also exposed.

With little time to spare, he analyzed quickly. Christian was advancing by approximately three steps every ten seconds. 'If he's one hundred meters away, he'll be on me in about three minutes.' He slid back down behind the tree, quietly made his way back to the huge decaying tree trunk and took position directly behind it. He had less than three minutes to finalize his plan of engagement.

After crossing the shallow water and entering the island from the rear, Christian slowed his pace. He surveyed the area where Marty crashed through the underbrush and saw no sign of life. Stopping twenty feet short of the fallen tree behind which Marty hid, Christian also considered using it as cover, but then hesitated. He picked a spot low on the tree where he could peer over the trunk then stepped over and eased his head into a safe position to look.

Waiting patiently, Marty saw the leading edge of the Rabbit's goggles come over the edge of the tree. He flicked his Bic lighter and simultaneously pressed the nozzle on the can of chigger spray. The alcohol and other chemicals in the spray ignited, sending a ferocious stream of fire toward Christian. The flame itself did no damage but, with the ultra-high magnification of his goggles, the flash completely blinded him. As Christian instinctively jerked his head back and away from the explosion of light, he lost his balance and fell head first against a broken and pointed limb protruding from the dead tree. With all his weight in motion, the jagged end of the limb struck him just behind the left ear. The surprise of the blinding light and the pain of the blow disoriented him, making him unable to control his fall or prepare any kind of defense. Within a split second, Marty bolted over the tree, picked up the paint gun, put a foot on top of Christian's chest, pointed the gun at him and yelled, "DON"T MOVE!!!" louder than necessary. Towering over the Rabbit, he reached for his ELT device, uncapped it and pressed the button. The extraction team would be on the way.

It was a defining moment for Marty in the back of the Blackhawk on the return to base. He felt bad for Christian, the hit he had taken from the tree limb had cut him badly and he was in wicked pain. The five trainees with fluorescent pink paint spots on their fatigues were sitting along one wall of the noisy chopper. They peered at Christian from time to time, lying on his back in the middle of the floor; his head being tended by a medic. Marty sat alone against the opposite wall, wet and muddy, covered with scratches and shivering in the air rushing through the open door. He was beat up. But he had graduated differently from the others. The casualty of his graduation was lying on the floor in front of him: the only true failure of the group.

2

The Girls

At 9:30 p.m., in Cruz Bay, St. John, U.S. Virgin Islands, it was well past normal closing time for the small rental car office and well past the time most single women leave work on a Friday. Anya Sutton was still there however, and once again silently bemoaning the fact that no-one else in the family works as hard as she does. Through the screen door she heard music out in the street. It came from *Fred's Discotec,* an open air dance club on the other side of the main square which makes up the heart of town. When the idea of heading over there crossed her mind, she left the pile of un-posted receipts on the counter, locked the front door, moved to the back room, disrobed, and stood under the shower.

The heated cistern water felt stimulating, provocative. Her soapy hands on her body provided confidence, validating her beauty, empowering her toward the night. She knew men couldn't resist her. Other women wanted what she had.

Over at Fred's, Anya's twin sister Yendi, a beauty in her own right but lacking the same genetic edge, already had the place whipped into frenzy. She wore overly suggestive clothing and her perfume was much too heavy, making her cheap, made-up, and therefore easily figured out. Her scent would alert any man instantly, but the good ones usually lost interest just as quickly. That's where Anya would come in with her seemingly authentic charm. Almost without fail, the best man of the evening would eventually be drawn to her; leaving poor Yendi to be entertained by the less worthy.

Tonight would be no different. Yendi heated up the place early; Anya walked in later, fashionably. She arrived in just two pieces of clothing and moved perfectly on the dance floor, providing seductive notions of what lay beneath her short black skirt and loose silk top. Any man she danced with would not be satisfied with just one dance. But she wasn't hasty, she'd spread her attention evenly, setting up a cool intrigue between would-be suitors, making them work to edge each other out. And the winner, if there was one, would be the smoothest of the lot. She wasn't attracted to impatience.

By midnight, everyone was loose and in full party mode. The dim light and thumping reggae hip-hop caused patrons to sway about the room naturally, more or less in unison. The open walls allowed a stray tropical breeze through occasionally, bringing with it the lilting skunky smell of ganja being smoked in the street. The party spilled onto the sidewalk, where nearly everyone stepped out at one time or another to partake in whatever roach was being passed around, returning to the dance floor a few minutes later with a mellower attitude.

One group didn't indulge. Anya noticed them earlier at the end of the bar. They were clearly military, on leave, wearing garish Hawaiian shirts; drinking, talking, laughing, but behaving as gentlemen. The most interesting sailor stood in the middle of the group, taller by three or four inches over the rest. He was handsome with short hair, and an imposing, muscular, yet trim build. The body language of the group told her he was the natural leader. His height made him visible from everywhere she danced and she tried deftly to catch his eye on a couple of previous trips to the floor, but he paid little attention. When he glanced across the way while engaged in conversation, his gaze paused at her no longer than it paused at anything or anyone else. It was his confident indifference that attracted her most.

Anya looked to her sister and nodded subtly in the sailor's direction, alerting her in a conversation only they understood. Yendi took up the challenge to engage him gamely, welcoming the lighthearted competition, one that had played out many times before. She strutted over to Midshipman Vincent Marini and planted herself in front of his tall frame. Smiling seductively and staring straight into his brown eyes, she slid her hand inside his waistline and pulled him onto the dance floor. Her actions spoke loudly of her intentions. The other four sailors cheered for him, standing on the sidelines, egging him on, chanting, "Go get her Vinny!" He answered with a crooked grin. They reveled in his prowess and high-fived over his success. Vinny was always the one who left with a hot woman. On board the USS Abraham Lincoln, he was a legend.

After a time of dancing Marini tired of the garish magnetism of Yendi and became entranced by the subtle differences in Anya, who replaced her sister playfully when the time was right. As their attraction gained momentum, Anya brushed herself against him discreetly in cadence with the music, previewing the fullness of her chest. She subtly unbuttoned his shirt one button at a time as they danced, exposing his ripped mid-section. Then she brushed against him time and again, examining the fullness of his arousal, testing the waters, deciding if she would take the full plunge, knowing all the while he was ready. They rubbed softly and chatted in a steamy cocoon on the floor. As the crowd thinned in the wee hours of the night it would be her call as to where they went from there.

Marini's mates had long since separated. Two of them had each found a woman as well, one was struggling to make time with Yendi, and one made his way back to the hotel early, destined to settle for self-pleasure with an adult movie on pay per view.

Jared Sutton, a tall, strapping West Indian man and the twins' older brother, sat alone at the far end of the bar in the dim light; stoned, drunk, surly and stewing. The twins loved their brother, they loved his kind and caring heart, his energy for liberating the West Indian people - when he was sober. But they knew the other side of him. Alcohol and weed brought out his intense, over-protective ways. They had warned him they would call the police if he interfered again. He watched from afar as they toyed with Marini, as they teased him and brought him to arousal. He wondered which one of them would be sullied by the white man's fluids tonight and, as the evening wore on, he figured it out. It would be Anya. He watched with contempt as she slipped out the side door with her prize.

As Anya guided Marini through the rental car lot next door to the club, he stopped her. They would make it no further. It was too dark; there had been too much rubbing, too much enticement, too much close breathing and sexy talk. The earlier gentle foreplay led to kissing now and groping by the door to a parked car, which in turn led to the back seat, where in short order Anya laid herself out passionately for Marini, taking it all. Their rapture was pure, animalistic; they devoured each other in uninhibited hunger. Their groans floated out of the car and across the lot. The passion was so energetic that Anya found herself, her head, being thrust against the opposite door, bumping into the handle each time he moved into her. At first, it was only slightly uncomfortable, not enough to outweigh the pleasure of his thrusts. In time though, the annoyance detracted from her pleasure and she needed to move, adjust, get into a position where it didn't hurt. She pulled herself up into him with her arms around his neck; letting his strength carry her, holding her away from the door.

As her orgasm arrived, she let go of his neck, unable to hold herself, unable to control her motions at all. With her release, the door handle again jabbed into the back of her head, breaking her pleasurable spasm, a frustrated and desperate 'ouch' took the place of one of the rhythmic moans she had been singing out. Hearing the distraction, Marini stopped to adjust, frustrated also, as close as he was to coming with her.

But he wasn't allowed to bring it back. From behind, crazed and demonic, Jared Sutton and two of his cronies grabbed Marini by the ankles and pulled him off her and out of the car. With his shorts wrapped around one ankle, he rolled in the dirt, still erect, too confused to avoid the toe of Jared's boot as it swung and buried into his stomach. The impact paralyzed him and he vomited.

He had no time to recover as another kick from another foot landed squarely and with full force in his back. The pain nearly made him pass out, or maybe it was the rapid exit of air from his lungs. Either way, Marini was defenseless, seeing green and knowing in his remaining consciousness, he was in for it.

Anya jumped out of the car in protest, yelling at her brother to stop. This wasn't Marini's fault; she wanted him there with her. Jared slapped her and she slammed hard against the car, dazed, then he returned his attention to Marini. Jared and his gang beat him badly, to unconsciousness, to the point where his face was completely smeared with blood.

Yendi, discovering the madness and fearful of what Jared might do if she interfered, watched from a distance until the pounding became unbearable. When she could no longer restrain herself, she ran up from behind and launched onto his back, digging her nails into his face. She was as crazed as he, swearing madly, wanting only that the cruelty would stop.

Jared struggled to take hold of her, finally succeeding in throwing her off over his head and sending her sprawling onto the ground, stunned by the impact. Reaching down with his huge hand, he grabbed her by the hair and reared back to slap her. Then he saw her face looking up at him, his little sister's face, horrified by what she knew was coming. Somewhere deep, he awoke from his insanity just in time - for her sake, for Vinny's sake.

He turned back to the bloody sailor and saw no response from him - no indication that life was still present. Jared lost interest in further beating, his rage replaced by a realization, a fear that he might have gone too far this time, that maybe this time, the bastard was dead.

3

Captain Ahab

In Guantanamo Bay, Cuba, it's hot and steamy every day in mid-June. In the back yard of his U.S. Navy provided home, Vice Admiral Allan C. Keeler lay in the shade on a hammock strung between two palm trees. A pesky fly kept him in a restless slumber as it continually landed and sipped from the tiny beads of sweat on his exposed chest and belly. He was about to give up the effort altogether and retire to the air-conditioned space inside his casa when his secure cell-phone, which he kept by his side at all times, gave off a warble.

"Keeler here," he said with a characteristic growl.

"Admiral, this is Stevens at the duty desk."

"What is it, Ensign?"

"Sir, I have a call on hold from a Captain James at the Coast Guard Station in Charlotte Amalie, St. Thomas. He asked for you…said it was important."

"What's it about?"

"He didn't brief me sir, just said he needed to talk with you and that it was a security matter."

"Do you have him on a secure line?"

"I don't know sir, he called me."

"Well call him back on a secure line and patch him back to me, I'll wait."

"Yes sir"

Keeler remembered the Coast Guard boys always panicked over the littlest things. The phone warbled a second time, "Keeler here," he said again.

"Admiral Keeler, this is Captain James, U.S. Coast Guard, Charlotte Amalie."

"I know who you are, Captain. You have a security matter in the Virgin islands on a Sunday afternoon?"

"Yes sir."

"Well I can't imagine why you're calling me, son, but go ahead."

James paused to phrase his words in a way that would express the importance of his case, without sounding like a freshman. "Admiral, have you heard of a group of radicals called the *Society to Free the Caribe?*"

Keeler couldn't imagine a true radical group operating in the Caribbean. "No," he answered with a chuckle.

"They're extremists. The members are scattered across St. Thomas, St. John, St. Croix, and some islands over on the British side. I've developed an informant on the inside. I think the group is planning some kind of disturbance, something to publicize their cause."

Keeler was incredulous. "What the hell are you talking about, an uprising? We don't have uprisings, not here in the Caribbean. Do you know what talk of that kind will do to tourism? Have you reported to Admiral Curtin in Washington?"

"No sir, you're the first I've told. I know you're an expert in counter-insurgency and hoped you might give me some insight. I have not alerted anyone in Washington because I'm afraid of what the response might be. The last thing we need down here is a destroyer cruising around."

"You are not thinking clearly, Captain." Keeler elevated his tone to a Full-Bird Admiral don't-fuck-around growl. "You get your ass over to your computer and fire off a report to your C.O. And don't get me involved in this."

"Admiral, it isn't that simple. You see one of your boys, a midshipman, was over on St. John on leave and got himself drunk, and..."

"I can't believe this," Keeler interrupted, "is this the first time you've seen a seaman get shit-faced on leave? And did you call on Sunday as a security matter to tell me about it?"

"But sir..."

"James, I am going to hang up now. If you have one of my sailors in your brig, get him on a supply boat to San Juan and I'll have our Security Force officers pick him up. And if I were you I'd contact Admiral Curtin, tell him what's going on and wait for orders. And leave the goddam uprisings to the goddam CIA."

"NO, Admiral!" James finally yelled, bordering on disrespect, "Admiral, please listen for a minute, sir. He raped a native. At least *they* say he did." This brought dead silence from Keeler and James continued. "Your sailor got into it pretty good at a local dance club and wound up with a West Indian woman who just happens to be the sister of one of the ringleaders of the SFC. It seems he started pawing her at the club, so she left. He followed her out into the parking lot, slapped her around, dragged her into an empty car and forced himself on her."

"Aw Christ. What's his name?" Keeler asked.

"Marini, Midshipman Vincent Marini."

"Where is he?"

"At our base clinic in Charlotte Amalie," said James. "Apparently the woman's brother, Jared Sutton, heard the commotion and ran to help her. He found Marini on top of her in the car and pulled him off. Then he and a couple of others beat the guy up badly. Another native found him balled up in a shopping cart in the parking lot at the local market and called me."

"Has he been arrested?"

"No sir, the police haven't been informed as far as we know. We collected the details from a bartender who was just getting off work when it happened; he and a couple of Rastafarians saw the whole thing and called me."

"What is Marini saying?"

"He can't talk." said James. "It's not like he's in a coma or anything, in fact the Doc says he'll be okay after a while. He has a few busted ribs and they broke his jaw and knocked out some of his teeth. They have to feed him through a tube for now and he can only see a little bit out of one eye."

"Jesus Christ. What does the woman say?"

"We can't find her. We spoke with her twin sister who said that the woman is too humiliated to speak with anyone. You know, some West Indians will persecute a women who has sex with a white man. It symbolizes slavery."

"So aside from the testimony of a native bartender and a couple of street junkies, do you have any other evidence that he raped her?"

"The Doc said there was dried semen on his groin…and vaginal secretion."

"Well, shit, Captain, the last time I had sex, the woman and I had semen and vaginal secretions on our groins too. That doesn't mean I raped her."

"I understand, sir," James replied. "There was also a note stuck in Marini's pocket. I'll read it to you.

'Just as the white man has raped our people throughout history, so this pig son of the white man has raped a beautiful child of our people. Just as this single deed has been avenged, so we will avenge your crimes against our culture.'

It's signed, James concluded, '*Society to Free the Caribe'*."

James allowed silence for a moment, and then continued. "So, you see sir, this is more than just a little trouble in paradise. I need some direction and I figured you were the best man to talk to. Do you still think I should notify Washington?"

"No," Keeler admitted. "If we blow the whistle on our man immediately, even if he *did* do it, we'll be giving them publicity. It'll help make a martyr out of the woman."

James felt validated. "Admiral, maybe I should contact my mole. He might be able to find out if the woman really was raped..."

"Mole? Forget the mole. Don't talk about this with anyone but me. They probably know about your informer. They'll feed you information through him to serve their purposes. Then, as soon as his usefulness is gone, so is he. The less you talk to him, the longer he'll live."

"Yes sir," James muttered.

"I'm going to send down a couple of officers in a marked aircraft to pick up Marini. I want you to put on a show that will make people think Marini is dead. In other words, we are coming down to pick up the body. I also want you to find the Sutton woman. Find out everything about her. Have her tailed. They'll figure it out, but they'll think it's consistent with a murder investigation. If they think Marini is dead, it'll confuse their plans and buy us some time."

"Have her followed, sir? I don't have anybody trained for that."

"Then do it yourself," Keeler said evenly, "and report back to me. I want to hear details of how you intend to move Marini and whatever you can find out about the woman by... 0900 tomorrow." James was beginning to second guess the wisdom of calling Keeler. It might have been safer to just report this to Washington and let Admiral Curtin deal with it.

"And, Captain," Keeler said.

"Yes sir?"

"You did the right thing."

"Ay, Admiral."

Keeler hung up the phone and dialed the duty desk. "Stevens? Call U.S. Marshall Willard Davis at the Justice Department in Washington. Use a secure line. The numbers are in my Outlook file. If he's not in his office; try to raise him at home. Connect me once you've made contact."

As Keeler sat on a kitchen stool pondering the events, he had the same misgivings as James; that it might be best to stay out of this thing and turn it over to Curtin. But he knew he couldn't. A scandal was brewing involving one of his men and therefore might also involve him. And, he remembered how it was for the Jamaicans when rumors of revolution sprouted in the late '70s. The Jamaican people didn't really want independence from the British; they just wanted a higher standard of living. It never happened and they suffered from the negative publicity. It took years for the tourism trade to rebound and he didn't want to see it happen again in the VI.

The phone rang. "Keeler here."

"Why the secure line?" Marshall Will Davis asked, "Whose wife are you sleeping with?"

Keeler laughed. "I figured it would be the only way to tear you away from your squeeze. How is Mary anyway?"

"It's *Kerrie,* you jerk, and she's fine, thanks."

Keeler decided that was enough small talk. "Will, have you ever heard of a group named the Society to Free the Caribe?"

"What's that, a new Rap group?"

"I'm not talking about that kind of group. I hear these guys are a little hornet's nest in the Virgin Islands. A seaman under my command stumbled into it while on leave. I need some background."

There was a long silence. When Davis spoke, there was trepidation in his voice. "First, tell me what you know and who told you."

Keeler summarized. His friend said little, except to ask for further details at certain parts. Davis seemed particularly interested in the

Sutton family. Keeler finished up in saying, "I think it might make sense for me to get involved, see if I can dissipate this thing before State or Interior gets down here and really makes a mess of it."

"What about Internal Affairs?" Davis asked.

"Have you ever seen what IA boys in dress uniform look like in the Virgin Islands? We'd be playing right into their hands. This *is* my area of expertise, you know."

"Yeah, I know."

"Will, I have a sailor who might see his next birthday in the brig and I'm not sure he should be there. He could be just a goat."

"Okay, I'll tell you what I can, but it's not a helluva lot." Keeler took out a pen.

"I've received a few classified advisories, mostly because we assign deputies to work with DEA."

"DEA is in this?"

"Yeah. Probably CIA too. The advisories always talk about the SFC in almost the same breath as the Medellín Cartel."

"These guys are peddling cocaine?" Keeler asked.

"I don't know, but the Assistant Secretary of State sent me an Information Request Packet yesterday, the main thrust of which was a directive to my office for estimates on how long it would take to have two Special Operations Group Deputies trained for undercover duty in the Caribbean. He also wanted to know about our field office on St. Thomas and what capabilities we have. I got this right after a DEA cautionary advisory, to the effect that their ops in the Virgin islands might be complicated by activities of the SFC."

"Complicated? What the hell does that mean?"

"Again, I don't know. Like I said, I get the DEA memos because we do joint ops with them sometimes. This SFC thing is so new, there's no deep background in the intelligence circulars; no history. But considering that State wants information on my assets, I figure something is coming pretty soon. We don't even have a field office on St. Thomas."

"Sec State wants undercover work? Why doesn't he just use CIA?"

"Believe it or not, CIA is stretched a little thin. And there's this thing, this law, about CIA not spying on American citizens. You've heard of law, right?"

"Who's going to train them?" Keeler asked and waited through the predictable silence.

"Train who? You mean my guys? Oh no. No way. You're not doing it. You'll turn them into agents and then they won't want to go back to being *just* a marshal."

"You want them to stay alive, don't you?"

"Yeah, but I want them back. If you get hold of them, they'll be gone for good,"

"I'll make them better."

"Yeah...and then you'll keep them."

"It'll work for both of us." Keeler was persuasive.

"I'll call you." Davis said, then hung up abruptly.

Keeler knew Davis would eventually see it as a good fit. He also knew he needed to at least make an effort to let someone know what was going on.

The Secretary of the Navy's office is an extremely busy place. The chances are that a vague advisory about the operation would sit unnoticed, especially if he sent it non-coded, unclassified. Keeler went to his laptop and wrote a cover-your-ass memo.

Dear Mr. Secretary:

In response to the possibility of improper conduct on the part of a seaman under my command, as of 1330 hours this day I have requested investigative assistance from the U.S. Marshall's office in Washington. A complete briefing will follow this investigation.

VA Allan C. Keeler

Guantanamo Bay, Cuba

6/14/13

Keeler emailed the advisory to the communications officer back at the base with instructions to file it on Monday along with the routine daily communiqués. This method would alert no one in particular, he thought, not even the clerks handling the filings, as routine advisories attract little attention.

The phone rang again, it was Davis. "That was quick," Keeler said.

Davis feared he'd regret this. "Where do you want the deputies to report?"

"Have them sent to me here at Gitmo. Don't send me any junk."

"First, we don't have junk in the Special Operations Group." Davis sneered. "Second, why don't you fly to FLETC in Georgia and pick them up yourself?"

"All right, I'll do that. And I'll remind you, these guys are going to get some of the best intelligence training available, so you get something out of this too."

"I figure the most I'll get out of it is that you'll solve the puzzle and I'll get credit for providing you with the talent to do it." Davis replied. "On the other hand, if you screw it up, it's not my department. I'm going to advise State that I'll have two undercover deputies trained and available at Charlotte Amalie in six weeks."

Keeler chuckled. "Hell, Will, they'll be trained in two weeks, they'll be veterans in four and this thing will be *over* in six."

"It better be." Davis was serious. "My two best, at FLETC, for your review, Tuesday, the day after tomorrow, 0800 hours."

"Thanks pal, I'll give you two shots a side at Congressional in the fall." Keeler said.

"I don't need two shots a side from you."

4

The Flyer

Pilots disagree about whether it's more difficult to fly low over water during the day or at night. Most say that it's more difficult during daylight because the smooth reflective surface of the water provides an unreliable altitude reference. But since the pilot can at least see something, he relies upon his eyesight instead of the radar altimeter, which could trick him into flying the aircraft into the water. Most pilots prefer flying low over water at night when they are not tempted to look out into the darkness. They then depend solely upon the reading of the radar altimeter, which is infinitely more accurate than the human eye.

This challenge notwithstanding, there is a safe zone between the surface of the ocean and about fifty-five feet above it. At this altitude, the deft of touch may fly, survive, and go undetected by radar continually monitored by U.S. agencies such as DEA and Homeland Security. But instant death is only an improper twitch of the hand away, as the tiniest error could cause the airplane to lose altitude, strike the water, and become mere flotsam scattered across the surface.

The safe zone is where highly skilled drug mules earn their living. Contrary to popular belief, these pilots aren't pot-head miscreants trained to do foul work for the drug Cartels, nor are they mavericks with black marks on their flying records or outcasts from commercial airlines. Most of them, the successful ones, are highly skilled and serious aviation professionals; some are former military pilots. They possess a love for pushing the envelope, are thrilled by the risk, and are able to command large sums of money for their services. They generally don't care what they're transporting. It's not about the cargo; it's about the rush of completing a mission behind enemy lines; getting the job done secretly and getting back safely. Each successful mission brings a big payoff, for sure. But the reward is soon forgotten; it is anti-climactic. Once a mission is complete, the next can't come too soon, as it's the rush from the action and not the result that feeds the addiction.

A mule usually receives part of his fee prior to take off and the balance upon delivery of the cargo. He knows that if anything improper should happen to the haul, or if he poses any security threat to his employer, the final payoff will be death instead of a bag of cash. To reinforce the point, the Cartel will stage a loss from time to time. In 2012, the St. Thomas police found a West Indian mule, Jacob Gainor, in a pool of blood on the Charlotte Amalie wharf. Gainor was trained in the British R.A.F. and became, for years afterward, a trusted pilot for the Cartel. But then he made the mistake of becoming too independent. After smartly and quietly accumulating piles of cash, he decided to start enjoying it. He demanded a lighter schedule. He bought a nice villa on a hillside overlooking Megan's Bay on St. Thomas and a new Porsche convertible, driving it to the airport with a little too much flair. He became indiscreet and, therefore, a security risk.

The Cartel decided Gainor would make a perfect example. On September 12, 2009 he asked for and received a night off from his normal Tuesday route between St. Thomas and Montserrat. In addition, his boss told him he should report to his contact to collect a bonus for many years of loyal service. When he went to meet his man that evening in Red Hook on the east side of St. Thomas, he discovered that his bonus was a Colombian necktie and a mouthful of his own genitals. The police found him later, his neck slit from ear to ear, his tongue pulled out through the opening, and his penis and testicles cut off and stuffed inside his mouth. The Cartel planted twenty ounces of cocaine in a closet in his villa for the police to find and then distributed a story within the organization that a shipment had been altered while in his custody.

So the hazards of being a drug pilot extend beyond the risk of low altitude flying. Retirement from this business comes at a time, generally, when the Cartel decides it's appropriate, and not before.

Conrad Sutton, however, the pilot at the controls this night, was a special case. The thrill had been gone for some time, he had accumulated a huge amount of cash, and he had developed other interests. The Cartel was so overwhelmed by his loyalty and quality service over the years, when he asked to retire, they said yes.

On this night, a particularly smooth night for flying, Sutton believed it would be his last at the controls of his well-worn and trustworthy Cessna 310; his last for the benefit of the Cartel anyway. As he scanned the instruments of the airplane, paying special attention, as always, to the radar altimeter, his memory traced back to the old days in the early 1970s. It was then that he first stepped into this life.

Sutton was born on the west side of St. John in one of a small collection of tin roof homes forming a village known as Calabash Cay. Not all the native children went to school in those days, but he did, at a Calvinist mission in Enighed (pronounced *anyhead*), and he proved to be a very good student. The missionary, Joseph Van Deek, sought out a college scholarship for him at the university on St. Thomas just a short ferry ride away. The boy excelled in engineering and upon graduation in 1970 was accepted into the U.S. Air Force and sent to training at Laughlin Flight School in Texas. Being an excellent student, with exceptional hand-eye coordination, pilotage came easy to him and he loved the thrill of flying.

The war in Vietnam continued to escalate and, after just twenty-eight weeks of flight training, he was strapped into the seat of an A-4 Phantom attack bomber and sent to southeast Asia, where he spent thirteen months in low altitude bombing and ground battle support missions. He earned the nickname *Yahman* from his fellow pilots, as that was his word for affirmative over the aircraft radio instead of "Roger". One afternoon during the rainy season, Sutton and a wing of three other A-4s were on a napalm mission in an area where the North Vietnamese Army traveled, just a few klicks west of Dac To, near the Ho Chi Minh trail in Cambodia. The attack wing would enter the area at two-hundred feet above ground level, four abreast. After release of their ordinance, the wing leader and two others were to peel off to the south. The fourth, in this case Sutton, would circle to the north and return. Slowing to 175 knots, Sutton would climb to five-hundred feet to take damage assessment photographs using the pod camera mounted on the belly of his plane. None of the pilots could understand the purpose of these pictures, especially after dispensing napalm. For in the short amount of time it took the damage assessment aircraft to circle north, slow down and climb, the area was fully in flames and producing dense black smoke. To make matters worse, the Viet Cong had quickly caught on to the maneuver. They had come to expect the return of one aircraft, so they simply waited.

"Gray Ghost to Yahman, is the film spent?" Sutton heard his wing leader over the headset. He felt the impact as a group of rounds hit the aircraft just after he released the exposure trip for the camera and although it seemed that he had full engine power, his flight controls were mushy and, within a few seconds, he could not make the jet climb.

"Yahman ta Gray Ghoost... yeah the can's full, but I taken a hit in the hydraulics, I think nobody gonna see these pictures, at the moment I cannot hold six hundred feet. I am, uh….maybe 4 klicks southwest of de target, heading two three zero at about three hundred knots. I gonna have to eject."

"Yahman, we'll call search, be safe, Gray Ghost out."

Gray Ghost quickly turned the other aircraft northwest to try to provide cover for Sutton and attempt to locate his parachute and ascertain his exact position. He then radioed search to scramble an extraction team and turned his plane to the southeast in order to make a second pass from the opposite direction over what he thought would be Sutton's position. All of them would soon have a problem with fuel. They would have enough to linger only a few minutes over the area and the extraction team was at least a half hour away.

Meanwhile, Sutton applied ten-percent flaps, helping gain him three hundred feet of altitude. At that moment, several thoughts went through his mind. He knew that with flaps out he could not maintain more than 150 knots airspeed, which would make him a sitting duck for VC ground fire. He also knew that, in this configuration and airspeed, he would not have enough fuel to make it back to base. Ejecting from the aircraft then, was likely to come sooner or later. But he had to wait until the last minute - until he slowed as much as possible - because at high speed and low altitude, the parachute might not have enough time to open and slow him before he hit the ground. He also knew that when he ejected, the G force of the parachute opening might cause him to lose consciousness momentarily as all of the blood rushed from his head to his feet, and therefore he might not be fully prepared to hit the ground properly when he landed. In the few seconds it took Sutton to analyze all of this, the F-4 had already slowed to 240 knots and was again losing altitude. He tried to apply more power, which in turn caused a tremendous buffeting in the airframe. He realized that the time had come, reached up to the canopy for the ejection mechanism, and pulled it.

Two essentials were in his favor. First, in the time between his communication with Gray Ghost and the ejection, another aircraft in the wing had returned to the point where the pilot could see Sutton eject and could pinpoint his exact position. Second, he ejected over a clear paddy area, so that when he hit the ground, there were no trees to impale him. However, being in a high speed descent in the parachute, when he landed, he was unable to control his impact with the ground. In the frantic collision, his right leg sank knee-deep into the paddy mud. The rapid forward momentum of his body bent his leg violently in the reverse angle, hyper-extending and completely destroying his knee joint.

When the extraction team pulled him out of the rice paddy, Sutton was conscious but in tremendous pain. They flew him back to base quickly and then to Hong Kong for surgery. After six weeks of recuperation, he received an honorable discharge from the Air Force and a hero's welcome when he limped off the ferry in St. John. He would limp for the rest of his life. His regional notoriety didn't escape the Cartel's notice and one day a rough looking Panamanian man with a pock marked face appeared at the doorstep of Sutton's family home, claiming to be the president of a Colombian air-freight company. He offered Sutton a job as a pilot with a very hefty salary attached. Later, Sutton learned the man's real identity. It was Manuel Noriega.

Sutton's reminiscing was interrupted by a harsh crackling voice in his headset. "Where is the little bird?" the voice asked.

Sutton clicked his yoke mounted microphone switch and replied "On the wing".

This timed and coded query was set up prior to Sutton's departure. He knew that the voice at the other end was that of Placido Orestes. He would broadcast on 131.45 megahertz at precisely 0400 hours, so that, given Sutton's scheduled departure time from St. Thomas; he would be approximately 125 nautical miles northeast of Bonaire when he received the message. If the first attempt garnered no reply, Orestes would broadcast again at 0415 and 0430. If no reply was received in three attempts, the mission would be scrubbed, and the delivery crew waiting at the small dirt airstrip thirty miles north of Cartageña would be sent back to an alternate position to await further orders. If Orestes received a reply, the crew would begin preparations for Sutton's arrival. Upon landing, he would be immediately ushered to a waiting car and driven to Cartageña. There, he would be fed and given a room, and allowed time to rest in preparation for the return trip at 1900 hours that same day. Solid sleep was essential, for the return flight from Cartageña to Montserrat was another five hours at the controls at fifty feet above sea level. While he slept, armed guards would stand watch over the aircraft until departure time.

The pickup for Sutton on this, his last trip to Cartageña, was 250 kilograms of nearly pure crystalline cocaine. Enough cocaine, after cutting, to supply Guadeloupe, Antigua, Puerto Rico and the British and U.S. Virgin islands with cocaine for about a week. When the shipment arrived at Montserrat, it would be unloaded and taken to a warehouse where workers would add about 50 kilograms of powdered sugar. The cut cocaine would then be repackaged into 27-gram allotments, one ounce, the amount normally wholesaled to street vendors. At this point, the wholesale value of the cocaine would be set. The wholesaler's judgment as to the market conditions and the quality of the batch would contribute to the valuation, but the price would usually be set at around two thousand dollars per ounce. At this rate, the take for the Cartel for this shipment alone would be $25.9 million dollars. All of it cash.

The pilot's mind shifted again as he saw the lights from the coast of Colombia about thirty-five nautical miles in the distance. He sometimes thought it strange that he was involved in the cocaine business. Occasionally, he would awake struggling, after dreaming about the damage the dreadful drug would cause. The guilt and shame would haunt him for a couple of days, but each time he would find some way to deny it. "Same shame," he often say in justification, "that my people been feelin under the feet of the rich men."

Like most West Indians living on U.S. territory, his life with white people on St. John was demeaning. For all of modern West Indian history, the defining element between the two races has been money. The whites have it, and the natives, for the most part, do not. There are some West Indians who like Sutton, had become successful. He owned and operated a charter flying service and car rental agency and others operated various businesses catering to the tourists. But they did this only by trading with the white society, on the white man's terms. This mode of business was, to Sutton and others, nothing more than a form of servitude. There were some whites in the Islands with whom Sutton had become what might be called 'friendly', but the friendship endured only for so long as he remained painfully aware of his place. And his place, like that of all other West Indians, is that he is a native.

Having lived for so long with this under-current of oppression and in spite of his business success, Sutton had lost all respect for and loyalty to the United States. He became a war hero turned bitter. This made him the perfect candidate for long-term employment by the cartel. He was an inconspicuous person, who simply went about his work and his life quietly. He never missed an assignment unless he was so ill he couldn't fly. He was very thrifty and saved almost all of the money he had earned over the years; as a consequence, there was nothing flashy about his lifestyle. He continued to live in the house where he was born and he spent most of his spare time raising and caring for a son and twin daughters. His wife died giving birth to the twins in 1985.

For nearly forty years Sutton carried out an elaborate scheme to build and conceal his fortune. On the third Thursday of every month he would fly to Martinique. There, he would convert his dollars to francs at three different banks. The francs would be deposited and wired to an account he owned at the Union Bank of Switzerland. For this service, Sutton agreed to maintain a rather significant balance in the three banks in Martinique. This manipulation served his purposes and maintained his cover, because certainly it would be normal that a charter pilot and car rental agency owner would have a checking account, and he was able, if necessary, to demonstrate reasonable equity for legitimate business purposes. The charm of the arrangement, however, came from the fact that any authorities that might be suspicious of him could not trace the transfers to Switzerland and the funds would be untouchable, should something untimely happen to him.

The extent of his wealth was unknown to anyone else, or so he thought. In fact, the Cartel people knew everything, but they were not concerned. The knowledge that he was inconspicuous gave them solace, and his wealth made it unlikely that money would tempt him to change his allegiance. They recognized his value and paid him enough so that he would not be tempted to do something else, and he served them impeccably. Thus, a solid balance existed. So when Placido Orestes, the chief enforcer for the Gallierga Cartel, learned from his sources that Sutton had accumulated in excess of forty-two million dollars in in his Swiss bank account, there was no issue. He had earned it through prudent service to the organization. They would monitor his activity occasionally, but if he went about his business quietly and continued to demonstrate regard for the ways and needs of the Cartel, he would never feel the presence of its watchful eye.

The total, to be exact, was \$42,643,322.32 according to the account ledger Sutton had seen during his last internet inquiry. Interest on this amount was beginning to compound at a prodigious rate and, over the last few months, Sutton had come to wonder what he would do with all that money and, indeed, what he would do with *himself* with all that money. When his thoughts turned to 'retirement' from time to time, he experienced the same hollow and weak feeling that any other man feels near the end when he realizes that his professional life as he has always known it is in its final stages. Sutton sometimes wondered if he'd be able to do anything well ever again.

As he flew the Cessna 310 into the mouth of the Magdalena River to the east of Cartageña, he felt that feeling, but put his angst aside for the moment. The rapid transition from flying low over water to flying over the rugged landscape of Colombia presented the most treacherous portion of the trip. He allowed himself the relatively generous altitude of one hundred and fifty feet once he'd flown two miles into the river basin, as both shores rose up quickly to more than a thousand feet and surveillance radar was not able to penetrate the valley. The particularly sticky part then confronted him quickly. About ten miles to the south of the town of Barranquilla, which sits on the west shore, a small tributary river meets the Magdalena. It begins as a roaring brook in the mountain rainforest some three-thousand feet above sea level near the city of Cartageña. It gathers volume and momentum from the mountain runoff and cascades down a series of waterfalls before reaching the river. The walls of this ancient tributary provided Sutton with the perfect hidden pathway to his destination: a mountain airstrip owned by the Cartel. As the radar altimeter was useless over this rugged terrain, he had to fly the path manually using his landing lights shining upon the treetops. He flew it flawlessly again that night, as he had done many times before, the challenge a little more enjoyable that time, knowing it would be the last.

As Sutton brought the 310 to a stop at the end of the airstrip and he pulled the two mixture knobs to full lean to stop the engines, he saw the silver Mercedes Benz, the usual ride to his resting place for the day.

"Buenos Dias," said Placido Orestes in greeting as he swung his tremendous fat legs out of the car. The man's profile revealed a lavish life he had come to lead and his jolly round demeanor obscured the ruthless methods he used to support it. "I am truly sorry to think that this is the last time I will be meeting you here." He looked at Sutton with kind intensity on his face, emphasizing the sadness in what was to be their last rendezvous.

"I am too," Sutton said with mixed emotions, "but it's time for me to give the nerves a rest, and maybe to enjoy a little bit the good things after all these years."

From early on, Sutton had practiced careful diplomacy with the Cartel chiefs. He learned how to present his side and yet maintain an air of humility: overstate honor and respect; understate his own interests. This had been very effective with Orestes and the two had become, if not exactly friends, like comrades in battle.

"Shoulder to shoulder," Orestes would say from time to time, "we have carried on the needs of the business. And when we die, all of Medellín will attend us." For Orestes, the two were living out a great drama. The business of the Cartel went well beyond the matter of making vast amounts of money. It had become a struggle against the United States and its influence in South America. For Sutton, this was a siren's song. He was an insightful man and a part of him knew that in the final analysis he would find no justification for drug smuggling. But Washington had committed vast resources to combat the flow of drugs, especially cocaine, out of the Caribbean basin. Each time he would mule a load of the drug somewhere, therefore, he enjoyed a twisted payback from white society. He also enjoyed the wealth that was building in his bank account.

"Come, my friend," Orestes said as he took Sutton under his arm, "someone special is waiting to talk to you."

"Who is that? I am not dressed for someone from Medellín," Sutton objected. "Why don't you tell me about that? They will think that I have no respect."

"Calm yourself, my little amigo," Orestes chuckled, and when he did his gravelly voice changed into a musical 'ha ha ha' and his big belly boiled up and down with each 'ha'. "Emilé Gallierga wants to show *you* respect."

Even at dawn, the humid air of Colombia was oppressive. By the time they reached the Mercedes, the small exertion that Orestes spent in greeting Sutton put the big man into a miserable sweat. He immediately hollered at the driver to turn the air conditioning on full and began mopping his face, forehead, and the back of his neck with a fine linen handkerchief from a box on the seat nearby. He was breathing hard and grunting from the effort. The cabin of the fine automobile had the musty sweet stench of the Cuban blunts that Orestes puffed incessantly and under his seat, the lush carpeting had heavy gray stains from the large chunks of cigar ash he let fall without concern. While Orestes mopped up his sweat, Sutton noticed his fingers were like the fat chicken sausages his mother used to prepare years ago, at home, on St. John. He figured that one day, the heart of the beast would simply be unable to support it all any further. Miles and miles of added capillaries throughout his massive legs and gullet would prove to be too much. One last gasp from the pump and that would be it. Placido Orestes would be, in the end, nothing more than three hundred pounds of bloated, life-less flesh.

"This goddam fucking car never stays cool enough," Orestes blurted, "and Miguel," he said to the driver, "you tell that putan dealer that if he doesn't get my car fixed so that I don't sweat my ass off all the time, I will send someone during the night to cut off his balls and then I will steal his wife…ha ha ha."

Sutton was mildly amused as Orestes ranted and raved about everything imaginable during the ten minute or so ride to the ranch. The more he spoke, the more animated he would become, causing him to sweat more, and in turn, swear more about the heat.

"Ah, Amigo, what a wonderful country this is, no?" he said as the driver turned the car down the long paved road and through the guarded gate to the estate. "Nowhere are there such mountains and valleys and splendid people. And of course the women, eh? Many fine young women: plump, firm, and delicious. Are they not?"

In fact, on several occasions Sutton had suppressed his attraction to the dark women of Colombia. Orestes always had several in residence at the estate and, when he tired of any particular one, he would send her down the road with enough cash to lend the impression that she had gotten the better part of the deal. This maintained his reputation for generosity, which assured him an abundant and eager supply of fresh company.

"I can think of no thing that is more beautiful than this spot," Sutton lied, "and the women here, they make the old men young. They probably make the young men old too. But sometime I think you come to my island and it could be that you will not leave." Another lie; he would never actually offer to entertain Orestes in St. John and he certainly wouldn't subject any of the women in his culture to the crudities of this man. He also knew that Orestes would never leave Colombia, at least not without a small army of guards to accompany him. There was no need for such travels; he could afford to bring all the pleasures of the flesh to himself here, inside of Colombia, where the strength of the Cartel kept him safe.

The Mercedes stopped in front of the grand entrance to the mansion where an affable young servant stood to the side and opened the door to the car. 'Welcome, Señor Sutton,' he said. Sutton had been here to the main house only twice. As before, the formal but warm greeting he received truly impressed him. Another Mercedes was parked to the left of the main portico. This one was very long and shiny diamond black, and guarded by a large man wearing dark sunglasses and clad in a stone colored suit; he was all business. The guard said nothing as the servant led them toward the mahogany steps, but Sutton could feel his glare and realized that the man had no desire for pleasantries. There were several others like him standing near the borders of the landscaped areas surrounding the yard. Their presence had to mean that Emilé Gallierga was in the house. Gallierga moved about the territory secretly and his attendance there today was certainly a compliment to Sutton.

"Please do not allow my guards to discolor the special nature of our meeting," Gallierga said as he watched Sutton climb the steps to the veranda.

"Thank you sir," Sutton replied. "You can be sure that dis is a special day for me indeed."

"You must be very tired from your trip. Placido has some splendid relaxation planned for you, so I will take only a few minutes of your time." He looked at an empty, cushioned wicker chair adjacent to him and motioned for Sutton to sit. A servant appeared and quickly placed a glass of iced mango juice in front of him and Orestes excused himself from the conversation.

"You know, Señor Sutton," Gallierga began, "over the years you have become a trusted and valuable asset to my organization."

"I have always tried to do my job and be on time." Sutton replied.

"You have been exemplary." The boss smiled. "It is for this reason that we have paid you so well over the years: evidence of our appreciation for your excellent service."

Sutton felt anxiety. "Do not worry," the drug lord continued, "if you wish, you may fly out of this country and never concern yourself about us again. You have demonstrated that you are a man of honor. You have also guarded your assets carefully and not behaved in any way counter to the interests of my business. Your reward for this, if it suits you, will be the freedom to carry on the balance of your life as you choose. If at any time you are in need of our help you may call us and our considerable resources will be at your disposal." His words eased Sutton's discomfort. In fact, he began to well up from emotion aroused by the man's sincerity.

"But..." Gallierga said with a smile, "it would be bad business on my part and a waste of true talent, if I did not attempt to in some way convince you to stay involved with us; perhaps expand your horizons, so to speak." Hearing this from one of the most powerful men in South America turned Sutton's sentimentality into fear. He moved to take a sip from the glass of mango. As he brought it to his lips, the ice clinked against the glass.

"You see, for as long as you've been involved in our distribution system, we have felt secure that our product, at least the portion in your charge, will be brought reliably to the marketplace. In fact, we have always considered you to be the strongest link in our supply chain. I am sure you are aware that your weekly trips between here and Montserrat represent the largest share of the cocaine distributed within the Caribbean basin. We are proud to remind you that not one shipment in your hands has gone anywhere other than where we intended it." Gallierga shifted in his seat to get closer to Sutton, as if to share important information meant only for him.

"Our problem has been with the distribution after the goods have reached Montserrat and passed on to local delivery. Since we are quite remote from the delivery chain, our control over this segment is not what it should be and frequently, we experience losses." The boss allowed a brief silence to settle in. "We feel certain that our losses would be reduced significantly, if you would consent to manage our entire transport operation in the West Indies."

The huge diamond on the ring finger of Gallierga's left hand mesmerized Sutton. It had to be at least five carats in weight, set in a wide gold band. The morning sun filtered through the trellis above them, occasionally reflecting upon the ring with such intensity it seemed to freeze time for a split second. The flash of light from this hypnotic image caused a few heartbeats to pass before Sutton could grasp the gravity of what Gallierga was asking. He collected himself quickly as he felt the Boss examine his face for a reaction.

"The way you think of me is a great honor." Sutton said, now momentarily in control, putting on his very best air of subservience. "But there are some things that I was going to do with the free time I would have now."

"You would be very richly rewarded, amigo."

"But I don't need no more money." Sutton turned his palms up, shrugging his shoulders.

"I've been told that you are interested in starting up an inter-island freight company, we could help you with this," the boss offered.

"Two, maybe three planes is all I need. But I have enough for that."

"I also understand that you, shall we say, sympathize, with a West Indian political faction. What is it called, the *Society to Free the Caribe*? It would seem that the proper financing could expedite your cause."

Sutton felt his face burn. Since the beginning of the SFC, he had tried to keep his name out of it, though it was his money that supported the group. If Gallierga knew this, others had to know also. "How much money is we talkin about Señor?" He asked quickly, moving on.

Gallierga perked up. "I propose that we upgrade the size of the aircraft and thus the size of the shipments, to perhaps 500 kilogram allotments. Once a load has been brought to Montserrat and prepared for distribution, you would then fly the splits to no more than say, five or six other locations. These would include San Juan, Charlotte Amalie, Montego Bay and a few others."

Sutton didn't flinch, he simply looked the boss in the eye, "But of course I would need more information before I could commit ta provide you with the type of service that you expect, and we could not be responsible for the handling of the negotiations or the collection of payments for the goods."

"Your only responsibility would be transportation," Gallierga replied.

"How much money is we talkin about, Señor?"

"To begin the discussion, we are prepared to offer you five hundred thousand dollars for each complete multi-leg delivery of five hundred kilograms. We would transmit the payment to any depository you choose." Sutton, unwavering in his reaction, didn't need more than a few seconds to imagine the tremendous amount of cash that he might accumulate. His curiosity with regard to the details had grown quickly.

"What I have in mind," Gallierga continued, "that is, if you find it interesting, and believe me, I don't mean to be presumptuous. But what I have in mind would be, well, a joint venture of sorts. It would be a branching out on your part. Your responsibility would be the care and custody of our product from the time it leaves Colombia to the time of delivery to our wholesalers. All of the operational components of this arrangement would be yours to maintain, as well as the security forces you determine necessary to aid you. Otherwise, all of our resources with regard to intelligence services, and shall we say legal assistance, would be at your disposal."

"I would own the airplanes?" Sutton was beginning to warm to the proposition.

"As I said, all of the operational components would be yours."

There was silence as Sutton worked to conceal his state of mind. His mouth was so dry he couldn't keep his lips from sticking to his teeth. He slowly reached for his drink; the ice clinking again as he moved it to his mouth. He took a sip and swished the fluid in his cheeks.

Gallierga broke the silence, "My friend," he said warmly, "the task is truly a simple one. Pick up a five-hundred kilo shipment from Mr. Orestes, deliver it to Montserrat; twenty-four hours later, pick up six two-hundred kilo shipments in Montserrat and deliver them to islands to the north."

"It might be that I could not arrange for all of the secondary shipments to go on the same day from Montserrat. Maybe I would need two or three days for dat." Sutton had slipped. He was already thinking about the intricate details of the missions, revealing his intention.

Gallierga rescued him. "My friend, the minor operational questions can be worked out between yourself and Orestes if and when the time comes. Please allow yourself some rest now and consider my proposal freshly after you return to your island. I do not expect an immediate answer."

Gallierga gave a sharp ring on a small silver bell on the table beside him and rose from his chair, signaling the end of the meeting. Before Sutton could stand as well, a beautiful dark woman appeared at the door to his left with a warm smile. Loose cuffs of soft white linen pants partly covered her bare feet and a thin leather drawstring held them perfectly at the upper curve of her hips. A fine woven tee shirt, the color of burgundy wine, ended irregularly just above the string line. Sutton imagined by the fall of her breasts and the looseness of her soft thighs that he was looking at all the clothes she was wearing. He made her out to be perhaps twenty-seven or twenty-eight and sophisticated, accomplished in a way unlike any of the other female guests usually in attendance at the estate. Her hair was dark silky auburn, styled so that the gentle curls fell loosely and teased at the suppleness of her chest, some of the strands were tucked gingerly behind her right ear. From her earlobe hung a delicate strand of gold, supporting a single ruby of perhaps two carats. When she walked over to them, a faint and inviting scent brushed him. Her aura made him self-conscious as he realized how he himself must smell from the long flight, augmented by the stench of Orestes' cigar that had imbued his clothing earlier in the car.

Gallierga spoke. "Señor, I would like to introduce you to Valisé, my niece." Sutton was confused that a member of Gallierga's family would answer a servant bell, and over the years many things about this culture had perplexed him. "She accompanies me occasionally on trips to the country and I wanted her to meet you. She is an astute judge of character. This is evinced by her distaste for Orestes and his vices." Sutton fought off a grin; Gallierga didn't conceal his.

"I am pleased to finally meet you, Señor Sutton," she said with confidence, "and now that my uncle has signaled that you are finished with business for today, it would be my pleasure to escort you to your cabana. I have taken the liberty to have a bath drawn for you and apparently the always-thinking Mr. Orestes has assigned someone to, shall we say, tuck you in." Her playful disdain made them all feel a little lighthearted. Sutton understood at once that Valisé was a well-educated and insightful woman; able, in mere seconds, to improve the polite but serious mood.

"The pleasure is all mine, Señorita, and I am honored that you would show me ta my room. But please thank Señor Orestes for me that I just need now to take the bath and go ta sleep."

She smiled and nodded approvingly toward her uncle as she moved to lead Sutton from the room. He thanked the boss for the honor of their meeting and followed as she glided down a stone path to one of several guest cabanas. Once there, she bid Sutton a restful sleep and left him. As he opened the door and walked across the clay floor of the sitting room, he saw the morning sun shine through the window to the bath area. He kicked off his shoes, removed his shirt and made his way in. As he walked through the door, he saw a young Colombian woman of perhaps eighteen years wearing a cream colored silk robe, sitting on a padded stool, one of her long legs inside the tub, one out. For a moment, Sutton took in the alluring vision. She moved her hand up her soft cocoa thigh and slid the robe from her lap to expose the beautiful, soft, moist place that some men would pay thousands of pesos to inhabit. She touched herself there, seductively, sighing at the sense of her own delight. She looked at him sweetly. "Yours, Señor?"

Sutton reached in his pocket, pulled out a fifty dollar bill and handed it to her, then nodded toward the door and said, "Gracias, you are most beautiful, but no thank you."

The smile on her young lips turned upside down. Grabbing the money and screeching a Spanish obscenity she withdrew her leg from the tub, splashing water out with it and marched out of the room. The racket of her voice reverberated in the hallway, continuing to curse loudly as she slammed the front door on her way out.

Sutton took a short bath, laid out his clothes for the return trip and eased into the big comfortable bed. He hoped sleep would come quickly, but couldn't help thinking that Gallierga's offer might be one he simply couldn't refuse.

5

An Island Comes Alive

The main gathering room in Gallierga's estate home had tall floor to ceiling windows that provided a panoramic view of the adjacent tropical mountains and the jungle valley below. It was from here that Valisé watched as Sutton's Cessna 310 aircraft flew into view, beginning his return that evening to Montserrat. The plane, containing 250 kilos of nearly pure cocaine, crossed her field of vision at eye level, splitting the air between the emerald green walls of jungle rising up from the tributary he had followed in from the Magdalena river the previous morning, now following it back again en route to the south Atlantic, the first leg of a journey that would eventually deliver the cargo to the noses of thousands of cash customers.

Within two years of completing her MBA at Wharton College, Valisé was able to elevate the Gallierga organization to the status of premier supplier of cocaine in the western hemisphere.

What was once a crude and wasteful yet inherently lucrative company had soon become, under her tenacious management, a finely-tuned and structured network. She preached the law of supply and demand in the marketplace. She insisted that the product not be cut extensively before shipment, so as not to reduce the purity of the cocaine, making her Colombian 'Pink' brand the most sought after by retailers: enabling them to increase profits by cutting it themselves. This allowed her to command a higher price for the product. She also enforced her disdain for the violence of the old days and argued for a more civilized approach in company operations. She accepted that, in part, they had to deal swiftly and, perhaps brutally, with an employee whose interest strayed from that of the company. However, she would not tolerate violence as a way of life. Most important, she preached, killing was simply bad for business.

Gallierga had always provided her with the finest life that money could buy. She attended boarding school at Phillips Exeter Academy and vacationed with her schoolmates all over the world. She summered in Venice, Paris and London and made frequent shopping trips to New

York and Los Angeles. She skied in Aspen in the winter and spent time in the south of France in spring. Gallierga had interests in several thoroughbred horses, so she would accompany him to The Kentucky Derby, Saratoga and the Breeder's Cup to watch the company horses run. In the process of all of this globetrotting, she developed friendships with American and European socialites and received invitations to fêtes at the most prestigious addresses. When she traveled, she took with her the latest in communication technology, enabling her to be in constant touch with the office while on the road. She was the perfect Latino version of the *consigliore*. She was beautiful, watched the business like a hawk, made shrewd decisions on legitimate investments and she represented her uncle impeccably. On top of all this, she was family.

This evening, as she watched the Cessna 310 climb up through the valley and pass through the notch in the mountains to the north, she wondered how she had come to be in this place; how she became involved with these people, some of whom, like Sutton, were interesting characters indeed. She wondered why it was that she had not met him previously. Then, as usual, she quickly snapped her mind clear of any thoughts about the humans she was involved with.

Valisé felt no authentic guilt about the product that her labs sent to market. The fact that Colombia had these natural resources, providing jobs and income for thousands of Columbians, gave her a perfect mental write-off. Was the production and sale of cocaine any worse than distilling alcohol? In her mind the answer was 'no'. The difference was that most countries had allowed that alcohol abuse was an acceptable form of escape, while snorting cocaine was not. The criminal element surrounded her product only because those countries made it illegal, which, of course, was also the primary reason that processing and selling it was so lucrative. The people and way of life in Valisé's world posed no moral dilemma that she couldn't handle, but the enigma of her heritage did. So as Sutton's plane became a speck in the distance, the nagging question of her family lineage set in again and brought with it a dull ache in her stomach.

The death of her parents was shrouded in secrecy. The story was that when she was two years old, her father, a lieutenant in the Cartel, and her mother, Gallierga's sister, took a vacation on the company yacht in the Virgin Islands. When a hurricane came up suddenly, the ship and all on board were lost. Gallierga then took Valisé into his home and raised her. Aside from this explanation, there was never any talk of her parents: no pictures, no keepsakes from their lives, no stories of the days before their deaths. All of the simple aspects of family life that most people take for granted, were a void to her. To inquire about these things was impossible, for her uncle admonished her and exhorted her to look to the future. "The past," he told her, "holds nothing for you but grief." It seemed that he couldn't comprehend her need to fill in the blanks. She yearned to identify with her parents, learn the details of their deaths, gain insight into her past and in turn, give her life context.

This kind of yearning was always a waste of time to Gallierga. The last time she had mentioned her parents he had become gruff and impatient, insisting they had been over this many times before. All records of the accident had been destroyed, he told her. The business could not risk the exposure that an exposed history would present. "But I would guard the history," she insisted, "in the way I guard all family secrets." Gallierga became inflamed and surly. "Further discussion will only undermine the tremendous trust we have built together; I will hear no more on the subject." She didn't understand his outlook; she felt her request bore no cost. As she continued to gaze at the panorama through the massive glass, she felt a chill as she again concluded there was something wrong with her family picture. Gallierga's behavior concerning the topic was unnatural. He had a subconscious reflex in his manner, as if there was a reality that he couldn't mold to his liking, a problem that he couldn't explain away. He was frustrated, or guilty. It wasn't the sorrow of a man who fell behind circumstances out of his control, but actual guilt, as if there was some aspect of her life that he had purposely altered, producing results that he couldn't later undo. Because he wouldn't even attempt to address her need for information, indeed, he made her feel wrong for wanting knowledge, the trickery evolved into a form of abuse. It produced in her both a ruthlessness that served her well in the drug underworld, and, a melancholic need for validation that did not.

Sutton's plane had long disappeared over the mountain when she heard the distinctive clicking of Gallierga's Italian shoes as he strode up the tiled corridor, past the enormous mahogany walled study and eventually to the archway leading to the gathering room where she stood motionless, entranced in confusion and growing anger over the sham that was her life. She felt his presence behind her and steeled herself to behave as if nothing was wrong. A drip of sweat trickled down the cleavage of her back.

"I was thinking, Vali," Gallierga said, using his favorite name for her when appealing for her help, "that perhaps your presence in Cruz Bay might convince our friend Mr. Sutton that staying with the company would be beneficial to him. He appeared to be positively entranced by you this morning. You might make the difference in his decision." He walked up behind her, cupped her shoulders in his huge hands and kissed her, a loving, paternal kiss on the back of her head. "And perhaps a field trip to St. John would be amusing for you as well, yes?"

She let an annoyed breath slip out as the practical part of her mind overtook the emotion of the previous few minutes. "I'm needed here, Uncle; there is much to do with the labs. I should be in Cartageña right now, inspecting the equipment. If I don't stay right on top of Orestes' people, they allow the acetone vats to build up dangerous amounts of sediment. Need I remind you of the explosion at the southeast plant last year? We lost millions from that one." He nodded and then shook his head, standing behind her as she spoke.

"I understand your concerns, but you must appreciate the importance of keeping Sutton in our employ. He is an effective routing tool; to replace him would take years, if indeed he could be replaced. We must convince him that his growth with us will give him what he covets. Our delivery capabilities would benefit immensely if he were to expand into a small air force of transports. He was a tenacious fighter pilot with an innate sense of duty. If he takes on the assignment, he will get it done. And proficient transport capabilities will carry much weight with our new Arab friends."

The mention of trade with Arabs disrupted the smooth argument that Gallierga had been building. She had no interest in this new dimension. "I don't think it's wise for us to become trading partners with these people from Yemen. By associating with them, we endanger ourselves in a way that goes beyond the DEA."

"I share your apprehension about the politics of Islam," he said, holding his hand up gently in protest, "but we seek from them only a slice of their tremendous trade. They seek from us only access to our markets. If we do this properly, we will reap a huge reward from their heroin, without having to produce it. They have the commodity; we have the horsepower. Since we are moving our cocaine anyway, we can move their heroin at the same time. The influx of cash will reduce our cocaine production and transport costs to almost nothing. The Arabs, Valisé, will be paying our bills."

It was difficult to dispute the model, but she was not comfortable with the prospect of dealing with men who might be related to terrorists. In fact, she was sure they were not Yemeni. They might have had a center of operations in Yemen, but they were definitely Saudi. She had traveled to Riyadh once in an exchange program. She learned something of the culture and gained the ability to recognize subtle differences within Arab nationalities. There remained, however, a great deal about the culture that she didn't understand and had no desire to. She saw the beauty of the relationship as a business model, but was suspicious of their motives and believed their ruthlessness went beyond anything even Emilé might comprehend. On the other hand, if Arab drugs were to be a genuine presence in their market, like it or not, it would seem wise to share in the profits as opposed to competing with them. She agreed that if they could control the path to market, they would be the gatekeepers, making the price of admission just low enough that it would not pay for the Arabs to build their own network.

Still, she had misgivings. "These men have a different culture to ours. They are motivated by things other than profit. They have, or many of them have, deeply religious callings. They might take risks, or ask us to, without concern for the consequences."

"I have met with these people," he replied, "and although I understand nothing of their customs, they have a feel for business, just like us." He placed his thumbs on his chest just under the lapels of his sport coat and made a steeple with his fingers, as he did customarily to present his most thoughtful image. "They know how to show proper respect for a business associate and they were impressed by our ability to deliver. They are not fanatics, Valisé; they are entrepreneurs, just as we are."

She was not convinced, but she relented, as usual. "I will always support your decision, you know that. If you are certain this is a good opportunity, so be it." She pursed her lips, a final indication of her dislike for the new trade partners, then she changed the subject. "How long should we give Señor Sutton to think about the offer before I call on him?"

"I think we should keep the prospect fresh in his mind," he replied, "and also impress upon him how important he is. Perhaps you should go tomorrow or Thursday at the latest."

She nodded in agreement and took another look at the splendor through the window. "Would you call the Pereź man and ask if the Hill House is available? I'd like to stay four or five nights, which would allow me to visit Sutton more than once, giving him time to think and respond to me directly. I'll ask Orestes to send word to Mr. Sutton that I'm coming in for a visit. Does that seem appropriate?"

He smiled, "It does indeed, my love. And I truly believe a few days on the beach will be good for you."

"Well, maybe you're right."

"Good, it's settled then, I will call Pereź and have the Hill House prepared for your arrival."

As Gallierga walked away Valisé turned toward the window and looked once more through the glass. The sun had nearly finished its escape behind the mountains and somehow her anxiety had disappeared as well. It was replaced by warm thoughts of St. John: the terrific beaches and the colorful sea life just a few feet beneath the surface. In Charlotte Amalie, St. Thomas, she would catch a ride to St. John on the Caneel Bay Hotel boat. The captain would surely remember her, but if not, a hefty tip would jar his memory, and cause him to welcome her aboard as if she were actually a guest at the resort. She looked forward to the exciting cruise across Sir Francis Drake Channel, especially after the stuffy plane ride. Only a few people travel on this boat, as it services the Caneel Bay Resort alone, so the atmosphere is relaxed and festive and the Piña Coladas are exceptional. The sea air is wonderfully fresh as the boat rolls over the rough swells of the channel, huge sprays of warm salt water kick up, occasionally hitting passengers in the stern, bringing smiles and excitement. A twenty-five minute ride seems like only a few minutes, during which the guests adjust their composure and acclimate themselves to the warm and salty sea air. They become less concerned with tidiness, how they look, and more appreciative of how they feel. And they know at the end of this, the last leg of a long journey, lies a spectacle they'll enjoy: a tiny island with steep mountains covered by tropical vegetation, parted by winding roads and small paths that lead to pure white sand beaches and warm, azure blue sea.

With the exception of Cruz Bay, the various towns on the island are nothing more than clusters of homes, with perhaps a small guest house here and there, and several small harbors where sailboats put in for supplies. The pace is so slow, no clocks are needed. It's either morning, afternoon or night. The exact hour doesn't matter. The family owned grocery store in Enighed opens, they say, at 9 a.m. However, that could really happen any time between 8:30 and 10:00 a.m.; depending upon what time the hired help shows up. The bar at JJ's Saloon closes at 1:00 a.m.; it says so on the sign, but it could be anytime between midnight and dawn, depending upon the mood of the owner and what time the last customer stumbles out the door.

In the late afternoon, if you sit in front of JJ's drinking a beer on his small patio that overlooks the town square in Cruz Bay, it's a people-watching spectacle unlike any other. The passersby are from every imaginable walk of life: Rastafarians practicing, that is inhaling, their religion; taxi drivers hanging around looking for a fare; American waitresses who came with the intention of staying a few months and stayed a few years; bronze beauties on the island for a sedate vacation and in town shopping at the quaint stores that line the streets; the occasional wealthy, middle-aged couple, staying at Caneel Bay where they are pampered and 'yuz sah'd' to death, out on a field trip, being led around by a native guide who swears it's all right to get out of the car. "You no gonna be attacked missus," he promises.

There are stock-brokers and nobility, islanders and tourists, singles and couples, blacks, whites, yellows, browns, all sharing the same narrow streets and sidewalks and trading lazy smiles. All of them are headed somewhere, sort of, but in no real hurry to get there. Tomorrow will be just like today, maybe a little longer, maybe a little shorter, but who cares? A tall lean muscular native policeman with a crisp white officers cap and shoulder epaulets stands on the corner watching over the proceedings, looking to all the world as if he might have been a cruise ship captain in another life. There is little cell phone service, no standing in line for anything, and no traffic to speak of. This is the essence of the Caribbean: life is good, time doesn't matter, and the sea is everywhere.

While Valisé day-dreamed Gallierga was busy making arrangements. "Pablo?" he asked into his cell phone, "It's Emilé Gallierga." The lls rolled off his tongue as he said his own last name with flair. "Buenos Dias, my good friend. How are your beautiful wife and family? Good? …ah good, my friend…yes all is well here. I thought that perhaps I would be in to meet with you tomorrow, if you have some time for me. I have news I think you will find interesting in regards to our meeting with our new partners.

"Yes, anytime in the afternoon is fine with me…Valisé? She is fine, working too hard, but I am proud of her. Pablo, this is why I called. She was hoping to take a few days on St. John, so I thought that if the Hill House was available, you might not mind her staying… "No, I know I don't have to ask, but I should never be so presumptuous as to take your hospitality for granted…there are some guests in the Road House? Two gay Americans, really? They will not bother her, nor her them. Ha, ha, ha…I should think there will be no problem, will there? No…ha, ha, ha. You are most generous my friend, she will be arriving tomorrow or Thursday…thank you, your generosity to my family will not be forgotten, and I will see you tomorrow myself, say around two? Good…yes, I will tell her, she thinks the world of you. Yes, I'll send someone around in the morning for the keys…ciao."

Pablo Pereź was a business associate, a Cartel member but in possession of only two laboratories and limited transportation contacts. His brother, however, was a general in the Colombian Army, so Pereź brought priceless political resources to the organization. The army, as far as the Cartel's business was concerned, was family.

Gallierga thought it strange that Pereź would be renting out the Road House. It might not be, perhaps he had extended his hospitality to a son of his American connections, for a few weeks with his boyfriend-lover. Gallierga shivered at the visual. No matter, he thought. The Road House is well below the Hill House and the two men would be of no concern to Valisé. He decided there would be no need to complicate her stay with a bodyguard. He would just call upon Randall, Pereź's man on the island, to keep tabs on her.

Three days later, as the boat swung lazily toward the mooring posts, steered by the expert hands of the ferry captain, the passengers queued up to cross the ramp to the dock. Valisé took a place in line with the hotel guests, who were anxious to get checked in and then to the beach for an afternoon swim. Wearing an ice blue oval neck tee slung low on one side, on top of white gauchos with sandals, she slung over her shoulder a striped canvas travel bag with leather piping and corners and a small round leather tag imprinted with a fashionable 'G'. She was seeing the world through dark blue Bulgari sunglasses, and a perfectly coordinated dark blue Boston Red Sox baseball hat shaded her face slightly. Her auburn hair, the red highlights glistening in the Caribbean sun, was pulled back and gathered loosely in a ponytail and slipped through the back of the cap. Her bronze skin made her appear as though she had spent her entire life on the island. She wore little make-up: it wasn't necessary.

When her suitcase came off the boat, she smiled and nodded at one of the bellman as he retrieved it and followed her. She would have pulled her own suitcase if need be, but was perfectly content to let someone else do it, here, in this splendid resort, as was the custom. She had the confident walk of a woman who wanted for nothing.

Various guests were enjoying a lazy afternoon in the gardens at the hotel. All of the men and most of the other women turned to watch as she made her way up the path from the dock, through the gardens and patio which front the hotel, then through the lavishly planted breezeway and toward the parking lot. The women noticed the little things: the Gucci sandals and knapsack; the gauchos, fitted by a designer; the Cartier ankle bracelet, hanging perfectly on the top of her left foot and sporting perhaps fifty alternating quarter-carat diamonds and emeralds. The men noticed other things: the gentle swing of her perfect hips as she glided along; the luxurious sway in her upturned breasts. She left behind an alluring, clean, yet slightly musky scent as she moved past. Her face could inspire an artist. Valisé had arrived in St. John, and she was, like the deep green paradise that surrounded her, spectacular.

Parked at the circle in front of the breezeway sat a white Jeep Wrangler with no top. Behind the wheel sat a large West Indian man, perhaps thirty-two or three, who, when he saw her, lit up a huge smile full of very white teeth.

"Miz Valisé, I was thinkin just the other day about when you be coming back ta the island," he said excitedly in a sing-song Caribe accent. "And then when I see your name on the sheet this mornin, de boss, he say, you be pickin up miz Valisé at the Caneel Bay today, you be taken the car ta her."

He jumped out of the seat as best a big man is able, and held out his big paw for her to shake. "It's a good thing ta see you; you make the sun happy ta be out."

Valisé pushed away his hand. "We don't shake, Randall, I've

known you far too long for that," she said as she hugged him, "it's so good to see you. Ahh," she exclaimed, "you brought me the Jeep with the good sound system. You are so thoughtful. God the ocean smells wonderful, Randall, can you smell it? And look at the hibiscus." Randall smiled and nodded, taking in her joy, watching her celebrate his island.

Meanwhile, the bellman, who'd been enjoying her excitement also, threw the suitcase into the back of the Jeep and asked, "You be comin down ta the big lunch buffet tomorrow miz? They be havin the grouper fish you like."

She handed him a sizeable tip and said, "How nice, thank you, I will, and will you be here to help me to the boat on my way back through?"

He nodded several times "Of course miz, thank you miz, just call ahead an I be lookin for you."

Randall held out the keys to her. "Wuz you gonna drive?" he asked, hoping she would decline.

She nodded and grinned. "Of course." Reaching for the keys, she jumped into the driver's seat, started the engine, revved it up a little, threw the shifter into first and let out the clutch a little too quickly. The tires chirped sportingly as the Jeep caromed away, with Randall not yet fully seated.

Randall worked for Perez. He helped with the house guests, taking care of the properties and other Perez assets on the islands, which included more than just a few vacation homes.

"You be stayin at the Hill House again this time, that right?"

"Yes. Oh, and before I take you back to town, would you mind coming up there with me to make sure that everything is on?"

"No problem Miz Valisé, the boss be pissed at me if ya not okay in the house."

The Hill House is situated partly up a mountainside about three miles east of Cruz Bay. The main road leading to it, barely wide enough for two cars, wanders along the base of the mountains around the back of Caneel Bay, Trunk Bay, and Cinnamon Bay and then turns to dirt and eventually ends at Leinster Bay and the Annaberg Plantation. The turnoff to the Hill House, just past Trunk Bay, is where the adventure really begins. The long driveway was paved about fifteen years ago, with asphalt that has now begun to decay enough to be bothersome, but not enough to merit replacement. The road is wide enough for one car only. It is really no more than a meandering path, cut into the side of a mountain formed volcanically millions of years ago. To one side is a steep cliff up; the other, a steep cliff down. Occasionally there is a wide spot in the road, so that if two cars meet head on, one can back up and let the other pass. On the worst of the hairpins, there are posts driven with wires between them guarding the outside of the turn, placed there with the intent of stopping a vehicle should it fail to negotiate the run. Any car that ventures off the side of the road for more than a couple of feet, and is not stopped by the guard rails, will careen over the edge of the cliff and tumble hundreds of feet down. A few have done so over the years, so negotiating this driveway requires slow speed and constant attention, especially after dark.

The Hill House has one of the most spectacular views in the world, a panoramic overlook of the bays on the north side of the island, Pillsbury Sound, the island of St. Thomas to the west, Sir Francis Drake Channel and the British Virgin islands of Tortola, Anguilla, and Virgin Gorda, to the east. The azure blue Caribbean ocean fills in the space between them all. The contrast between the blues and greens is surreal, reminiscent of a retouched postcard, making the viewer want to reach out and grasp it, to be certain it's authentic. The house is carved into the side of the mountain, with a deck and glass-laden front, allowing the picturesque view to be enjoyed from every room in the house. A lap pool sits in what would normally be thought of as the back yard; in reality, just a hollowed out portion of the mountain. Lush greens and tropical flowers surround the pool area and blooming vines climb everything vertical, seeking sunlight filtering through the trellises. Presumably the pool is necessary because the trek up the hill from a day at the beach is quite harrowing, and one must cool down again after returning. The atmosphere in the garden is so majestic, however, it's hard to imagine ever having a reason pressing enough to leave in the first place.

Pereź completely renovated the property in the late nineties. The colors and furnishings were updated every couple of years, so it was always in fashion. It's the type of place the rich and famous would think of as an upscale camp. Most mortals would never have the opportunity to sleep just one night in such splendor.

The Road House, another Pereź property, sits at the base of the mountain, resting on the corner of the Hill House driveway and the

Annaberg road. Directly across the Annaberg road from the Road House is a narrow path that winds down to the ocean and lands on the eastern end of Trunk Bay. As Valisé zipped along the bumpy road, unconcerned about her destination or keeping the bouncing Jeep on the correct side, she saw the familiar hibiscus trees surrounding the porch of the Road House; a welcome sight. The landmark came upon them quickly, signaling an immediate need to slow down and turn. Knowing she wasn't fully focused on driving and they would have to make a reckless turn at the speed she was traveling, Randall raised his hand, grunted and pointed at the driveway, hoping she would just miss it, stop and go back. Undaunted, Valisé cut the wheel to the right and slid into the driveway amidst screeching tires and flying rubble. In the force of the turn, Randall nearly came out of his seat and over onto her side of the Jeep.

They were shocked to find a dark-haired white man standing in the middle of the drive, slapping his scuba fins together. She was moving much too fast to stop, so she to swerved to avoid hitting him and sent him scurrying to the side of the road out of the Jeep's path. He slipped and fell into the sandy parking area for the house.

"ASSHOLE!" he yelled as he rolled. He had a good look at Valisé when she was heading right for him, but at the moment, was not impressed with what he saw.

She managed to bring the Jeep to a near stop. Looking back, she saw that the man wasn't hurt, yelled "SORRY," and continued driving. She watched in the mirror as he stood up and brushed himself off.

"That is one of the *fellahs* that the boss be letting ta rent the Road House." Randall informed her. "I bring one of them over here last week. They gonna stay for two, three months is what the boss says. They sure is nice boys," he remarked, rolling his eyes.

"Randall," she replied with a smile. "Why are you so silly about gayness? Is it because thinking about being gay makes you feel more in touch with yourself?"

Randall paused, looking befuddled, "I don't know what that is Miz Vali, but I know that THEY is not gonna be more in touch with me! ha ha ha," he said, tickled by his own word play.

When they arrived at the Hill House a minute later, Randall secretly thanked the Lord for allowing him to survive the ride with her behind the wheel. They made a quick tour of the house, checking to see that the plumbing and lights worked, the cistern was full of water, the pool had been cleaned and the refrigerator was stocked. Randall stood at the counter in the kitchen and opened a porcelain cookie jar, one of several matching and incremental in size. "There be something in here for ya Miss Valisé, you know, just in case ya need ta chill." He smiled slyly as she looked inside the jar and saw a baggie of cocaine, perhaps a quarter ounce, a razor blade and a small round mirror.

"God, Randall, thank you, you are so thoughtful. But I don't normally use it. I don't care for the side effects."

"Well," he said, okay, but I leave it here, just in case. You never know."

"Thank you, you're right, you never know."

Satisfied with the status of the house, they hopped into the Jeep for the ride back to town. At the end of the Hill House Road, waiting for an oncoming Jeep to pass before turning, Valisé saw the man again, sitting on the front porch in a bamboo chair with his feet propped up reading a paper and drinking a beer. She looked directly into his eyes as she passed. Neither said a word nor exchanged expressions. As she turned the corner and began to accelerate down the Annaberg Road, she thought, 'Hmmm, he doesn't seem gay to me.'

6

Boys in the Band

Unlike the Caneel Bay boat, on the public ferry they don't serve Piña Coladas en route to St. John. Marty Becker threw his suitcase on top of a luggage rack and slid himself onto one of the aluminum benches inside the ship. The captain fired up the old diesel engines, backed the ancient craft away from the gangplank inside the harbor at Red Hook, spun it around 180 degrees and slowly chugged out to the open water of Pillsbury Sound. Leaving the harbor Marty lost track of time, which tends to happen in the VI, thinking about how the world seemed so simple here. He looked out across the channel at the bright sun reflecting on the water and was mesmerized by the deep green islands interrupting the horizon; just a faint line between the blue of the sky meeting the deeper blue of the sea. As the big engines droned along, pushing the craft steadily over its route to St. John, he became entranced by the colors and the noise and the smells. Then he remembered Admiral Keeler's final orders, the words hung in his mind: 'Blend in, but don't get caught up in the place. Remember you're there to do a job.' The contrasting words felt like a cold wind against his skin.

Indeed, when Keeler arrived at FLETC, The Federal Law Enforcement Training Center, twenty days prior, and selected him and John Christian for this mission, Marty didn't imagine himself here. Then when they immediately began intensive training and mission briefing at Dog Island, learning how to disappear in plain sight, to be conspicuously inconspicuous in an upscale tourist environment, to transform themselves from cowboys into actors with a real life role, the idea of his immediate future was filled in for him but his arrival there remained a distant fantasy. Now, sitting on this old boat, churning his way across a channel between islands he'd never heard of before, feeling the sweat and salty air mix on his face and coat his hair with an oily blend that somehow felt natural and quite in tune, the story came to him in three dimensions. The camera was finally rolling and he was a headliner. As quickly as he felt the reality of it he also felt the budding urgency and determination to get it right. He was no longer just traveling to an idea, he was in it.

The boat engine began to slow and Marty broke from his daydream to see that they were approaching the mouth of Cruz Bay harbor. The entrance is merely a parting of the rocks about two hundred meters wide and the big ferry rolled into port over calm water, as the ocean swells don't flow directly into the mouth, but across it. The surroundings fully fleshed out the mental sketch Keeler had given him. Inside the lagoon-like port, coconut trees grow all the way down to the water's edge. A dozen or so schooners rolled gently in the wake as they chugged by, and up by the ferry dock he could see the activity of passengers waiting to catch the return ferry ride to St. Thomas. Cruz Bay is a small village. A ferry pulls in every hour on the half-hour and each arrival is an event. St. John style taxi cabs, a small pickup truck with bench seats in the bed and a frilly tarp framed over the top, sit at the curb above the gangway. Village children ride their bicycles looking for a handout from the tourists walking off the dock. A friendly street vendor hawks her T-shirts and island jewelry. Tourists arriving and those departing on the next ferry intermingle, slightly confused, some of them not sure which line to be in or in which direction to turn. Native and white workers coming and going on the ferry have more of an agenda in their gait and are easily discernable as people who actually live here.

Christian had arrived the night before and was waiting at the dock. This first act was drawn up to advertise, when Marty arrived, that they were lovers. They would be just another couple meeting for an escape in paradise, and when Marty appeared at the top of the ramp he dropped his suitcase and they embraced in a full spread close hug. Christian thought it was fortunate that Randall happened to be hanging around in front of JJ's Saloon at the moment. It was perfect timing. Randall announced to the others outside JJ's that, "There be some nice American boys staying at the Road House and the partner he just come in and I not be going down there ta the Road House alone for nuttin…ha ha ha."

In the car, Marty and Christian talked strategy, awkwardly at first, but they were soon able to forget about what they had just done and concentrate on the mission. According to intelligence provided by Captain James, the Sutton woman- the alleged rape victim, worked with her brother and twin sister at a local car rental agency in Cruz Bay, owned by their father. The old man, Conrad Sutton, also owned a small charter aircraft business and therefore traveled frequently. The siblings ran the car rental agency pretty much without him. They all lived in a modest but clean bungalow up in the mountain off Centerline Road.

Captain James thought it strange that the father and children still lived in the same house, but none were married and didn't seem to have significant others. Their mother died giving birth to the twins. The elder son, Jared, was a quiet sort, introverted, although there was usually a group of men his age milling around the car livery. In fact, the same basic group was observed hanging out there on consecutive days. It appeared that none of them are employed, but none of them seemed to be lacking for money.

James had followed Jared the previous Saturday evening as he boarded the ferry for St. Thomas. He got off in Red Hook and spent the evening nearby at a place called Coki Beach, at a party. There were no whites in attendance. The music, James said, was a jagged blend of reggae and rap. The lyrics were hard to understand because he had to keep his distance, but he thought that some of the words were about slavery and white money and a 'whitey be too good for you' sort of thing. In any event, it sounded angry and grew more so as the night wore on and the rum and marijuana took effect. James said it became evident that Jared was one of the ring leaders of the SFC and the beach party was perhaps a convenient and surreptitious place to hold an organizational meeting.

He also shadowed the alleged rape victim, Anya Sutton, on and off for a few days and it didn't appear that she was suffering from any trauma. She did seem quiet and business like, similar to her brother. It was difficult to keep track of her, James admitted, because he had the station to run and regular patrols to operate and she was, after all, a twin. However, he concluded that she was influential in the family business, and appeared to be the one in charge at the rental office.

James told Christian that he took the sailor, Marini, out of the clinic and off the island in a body bag, as directed by Keeler. His mole said the locals were buzzing about the dead sailor and everyone assumed the death resulted from Jared's beating, probably a key factor in why there had been no public claim of rape. Perhaps Keeler's strategy had worked. Jared would not want to be the subject of a murder investigation, even if his action was purely in defense of his sister's honor. Hence if he, or *they*, meaning the SFC, began to make noise about the rape, surely Jared would be arrested for murder and jailed at least until the affair was sorted out. Jared probably thought, says James, that he had some kind of uneasy truce with the U.S. Navy. He had to be worried, however, that the hammer might drop soon. James had discovered other interesting and complicating factors in the process.

As part of the investigation into Anya, James directed his informer to alert him anytime Sutton was leaving the island at a strange hour. One night, after one such alert, James tailed Sutton to see where he was going. Sutton caught the last ferry from St. John to St. Thomas at 2300 hours. This was unusual, since there would have been no ferry back to the island that night and he had no girlfriend and no known relatives on St. Thomas. James picked up his trail as he got off the ferry in Red Hook and followed him to the airport. Sutton got into his Cessna 310 at 0145 and took off to the southwest. A call to air traffic control at St. Thomas Airport confirmed that N113CS, Sutton's aircraft tail number, had taken off Visual Flight Rules with no flight plan filed. VFR is the simplest form of flying: it does not require a flight plan so there is virtually no air traffic control for VFR aircraft. It is against federal regulations to fly VFR on a commercial flight, that is, while ferrying passengers. So, Sutton could not have been flying a charter flight. Of course, James thought, he could be on his way to *pick up* passengers and planned to file an Instrument Flight Rules or IFR flight plan on the return trip: a perfectly legal maneuver, but this didn't make sense. The safest way to fly, especially over water, is to file an IFR flight plan and be in contact with air traffic control during the entire flight. If he was going to file at the passenger pick-up point, why wouldn't he do it first, file the entire plan at one time and then just activate each leg as he took off? All things considered, the flight appeared suspicious.

The next morning, James went down to air traffic control at Cyril E. King International, the St. Thomas Airport, identified himself and declared that his investigation was covered under the Federal Homeland Security Act. He didn't tell them who or what he was investigating, being careful not to reveal the subject of his inquiry. He requested the air traffic log for the previous twelve hours and noted an entry in the log: 0147 hours, N113CS, departure VFR. There was no entry for the return of N113CS. He then asked for a video copy of the radar screen for the period 2330 hours to 0300 hours on the previous night. At the screen time of 0147 he saw the radar blip of Sutton's aircraft. His transponder was reading 1200, the standard VFR squawk frequency. He took off and climbed out to the southwest on an approximate heading of 230 degrees. The blip stayed on the screen for about 15 minutes and then completely disappeared. James had sufficient training with the DEA in Quantico to recognize this maneuver as behavior consistent with a drug mule, because it indicated that the pilot had slipped below the altitude where the radar could continue to detect him.

"So," Christian said as they sipped a beer on the porch of the Road House, "maybe Sutton took off to pick up passengers somewhere, or shit, maybe he went to visit a girlfriend on some island to the south and he doesn't like to deal with customs. But I agree with James, it's suspicious."

"Man," Marty exclaimed, "this is a long way from where I thought I would be six weeks ago."

"Yeah, it sure beats chasing you guys around the marsh with a paint gun," Christian answered. "Ironic, if you hadn't flashed that fucking blowtorch in my face, we'd probably still be there."

"Yup, you owe me." They both laughed.

It wasn't made clear who was in charge between the two of them, but since Christian was senior over Marty by two pay grades, he was senior, period. Marty perceived however, that Christian didn't feel like he was in charge of this investigation. He frequently left room for Marty's opinion when they talked and they joked more than he would have expected. It was as if Marty was the little brother on an adventure; as if he had natural predatory instincts that Christian always had to work at. Marty never felt as if there was competition between them; their strengths complemented each other. So, if he had to have a partner, he decided, Christian was about the best he could imagine.

"We gotta get into that office," Marty said, "see if there's anything in there related to the SFC."

"Well, there's not much we can do until tonight." Christian said. "I thought maybe we'd go into town, have some dinner and then scope out the bar scene. We can look for the Suttons, maybe case the rental office afterward."

Marty stared at him for a second, "I'm glad we didn't have to kiss."

"No way am I kissing you," Christian said. "I'd puke."

"Fuck you. Hey, think we can just be bi?"

Christian laughed. "Nope, we're a couple."

"I'm going to want to meet a woman. You know, we were in training all that time then went right to Dog Island with Keeler. I mean shit…"

Christian nodded. "For now we have to play the role. Don't even look."

Marty grumbled in agreement.

"I'm going to update the Admiral." Christian said as he got up, "Since you have a few hours, you ought to go down to the ocean, clear your head. Take the snorkel gear, it might be the only down time you have for a while. There's a path across the road that leads to Trunk Bay."

Marty grabbed the snorkel bag, stuffed a towel in it and a couple of cans of Coors still hanging in the plastic ring. He took a few cigarettes from Christian's pack of Marlboro Lights and put them inside the towel. As he made his way across the road and down the ancient path, a path that the Caribe Indians had used for centuries but tourists rarely saw, he reflected upon his assignment, on where he was. He couldn't remember where he thought he'd be, but it surely wasn't there, walking a sandy path, seeing the flickers of sun on his arms as it filtered through the shroud of the jungle above. At one point, a mongoose scooted across the path in front of him.

"Christ," Marty said as he flinched in surprise. Then he recalled that Keeler said there were no snakes here on account of the mongoose. "I'll take it," he concluded.

The jungle trees thinned a short distance ahead and he could see the contrasting blue ocean through breaks in the foliage. The opening exposed a white sand beach awash in sun, receiving gentle ocean swells rolling in. This part of the bay was deserted. The tourists and sun worshippers were on the far side, at the Trunk Bay National Park beach, perhaps a mile away. In the middle of the bay a huge stone monolith jutted from the water, towering a hundred feet into the air and twice as wide. It could not be mounted or walked on unless you were to swim out to it with mountain climbing gear, drive pitons and scale it. Swells crash against it relentlessly, so a boat cannot be tied to it.

Marty imagined that at one time or another a bunch of guys probably figured out a way to climb it and look out over the ocean, just to say they'd done it. Snorkeling swimmers circled a hundred feet or so from the rocky buttress, the rock itself the foundation of the coral reef below. There were several sailboats floating in calmer parts of the bay, probably moored there for a day trip of partying.

He dropped his belongings in the shade of a low hanging leafy tree at the edge of the jungle. As he approached the water, he checked for coral close to the beach. When he saw no danger, he ran into the swells and dove, instantly feeling a rush as the water enveloped him, then felt his skin prickle into goose bumps when the initial chill hit. As he swam further into the swells, the water and the sun blended into a smooth comfortable blanket. Rolling over onto his back, the buoyancy of the salt water made it effortless to float face up. The hot sun beat on his face and chest. The swells moved his body up and down. The salt water in his eyes stung slightly and, mixing with the intense light of the sun, blurred his vision into bright silvery strands of crystal blue sky and the screaming yellow ball of the sun itself. His ears, just under the surface of the water, heard only the white noise of the ocean as it moved under him toward the shore and back again. His heart beat in the background, slowing, relieved of its work by effortless floatation, and, for just this moment, he was completely relaxed.

After a spell he swam back to the beach, chugged half of a beer and grabbed the mask, snorkel and fins. John was right: the undersea life was intense and the water incredibly clear. As he held his head below the surface, sealing out humanity, another world was exposed: colorful darting fish, aqua blue gars slipping near the surface, barely distinguishable from the water, long strands of seas grass shifting gently in the current. In twenty feet of water, he spotted a sea turtle on the bottom, grazing. He decided to swim down, just to see how close he could get. Being so buoyant in the salty water, he had to work hard to get to the ocean floor. The turtle, of course, wanted nothing to do with him and as Marty approached to within a couple of feet, it scooted away, being remarkably quick for such a large loping creature. Marty kicked and pulled himself through the water faster and was just able to get his hand on the turtle's back, to touch him before he moved away. He chuckled under the water, but as he turned upward toward the surface, another resident of the quiet bay disturbed his fun. Nearby, perhaps thirty feet to his left and angled slightly toward him, floated a silvery blue barracuda four feet long; motionless, hovering, taking in the action between Marty and the turtle; curious, but, thankfully, not interested. In scuba class he learned to never take a barracuda lightly, though one rarely attacks a human. Marty understood he wasn't really in danger; he was comfortable enough with the ocean to take it in stride and enjoy the opportunity to see such a predator up close. He allowed himself to float slowly up to the surface and began to gently kick back into shore. There, he sat on the beach into the late afternoon, drank the beers, smoked a couple of cigarettes and pondered the Suttons.

Considering Captain James' suggestion that the car livery appeared to be a drug operation, he wondered how the Suttons could carry-on with it so easily, and what relationship drugs might have with the SFC. He wondered if the SFC could be politically pure. Could they possibly be so juvenile as to imagine driving the U.S. from the Virgin Islands? It was inconceivable. If their objective was more realistic, if they were seeking, perhaps, legitimate local control over the territory, why would they want anything to do with the dirty business of smuggling drugs? From the other side of the equation, he saw a more puzzling problem: why would serious drug smugglers want anything to do with a noisy political group? Given no logical answer to either question, he concluded that the SFC could only be a front, a scam to build power, ostensibly for the purpose of forcing a political agenda, but actually to operate and protect a smuggling operation.

Marty picked up the snorkel gear and made his way back to the house. Having been at the beach for three hours, the sun had tweaked his skin into a minor burn. He was feeling crusty, but also fully refreshed and tuned in. When he reached the Annaberg Road, he threw the beer cans in the trash barrel at the end of the driveway and began slapping the fins together to knock off the sand before going into the house. He was standing just off the driveway on the edge of the Hill House Road when a white Jeep convertible appeared, screeching around the corner, and heading straight for him. He jumped to the side into the parking area and fell, saving himself from being pressed up against the grill of the vehicle, which surely would have ruined his day.

There, on the shoulder of the Hill House Road, rolling in the sand, Marty met Valisé.

7

Arabian Snow

In Keeler's office back in Guantanamo Bay, the secure phone rang directly at his desk, not coming through his secretary. This meant it was from Washington. He picked up the receiver.

"Keeler here."

"Admiral Keeler, this is Admiral Curtin's Adjutant. Are you in a position for a secure conference call?"

"Yes," Keeler replied, "who else is on the call?"

"It will be Secretary of the Navy Admiral Curtin, U.S. Marshall Davis, National Security Advisor Andrews, and Deputy Director Intelligence-CIA, Nardacci."

"Christ, you could have given me a heads up. Go ahead, patch me in." It took a few seconds for the switching to occur before Keeler heard the faint background hissing that accompanies the beginning of a secure conference call.

"Allan, this is John Curtin, how are you?" He didn't give Keeler a chance to answer. "With me is Will Davis, who of course you know. I think you've met National Security Advisor Peter Andrews and Mike Nardacci, Deputy Director CIA."

"Yes, hello John, good morning gentlemen, I've a feeling you didn't call to check the weather here in Gitmo. What can I do for you?"

"Allan, Peter Andrews here."

"Good morning, sir".

"Allan, we need an immediate briefing of your group's activity on St. John. Will Davis informed us you have two of his deputies down there under cover investigating an alleged rape and the SFC."

"That's correct sir."

"There's more involved here than you know at present, but we need your information first. Please fill us in."

"Yes sir." Keeler paused to pick a point of beginning that would meet the hurry-up mood he sensed on the other end. "Will's people arrived on Tuesday and are beginning to gather intelligence. Presently, it's a guessing game of who's who in the SFC organization. Drug smuggling might be involved. The rape investigation, although it remains a part of the scope, is really not the only focus at this point."

"Go on," the NSA said, demonstrating he wanted detail.

"We have extracted the sailor who is alleged to have raped the Sutton woman," Keeler continued, "although no one has formally alleged anything yet. The sailor claims she left the bar with him willingly and they had consensual sex in a parked car. While they were in the act, someone pulled him off her and beat him. His injuries appear consistent with a defenseless attack. I have him under guard at the hospital here in Gitmo; he's in pretty rough shape. The St. John police are not involved or even aware that a rape occurred as far as we know and I haven't asked JAG to investigate yet. Captain James from the Coast Guard in St. Thomas moved the sailor off the island, creating the impression that he had in fact died from injuries inflicted by Jared Sutton during the beating. Sutton hasn't asserted the rape charge any further than a note promising revenge. Speculation is that he now fears a murder charge might be pending, or at least an extensive investigation. As far as the public is concerned, it's likely people think it's a military jurisdiction and the island press doesn't like to go front page with a murder story; it's not good for business. Sutton, the father, operates a rental car and charter airline business on St. John. James carried out surveillance of him and his family and it appears that Sutton's plane carries more than just tourists, but that is only speculation at this point."

"Now we have the Coast Guard involved too?" Mike Nardacci from CIA asked grumpily. Keeler wondered if they might get around to this.

"It's not that we *have* James involved, Mike," Keeler replied. "The bartender who peeled my sailor off the street brought him into the Coast Guard station. Therefore, James *is* involved, and it's fortunate for us. Because of him, we're much further ahead, information-wise."

The DDI didn't reply to Keeler but addressed the National Security Advisor. "Peter, I'm confused here. We have a navy admiral directing a covert operation commenced by U.S. marshal deputies and a coast guard captain. Whose department is this? This is something that my shop should be handling; I should send two agents down there to replace the marshals and a get a field officer to take over for the admiral."

NSA Andrews knew Allan Keeler well, knew that he was a trusted deputy of Colin Powell back in the day, and that he was an experienced and effective counter-intelligence officer. "Mike, the President cannot allow CIA to spy on U.S. citizens and FBI is too starchy for this environment. I asked Will Davis to prepare a couple of his people for undercover work on the SFC matter even before Admiral Keeler got involved. It was fortuitous for us, in a way, when the rape claim against one of his people surfaced, because Allan is a perfect fit. In addition, if the Islamic connection turns out to be anything, his mid-east experience will be a welcome asset."

Keeler's head snapped. "Sir, Islamic connection? What am I missing?"

"It's just evolving now Allan. We'll get you a package within twenty-four hours."

"Thank you, sir," Keeler said blandly, and then added "I could use some back-of-the-house support from CIA; would that be acceptable, Mr. Secretary?"

"Yes, I don't think the President would have any problem with you using CIA resources, I mean, you have before. But I don't want any agents directly involved."

"Yes, sir." Keeler directed his talk to the CIA director. "Mike, I need a courier and some electronics, mostly encrypted communications gear. The only secure link I have with my men is through the Coast Guard station, which might be unreliable. Do you have a field office in Puerto Rico?"

"No, I have nothing in San Juan," the CIA man said with some frustration, "but I have one in Tortola in the British Virgin Islands; it's at the consulate in Road Town. I'll set you up with a code package and a courier group."

"Thanks." Keeler thought this was going pretty well. Andrews did all the work for him, keeping CIA out of the front end of the operation.

"All right, gentlemen," Andrews was moving along, "this operation is classified and operating under the code name 'Arabian Snow'. Any paperwork to and from the field is 'eyes only' for the people present and of course, the President. It is also 'need to know' for everyone. Some of you may not need to know all aspects of the operation. Allan, you'll get the file via courier within twenty-four hours. The president is anxious for details and I don't have much to tell him. I need a solid detailed briefing within seven days. I don't want to walk into the Oval Office next Tuesday morning with an update that begins '*we think.*' I need facts, Admiral."

"I'll do my best, sir."

"I know you will. Contact me directly with your findings."

"Yessir." the conference call went dead.

"Fuck," Keeler said aloud, "an Islamic connection?" He sat at his desk and began a flow chart of the mission, writing in the margins questions that needed answers. Within thirty minutes his phone rang again: it was Will Davis.

"Keeler here."

"Keels, it's Will."

"Jesus, talk about getting blindsided." Keeler said, sounding edgy but excited.

"I know, sorry. They called me in this morning and wanted an ops scenario right away. They didn't like hearing from me that your intelligence to date is sketchy; they decided to hook you in also."

"Why is the NSA in such a hurry? These guys, the SFC, they don't represent a clear and present danger, do they?"

"Foreign policy is in trouble. The president has Congress so far up his butt he can taste English Leather. The Republicans are looking for anything to throw in his face."

"What's the Islamic connection? Has CIA been on the SFC for a while? Why didn't you tell me I stumbled onto a black op?" Keeler was starting to get revved up.

"It was 'need to know', Keels," Davis protested, "I didn't have the authority to discuss it when you first called. After we talked, I told the NSA that you were getting involved, which he favored. So I knew you would be brought up to speed before too long anyway."

"Okay," Keeler said, sufficiently stroked, "so what is the Islamic connection?"

"It's involved. Your file will have full details. The bottom line is this: the Saudis tipped us off to an al Qaeda fundraiser named Muhammad al Jamal, who, according to them, reported directly to bin Laden before we killed him. Now he reports to al Zawahiri. CIA hasn't captured or neutralized Jamal because they want to follow the money. They want to give him some rein and get a lead on any other trail he might uncover. They crosschecked the Saudi story by interrogating prisoners recovered from Afghanistan and parts of it check out, so they've stayed on him for the last couple of months. Turns out that a few weeks ago, al Jamal traveled to Buenos Aires and met with a Colombian by the name of Gallierga, Emilé Gallierga, ever heard of him?"

"Yeah, of course," Keeler replied, "he's a Cartel strongman."

"Right. He controls at least seventy-five percent of Colombian cocaine production; he and his niece. So, CIA followed al Jamal and confirmed that much of the money he raises for al Qaeda comes from smuggling heroin. Now they believe he's set up a deal with the Cartel."

Keeler became anxious. He had to file a report and he had to construct a secure means of communication with Becker and Christian, to get a handle on what they had learned the last few days, before he could file it. He had pressing things to do.

"This is a fun story, Will, it really is. But I have just a couple of things to do."

Davis ignored him. "CIA called in DEA to find out what they know about Gallierga's operation. Their information is incomplete, but they think Sutton and maybe his kids are mules for the Cartel." The light went on in Keeler's head.

"Holy shit."

"Yeah, you can imagine the house of horrors the National Security Advisor is building. When an undergrad goes to the Caribbean on spring break and buys a bag of coke, the money could filtering back through the Cartel to al Qaeda. The SFC might also receive funding from the Cartel but, in order of magnitude, the last thing worrying the President is a little revolution in the Virgin Islands. He simply can't stand the thought of drug sales in the U.S. funding terrorism."

"I get it."

"Problem is, the NSA can't use CIA assets because the Suttons are American citizens. DEA isn't qualified for this kind of intelligence gathering. FBI *really* is too stiff to undertake a covert operation in St. John and continental security issues have them tied up anyway, so that's how I fit in. They liked the idea of the Marshals Special Ops unit in deep cover on Sutton and maybe uncovering the SFC at the same time. They also liked the fact that you were directing it, especially the President."

"You don't have to blow smoke up my ass Will. I'm already here." Keeler said.

"I'm not. You wanted to know the background, right?"

"Yeah, okay"

"I don't think we're going to get much help from Mike Nardacci."

"I know Mike." Keeler replied. "He was the station officer in Cairo during Desert Storm." Keeler remembered him as being a little arrogant. "He'll be okay."

"Yeah, well, be careful. CIA is under scrutiny. Terrorism is their reason to exist. Mike does not like to get left out. He'll probably be happy if you, that is, *we*, fall flat on our faces."

"I'll keep that in mind. How far am I supposed to go with Arabian Snow? What's the ultimate objective?"

"I don't know what to tell you. Maybe there'll be a detailed mission statement in your packet. If not, I guess it's our call. First, let's explore the connection between Sutton and the Cartel. We'll report on that, if they want more, we'll give them more."

"All right, I'll get it rolling. I'm a long way away from a decent report." As they spoke, Keeler had been thinking ahead. "Do me a favor, willya"?

"Yup, what is it?" Davis figured this would define his part in the mission: he'd support Keeler.

"Call NSA and ask him to send the diplomatic pouch to the CG station in St. Thomas. Oh, and tell Nardacci that I won't need the courier right now. I can't get the job done from here, I'm going down there."

"All right." Davis smiled at the thought of himself as back-up to Keeler in the field. "CIA is going to *love* that news. I assume the CG has a secure line with a scrambler?"

"Yes."

"You'll be hearing from me." Click.

Keeler picked up his office phone and rang his assistant. "Stevens? Come in here, please."

"Yes, sir." Stevens was at his door with a note pad in seconds.

"Sit down." Keeler didn't wait for him to sit before starting in. "I'm going to be taking a couple of weeks leave. Call Commander Gaige and ask him to meet me here at eleven hundred hours for a short meeting before I go. He'll have the bridge in my absence." Stevens didn't look up; he just nodded and took notes. "I want a twin engine turbo-prop: see if there's a UC-12M Heron with no markings that can be fueled and ready to go at twelve hundred hours."

"And a pilot, sir?"

"I'll be flying myself."

"Sir? An escort plane then?"

Shit, Keeler said to himself, nobody likes to see an admiral off alone. "No, I don't need one."

"Ay, sir. And the destination, sir, for the forwarding log?"

"I'm not going to log a destination. I'll be in the Caribbean; I'm meeting a woman friend there. I'll check in with you as needed."

"Ay, sir."

"That'll be all, Ensign. Tell Gaige to get his butt over here."

"Ay, sir."

Adrenaline coursed through Keeler's veins. After waiting around for much too long, he was back in the saddle.

8

Sanaa

On a narrow stone and dirt side street in the small city of Old Sanaa, Yemen, a slight bearded man in a linen robe walked smoothly between the rows of jagged masonry structures that line the street. The buildings, homes, are hundreds, maybe even a thousand years old. Occasionally, a street number or a family name sits above a door. But most streets are not named, so there is no means for an outsider to find an address.

The bearded man is not an outsider. He is a freedom fighter; making his way directly toward one of the old houses and defiantly serious about the life he leads, certain that Allah has blessed it and approved his jihad; hoping that he will be rewarded soon with eternity in paradise in the company of seventy-two virgins.

He is a messenger, one of a special few who deliver coded instructions sent to the now fragmented but still powerful al Qaeda organization. The messages are meaningless to him. He is but one tiny pawn in a fanatic struggle to whittle away at the State of Israel and nation of Satan in the west that supports it. The enemies of his Jihad, the Americans and other westerners, do not understand that the people of Islam, his Islam, have no desire to be guided by western ideals or morals. His people do not respect any culture but their own, and believe that those who want to 'westernize' them, are fools. Their jihad is all that matters, and they'll take any course of action against Israel that their interpretation of the Quran will ordain. Their interpretation, of course, is fluid.

He walks down the street looking just a few feet in front, with no need to navigate. His familiarity with the route is so ingrained that a look further ahead is not necessary. The old buildings to his left and right are strung together by a spider's web of telephone and electrical lines, installed sloppily in no organized fashion. This eyesore is the rallying cry of older fundamentalists who oppose modernity; who speak openly about going back to the days of a clean market town, without electricity, telephone, automobiles, or the trash left by foreigners: people who live outside of town and come in by day only to work or to go to market.

He has no concern for such issues. He is not a foreigner and he has no desire to return to the past. His goal is to slash and burn his way and the way of others like him into the future. The future is Allah.

Heavy sandals on his feet allow him to manage the rough cobbled street with ease. There are no sidewalks, no street lights, no driveways, and no crosswalks. A young man driving a dirty car wildly and without regard for pedestrians interrupts his walk. He yells at the driver to slow down; the man yells back a string of obscenities. For this one moment the freedom fighter lapses back into being just like any other inhabitant of this culture; a culture much older and in many ways more complex than most on earth and understood by very few on the outside. It is a society where necessity is the primary human motivation and where religious law carries more weight than municipal law. As in any community, there are arguments over everything. But here these are settled most of the time by a council of elders and sometimes by the slice of a knife in the throat while an opponent sleeps. It is a grimy, dangerous, and dark, yet sometimes colorful and animated urban environment.

It is also an anonymous environment. During the daytime, in houses sheltered from the pounding sun, and at nighttime, in narrow dark alleys, groups of bearded men with automatic weapons slung across their shoulders meet and plan. Christians and Judaists would call them terrorists; a small minority of Muslims see them as missionaries. The townspeople know everything here, and they know nothing. Some practice jihad, but they don't explain it or even speak of it by name. They pretend not to notice. It is, simply, the struggle for Islam.

Today, the messenger is en route to pick up another set of orders to disseminate. These will be instructions from Mohammed al Jamal to the al Qaeda heroin network. They are a jumbled dialog of parables which, once decoded, will direct shippers to change the route used to transport al Qaeda heroin from Afghanistan to market in the west.

The making of heroin is a tedious process. In the fields, farmers pick the opium poppy seeds, milk a dark tar-like substance from them, form the product - the raw opium - into small bricks, then take the bricks to market and sell them to the highest bidder. Many of the bidders are al Qaeda members, some are not, but al Qaeda usually has the most money to spend. At a refinery, the bricks are boiled into a paste that is then filtered and distilled. In the final step, hydrochloric acid and ether perfect the end product. The procedure is time-consuming, expensive and very dangerous, causing so many explosions that al Qaeda has taken up directing the refining itself, both to ensure a steady stream of quality product and to see that the raw materials survive the process. There are no fire insurance policies in the heroin manufacturing business.

For many years, the refined heroin was shipped west to Europe and beyond primarily over-land through Iran, Turkey, Eastern Europe, Italy, France, and England. Those shipments bound for the U.S. had the additional journey across the Atlantic Ocean with the final challenge coming in the passage onto American soil. After 9/11, however, transport became even more difficult. Land routes from Afghanistan to Europe were no longer reliable. The Turkish border had grown too rigid; the Iranian trails had become dangerous; and the Caspian Sea was patrolled regularly by Greek and Italian navy gunboats. More detailed manifests were required for cargo brought into the U.S. and other ports, and ships became subject to indiscriminate search everywhere. Subcontractors who transported for al Qaeda ran greater risks of capture and loss and thus charged more for their services.

The war that bin Laden carried out on U.S. soil made the world smaller for al Qaeda. This was expected. But the western response restricted more than his movements, it tightened the noose on his drug income as well. This was an unanticipated backfire.

After bin Laden's death, his former lieutenants, al Jamal and al Zawahiri, purchased their own shipping vessel and changed the route of heroin transport. It would now be sent over land east from Kabul to Rawalpindi, then south to port in Karachi, on the Arabian Sea; then loaded onto a small but very sea worthy al Qaeda cargo vessel. The ship would steam south to Madagascar, around the tip of South Africa, north into the Atlantic, and then west to South America to a small atoll off the coast of Columbia, about fifty miles northeast of Cartageña. There, the product would be off-loaded and turned over to the care and custody of Gallierga for final smuggling into the United States. After dropping off the heroin, the al Qaeda ship would continue into port at Cartageña, where it would unload a perfectly *bona fide* load of

Arabian coffee beans and return with a perfectly *bona fide* load of Columbian coffee beans.

Gallierga would complete the transport of the heroin, bringing it to market in the western hemisphere. For this service, al Jamal agreed to pay Gallierga one-quarter of the wholesale value of the heroin. This bench-mark would fluctuate some with the market and with the quality of the product. But the initial value was set at $100 thousand per kilogram for the purpose of calculating the commission. For a 660 kilogram shipment, approximately 1,450 pounds, the wholesale value would be approximately $66 million, resulting in a commission for Gallierga of $16.5 million.

Historically, the western over-land route for al Qaeda heroin limited each shipment to 30 kilograms, or approximately 70 pounds. The goods had to be transferred many times: from mule to car to truck to ship, back to car, back to ship or plane across the Atlantic, and back to car in the U.S.; that is, if the goods made it that far. Typically, one of every two shipments became delayed, stolen or confiscated in transit. The new route, al Jamal believed, would regularize the flow of heroin to the U.S. and greatly reduce inventory shrinkage. Just five 660 kilogram shipments per year would yield al Qaeda almost $250 million, five times the revenue produced in the old days. The fee paid to Gallierga for transport was relatively cheap insurance, given the amount of income projected. Al Jamal thought of it as a bargain.

The small bearded messenger entered a rundown building through a worn wooden door. He saw al Jamal seated at a mahogany plank desk in the corner of the dark gathering room.

"If Allah will permit, al Jamal, I am here to do my duty as you so direct." He bowed in respect.

"Allah is great," the chief said without looking up from what he was writing, "and he bids you to relay these words of jihad." He handed the man a cell phone and a list of country codes and phone numbers to call. Each number had a corresponding message to be read. He also handed him a packet of money. "Call each number until you hear a human voice on the other end. Read each expression slowly and clearly. Ask the listener if it is understood."

"I have done this for Allah many times, my Captain. I understand the procedure."

"Do not make the calls from here," al Jamal told him. "Go to

Riyadh. In the packet are one thousand Riyal notes for your costs. Do not allow yourself to be followed. Do not allow yourself to be captured alive." He looked at the little man directly in the eyes, without blinking, as if searching out his loyalty. "The lapdogs of Satan are listening to us," he continued "the Americans: the CIA, they are here in Sanaa, and they search for anything that might lead to us. Have you been followed?"

"There are no infidels following me."

"Do you know that Allah watches over you?"

"Allah sees all."

"Are you loyal to only the Great One?"

"My loyalty to him is so complete that I continually regret the smallness of my tasks." the messenger pleaded: "let me take something to the dogs, my Captain, let me take an important package to them. Let me mix my blood with theirs in the streets. Praise Allah."

"Praise Allah," said al Jamal, "and praise your jihad. But your service is needed in this world, for now. Discharge your duty well, your time to deal with the ministers of Satan will come and Allah will welcome you."

"Praise Allah," said the little man as he nodded and backed out into the hallway where two large guards were stationed almost invisibly in a recess of the wall. They stood motionless with automatic rifles slung across their bellies, watching him, ready to react to the slightest impropriety. He slid back out into the blinding light of the day, pulled the tail of his turban across his forehead to shield his eyes from the sun, and strode quickly down the street toward the train station.

The three hour train ride to Riyadh was hot and dirty, but he didn't notice as he prepared for duty by committing the messages to memory. The meaningless nature of the parables gave him great comfort. He knew that because they meant absolutely nothing to him, anyone on the outside would be likewise in the dark. The messages may be heard with the listening devices of the infidels, he thought, but they would not be understood.

Once in Riyadh, he walked along a busy street in the center of the city and made his first call.

"Are you there?"

"Yes," the listener replied. "Praise Allah."

"Praise Allah."

The man on the other end waited in anticipation for the message, listening carefully to be certain that it matched what al Jamal himself had provided in the weeks prior.

'In the middle of a field stands a lonely goat.

It moves suddenly, frightened by a tiger.

The last sound it makes is a single bray.

The last thing it sees is the hunger in the tiger's eyes.

"Have you heard the message?"

"Yes," the listener replied.

The messenger pressed END on the cell phone. He knew from the country code that the call went to Afghanistan. That was all he knew. The listener, the foreman of the heroin packing crew, understood it all. He was the al Qaeda operative who directed the shipping from a processing plant in a southwestern section of Kabul. The coded message told him to make final preparations for the next shipment, a very large one, to proceed to Colombia through the southerly route around the tip of South Africa. It also told him to expect contact by the cargo handler and to deliver his load to a container ship docking in Karachi within a few days.

The messenger had several more calls to make, but he would wait a half hour or so to make the next. He turned and walked leisurely toward the market in Riyadh, as did the CIA agent who was now shadowing him. The agent remained thirty meters behind and crossed the street frequently so he would not be seen more than once in the same relative location.

The agent also knew the country code that was dialed, because of the pencil he had tucked behind his ear. It was actually a powerful directional microphone connected to a hand-held computer hidden in his coat. When the messenger made his last call, the pencil microphone picked up the tones generated as he depressed the number buttons. Based upon the pitch of each tone, the hand held device displayed the numbers the man dialed. The spook then forwarded the number to a CIA station office located in the bowels of the American Embassy in Riyadh. At the station, the surveillance clerk looked at the number appearing on his monitor and matched the country code. 'Big surprise,' thought the agent, when the clerk's voice said "Afghanistan," in his earpiece.

The eavesdropping session didn't provide much else. The CIA now had the cell phone number of the al Qaeda operative in Afghanistan, but it was a number they had intercepted before. The pencil microphone also picked up the expression recited by the messenger, but it was so oblique that no one could make sense of it. In fact, most of the veiled conversations they picked up were so metaphorical they shut out the rest of the world completely. The CIA had the best cryptologists in the world working on this strain of al Qaeda communiqués, but to date, nothing of value had been decoded.

The agent had come to believe the business of following these people was a waste of time. "We know they're al Qaeda," he said to his station chief, "why don't we just pick em up? Bring em in for interrogation. We don't have any international law issues; al Qaeda isn't a country; there is no diplomatic immunity. Let's just herd all these guys into a pen and let them rot till they tell us what we want to know." The station chief was not receptive. But once, after a couple of whiskeys, the agent was told the real logic. "Look, every time we pick up an operative, we might get some information from him, but most of these people don't even know what they're doing; they're just given a bunch of mumbo-jumbo to distribute. If we bring them in, we could cut off a potential trail. We need to follow along and see where they lead. Maybe we can put together the puzzle. Maybe sometime we'll get to the bigger fish. We know that al Qaeda is shipping heroin and they produce it in Afghanistan. This isn't about drugs, although it wouldn't be a bad thing for us to intercept a pile of al Qaeda heroin. This is really about war dollars. If we can't flat out defeat al Qaeda, maybe we can starve them. Maybe we can follow their smuggling trail and secretly intercept either the drugs or the money. If we get the drugs, we'll throw it in the ocean. If we get the money, we'll use it to pay others to inform on them. But if we get the money, they can't use it to buy cell phones, AK-47's, stinger missiles, C5, and they can't use it to put a bunch of kamikazes on jumbo jets."

The little bearded man stopped to make another call.

"Yes," said the voice on the other end.

"Allah is great,"

"Praise Allah," said the voice.

"The white tips of blue oceans cast a spray of salt into the wind.

A great pelican flies low over the water.

It dives after a silvery fish.

The fish grows suddenly large and eats the pelican.

"Have you heard the message?"

"Yes."

The messenger pressed END on the cell phone and continued his walk. This message was heard by the next link in the chain, directing the cargo handler in charge of the al Qaeda ship in Karachi to contact the shipping foreman, receive the heroin, and then immediately embark for the coast of Columbia via the route around the southern tip of Africa.

The bearded man, pleased with his work so far, hoped he would get his reward from Allah someday. But until then he looked forward to the earthly pleasures of Riyadh. He had plans for the evening. When his day was complete, he would make a visit to the east of the city, where the Bedouin women set up tents and the Greek liquor flows freely. Islam, like most religious cultures, has its share of contradictions. The pleasures of the flesh can somehow be reconciled in the mind of even the most devout believers. As long as no one else knows, the devilishness can be kept a secret between the spirit and the follower. The sin can be paid for later.

It was nearly time for mid-afternoon prayer. The messenger selected his Kiblah, the direction to Mecca, rolled out his rug, knelt down and began to pray. He arched his back high while on his elbows and knees, in complete submission to Allah.

The spook heard the latest message. "What a bunch of shit," he said, then watched as many began to roll out rugs, feeling awkward at times like this, as though it was rude to go on with business while others were in the privacy of prayer. He admonished himself for worrying about his lack of courtesy at the moment.

The country code on the last call was Pakistan. The clerk told him the number was not already on file.

"Can you get a satellite tasked onto his cell phone next time if I get the coordinates?" he said into the Bluetooth microphone button on his lapel.

"Maybe," the clerk replied, "is he still talking?"

"No, but if he's true to form, there'll be a few more calls before he's done today."

"I'll connect with Comsat control and see if we have any real estate available up there." The clerk replied. "Give me your current coordinates so they can target you."

The CIA man pressed the Global Positioning Satellite search button on the miniature computer in his coat pocket. The GPS function triangulated between three navigational satellites and his exact position to within about two feet came up on the display: 29 deg 39 min 18 sec N, 46 deg 42 min 55 sec E.

"Ok, I have it," the clerk confirmed. "I'll be back with you in a few minutes."

"Don't waste any time, he's almost finished with prayer and he'll probably make another call right away." The clerk had already left the line.

The messenger stood up and carefully gathered his rug. After rolling it perfectly and using the rope to sling it across his back, he walked slowly but steadily on his way again, in the general direction of the public gardens at the political center of town. Off in the distance, the CIA agent could see the great thoroughbred race track, built by the Saudi aristocracy. The huge iron gates were visible in front and the ornate grandstands behind formed a backdrop. He heard the tell-tale hiss in his ear that always preceded the clerk coming on line. "We have the satellite tasked to your coordinates," the clerk informed him. "Give me the 13577 ident code on your hand-held, so we can target you." The agent had the code programmed in as a speed dial. He hit 1-1 SEND and the micro-computer spat out the ID code. There was a short pause and the clerk came back on. "Uh, okay, okay we have you. You'll have to get within five-meters of him in order to track his cell, and you've got to feed me the country code and cell number he calls first."

When the satellite was tasked onto the agent, it was able to pick up other radio frequencies in the immediate area. By matching the tone code of the messenger's cell phone and the frequencies emanating from it, a trailer code could be assigned to the frequency string. The signature of this trailer code would then be copied simultaneously to all twelve 'listener' satellites throughout the Middle East. As long as the listener on the other end of the call was using a cell phone, the frequency would emerge from a cell tower and could be tracked to its destination. The difficulty lay in getting close enough to the source to pick up the group of frequencies, and to then 'manually' tag the desired string.

The agent had to gain on the Arab quickly. The generous lead he had given him was now a hindrance, as he needed to be close enough to send the tones and start the tracking. The man would be ready to make a new call soon.

At the edge of the public gardens, wooden benches were scattered along the sidewalk and along paths through the grass. The little bearded man walked a few hundred meters into the gardens, found an empty bench and sat down. He pulled a tin of dates from his coat pocket and began to eat leisurely. The temperature was a comfortable 81 degrees, cooler than usual for late June. The agent took a seat on a bench about thirty meters from his contact and read the Arabic newspaper he brought with him. His eyes were hidden from view by the sunglasses he wore, so it couldn't be seen that although his head was tilted down toward the paper, his eyes never left his mark for more than a few seconds. On the hand-held, he dialed a silent alert to the station clerk and gave him the 13577 code again, advising the clerk to 'stand by'.

The messenger snapped the cover on the tin of dates and put it back in his pocket. When he removed his hand again, it held the cell phone. The CIA agent began to fold up his paper, as anyone would normally do before standing. The timing for this would have to perfect. He would have to get close without slowing his gait noticeably or in any way tipping off the messenger that something was amiss. He watched him holding the phone. At that instant, the agent got to his feet and pointed his head toward the phone. He walked as smoothly as possible while the man was punching in the phone numbers. When he saw him finish dialing and press what he imagined was SEND, he depressed his also and sent the clerk the numerical value for the country code and the phone number.

"Got it," the clerk said into the agent's ear. "Holy shit, this number is in Colombia, get as close as you can."

Back at the station the clerk frantically typed the tasking sequence so that all 105 U.S. listening satellites would have the frequency group, not just those perched over the Middle East. When the frequency emerged from a cell tower in Colombia, he would need a satellite in geo-stationary orbit there programmed with the information necessary to recognize it.

The agent walked toward the Arab and intentionally dropped his paper; allowing time for the cell phone to connect. When he stood up again, the messenger had begun to speak, this time slowly, in very forced Spanish. The agent used his head to point the microphone and lingered as long as he could.

"I have a message from Allah.

"A bird is in flight,
  It travels over many oceans,
  To land in soft warm hands,
  The third holy day after Ramadan."

This message, sent to Emilé Gallierga, would be the Arab's final call. It relayed that the heroin shipment had begun, the approximate date of its arrival, and that he'd soon receive further instructions.

Within a few seconds, the agent heard the clerk on the line. "We have the frequency tagged. Now get lost." He began to walk away at the same speed at which he approached. But he managed only a few steps before the peace of the park was disrupted by a blur by explosive gunfire. He watched as two Arabs with automatic pistols appeared from behind a parked Mercedes van and opened fire in the direction of the little bearded man and, therefore, toward himself. He saw several rounds hit the messenger, one of which caused the right half of the man's face to explode.

As the agent fell to the ground instinctively, his hand went under his armpit to unsheathe his pistol. He felt a burning sting in his right hip, followed by the complete numbness of his right leg. He managed to pull his weapon out and get off a few shots at the attackers and saw one of them fall to the ground. The other ran back for cover at the van to reload his weapon.

The agent tried to crawl in the direction of the mortally wounded messenger, knowing the cell phone might hold memory of other calls to other numbers. But his progress was slow, handicapped as he was by his right leg. The remaining assassin was returning, coming toward him in retaliation, firing shots on the run. The agent managed to avoid the spray of bullets spitting all around him while rolling toward the little bearded man, trying to get to the cell phone. He realized the shooter had unwisely spent another magazine with the notoriously inaccurate MAC10, and he was not hit again during the wild barrage of fire. The Arab threw down the empty pistol and continued his charge, frantic to complete the kill, as a siren rang in the distance.

The agent got to the phone and found it was nothing more than a fractured mess. One of the attacker's bullets had struck it before hitting the little bearded man's face and the impact had destroyed the fragile electronics inside. There was no time left to gather the pieces as he looked up and saw the remaining shooter running at him in a rage. Strapped around his ankle on his left leg was a six-inch fixed blade knife. He unsheathed it just as the attacker drew near. As the Arab leapt through the air, arms extended, screaming in Arabic, diving in attack, he brought the knife up to meet him. It found its mark in the man's throat. The agent took the entire brunt of the attacker's body as it landed on him, but it was of no import. The knife had punctured the man's neck and severed the jugular vein. He lay motionless, partly on top of the agent, his heart issuing blood from his neck in pulses, his body in spasm as the light of day left his eyes, his lips mumbling an unintelligible Muslim prayer.

The agent, encumbered by his useless leg, struggled to get out from under the body of the bloody attacker. Once free, he reached into his jacket pocket, found the miniature computer still intact and sent the code '5-5', informing the duty clerk that he was going 'diplomatic'. He then quickly picked up and pocketed as much as he could of the shattered cell phone, pulled out his State Department credentials, and waited for the Riyadh police to arrive.

Within seconds a policeman approached with gun drawn, pointed directly at him. The CIA agent held up his credentials and said in Arabic, "I am a representative of the United States Government; I have diplomatic credentials. These men attacked me and I was forced to defend myself. I demand diplomatic immunity and I will not participate in your investigation. I don't need medical attention. Don't touch me; an official of my government is on the way."

9

Stings

They took a table on the deck of an Asian fusion restaurant overlooking Cruz Bay. Marty sat against the rail and took a swig from his beer, pondering on the one hand how he should behave in order to appear gay, and on the other, how to avoid doing it. Keeler's creativity had become annoying. The role was especially challenging here, in St. John, where women give new meaning to the term comfortable clothing.

The waitress arrived at the table; the latest contributor to his frustration. "Hi, I'm Julie. Welcome to Asolaré," She said. "We have some great specials tonight."

"Are you from New York?" Marty interrupted her.

"Jersey, well, a long time ago. Why?"

"The accent." He returned her smile and edged away from the railing, leaning on his elbow in her direction; seeking more clarification of her background. Christian gave him a nudge under the table.

"Yeah, I hear that a lot. I came here three years ago for a writer's workshop, and, well, never left." She shrugged her shoulders and smiled again.

Christian interrupted. "I'll have the Chilean sea bass, and can we see a wine list please?"

'So gay,' Marty thought. The waitress smiled at him again, indicating her willingness to continue this later, and then turned her attention to his partner.

"Okay." she said warmly.

Marty looked at his menu and didn't see a word, wondering what time the place closed and how he would manage to get away from Christian long enough to get back. "I'll have the wahoo," he said finally. "It's not too hot is it?"

"No, it's nice," she replied. "It's got good heat."

"I'll bet it does." He paused. "And uh, how late does this restaurant stay open anyway?"

"Eleven, I'm usually out the door by eleven thirty...there's a great reggae band at *Fred's* tonight."

"Oh, we have to be in bed early tonight," Christian interrupted. "Such a busy day planned for tomorrow."

"That's a shame," she said, scribbling on a napkin, then handing it to Marty. "Just in case you change your mind, here's my cell, you might need directions." She looked back at Christian and said, "I have tons of gay friends, you'll have fun too."

"Thanks Julie," Marty said as she glided away, imagining himself walking out of the Road House later on, right about eleven o'clock.

While they ate, their conversation turned to the car rental office. When he was there to rent the car, Christian noted there was no evidence of a security system. Wearing the headsets that Keeler had given them, one of them could sit outside the offices hidden in the bushes or in the car, while the other broke in and gathered evidence. They decided Christian would be the best lookout, since he had been on the island longer and was more likely to recognize the key players. The headsets would allow them to be in constant contact in case anyone showed up. Marty would carry a digital camera that requires a flash, so he'd need to check with Christian each time he took a picture lest someone see the pop of light. Of course, all this presupposed that there was something inside the office worth the effort.

After dinner, they walked back across the town square, entered JJ's Saloon through an old wooden screen door and took a seat at the bar. Randall was at the other end with a couple of cronies. When the 'couple' sat down, Randall's buddies looked up, then glanced at him in amusement. The music was reggae with attitude. Some of the patrons were white; most were not. Christian ordered rum and coke, Marty a beer. Being new to town, Marty recognized no one; Christian recognized only Randall. During conversation, Christian looked up once to find Randall peering at him while talking to another man next to him, chuckling, and then shying away after being caught. He tipped his finger to his brow and Randall, apparently embarrassed, returned a nod. The cover was working perfectly. Unfortunately, there were no Suttons to be found there.

They finished their drinks and made their way back to the car. Christian drove around the large one-way square that defines the center of the Cruz Bay shopping and restaurant area. At this time of night all the shops were closed, and the street was dark and mostly quiet save for the bars, including Fred's Discotec, which were beginning to gear up for the evening. When they slowed for a stop sign on the far side of the block, Marty slipped out of the car while it rolled slowly to a halt. Christian made a left turn to go down the backside of the block, the last part of which is terraced into the hillside and runs above the Sutton parking lot. Marty made his way to the lot on foot, skipped down the bank, and then crossed the lot between parked cars, sticking to the shadows from the lights of nearby restaurants filtering through the trees. Standing in the darkness, he analyzed the front of the building. There was a bright white mercury vapor light mounted on the side that fully lit the front door and stairs to the deck. Marty knew he would have to work fast. Speaking into the Jawbone transmitter mounted on his left ear, he asked Christian, "how's it looking, all clear?"

Christian, hunkered down in the car with just his head poking up over the dash, said, "You're all clear."

Marty followed the shadows to the far side of the building, opposite the light, and cautiously poked his head around the corner. He could see the lock from where he was standing and recognized that it was an inexpensive tumbler type, of the school locker variety. He made ready the little pick in his pocket in case there was a secondary lock in the door handle. If an alarm sounded when he opened the door, he would have to bolt and the operation would be a bust. Worse, it would also alert the Suttons, making them aware that someone is interested in their business.

Christian saw Marty start for the door. "Still clear." he said.

Marty jumped up onto the deck and moved to the lock. There was, in fact, a secondary lock in the doorknob, so he quickly set to work on the combination lock first. He put his ear down close and turned the dial fully two times to the left, then turned slowly right until he heard the first tumbler fall; one full turn left and slowly continued left until the second fell; then slowly right again. When the third fell, a bead of perspiration ran down his nose and dripped to the floor. He pulled on the lock and it clicked open. "Still clear?"

"Good to go."

Marty started in on the other lock with the slender pick. He fed it into the lock cylinder and jiggled and scraped for about fifteen seconds until the lock opened. He removed the combination lock from the hasp, opened the door, slid in and closed it behind him. He felt along the top of the door for wires leading to door contacts and looked carefully along the ceiling for the tell-tale blinking red light of a motion or infrared sensor, indicating an alarm system had been activated. There was nothing. The light from the outside flood lamp shone in through the glass and someone had mistakenly left the bathroom light on, spilling out enough light to allow him to maneuver in the office. He spotted a row of file cabinets. Using a tiny penlight he read the labels on the drawers: SALES, VEHICLES, RECEIPTS, INSURANCES, etc. He opened a couple of drawers, found the contents were as labeled and contained nothing of interest. One of the lower drawers was labeled CHARTERS. Inside it, he found several years of files beginning with 2001. Opening 2013, he saw only four receipts for aircraft charter services. He spread them out on the desk and reached for his digital camera. "Is it okay to use the camera?" he asked Christian.

He came back immediately, "All clear here". Marty snapped off a picture, reassembled the file and returned it to the drawer.

A flat screen monitor sat atop the most prominent desk. He moved to the seat before it and pushed the power button on the box. In a few seconds, the screen came to life, displaying several program icons and shortcuts to files. As he read them, one labeled 'Society' drew his attention. He double-clicked it and a file opened with several sub files. Of these, he opened the one labeled 'Members'. A list of names, addresses and phone numbers came up; some even had e-mail addresses. He figured it had to include about five hundred names. A printer sat on the desk; powered up and with paper in the cassette. He clicked 'print' and it began to spit out the first of fourteen pages. As this file was printing, he took the opportunity to look into other files: 'Donors', 'Inventory', 'Contacts', and a few others. He opened the 'Banking' file, and a spreadsheet appeared entitled Caribe Sovereignty Bank, with an account number. There were long columns with deposits and withdrawals listed and on the third page an ending balance of just over $100,000. The 'Inventory' file was much more telling. Another spreadsheet appeared, listing all manner of weaponry, including, 'automatic rifle, quantity 55, grenade launcher, quantity 13, C-5-3# block, quantity 32. On the far right was a column identifying the location of each item, which, Marty assumed, were street addresses where members stored the items. He selected 'print' just as Christian's voice came into his ear.

"I think you're gonna have company. Get out of there."

He looked over at the printer as it started and began the process of shutting down the computer, hoping the print job would finish regardless. The printer spit out the last page and came to rest. He grabbed the pages from the tray, stopped at the monitor for a moment to confirm it completed the process of shutting down, moved to the door, slipped out and re-set the padlock in the hasp. He ran across the deck to the railing and with one arm as a fulcrum leapt feet over rail into the bushes below. He crouched there silently and listened.

Christian's voice came across the headset, "It's Anya and…it must be her sister, they look identical. They're coming down the driveway; be at the door in ten seconds."

Marty whispered "Roger" and waited for the twins to enter the office. After they went in the door and the lights went on, he wondered if he had disturbed anything that might appear unusual. He replayed his steps in his head, but could think of nothing. "There's a lot of material in there, maybe we ought to wait till they leave and I'll go back in," he said to Christian in a whisper.

"Did you get anything at all?"

"Yeah, I got some files. The place is rich."

There was silence for a few seconds. "No. Let's pull the plug on this and come back another time."

Marty was sure he had solid evidence that the SFC was administered from the office, which brought him to the next step. If Sutton had an email address, he should be able to hack into the computer and get the rest of the files, a much safer proposition than going back in person.

"All right," Marty whispered. "I'll meet you at the stop sign."

As Christian started the car Marty stood up carefully and made his way out of the parking lot in the shadows. Once in the street he maintained a casual, moderate gait. At the stop sign, he waited in the shadow of an adjacent building and lit a cigarette. When Christian rolled up in the car, Marty slid in. Neither of them said anything until after they drove around and passed the office once more and didn't see any problem.

"What else did you see?" Christian asked as they drove past JJ's.

"There's a file on the computer titled *Society*, with a sub-file for a bank account with about a hundred grand in it, a list of inventory including rifles – AK-47s, C5, grenade launchers, all kinds of goodies. I printed some of it, but there's a lot more."

"Good. We have to update Keeler," Christian said, "see what he wants us to do next."

Marty nodded, "Ask him to get us a laptop with hack-ware. I'll send Sutton an email with a worm attached and it'll feed us back everything."

Christian pulled the satellite phone from his pocket and dialed Keeler. He spoke while he drove, informed him of their findings in the office, describing the contents of the files, and then asked him for direction. The admiral told him to see if they could quietly pick up Jared Sutton in the morning, follow him, but not do anything proactive. He ended by saying he would be back in contact tomorrow, late morning. Christian stopped the car in the driveway and turned off the engine.

"He doesn't have a clue what to do. He didn't say that, but I can tell. When your CO says 'blend in' or 'lay low', he means, 'I don't know what to tell you; I have to check upstairs'." Christian let out a small chuckle. "So until he gets back to us, we're supposed to tail Jared."

"And do what?" Marty scoffed. "Watch him go back and forth between his house and the office? We know the SFC is armed, but they're not going to assemble in the square and set off an explosion tomorrow. It's not imminent. We should be working on Sutton. If there's a connection with the Cartel, he's it. I took digitals of his charter receipts for 2013, there were four trips of record, for all of 2013, John, *four* trips."

They sat in silence, contemplating, feeling the pleasant Caribbean air drift by. Christian considered the admiral's orders. Well, he thought, we could stake out the Sutton home, that way if Sutton comes and goes, we might be able to figure out a little more about him, and we wouldn't be disobeying a direct order. Jared isn't the Rabbit in this investigation and Keeler knows it, but he wants to keep us out of the mix until he figures out how far we're supposed to go.

"I'll head to Sutton's house tomorrow." Christian said. "Maybe you ought to hang around the area of the rental office. If Jared's at either place, we can tail him and see where he leads us, while we wait for Keeler to call. Meanwhile, we can look for the old man too."

Marty understood the strategy. "I was actually thinking about going back into town tonight, to see what the sisters are doing."

Christian looked at him skeptically. "Don't fuck up!" he said. "Don't be chasing after that waitress. I'm going to drive by Sutton's house. I'll drop you off on my way."

Marty lit up another cigarette as John started the car again. As they pulled out onto Annaberg Road Christian repeated his warning, "I mean it, don't fuck up. Don't be whoring around when you're supposed to be gay."

"I got it."

Marty got out of the car by the ferry docks, and then walked past JJ's toward the Sutton office. The inside lights were still on. He slipped into the dense underbrush down the street and negotiated his way to the back of the office.

At the back of the building he proceeded carefully and went past the line of windows until he found one where he could hear someone talking. The bamboo shades were down, covering most of the window, but he could see through a break in the slats. One of the sisters was sitting with her back to him, at a computer, looking at what appeared to be mapping software. It wasn't clear, but it looked like an island on the screen, not St. John though, a different island, long and thin. The other sister was on the couch thumbing through a magazine. He could see that the figures on the page were men. He strained to see more detail. It was an army uniform catalog.

The twin seated on the couch looked up, annoyed and said, "Randall have that woman he wants us ta meet, I told him that we be there at eleven, we need ta get goin."

The other sister said nothing, keeping her focus on the computer, "The airstrip at Montserrat is only thirty-six hundred feet long," she said after a moment. "Papa says that the new plane will get down in that okay, but he'll be needing forty-five hundred feet ta get back up, especially if it's hot and the plane is fully loaded. We might have ta stage the new distribution somewhere else."

Marty figured that the woman on the computer was Anya; she was well-spoken, and her body language demonstrated she was the dominant half of the pair.

"Fuck the Montserrat crew anyways," the one on the couch said, "they all assholes. And it seem like all the time they be takin too much time ta load the plane."

"If Papa signs on ta the new deal with the G man, we're going ta need them, that is, if we still fly through there. There won't be time ta train new help." Anya clicked the computer off and stood up. "Be on your best behavior with the Gallierga woman. Papa wants us ta give her a proper welcome." She curtsied mockingly. "Let's go."

They started turning lights off. When Anya turned to shut off the last table lamp, her silhouette was accentuated by the change of light in the room. Marty saw then that she was attractive in a rough-around-the-edges sort of way. She wasn't exactly tough looking, more smart and shrewd. She'd been around the block a few times, but beautiful nevertheless, and a little older than was reported: Marty put her at maybe twenty-nine. He was trying to picture her as a rape victim. It didn't fit.

The twins set the lock in the hasp as they went through the door, walked down the deck stairs, took a left, and went through the parking area up to the street. Marty remained perfectly still in the bushes, but wearing casual dress shorts and a pale yellow tee, he didn't exactly disappear into the shadows. He benefited from the fact that the sisters had just come from a well lit room and their eyes had yet to adjust to the darkness. They sashayed up the driveway, with Anya just in front. After they were well past the lone street light at the corner of the lot, Marty slid out of the bushes and followed leisurely. About half way down the adjacent block, they took a quick left and up the stairs to a second floor open air bar. Mellow Reggae music drifted over the balcony. A sign hanging from the bottom of the deck read 'Grumpy's.' A second sign hooked below read, HOURS: *Whenever I Feel Like It*. Marty waited for what he thought was an appropriate amount of time, then climbed the stairs and walked onto the deck. The ceiling consisted of a green awning stretched over an aluminum frame with the edges of the deck open to the starlight above. Across the floor and to the right was the bar with a side hall leading to the kitchen. Large folding doors, apparently used to secure the bar area at closing time, sat in the open position fastened to the wall at each end of the bar. The tables were filled with young and middle-aged, mostly residents or natives, with a few tourists sprinkled in.

Grumpy's was clearly a local's bar. An unshaven crusty-looking, overweight man in huge Hawaiian shorts and a white tee shirt sat shoeless at the end of the bar. His feet were cruddy and the crack of his buttocks was exposed above the top of his shorts as he sat facing away from Marty. This must be Grumpy, Marty mused, the St. John version of Norm, and walked past him to a vacant stool. He sat down and looked for the bartender to order a beer.

The Sutton women were standing at the bar a few spots away, talking to Randall and a Latino woman who were sitting on stools. The collective conversation and music on the deck were loud enough that Marty had no chance of eavesdropping on what was being said from where he sat. He did hear Randall's deep, staccato, 'ha ha ha,' laugh, and surmised the meeting had a mostly social tone. The bar was warm and comfortable. The patrons were jovial and the music engendered a friendly sexiness in the atmosphere. Marty found it easy to smile, which he did confidently when he caught the Latino woman stealing a glance in his direction. She appeared strangely familiar. Seeing Randall with her brought it all back: 'the woman in the Jeep.' He suddenly felt embarrassed, remembering that he had called her an asshole, loudly. But she continued with the eye contact. The bartender approached and Marty turned his attention from her and raised his head to tell him what he wanted, but he was interrupted.

"The lady would like to buy ya something, what ya like?"

Marty had been about to say "Bud-Light", but then re-thought his choice and said, "Captain Morgan, rocks`, splash of club soda, double lime."

The bartender nodded and moved off to make the drink. Marty looked over at the woman who was turned from him talking with Anya and being, at this point, a most gracious listener. His eyes lingered briefly on her silken auburn hair and the golden tan of her back exposed to the warm evening air. He suddenly became conscious of the fact that he still had the dark green tweed shorts and v-neck t-shirt he had worn to dinner, and figured he must look disheveled from having been in the bushes tonight. But then he glanced casually in the mirror behind the bar and thought that the image didn't look too bad, all things considered. He had certainly benefited from the sun earlier in the day.

Marty reached for the icy glass of rum set in front of him and took a long sip. As he looked up, the woman had finished with a round of talk with Anya and caught his glance. He tipped the glass slightly toward her and nodded a thank you. She smiled as she put her delicate bronze hand on Randall's shoulder; Marty could see her lips form the words "I'll be right back" near the big man's ear. As she turned her legs from the barstool and stood up, the complete brilliance of her beauty unfolded. The front of the pale gray top that had so exquisitely exposed her back to him before was resting gingerly atop her firm up-turned breasts. Below, she wore black silken blousy bottoms that tied low at the outside of both hips, and were cut down the outside of both legs, held together by an occasional loop tie down to the knee. The legs tapered sharply to her ankles. Her tummy puffed out perfectly, softly at the navel, which was pierced with a diamond strung on a delicate gold chain. The diamond swung gently on its leash as she moved. Her waist and hips were shaped so as to provide the ideal slope for the pants to rest precariously but at least for the moment, securely. As she turned toward Marty, she glowed. The rest of the room became muddy green in his peripheral vision and the music blurred in his ears. She smiled as she took the last few steps to him with a radiance that forced him to smile in return. Her walk up to him felt natural, like he knew her already.

She held out her hand. He managed to raise his hand to meet hers without too much hesitation and returned the handshake. She grasped his hand firmly but gracefully. It was slightly business-like, but pure woman.

"Hello, I'm Anna Maria Santiago. I nearly ran you over this afternoon and I'm very sorry."

Admiral Keeler provided cover names for Marty and Christian before they arrived and Marty recited his flawlessly. "Peter Smith," he said, "and I'm okay now that you have plied me with alcohol. But please, do let me know before you leave, that is, if you're going to be driving anywhere near my place tonight." He elevated one eyebrow playfully.

She chuckled. "Yes I am, and I would be more than happy to drop you there if you like. If I'm not mistaken, it's right on my way."

"No thanks, I've got my eyes on a relatively safe taxi outside, you know, the one with bald tires and only one headlight."

She chuckled again, but changed the subject. "What are you doing here, Mr. Smith?"

"I'm a writer. I'm working on a book about the slave trade and the sugar industry in the early nineteenth century."

"That sounds very interesting, but I meant, what you are doing here at this bar, you're gay aren't you?"

Marty liked the directness. "Funny how they make bars in gay and non-gay versions, isn't it?"

"Yes, funny," she said, and gently touched his glass with hers, accepting his caginess.

"And what are you doing here, on the island that is?" he asked.

"I've been coming here since childhood. I'm a venture capitalist in Colombia, South America, just taking a few days of vacation. I love it here."

"I see," he said, "I mistook you for a stunt driver, practicing running old Jeeps up onto two wheels."

She chuckled again, and he added, "It is beautiful though, and a peaceful place to work; I might stay here a couple of months."

As they continued chatting and trading friendly banter, she had come to rest on the edge of the barstool next to him, seemingly relaxed, but then stood up, as if suddenly distracted. Randal had been peering at them. "Well, it was very nice talking with you. And again, I'm very sorry that I caused you to fall into the ditch."

"You have to leave so soon?" he asked.

"Yes, I have to return to my friends. I do hope to run into you again…well, not run *into* you, but…." They both laughed.

He watched as she stepped toward the twins, then turn and glide over to Randall who immediately guided her back into her seat with his massive hand on the base of her back, signaling to everyone in the room, most of all Marty, that she was under his protection. Marty finished his drink and reached into his pocket for a couple of dollars for the bartender, then stood up and walked over to the door, turning slightly in her direction before going out. He caught her eye and held it for a second until they were interrupted by Randall's questioning look, then he turned through the door and left.

Marty hopped into one of the open-air tourist cabs that would be heading down the north shore road and lit a cigarette. The ride to the Road House seemed to take longer than he remembered, probably because he was anxious to get there and get in bed. There wouldn't be much to report to Christian. He'd talk about the Sutton twins and the fact that Randall seemed to have a special visitor in town, but he decided not to mention his encounter with her. As the taxi approached the Hill House he tapped the driver on the shoulder and got out when they stopped. The house was dark, except for the porch light. The car was in the driveway; Marty felt the hood as he walked by and it was cool. Surely Christian was asleep by now. He walked in the door that led to the kitchen, switched on a table lamp and made his way to the room he'd chosen for his bunk. He stripped off his shorts and shirt, set the alarm clock on his cell phone for 6:00 a.m. and put it on the stand next to the bed. An early morning swim would be a good way to start the day.

The alarm wasn't needed. When the sun first cast a yellow-pink glow into the eastern sky the next morning, he was awake in seconds. The tropical forest around the house was alive with creatures and their chatter invigorated his rise from bed. He followed the smell of coffee out to the kitchen and silently thanked Christian. He looked outside and saw that the car was not there. Christian must have gone for the paper and some breakfast. With just a mug of coffee, his swim trunks on and a towel slung over his shoulder, he walked out the door and across the Annaberg Road. The sand on the path down to the sea felt cool to his feet this morning, retaining the relative chill of the air from the night before.

The beach was deserted, save for a lone figure running the sands on the far side of Trunk Bay. He laid his towel out, sat down with his knees under his arms, and finished the cup of coffee, watching as the sun rose over a hilly island peninsula to the east. A slight whisper of a breeze came in from behind, a south wind, indicating it would be very warm today. He watched in relative silence as the first ferry of the day trundled off in the distance, headed toward the British Virgin Islands through Sir Francis Drake Channel. He stood up, went to the edge of the water and began to trudge in aggressively against the swells, then hit the surface face first and swam rhythmically toward the center of Trunk Bay, counting his strokes to estimate a half mile, after which he would turn around and swim the half mile back. A fair workout for the morning.

He enjoyed the high salt content of the Caribbean water. He felt particularly buoyant here and found himself more powerful, able to get to his breath…stroke…stroke…breath regimen easily. After a few minutes of this rhythm his endorphins took over and the activity became effortless. His mind wandered to the night before; to the Sutton twins and Randall; to the way those characters were tangled together in the drama. He thought it ironic that the pleasure of meeting the woman, Anna Maria, in the social joviality of the bar last night was connected to a devious and ugly business like drug smuggling. It reminded him of how duplicitous people could be; how he himself could carry on as if it were a casual meeting, when the end game was really, it seemed, selling poison to the addicted. Shrugging off the incongruity, he thought of the woman again. It seemed as if she was attracted to him too. He wondered if every man who met her felt that way.

Breaking from his fog, Marty realized he had forgotten to count his strokes. When he looked up in order to get a feel for how far he had come, he saw that based upon the position of the rock island in the center of Trunk Bay, he'd gone further than he planned. He did a kick turn to change direction and began his return to the point of entry, once again finding his rhythm and his stride and getting back on task. As he drew near to the place he entered the water, he opened his eyes to look for the floor of the ocean, expecting it to be rising up beneath him. Then a cloudy translucent mass appeared directly in front of him, quickly, so that he had no idea what it was or his distance from it. Instinctively, he used his arm to brush it aside, and then he felt the slithery tentacles drag across his arm, shoulder and chest.

The searing pain put him into a panic. He accelerated as fast as he could toward shore. The burning was excruciating. He was dizzy and out of breath, which in turn brought about more panic until he felt the sandy ocean floor beneath him and was able to stand in waist high water. He thrashed to the beach, yelling, "Fuck...Fucking jellyfish." Struggling against the swells to get the last few feet out of the water, he sat in the sand and surveyed the damage. "Shit..." he cursed again.

Long purple welts began to rise up on his arm, on his right shoulder and across his chest. He couldn't see his back, but knew from the pain that it wasn't good back there either. He sat with his head between his knees, breathing hard, trying to confront the pain, which felt like someone was holding a flame on him. He struggled for control. Then he felt a hand on his head. He looked up through the salt water and tears that filled the gaps between his eyelids and saw the blurry silhouette of Anna Maria kneeling next to him. It was hard to make out the details of her face with the bright sun and the sting in his eyes.

"Christ, where did you come from?" he asked.

"Shhh…I was running the beach and saw what happened." She stroked the back of his head. "I have something that will help. The jellyfish can be nasty when there's a south wind. Lie on your side and try to relax."

He reluctantly rolled over onto his side. She unscrewed the top from a small jar containing a green pasty substance that looked like guacamole. She scooped out a large amount with two fingers and rubbed it gently on the welts. At first the pain worsened from the friction, then more stinging, then he felt numbness.

She continued to apply the ointment on his wounds whispering, "Try to relax, you'll be fine; this will make it go away."

Within moments the pain was nearly gone, but he was exhausted and felt limp. He managed to open his mouth. "What is that stuff?"

"It's an ointment from my family farm. We use it for sunburn and scrapes, and it works wonders for jellyfish stings. Now close your eyes and try to sleep." She held the back of his head out of the sand with her free hand and continued to use the other to finish smearing the ointment. He looked at her through blurry eyes and could make out steamy perspiration on her brow and upper lip. She had no make-up on and her hair was pulled back. He managed a weak "Thanks," and fell off into a trance.

She watched as he drifted off, repositioning herself so that the fleshy part of her calf supported his head and marveled at how the drug had worked its wonder. As her eyes surveyed the lines of muscles in his arms and shoulders, she took a moment to enjoy the view. Salt water and perspiration beaded up on his face. He was tight everywhere, and although she was sure he was drifting off, his muscles remained clenched from the adrenalin and the pain of his struggle. She used the corner of her towel to wipe his face and noticed his skin glistening with salt and perspiration in the sun. She looked at his chest and the way it met the base of his neck; found herself imagining the feel of it against her and the scent of his oils. She saw that the tension made his nipples taut, covered lightly as they were with delicate tufts of curly hair that began there and led down his stomach, disappearing into his trunks. She looked at his face and admired his strong chin and full lips. Kissable lips, she thought, and imagined hers on them; how they would feel; how he would taste. Arousal began to build in her. She prodded herself from this dream; only slightly embarrassed that she had secretly taken advantage of this man, this supposedly gay man, without his knowledge and consent. She rolled her towel and gently replaced her calf with it under his head. Then, with one last inspection of the welts on his arms and shoulder, she left him, walking off in the direction from which she came, his profile and the feel of his skin pressed into her memory.

When Marty awoke sometime later she was gone, as were the welts on his skin. All that was left to remind him of the ordeal were the dried remnants of the salve and another searing memory of the magical woman. He staggered to his feet, picked up the towel she had left under his head, looked at it and thought, 'Perfect.' He walked down the beach to where his own towel lay, picked it up and made his way back to the Road House.

10

The File

Admiral Keeler sat in a standard issue U.S. Coast Guard office chair at the station house in Charlotte Amalie, St. Thomas, U.S. Virgin Islands. An antiquated window air-conditioner whined away behind him as he shuffled case notes on a desk setup for him hastily when he arrived the day before. The admiral wore an aqua blue shirt with the sleeves rolled up and khaki shorts with leather sandals. He hadn't shaved in a couple of days, and, despite the fact that his legs were as white as rice, his attempt at going plain clothes wasn't half bad; craggy good looks and a two-day beard made him look civilian.

He pushed back from the desk in the squeaky chair, put his feet up, and thought about the Suttons. While looking through the tall office glass of the converted sugar depot and past the Coast Guard vessels moored in front, then across the blue water of Charlotte Amalie Bay, he saw a cruise ship steam out of the harbor to open sea. Earlier in the morning he had put a call into National Security Advisor Andrews, hadn't heard back yet, and he was fighting impatience. His satellite phone, resting on the desk, warbled with a call. He thought that it might be Andrews, but it was Will Davis.

Keeler picked it up. "Will, what's going on?"

Davis was all business. "This morning, at approximately 1600 hours Saudi time, CIA tasked one of its listener satellites onto a cell phone in Riyadh. They had an agent in direct proximity of the caller, a known al Qaeda operative. The call was traced to a cell number in Colombia. They don't figure the al Qaeda guy was talking to his cousin."

"Well, ok, but really Will, he could have been talking to anyone, he could have been ordering a new serape from a mail order house."

"Yeah sure, it could have been anything, but it wasn't. They got the conversation on tape and it's in code. More important, the

Colombian cell number is one that is known to belong to Gallierga's group."

"Ok," Keeler allowed, "so an Arab called Gallierga. What else?"

"Operationally, Andrews and his group want us to upgrade the time frame for our report. They want to sniff out these guys from every side, and our angle is pretty hot at the moment."

Keeler clicked his tongue in frustration, "Do they want an interdiction or do they want intelligence? If they want interdiction, we'll just slip into the Sutton house, pick em up, take em to a detention cell and interrogate them. If they want non-invasive intelligence, it's going to take some time. Christ, Will, we just got here, I thought I had a week…."

Davis interrupted him. "Andrews wants rapid intelligence and he wants you to prepare for interdiction. The point-to-point goes something like this. SFC to Sutton to Gallierga to al Qaeda. It could be drug smuggling, it could be something else."

Keeler was silent as he made notes on his own flow chart while Davis spoke.

"One other thing I learned this morning…" Davis added.

"What?"

"The Cartel has people in the VI, well, on St. John for sure."

"How do you know?"

"DEA picked up a name, it's an alias they know, *Anna Maria Santiago*. She went through customs in St. Thomas."

"When?"

"Yesterday. She flew in from Bogotá, passed through customs, took a taxi to the port at Charlotte Amalie, then got onto the Caneel Bay Hotel boat and rode to St. John."

"Who is she?"

"Anna Maria Santiago is actually Valisé Gallierga."

"Related to Emilé?"

"Right. Officially she's his niece. There's some analysis that she might be his daughter, an illegitimate daughter born out of Gallierga's dalliance with a house maid."

"Whatever, where is she staying?"

"They don't know. They had to let the trail go at the dock in Charlotte Amalie because they couldn't have boarded the Caneel Bay boat without blowing cover and they didn't have anyone in position to pick her up when she got off."

"Christ, what kind of an outfit are they running down here?" Keeler was incredulous. He couldn't imagine it. "They get a relative of the biggest drug boss in the western hemisphere on an itty-bitty island, not even in a city mind you, but on an island; she gets on a boat, a *one way* boat, to a known destination and… they lose her?"

"Listen. When she left the airport, they couldn't have known where she was going. And they don't have agents waiting around gangways in the hopes that a drug kingpin, or his niece, will pop into St. John."

"Have they found her yet?"

"No, but St. John is a small island and it shouldn't be too difficult. They say she's fucking beautiful."

"Ask Andrews to call them back," Keeler said.

"What?"

"Ask Andrews to call DEA and get them off of her," Keeler said with some urgency. "They'll blow cover. What do they think she's doing here anyway?"

"They think she's on vacation."

Keeler thought about it for a moment. "That might be, but you can bet she's not alone. Gallierga isn't going to let his niece or whatever the hell she is run off to the islands by herself. Christ, did you ever see those guys in the DEA office next door? They all look like they just got out of a barbershop. Get them off her, Will."

"Ok, I'll call Andrews and advise him to take it through channels."

"Tell him to hurry."

"This is Washington, Keels, nobody's in a hurry here."

"Well, if she gets a whiff of DEA on her butt, this op will be over fast."

"Alright, relax, I'll get it done."

"What's her role in the operation?" Keeler asked.

"She's the business manager, like a Chief Financial Officer."

"Shit, there's probably a half dozen people keeping an eye on her."

"DEA says no other known names were flagged at customs. And she was alone all the way to the boat."

"They've got people *here,* Will, natives. You can bet on it."

"Did Becker and Christian give you anything last night?" Davis asked.

"Yes. They broke into the car rental offices and discovered the Suttons are not only members of the SFC, they apparently *are* the SFC. Becker found, among other things, an organizational list with cell phone numbers, email addresses, and inventory files itemizing weapons and cash. He took a copy of the list and he's going to work on getting into the hard drive on the office computer. There might be some emails there that will give us something. I need a lap-top with basic hack software down here, so that he can get into the computer over the internet. I don't want them to break into the office again, it's too risky."

"Weapons and cash?"

"Yes."

"I'll have the laptop in your hands by tomorrow morning."

"Good, and get me an encryption modem too. We could be scanning and trading documents. We need the capability."

"All right, I'll do my best, we'll talk later."

"Call Andrews," Keeler said yet again.

"I will, I will." The marshal clicked off.

Keeler pushed his chair away from the desk, walked over to James's office and stuck his head in the door. "I need your thoughts on something," he said.

"Sure."

"I need to take a room on St. John; to be closer to the Suttons and my people over there, any suggestions?"

James thought for a minute, checking out Keeler's look. "Well sir, you look like a tourist, so maybe you should just go with that."

"Cripe…is it that bad?"

"No sir, not bad at all. But the fact is you don't look like you live here. Check into the hotel at Caneel Bay. It's very private. The only West Indians there are the workers. You can get a beach cabana with a phone line and an internet connection and nobody, I mean nobody, will know who you are."

"How expensive is it and can I get in there on short notice?"

"It's pricey, probably a grand a night, depending on where you stay in the compound. I doubt it's full, there's always a vacancy at that kind of place."

"A grand a night? Do they have anything a little lower scale?"

"I doubt it. But I think all meals are included and the food is supposed to be spectacular."

"Well, that's great, but I'm not here on a food tour."

"I can't think of anywhere else on the island that would guarantee you anonymity."

"All right, I'll check it out. What about transportation?"

"Why don't you rent a car from Sutton? You'd get to check out the operation."

"Good point."

"Oh, and, Admiral? You really ought to shave before you go; nobody staying there has a two-dayer; and get on the Caneel Bay ferry at the docks, it'll look like you just came from the airport." Keeler turned and grumbled something about thinking the beard would have made him fit in better.

In the time it took for him to shower, shave and redress, Will Davis sent him a text message. It read, 'C DEA A.I.C. 4 A.M.S. FILE'

Keeler struggled with the cryptography for a few seconds, but then figured it out. 'See the DEA Agent in Charge for the Anna Maria Santiago file.' So on his way out of the building he put in an appearance at the DEA office and introduced himself. The wheels of government in DC worked quicker than Will Davis let on, because when Keeler walked in the Agent in Charge had just hung up from talking with his Deputy Director in Washington and begrudgingly handed over the dossier. Keeler looked at the heading, which read: 'VALISE GALLIERGA AKA ANNA MARIA SANTIAGO'. The front of the folder was stamped **EYES ONLY**. Keeler left without saying anything.

En route to the docks, with a suitcase on wheels in tow, he stopped and bought a khaki baseball cap and put on his sunglasses. When he walked up to the Caneel Bay ferry, the ship's steward – the same one who had welcomed Valisé to the island just a couple of days prior, approached him. "Are ya checkin into the hotel, sir?"

"Well, I hope to, pal. Do you know if there's any vacancy?" Keeler smiled as he slipped the steward a twenty.

"I believe they is sir, welcome aboard. They have the piña coladas in the galley, sir, if y'are thirsty. We be sailin in just a few minutes." Keeler smiled and thanked him. He took the steward's advice and stopped in the galley for a drink on his way to the front of the boat.

The ride to Caneel Bay was pleasant enough. The two piña coladas he drank didn't hurt. The steward was right; there was room at the inn. The bellman drove him via golf cart to a beautiful spot on Hawksnest Bay, right on the beach. James was right also: the place was incredibly quiet, and expensive, $1,137.00 per night. He checked in as Dr. Wilton Peck with a Philadelphia address. After unpacking his meager belongings he walked back to the main building, about a half mile away. Then he took a taxi from the hotel to Cruz Bay and walked up to the window at the office of Sutton Island Rentals.

There was no one behind the window when he looked in, but a few men were hanging around the yard on stools and upended buckets. He walked over with casual confidence, feeling out of place but trying to pretend otherwise. "Do any of you guys work here?" he asked. One of the men waved his hand and pointed to a woman on the other side of the sandy parking lot, hosing down a white Jeep with no top. Keeler started off towards her, assuming this would be Anya Sutton, the alleged rape victim. She noticed him coming in her direction, motioned him on with the hand holding the sprayer, and then held her other forefinger up as if to say 'Just a minute'. She leaned inside the Jeep with the sprayer and shot water underneath the two front seats in a hard stream, presumably to wash out the sand left by the feet of the previous renters. Lastly, she hosed off the surfaces of the seats proper, clicked the sprayer off and walked over to him. She gave him a smile. "Good afternoon, sir, what do you need today?"

"Hi." Keeler said casually. "I want to rent a Jeep for a few weeks, do you have one available?"

"You can have that one right there," she nodded toward the one freshly washed, "it's new this season."

"What's the rate?" he asked.

"Do you want it for more than twenty-one days? The monthly rate is cheaper."

"Yeah, ok, what's the monthly rate?"

"That one's a standard, can you drive a standard?" she asked, giving him the impression she was concerned about his qualifications for driving the car.

"Yes, I prefer a stick," Keeler answered evenly.

"We drive on the left here, remember that."

"I will."

"Do you want the collision insurance?"

"Don't need it, comes with my credit card."

"You'll have ta sign a waiver."

"No problem," he said and gave her a steady but expressionless look which conveyed no impatience on his part, even though he was dying to say, 'What's the fucking price?' She had a sense of this, but didn't blink.

"Where are you staying on the island?" she asked.

"Does it matter?"

"It costs more if you park it on the street," she answered.

"I'm staying at Caneel Bay," he relented, "they have a parking lot." He realized that he just gave himself away as someone with money, which was her intention. She was smooth.

"I have ta go check the chart for the monthly rate." She walked up the wooden stairs to the deck leading to the door to the office. He followed her to the deck and waited while she fiddled with the combination lock, hooked loosely on the hasp. As he watched, Keeler thought Marty must have breezed through that lock; he used to crack them himself in grade school.

She went around the corner through a small swinging door, came back out on the other side of the counter and began to thumb through the pages of a loose leaf note book, as if looking intently for the detailed information she couldn't possibly remember. Keeler took an obvious look at this watch. It was a gesture she'd seen hundreds of times. "Let's see," she said while running her forefinger down a column of the page, "is there a discount on that one?" Keeler knew there would be, of course. "YES," she said showily, "that one normally goes for eighteen, but this month I can give it ta you for fifteen."

"Fifteen what?" Keeler said with a twisted look.

"Fifteen hundred," she said sweetly, "for the month."

"Fifteen hundred dollars?" Keeler asked with incredulity.

"It's brand new," she argued.

"I don't want to be proud of it; I just want to drive it."

"Well…" she gave her shoulders a shrug and followed it up with silence.

Keeler broke it, "The rental place over by Mongoose Junction advertises them for two hundred twenty-nine dollars a week. I saw it in the island Shopping Guide. Even if they don't give me a discount for long term, that's only a little over nine hundred for the month."

"Their Jeeps are much older and they have bald tires," she nodded conclusively.

"Are you telling me they rent cars with bald tires? I can't believe it."

"Go see for yourself, but I tell you, bald tires on these roads…" she shook her head.

"I'll give you a thousand bucks for the month and I need to be able to put the top on," he came back, weary of the nonsense.

"The top is in the back behind the seats. You'll only need it if it rains, and it only rains in the afternoon." She said.

"I want to be able to get out of the sun while I'm driving." He watched her ponder his offer with great sincerity.

"So, a thousand for the month then?" he pressed.

"I'll print you a contract. Can I have your driver's license and major credit card, please?"

Keeler gave them to her and watched, but not obviously, as she went about the familiar business of getting the rental paperwork together. He could tell from her body language this was not a woman who had recently been raped. She was beautiful and tough and quite in control of her world. He imagined her instead, taking a drunken sailor back to her house, throwing him down on the bed, playing with him just long enough to get him hard and then fucking the breath out of him.

Keeler made mental notes about details of the rental office. The exterior of the building was old-fashioned with a tired look, but the interior was clean and orderly. The computers were all new with large flat panel monitors; a collating photocopier sat in the corner; the file cabinets were made of solid mahogany and the counter tops were polished granite. A large flat-screen television was mounted on the wall and it was connected to a Bose music system. On the dropped desktop behind the counter sat a King Gold Crown base station VHF radio system that was used, he imagined, for communicating with Sutton when he was in the air with the charter plane. There had to have been a hundred grand in electronics and computers in this office and just an old rotary padlock on the door? That seemed strange, he thought. But then again, when you control all the criminals, you probably don't have to worry about them breaking into your office.

"Here's your contract," she said, "I'll need your signature here, and here on the credit card slip; your initials here and here." He signed where she directed.

"Here are the keys, enjoy your stay with us, Dr. Peck. You're here for quite a while, yes?"

"I'm writing a book. I enjoy the quiet of Caneel Bay."

"Ah yes, wonderful place," she smiled. "People here say that God created Caneel Bay for *us*, but we must have pissed him off because he turned around and gave it ta the white man." She smiled warmly to make him think she was joking.

"Say," Keeler came back, "you have a charter airplane? If I wanted to fly around the islands, just to see the sights, could you do that for me?"

"Well, I don't fly the charters. My father does. He is very experienced, a decorated Vietnam Air Force pilot."

"Really?" Keeler was aware, in fact, of Sutton's war experience. "What kind of plane does he fly?"

"He has a Cessna 310. But if you wait a couple of weeks, you can go up in his new one, a Beechcraft Baron."

"A brand new one?" he asked, "like the Jeep?" They both smiled.

"Yes Doctor, like the Jeep." He had the feeling that Ms. Sutton was, by the tone in her voice, flirting with him subtly. He liked it in spite of the circumstances.

"I'll come back to see him about a charter. Is he around at any particular time of the day?"

"Mornings, but you could just call him, umm, or call me, I can arrange it for you." She stuck a business card between her lips briefly, raised both arms to pull her silky hair back with both hands, and wrapped it with a band. Her moves accentuated her body and Keeler was beginning to feel blood pumping in his chest and face. When she walked toward him her scent was uplifting.

"My name is Anya. Call me." She handed him the business card.

"I'll do that," he said slowly. She extended her hand for a shake and he took it. "Thank you, Anya, I'll take good care of the Jeep."

He turned and left through the screen door and headed toward the car. Out of her presence he snapped to his senses and realized that a brand new Beechcraft Baron, fully rigged with avionics and interior finishes, would run about nine hundred grand: not an airplane that could be supported by a one-man island charter company.

Keeler drove the Jeep up the small hill that formed the driveway into Sutton's and slipped the clutch perfectly to keep the vehicle held in place while waiting for another car to pass on the street. Once clear, he engaged the clutch further so the Jeep mounted the crest of the hill and accelerated smoothly down the narrow street. Anya watched him from the lot. Having seen tourists drive out of the lot in Jeeps for years, she could tell that he was no stranger to machinery. A *doctor?*

Similarly, Keeler had his doubts. He was thinking there was a lot of money passing through that rental office and it wasn't coming from two hundred fifty dollar a week Jeeps.

He drove down the Annaberg Road to meet Marty and Christian at the old sugar mill. In fact, he trailed them by just a few minutes. The view of the ocean as he drove quieted his thoughts momentarily and he reminisced about the last time he travelled this road. He had just returned from Desert Storm in early 92' and was still tenuously married to his ex-wife. She had thought a visit to the Caribbean would be good for them, to rekindle their relationship after his long absence. The serenity of the place shocked him at the time. It would be easy to get side-tracked here and forget the civilized world, just eight hundred miles to the north. Easy, that was, if he had been fully committed to his marriage. But the plan didn't work, it couldn't have. He had been away in the Middle East for nearly fifteen months, serving George Bush and Norman Schwarzkopf and frankly, he couldn't wait to get back to work. He was a young man then, just thirty-one years old. The thrill of his career stood above all else.

When he negotiated the hairpin curve where the road reached a precipice overlooking Cinnamon Bay, he remembered being down there with his wife, how they made love late one May afternoon in the soft swells rolling into the quiet beach below. The moment was magical. But she hated his work. She wanted a farmhouse in Virginia; he wanted an undercover assignment on the other side of the world.

The meeting with Becker and Christian was set for the old sugar mill at Annaberg Plantation at 4:00 p.m., and Keeler was a little late. When the pavement ran out and changed to dirt, he slowly drove up the rough stone trail which that ended at the sugar mill ruins and marked the eastern most point of Annaberg Road. To go any further east on St. John, at least on the north shore, requires going on foot.

Keeler parked the Jeep near a small grove of coconut trees and walked up the hill toward the ruins of the main mill. There were a few other Jeeps parked among the trees, signs of other tourists taking in the sights of St. John's only historical landmark. He found Marty and John sitting with their legs dangling over a stone wall, appearing to gaze out at the blue ocean hundreds of feet below; looking to the world like a couple enjoying the afternoon sun. With no one else around, Keeler walked directly over to them. He leaned against the wall beside them and got right down to business.

"A few things," he said. They listened without saying anything. "First, I met the Sutton woman today when I rented the Jeep. She doesn't appear to be recovering from rape. Based on that observation and the intelligence you obtained in the office last night, we're going to proceed under the assumption that the rape is a hoax and the car rental office is a cover for the SFC. We will also assume the claim of rape is a cover-up of some sort, conveniently designed to discredit the U.S. in the eyes of West Indian citizens. Any further political intentions of the SFC are unclear at this time. One of our objectives will be to uncover and define those intentions. However, this is not our immediate task."

Marty and John were fully engaged; apparently the mission had changed. Both of their heads were turned toward Keeler as he adjusted himself on the wall before continuing.

"Second, through satellite surveillance, CIA has determined that there is communication and planning in progress between al Qaeda and the Colombian cocaine cartel." He went on to tell of the episode in Riyadh and explained that the interception of the cell phone message was evidence enough for CIA and the State Department to form this hypothesis.

"Third, the intelligence you have gathered vaguely suggests that Sutton and the SFC and maybe other V.I. locals are associated with the Cartel, possibly engaged in cocaine smuggling and distribution. One part of our primary mission is to determine the nature of this association and where the smuggled product, if any, originates. We will extend our research to associated al Qaeda connections if and when they surface. For the moment, this mission is intelligence only, but interdiction is possible depending upon the results of our research." He paused to check the time on his cell phone, allowing this disclosure to sink in. "Next," Keeler continued, pretending not to notice that both his agents had become more rigid. "DEA has determined, through customs manifests, that a high ranking Cartel member is currently visiting St. John under an alias. They think the purpose might be just a vacation. Regardless, DEA tailed the alias from the airport on St. Thomas to the Charlotte Amalie harbor and then lost contact at the Caneel Bay ferry to St. John. Apparently, they didn't have anyone set up in Cruz Bay to continue the tail after the boat put in. Part of our primary mission will to locate the Cartel boss and determine her business, if any, with the Sutton outfit."

"*Her,* Sir? The Cartel member is a woman?" Christian asked.

"Yeah," Keeler said, "and she shouldn't be too hard to find. Here's a file on her. They think she's the daughter of the Cartel's heaviest hitter, Emilé Gallierga. Well, they're related somehow. Anyway, she's the general manager or the consigliore, at the top of the organization."

Marty and Christian looked at the dossier while Keeler continued. "The alias is Anna Maria Santiago; her real name is Valisé Gallierga, keep one of the pictures for reference."

Christian, generally a man of understatement, said, "You're right, she won't be hard to find, she's gorgeous."

Marty leafed through the file casually, controlling his reaction. On the inside, he burned with anguish, cursing himself. The mood of the meeting was about to change. "We won't have to look for her," he said casually, "I've already met her."

Keeler became interested, but then looked at him askance as he wondered how Marty, in only a day and a half, could have become acquainted with the target.

Christian was incredulous. "Where?" he asked cynically, as if to inform Keeler that this was all news to him.

Marty related the two stories, the first on the road when Valisé almost ran him over and then the jellyfish incident just that morning. He left out the part about chatting with her the previous night at Grumpy's. He did describe in detail his second visit to the car rental office and the meeting the Sutton twins had with Valisé and Randall at the bar.

"So you talked with her on the beach?" Christian asked, clearly annoyed that he was not apprised of this.

"Yeah, she was pretty friendly and the salve or whatever concoction she used really worked on the jellyfish stings. She told me she was a venture capitalist here on vacation. I introduced myself as Peter Smith, a writer. We made some small talk. She thinks we're gay, asked me about it, in fact."

"She mentioned your gayness? Why would she do that?" Christian asked, now fully incensed. Keeler turned to Marty, letting him respond.

"I don't know why; maybe she doesn't buy it," Marty answered peevishly. "Look, the fucking jellyfish stung the shit out of me; she showed up; what was I supposed to do, run?"

"You're supposed to tell your partner," Keeler said.

"I didn't tell him because there was nothing to tell, Admiral. I followed the twins to the bar where they met Randall and the woman. I had no idea that she was a Gallierga. She's dark, she looks native. I had one drink and left. It was a minor detail."

Christian looked again at the photo of Valisé, then pointed at it. "There's no way you can tell me you believe *this* woman looks native," he said, knowing Marty's explanation wasn't lining up. "Your bullshit stinks really bad, Becker. I'm not going to have it. I'm not going to have a partner who doesn't…"

"Christian, shut up," Keeler interrupted, worried that this would escalate further. He knew of their history in the Georgia marsh. Then he turned to Marty. "Look, Becker," he said toughly, "you get this straight right now. There's nothing too minor for Christian to know about. My guess is that what happened wasn't *minor* at all, but I don't care about that at the moment." Both Marty and Christian listened with their heads up and eyes looking straight ahead; the position a soldier takes when getting dressed down.

"This is about trust," Keeler continued, "I'm going to give you ten seconds to get your mind straight, Becker. If you don't get my message real quick, your ass will be on the next plane back to the states. You can then explain to Marshall Davis about how you fucked up this operation in less than two days. Do you understand me?"

"Yes, sir," Marty answered.

"How is it you understand me?"

"My partner has to know everything."

"Can I hear that again?"

"My partner, Christian, has to know everything."

Keeler exhaled then paused for an uncomfortable time, in emphasis, letting them squirm. He knew that Marty would get a second dressing down from Christian later, but the split had been repaired. It could be worse, he imagined. Not only had they located the woman, but they had established contact. The wheels were turning in his head as Marty and Christian waited for him to continue. "Okay," he said after a moment, "So we know where she is. Do you really think she believes that you're gay?"

"I...I don't know, sir. She asked me about it sort of skeptically. I don't know."

"Wait," Christian said. "If you were so screwed up on the beach, suffering from the jellyfish stings and all, how did the conversation begin about your gayness? I mean, did you lay around in the sun afterward and share a glass of guava juice with her?" He knew there had to be more to the story, and he wanted it right then.

"She asked me about being gay in the bar, last night, not on the beach," Marty answered contritely. "She bought me a drink to apologize for the incident in the road; then she came over and introduced herself. She asked me about it then." Marty recited the rest of the conversation exactly. Christian said nothing more once the story was complete, but didn't attempt to disguise his contempt.

With the complete knowledge of what happened, Keeler proceeded to cobble together a plan B. He wondered why Valisé was interested in the topic. It seemed to him that questioning Marty about his sexual orientation was bold line of inquiry after having just met him. He deduced that she probably didn't believe the rumor, hence her confidence in talking about it, and she must be interested from a personal standpoint, otherwise, she would have had no curiosity in what he was: she simply wouldn't care.

"I want you to meet her again," Keeler said. "Go up to her place, tell her you want to show thanks for her help on the beach; tell her you want to take her to dinner or something, anything. Do you think you can engage her?"

"Engage her, sir?"

"Yes, Becker, get her to like you. Ask her out. Try to romance her. Get her into bed. Do you think it's possible?"

Marty was ambivalent; worried about his ability to do it *only* as part of his job. "I'll do my best, sir," he responded.

"You'll need to modify your cover."

"I could talk about Christian: that he's my literary agent, and he's gay, but I'm not. I'll say it helps when people believe I'm gay too, so they leave me alone while I'm writing. "

"That might work," Keeler said.

"Yes sir."

"Just be sure you understand the seriousness of your situation. You have to be convincing or we'll lose her. Just as important, if you're exposed, you'll probably be dead before you know it and you could take Christian down with you. She might, in fact, already know who you are. The Cartel is very astute. Their intelligence capabilities rival that of some countries."

"Yes, sir."

"It's imperative that you keep Christian informed on *all* your activities. If she as much as nibbles on your ear, I want him to know. I want him to know what color her toenails are. I want him to know everything," he said pointedly.

"Yes sir," Marty said quietly.

"Christian, I want you on Sutton. If he's not on the island, find out where he is. We need to determine his destination the next time he flies out of St. Thomas. I have my own plane here, so I can follow him. But I have to know when he's leaving; it will probably be at night. Our satellite phones are encrypted and safe to use, but not in public. Rent a second car; you'll be going in different directions."

"Ay, sir," Christian said.

"Okay, that's the situation. I'm going back to the hotel for a shower and a talk with Will Davis. Then I'm going over to the St. Thomas airport to scope out Sutton's plane, if it's there. If it is, tomorrow I'll try to book a sightseeing tour with him. I want to hear about everything and certainly the instant you have his computer hacked. Are there any questions?"

Marty spoke up, needing some clarity. "If I can make uh….progress with the woman, what am I doing? Are you saying you want me to try to turn her?"

"That's not likely," Keeler said. "You look and listen; glean bits of information from her that might indicate what she's doing here, what she does in Colombia, who she knows here, who else is with her. Try to get her to relax. Listen carefully for hints about her life or family. See if you can detect a weakness that might be exploited. You studied psych-interrogation; modify it to fit the circumstance. Try to work your way into her confidence. Take it as far as you can go, safely."

Marty nodded, but he was beset by the challenge of cultivating her.

Christian's mind was moving. "What do you think the al Qaeda role is here, sir?" he asked.

Keeler looked at him intently. "I'm reluctant to speculate. I don't want us to operate from any preconception. But it seems logical that it's about money. I think al Qaeda is partnering with the Cartel in drugs and the Suttons are mules. Let's hope its *only* drugs that they're smuggling."

11

The Schedule

The cell phone rang. Gallierga checked the caller ID window and saw 'UNAVAILABLE'. The caller was not from within the company circle, and there was but one person outside of it with his number.

"Yes," he answered in monotone. He heard a hiss in the background and waited. Finally, a voice asked, "Is this the Hotel California?"

He knew it was al Jamal without being told, and Gallierga chose his words carefully, then replied: "Yes. You can check out any time you like, but you can never leave."

Al Jamal had much to discuss and detested speaking openly on a cell phone, but there was no choice. A few days earlier, Gallierga received the coded cell message from Riyadh informing him that the shipment had commenced. The current call would be a discussion of the details. Al Jamal got right to it.

"On or about what you call July 15, nine days from today, our vessel, the *Dover Mist*, will arrive at the agreed upon location. As the ship nears the rendezvous point, and beginning at 1300 hours GMT on July 14, the captain will broadcast a message on frequency 121.45 megahertz. The message will be repeated every thirty minutes until contact is made with your people." Gallierga jotted down notes as the man spoke. "The message will be '*the moon and stars are shining brightly*'. The response from your man will be '*except for the one*'. After this contact has been established, your employee will dial the following cell phone number: 10133-433-3720, putting him in contact with the captain of the steamer so that specific transfer details can be discussed. If there is some problem with the communication, the steamer will circle the area for four hours, whereupon the message will be repeated. Do you understand all of this?"

"Yes."

"The shipment will be six hundred forty packages of one kilogram each. We have set the wholesale market value to be ninety-five thousand dollars per kilogram or sixty point eight million dollars for the entire shipment. As agreed, your twenty-five percent share will be fifteen point two million. You will furnish a Swiss Bank account number, whereupon one half of your fee will be deposited once you take control of the product. The balance will be deposited upon delivery to our agents in..."

Gallierga interrupted him. "You have altered the figures we agreed upon, my friend. We assumed the market value, for the purpose of calculating my fee, to be one hundred thousand dollars per kilogram. That would make the value of the shipment sixty-four million, and my fee sixteen million."

"Yes, that was our original agreement," al Jamar conceded, "but market conditions have changed and we must devalue the product slightly."

"I do not think the market has changed so much." Gallierga rejoined. "Producers in Venezuela are regularly selling South American heroin at one hundred ten thousand dollars per kilo and theirs is widely known to be inferior in quality to your product. More importantly, my cost and risks do not vary with the market; neither does the quality of my service or the value of my protection. I will not perform the service for less than the fee we agreed upon at the outset." Gallierga's voice showed no change, but it was clear there would be no negotiation of the fee. Al Jamal allowed a dramatic pause.

"Very well, it will be as we agreed earlier, but we have an additional request. One of our agents must accompany the shipment."

"You want us to transport a passenger as well? I'm sorry, my friend, but for security reasons this is not possible. We have weight considerations for the aircraft." Gallierga quickly realized that this was all al Jamal was after to begin with.

"It is critical that a representative of ours be in Miami to supervise the delivery and finalize the distribution of the product. This will be the only time that we will make this request. Surely you can understand. We are talking about a transaction worth nearly sixty-five million dollars."

Gallierga ignored this approach and returned to practical issues. "The airplane we use has weight restrictions and you have almost doubled the size of the shipment we originally discussed. Now you want to add the weight of a passenger. It isn't possible."

"Surely Señor, for sixteen million dollars, you can make use of a larger aircraft."

"It is not just the cost of the aircraft, my friend, it is the ability of the aircraft to maneuver, to fly under the radar of the DEA; moreover, the airplane's ability to get in and out of a small airport at an intermediate distribution point. A shipment this large will not be brought into Miami on one airplane, it will need to be split up and transferred to two or perhaps three smaller aircraft."

Al Jamal became nervous at the thought of transferring the goods en route and Gallierga could hear the strain in his voice. "I was not aware that you would split the shipment."

"I was not aware that you were going to send nearly three quarters of a ton of product in this first run."

Al Jamal had no options, but played every card he was holding. "You will have the entire product at the designated drop off point in Miami at the same time, is that correct?"

"With all due respect, Mr. al Jamal, when you contract with my company, you can depend upon our capabilities. We will designate the exact time when the entire product will be delivered. Of course, this will be within a close tolerance of what you require. But we will set the exact time. There are risks, as you are aware, and I am bearing those risks. By sending one of your agents with the shipment you are increasing my risk; yet I am hearing of no offer for additional compensation. What you're asking, I believe, is to make use of my facilities to smuggle one of your operatives into the United States. The product you send is not traceable, so to speak, should some mishap occur. However, your operative is, and he would become a security risk to my company if he fell into the hands of my enemies."

"We have a common enemy in this venture," al Jamal responded.

"We may have a common enemy for the moment. But again, with all due respect, we have different ventures. And I have no wish to be associated with your ventures except as a paid courier for your product. To be allied any other way would be very bad for business, as you can imagine. If it were discovered that we are helping to bring your operatives into the U.S., this could be construed by some as an act of war. And this would bear consequences far more grave than the mere loss of a shipment to the DEA."

Al Jamal was persistent, "If you will allow my agent to accompany the goods, I will increase your fee on the next shipment to thirty-five percent."

Gallierga chuckled. "Ah, so now you want me to perform added work, very risky indeed, and you want it on credit? No my friend, I will carry your agent for an additional five million dollars, deposited in full, at the same time as the deposit for the transport of the product. And please be aware, that should some mishap occur, your agent will be disposed of before we allow him to be captured."

"I would expect nothing less," al Jamal replied.

There was a long pause as he gave an uncomfortable silence one last chance to work on Gallierga, but in the end he realized he was without options. "It is agreed then. You will be hearing from my people on July 14. I will call you during your transit period to confirm that all is going well."

"Agreed," Gallierga replied, masking his pleasure over the victory. "But be certain that you deposit the proper amount in sufficient time for my agent to confirm the funds have been collected. We don't want any delays during the delivery."

Al Jamal sneered. "You seem as though you don't trust my word, Señor. Funny, since you will have sixty-four million dollars worth of my heroin and one of my agents as collateral."

"I don't want your heroin or your agent, my friend. I only want my fee. And I want our relationship to be mutually profitable and long lived."

"I will meet the payment terms, Señor," al Jamal said, and the line went dead.

Gallierga smiled as he turned off the phone and looked out across the City of Medellín from the fortieth floor of his penthouse. How pleasant, he thought, that the Yemen connection had conveyed such a lucrative transaction so soon. It seemed likely he would need to pay Conrad for two transits, instead of just one, but that was a relatively small additional expense. He calculated that his net profit on this transaction, including the bonus for transporting the passenger, would be approximately twenty million dollars. This was ten times the profit he would normally realize on a single shipment of cocaine, although admittedly, delivering to Miami elevated the risk significantly.

After the exact date had been established, Sutton came to mind. He must call to impress upon Valisé the urgency of obtaining his agreement to stay on board. He opened his contact list and pressed the button for her cell phone. At the other end, she recognized the caller ID.

"Hello Uncle, it's beautiful day here in the islands. How are you?"

"I'm fine, love. Are you enjoying your holiday?"

"Yes, wonderful. I ran the beach this morning, it was very peaceful. Randall has been helpful, keeping an eye on me, as you know."

"He's a good boy, that Randall. We're lucky to have him."

"Uncle, I don't need his protection. It's handy to have him around; he takes care of the details, but he can be a little possessive."

"He's doing his job. Have you had a chance to see about meeting with Sutton?"

"Randall and I met with his daughters last night. They are, well, different, but very welcoming. I'm seeing Conrad this afternoon. Randall is coming by in a few minutes to pick me up. Has there been some further development?

"Yes. It is imperative that we keep Sutton engaged. In fact, there is a transaction scheduled to commence very soon, probably within a few days. So you must get his agreement and express the need for him to begin planning immediately."

"I'll talk to him. But we don't want to appear needy."

"True. But the stakes are large."

"I feel confident he'll stay with us." Valisé shook her head, shaking off a sudden trace of compassion for Sutton's peculiar political cause and the cash he would need to pursue it. "Uncle, I have to get ready, Randall will be here soon."

"Be perseverant with Sutton."

"I will. I'll call you tonight, ok? Ciao." She clicked off the phone.

When Randall arrived at the Hill House, Valisé met him at the door and told him she wanted to drive. He agreed halfheartedly. The fact of the matter was that Randall had never been able to refuse her anything. Her charm simply conquered his will to disagree. Like other men, Randall harbored a secret love for her which could never be exposed. He was a willing slave.

She hopped into the Jeep dressed casually, wearing simple khaki shorts and a green fatigue shirt tied at the waist over a black tee. She also wore dark leather hiking boots; the whole of it gave her a chic militant air, which Randall had not seen before. Sitting in the driver's seat, she pulled her hair back so that the wind wouldn't make a mess of it and put on her baseball cap. Randall climbed into the passenger side. She turned the engine over and shifted into gear as he settled in. He directed her to head back to town where they would get on Centerline road and drive toward the south shore of the island.

As they began to climb Mount Bordeaux on the winding two lane road, Randall pointed her to a sandy drive that snaked down toward a bay called Hurricane Hole. There were steep turns not unlike the Hill House Road, except there were no protective guard wires or posts. As they descended through the dense vegetation, breaks in the canopy provided glimpses of the ocean at the bottom, where the road would eventually lead them. Valisé was enjoying the drive, feeling as though she was repelling the cliff in a car. Randall grunted occasionally, on particularly sharp turns, from fear she would not fully negotiate one and they would slide off the edge, tumble over and over again, until finally coming to rest in the sea.

They arrived at a relatively flat spot in the landscape where several modest but well-kept West Indian homes were spread out a comfortable distance from each other. He pointed to a white one with red hurricane shutters and told her to pull up to the side. The front porch was surrounded by bougainvillea and hibiscus in full bloom and a yellow cat lay sleepily on the front steps. Quite charming, Valisé thought to herself. There were roosters and chickens running loose and young boys playing stick ball in the road, slightly perturbed when they had to move to let the Jeep by. She smiled at them and upon seeing Randall in the seat next to her, they yelped with glee and began to call his name. Whenever he came there, he brought a bag of candy from Cruz Bay. Today, Mary Janes and Tootsie Rolls were his treat and, as he cast them out, the kids scrambled for a prize, yelped, and called his name over and over.

Valisé got out of the Jeep and followed Randall to the front door. It wasn't necessary to knock, as Sutton met them there with a welcome smile and a warm handshake. After exchanging greetings, Randall, knowing his place, excused himself politely. Sutton led Valisé to the open air sitting room in back of the house and handed her a glass of iced mango with a pinch of cinnamon on top.

"My uncle told me you would never forgive us if I was on your beautiful island and I didn't pay you a visit," she stated.

"Your uncle is a great and thoughtful man, and I am proud ta have been associated with him all these years."

"Have you had a chance to think things over? We truly need to continue our association."

"Well, yes, I was thinking that maybe I stay on for a while. But I has some things that maybe you could answer for me."

"I'll try." She said positively, suddenly relieved that he was saying yes. But she displayed no change in emotion.

"I was thinking that maybe I would do this work for one more year and after that you would not ask me ta continue any more, but let me be ta do the things I want. Is that agreeable?"

"That will be fine, Señor Conrad." Secretly, she was hoping to be out of this business herself by then.

"I was also thinking that, well, this is a dangerous thing that we do and something could happen ta me at any time. And if that happens, would you promise ta take care of my daughters and make sure that no one from the authorities comes for them?"

Valisé was elated by this, easy negotiating, so far. "I would use all of my company's resources to protect them, you have my word. At the very least, I would guarantee them safe haven in Colombia."

Sutton took pause when he thought of his daughters being subject to the likes of Orestes, but he continued, "and there is the matter of the money."

"Ah," she said with a grin, "was my uncle's offer not sufficient?"

"No, no the amount is fine. But I want ta be sure that my family gets all the money that I have if something happens ta me. I mean, they have no idea of the whereabouts of my savings, or the amount that I have. No one does, I think." He looked at Valisé slightly askance, searching for an answer to his probe; wondering how much the Cartel knew of his personal life. He received from her only an innocent, uncertain look followed by a slight tilt of her head, as if to convey a wish that he clarify his meaning.

"You see, I don't want them ta have the money now; maybe they use it for things that are not the best things. I want you to guarantee the safekeeping of my fortune, and that my children will receive de money if I am killed."

"My company cannot guarantee that," she answered stiffly.

"I know that, but *you* can."

"Why would you trust me in such a way?"

"Because I think that in spite of the ugly nature of the business and the ruthless people you work with, you are a sincere woman. And I think that you possess an honor and nobility that is different than the company you keep. The amount of money I am talking about is no more than a month's worth money for your company, but it is a lifetime of work ta me and my family. It mean nothing ta you but it is the world ta me. I ask myself, 'why would you take away my world for something so little ta you?'"

"I wouldn't."

Sutton nodded and retrieved an envelope from under his seat cushion. "Here is the access number for the bank account I keep in Switzerland. Before each mission, I will give you the password, good for one transaction only. If all goes good, you deposit my fee when I complete the mission, using the password for that mission. If something happens ta me, you withdraw all the money and give it ta my daughter Anya."

"Señor Conrad, I will honor your request and execute it if need be. You have my word." Given the volatility of her world, she knew that no such pledge could be absolute. But she was honest in her intent.

"You may tell your uncle that I await his direction for the next mission." Conrad replied.

"He will be very pleased."

She made an appointment to meet again the following day, after she had time to talk to Gallierga and ascertain the details of the coming mission. Randall rejoined her outside, and they began the drive back to the Hill House. She felt a sense of accomplishment, but foreboding accompanied her relief. Perhaps Conrad was more intuitive about this venture than she. Perhaps he was wise to plan for an uncertain future. Perhaps, she thought, she should be doing the same. Her head was swimming. They didn't need the Arab partnership.

As of her last balance sheet update, company assets sat at slightly more than one billion dollars. Of this, some $750 million was in cash or readily marketable securities. Company net income from returns on investments – perfectly legal returns – would soon exceed thirty million dollars per quarter. In another year at the current operating level, returns on legal investments would outpace income from cocaine operations. That, it seemed, would make the cocaine trade too risky an enterprise, losing its attraction as a profit center. It would make sense to sell off the cocaine business in the near future and focus on more profitable ventures. She often thought of the legacy of Joseph Kennedy, who used bootlegging during the period of U.S. prohibition to springboard into legitimate fortune and global influence. This was her model. Gallierga was drifting away from this possibility. By aligning themselves with the group from Yemen, he could be closing the door on legitimacy.

Arriving back at the Hill house, Valisé bid Randall goodbye and promised to meet him later for dinner in town. She sat in the wicker chaise lounge on the deck and looked out over the Caribbean as the sun inched its way toward the horizon. She began her transformation from business woman to relaxing tourist, sipping a pummeled orange drink, made from crushed fresh orange drowned in tequila. She was entranced by the colors the sun produced where the sea met the sky. Footsteps in the gravel drive below interrupted her peaceful state. A polite knock on the mahogany front door followed. As she glided through the kitchen in bare feet, glass in hand, she saw Marty standing outside the screen with a friendly smile on his face.

"I wanted to return your towel from this morning." He held it up as evidence. "I thought that maybe dinner tonight might be suitable thanks for saving my skin." He smiled. "I didn't know how to call you, so I just walked up the road."

She was interested in this outsider, this *Peter Smith*. The rule was that her man would come from within the company. But she found cartel men, for the most part, unable to match up with her superior intellect. From time to time she tried to satisfy her need for company with a handsome, though simple, son of one of Gallierga's lieutenants. She'd allow herself to be dated, wined, dined and entertained by him as best he could. But there always came the time in the night when she realized, yet again, that he was boring and un-inspiring. So she took care of the earthy part of romance in the comfort and security of her bedroom suite; alone with a vibrator and an image of someone else.

She had no real lover, no confidant and no friend. She had become vulnerable.

"How nice of you to visit me," she said, smiling politely, and extended her hand to greet him as she opened the door. The hangover from her inner drama earlier remained, but she was open to the possibilities presented by this man. "I'm so sorry, please remind me, is it, Mr. Smith?" she asked properly.

"Call me Peter. I really do want to thank you again for this morning. I would have told you then, but I woke up and you were gone."

"You were sleeping pretty soundly. I thought you would be fine. And as I can see, you are."

"So I am," Marty said. "And I would like to show my appreciation. May I take you to dinner or maybe you could show me some of the island? Perhaps we could get a boat and see another island."

"Oh my, what a grand repayment proposal for such a small deed; aren't you afraid of the ocean after this morning?"

"Not as long as I'm with you, and you're armed with your magic potion."

Her budding interest bled faintly through the indifferent posture she took, standing arms crossed in the doorway, leaning against the jamb, the open screen-door resting against her arm as she spoke. She resisted giving the impression that she would be quite so readily available and Marty didn't expect to come away from the visit with a plan for that night, but her playful wariness didn't prevent him from standing confident, waiting for a straight answer.

"Well," she smiled again, "I wouldn't want to be responsible for you shying away from the ocean. I have access to a boat; maybe a day-sail tomorrow? I know some great spots for reef, we could snorkel, and lunch."

A red flag went up. Marty wasn't about to be 'toured' around the islands with her bodyguard and crew. "No jellyfish?" he asked.

"No guarantees," she chuckled.

"Well, how about if I get the boat?"

"Do you mean sail it ourselves?"

"Yeah, why not? It'd be fun."

"You must want to work at this."

"It'd be a working lunch."

"I'm not sure that I should sail alone with you just yet, Mr. Smith. I don't know you very well."

They stared into each other's eyes, testing the others confidence by not breaking away.

"Well enough, I think," he said without blinking. "You held my head in your lap this morning and rubbed your magic potion on my wounds. Very few know me that well."

"Yes, pure charity though, answering a distress call, or perhaps guilt for almost running you over. But I don't *know* you, Mr. Smith."

"Do you want to?"

"Maybe."

"So can I pick you up at, say, nine in the morning?" He smiled his best smile and it served to disarm her one click further.

"Nine is good, but I'll meet you at the docks." Then she remembered about Sutton. "Oh, I have an early meeting, can we make it ten?"

"Ten it is." He stepped away and down the stairs to the dirt drive, turning back to her a few meters away. "What shall we drink?" he asked.

She smiled at his eagerness, "I like mango in the morning, add a little rum in the afternoon."

He raised his hand in the air and put on his best pirate voice, "Ay, Mango 'n' rum fer me lady." She waved to him and chuckled as she allowed the screen door to swing shut and went back into the house.

Sensing it was past the time she should have called Emilé to advise him that the meeting with Sutton had gone well, Valise retrieved her cell phone from the glass table next to the chair where she sat on the veranda earlier, intending to dial him up. Before entering the number, she hesitated, and considered the wisdom of calling him before she had more time to digest the new development: her 'date.' She decided it would not be strategic to inform Emilé of her plans for the next morning with Peter Smith. In fact, she decided against informing him of anything at all until she was ready; until she was feeling less anger toward 'the creep'. She rested the phone back on the table and took another sip of her tequila.

Keeler's cell phone rang. He flipped it open and said, "Go ahead."

"Sir, Becker here, I have a date with her."

"When?"

"Tomorrow morning. I need a boat. A small catamaran, single mast, stocked with food and drink, mango juice and rum. I also need snorkel gear, charts of the island, and…"

"Hold it, Skipper. Why can't you just take her to lunch?"

"Sir, she's not a *just lunch* kind of woman and it's the first thing that came to mind." Shit, Marty thought, why didn't I just let her provide the boat?

"Listen, Becker, do you have sailing experience? The waters around these islands are full of reef and wicked currents. I can't let you take off with this woman in a little boat. She said *yes* to this?"

"Yes, sir."

"Well, we're gonna have to charter something. I'll ask James to put it together. Mango juice and rum? Unfuckingbelievable. What time and where?"

Marty was grateful for the charter idea. "At the Cruz Bay dock, at 10 a.m. She'll be pointing the way. I figure maybe we'll get back to port around sunset."

"Sounds lovely Deputy, really."

"I understand, sir, I'm focused."

"I imagine you are." Keeler said dryly. "Where is Christian in all of this?"

"He's trying to locate Sutton at the moment. He'll call with a report."

"I'm sure he'll be pleased to learn that you are doing all the dirty work."

"Yes sir, I can't complain."

"Just watch your back."

"Yes, sir."

"I'll call you later with the details on the boat." Keeler clicked off.

12

The Dover Mist

In one of the small forward berths of the Liberian registered ship Dover Mist, a young bearded and scrappy Pakistani man, Yelsi Ribindi, was having great difficulty arranging his prayer mat, his sajjāda, for mid-morning prayer. The Dover Mist, the first in the al Qaeda fleet, was a small cargo vessel, only 195 feet in length. And it was heavily laden this voyage, carrying a payload of 3,500 metric tons of Arabian coffee beans and an additional, relatively small, but considerably more valuable cargo: 660 kilograms of nearly pure Afghan heroin.

The ship was managed by a crew of eight: pilot, co-pilot, navigator, two machinists, a plumber, an electrician, and a cook. Ribindi was the only real passenger. The electrician and the cook were a couple and hence the only two men on board who were really having any pleasure at sea. There were four other souls on board: two armed agents from the heroin seller, al Qaeda; and two matching Sicilian thugs representing the buyer, the Abruzese family of Miami. The four of them were aboard to watch over the heroin at all times, in shifts, two at a time, one from each side, until it was handed off to Gallierga.

The heroin was tested by the Italians just prior to leaving port at Karachi. It would be tested several more times before reaching Gallierga's people, as an assurance there was no tampering with the product in transit. Each time the product was tested, the guards would notify their respective bosses that the product was secure. Each time the bosses were so notified, 25 percent of the value of the purchase, or roughly $16 million, would be deposited into a secret bank account in Syria. In this way, the further the shipment progressed along the route, the more interest the purchaser had in guaranteeing the safety of the voyage. The first en-route testing revealed that the heroin was as promised: averaging between 96 and 98 percent pure. Hence, the first $16 million was deposited in the account as agreed. Upon departure from the Madagascar waypoint, the two thugs from Abruzese randomly tested 12 kilos again. This time, the purity per kilo ranged between 97 and 98 percent. Again, $16 million was transferred to the account. At this point, al Qaeda was in possession of all of the cash necessary to pay Gallierga and cover all production and transport costs. Upon delivery of the entire shipment in Miami, when the final payment was transferred to al-Qaeda, the net profit for the sale would be somewhere in the $40 million range.

The waters around the Cape of Good Hope were rough that night, due to a stationary low pressure 300 miles to the southeast, causing the relatively light Dover Mist to roll heavily in the 25-foot swells. The ship was not designed for very long voyages or high seas. It was originally built to carry cargo between the British Isles and the continent of Europe. Before al Qaeda bought it, the ship was used between North Africa and southern Europe, across the Mediterranean Sea. It had little commercial use for anything other than shuttling over small seas or channels, as the payload was relatively small and the size of the ship made the open ocean a risky place to be.

Ribindi struggled with his sajjāda as the ship rolled and yawed, and he was unable to kneel properly and maintain concentration on his prayer. Attempting to find his Kiblah was useless as he couldn't really determine the proper direction to Mecca, so he just proceeded with prayer anyway, hoping that Allah would hear at least some of it. He divided his concentration between the prayer and clutching his precious steamer trunk, trying to make certain that it would not be disturbed by the unpredictable motion of the ship. Concern for his own safety was not paramount, as he believed Allah would deliver him to complete the mission. It was, after all, by Allah's command. There was no need for concern over the safety of the ship.

Inside the steamer trunk were 220 syringes. Each syringe was filed with approximately 30 milliliters of ricin, enough of the toxin to kill more than a thousand people. So within the steamer case, judiciously protected by Ribindi, there was enough poison, if administered properly, to kill between 200 and 250 thousand people.

Ricin is extracted from the bean of the common castor plant and is therefore fairly easy to produce. The poison may be ingested in almost any way and works relatively slowly. Within 24 hours, a victim will have intestinal pain and bloody diarrhea. Within 36 hours, the stomach and intestinal walls will be unable to absorb fluids and abdominal bleeding will increase. Within 48 to 72 hours, the loss of fluid will be so severe that vital organs will begin to fail. Shortly thereafter, the victim will die from loss of blood and dehydration. Death is gruesome.

Ribindi was told that his mission was to deliver the toxin to a select group of American people; a group who would unwittingly ingest it mixed with their heroin. He would be the emissary of death. After the product was shipped, but prior to the time it was *cut* with powdered sugar, at an opportune time, he would gain access to the heroin, use the small syringes to put a tiny pinprick in each one of the 1 kilogram bags, and inject 10 milliliters of the liquid. Later, when the sugar was mixed in, the ricin would be mixed in thoroughly as well. Ribindi was told to wear goggles, rubber gloves, and a respirator when doing this, for just one renegade micro-drop of the poison would kill him.

This WMD was not a dirty nuke cooked up in some hidden laboratory; not a pot shot chemical bomb designed to cloud an American city with deadly gas; not a complicated, costly and risky hijack of American airplanes. It didn't require an elaborate and expensive delivery vehicle, or involve huge quantities of explosives. It was conceived in simple organic science. It was, in the mind of al Zawahiri, an elegant and relatively cheap way to bring horror to the people of Satan. It was beautifully ironic too, as al Qaeda would be paid for the heroin long before the toxin had time to do its dirty work.

The real genius in this act of war was not the act itself. It came with negotiating the sale of the heroin, engineering the payment terms and the safe transfer of cash from the buyers, and sub-contracting the delivery into the United States. All of this was expertly crafted by al Zawahiri, who contemplated that after a quarter million American pigs were lying in hospitals, shitting out all of their blood, withering away like prunes until death overtook them, he alone would receive the highest praise of Allah and the respect of his brethren for this great act of Jihad. He regretted that his act would not strike directly at the leadership or economic structure of the enemy's society. But it would surely cause massive fear and panic in the hearts of Americans and others.

In spite of his youth, Ribindi was shrewd and fearless. He was selected by al Zawahiri himself, and instructed in the minutest details of the operation: how the money transfer would work and how the heroin would be tested during transport. He practiced administering the injections, getting accustomed to injecting exactly 10 milliliter amounts of fluid, repetitive times. He became so adept at it that with his eyes closed, he could tell almost exactly how many milliliters of solution had been spent, just by the position of the plunger and the weight of the syringe between his fingers. He practiced until he was able to inject more than 10 bags per minute, actually using more time to pick up and dispose of syringes, than in performing the injections. He learned how to plunge the needle into plastic bags of flower without tearing the bag, and without spilling the liquid.

Ribindi applied his intellect in deciding the perfect moment to begin the real work, targeting the time just after the last test, but before the heroin was transferred to Gallierga. This could not be scripted beforehand; he would have to use his training and intellect to select an opportune time.

It was convenient for him that the heroin wouldn't be covered in coffee, or even crated too securely until it arrived in Colombia. The Mafia buyers insisted on this arrangement, as they needed access to the product for testing several times during transit. Apparently, they trusted Gallierga, because they asked for no further testing once the heroin was in his custody. This made al Zawahiri certain that Gallierga had a side contract with Abruzese. But it made no difference, in fact, it further insured the safe delivery of the heroin to the ultimate destination.

Ribindi was not yet finished with prayer when he heard someone struggling outside his berth, trying to make their way down the hall. There was a loud rap on his door. "Ribindi, we need your help. Get your ass down to the hold. We have to stretch out the bilge pump hoses to get the water out."

"I'm in prayer, go away," Ribindi answered in frustration.

"I don't give a fucking shit if Allah himself is in there with you. Get out here and down to the hold. Water is coming in through the vents. The special cargo could be threatened."

Ribindi opened the door and stuck his pistol in the face of the machinist, who fell backward across the small corridor in fear. He used this opportunity to move closer, putting the gun directly against the man's forehead. The ship rolled violently, causing the gun to bump into his head and drive it into the wall with a thud. He groaned in pain.

"I told you, you slime pig, do not to disturb me. Get the guards to help. If you interrupt my prayer again, I will scatter what little brains you have onto the floor where you stand, and Allah will bless me for it."

The man, fighting both fear and the heaving of the boat, managed to get to his feet and scamper down the hall, bouncing off the walls while looking back at Ribindi with an ashen face. The Muslim returned to his berth, slamming the door violently behind him. He knelt again to finish his prayer.

There was, in fact, general mayhem in the cargo hold. Everyone except the pilot was down there working feverishly to get the bilge pumps to operate at full capacity. The four guards however, would do nothing. They trusted no one on board, let alone each other, and refused to move from opposite sides in front of the storage locker which held the heroin. The water streamed in from large vent holes cut into the ceiling of the hold, leading to the outside, terminating in an upside down macaroni-shaped spout on the deck. The weather was so violent topside that seawater was being blown up inside the macaroni vents, then falling down onto the floor of the hold. To combat the flooding, the bilge pumps were fired up and suction hoses were being stretched out to remove the water. When the ship yawed to the right, a sheet of water would flood up against the door to the locker and then recede as the ship yawed in the opposite direction. The crates of coffee beans stacked in the center of the hold were sitting constantly in a few inches of water, but the crating material was so stout that there was little fear of water seeping into that product.

Of the four guards, the two from the Abruzese camp were the most fearsome. They would kill everyone on board if need be, and then sail the ship themselves. They had no regard for anyone, including Ribindi. In fact, they were convinced he was up to no good and were very suspicious of him. He did nothing of any consequence as a part of the voyage, except to guard the trunk. Moreover, while they would be required to part ways with the heroin once it was transferred to Gallierga, Ribindi and his trunk were continuing on with the shipment. He spoke to no one except in the most necessary circumstances, and spent most of his time in his berth. He hadn't showered in days and he smelled awful, the odor becoming so rank that anyone merely passing by him stopped breathing through their nose momentarily. If either of the Mafia thugs could find an excuse, they would simply shoot Ribindi in the head and throw him overboard.

They held similar disregard for their counterparts guarding the other side of the door, making the assumption the al Qaeda agents were planning to kill them any minute and keep the heroin and the money for themselves. The al Qaeda agents were scruffy, black-bearded, killers; equals to the Italians in the brutality department. At best, there was a fragile truce in the cargo hold, with a mutually assured destruction theme. They remained alive as long as neither side carried out a first strike.

The objective though, was much larger than what the four pawns could imagine. Only Ribindi knew the real end game, so he was the real threat- not to the cargo, but to those who guarded it. He would assure that the heroin was infested before it left the ship. He would kill them all, perhaps be killed himself, if needed, to make it so.

Ribindi charted the guard's habits carefully. He watched as they guarded two at a time, in four-hour shifts. At one point he had observed two of them from opposite sides attempting to construct a crude conversation; as if they had become so bored with the tedious task, they needed to find something to talk about. It was almost as if they had forgotten, momentarily, that they weren't on the same team. He watched in amazement during one shift as one of the Mafia thugs left his al Qaeda counterpart alone while he went to the galley. He returned with two cups of the cook's tea. He handed one to the al Qaeda and received a nod of thanks in return. 'So much the better,' Ribindi thought. If they dropped their guard, his job would be easier.

When the ship turned north after rounding the tip of South Africa, the violent storm system gave way to high pressure. For several days, the ship steamed along on smooth seas and made good time at nearly twenty-five knots toward Colombia. Early in the morning of July 11, the day they were to rendezvous with Gallierga, under the careful watch of Ribindi and the two al Qaeda agents, the Abruzese pair opened the door to the heroin locker and picked 12 kilos from one of the pallets for the final test. By this time, they thought it a pointless exercise, as they had personally kept watch over the shipment for nine days and were certain no tampering had occurred. They were unconcerned that some of the kilos they chose that morning had already been tested previously. Ribindi watched as the vials of solution and heroin were carefully mixed and then as the mixture became a deep pinkish violet. He listened as the two Mafiosi spoke in Italian and nodded, approving the test. When the bigger one called his boss on a satellite phone to report the positive result, the conversation ended quickly, a sign that Ribindi was waiting for.

After the testing was concluded and the guards returned to their posts, Ribindi went to his berth and retrieved a one kilogram bag of powdered sugar, wrapped identically to the heroin in the cargo hold.

He held it under his arm, picked up his 9mm pistol, stuck it in the rear of his waistband, and walked hastily out of his berth. In the hold he found two of the gunmen, one from each side, lazily guarding the door to the storage compartment. He walked directly to the al Qaeda agent on duty, threw the bag of heroin at his feet, and began screaming at him in Arabic with all the anger he could muster, using great animation so that the Italian would have no doubt of the message, regardless of his inability to understand the language. Ribindi continually pointed toward the berth area, while holding up four fingers of his other hand, making it easy for the Italian to interpret: there were four more bags of heroin stowed away in the al Qaeda berth.

The angered and indignant guard screamed back at Ribindi, "You are a liar! What is wrong with you? What would make you accuse me of this?"

Ribindi looked over at the Abruzese gunman and back at the accused with a nod. When he did this, the al Qaeda thug adjusted his weapon, prompting Ribindi to pull his pistol from his waist band also. In like response, the al Qaeda thug swung his weapon around to face Ribindi, which the Italian interpreted as an intent to shoot. The Italian quickly pulled his weapon up and let off a small burst at the al Qaeda guard. Blood sprayed about as the man's chest exploded. He fell back against the wall, his trigger finger pulling as he went down, spraying the hold with ricocheting bullets, but neither Ribindi nor the Italian were hit. Ribindi dove for cover and came to a sliding stop on the floor some twenty feet from the mayhem.

Having heard the argument, the other al Qaeda guard was rounding the corner when the volley of bullets hit his partner. He skidded to a stop, raised his own weapon, and sprayed the Mafia shooter with fifteen rounds in a mere two seconds. The Italian spun in a circle from the impact and fell hard against the door to the hold, finally slumping to the floor. His heart continued to beat, pumping out flood through the holes in his chest. In perfect timing, as if Ribindi had scripted it himself, the other Mafia guard arrived to see the al Qaeda guard fire a stream of bullets into his partner. He reacted instinctively, without questioning what was going on. He was only a few feet behind the remaining al Qaeda thug when he raised his weapon. Ribindi was balled up with his back against the wall of the hold and watched as bullets, fired from behind, emerged from the Arab's chest and continued on to ricochet off the wall just above his place of refuge.

The Italian, the last shooter alive, ran to where his partner lay still oozing fresh blood, and tried to make some sense of the scene. Ribindi seized the opportunity. He got up on one knee, pointed at the bag of sugar on the floor and yelled hysterically in Arabic, "He stole the goods! He stole the goods!" The man walked over to where the fake heroin lay and with his back to Ribindi, bent down to pick it up. Ribindi pulled out his 9mm and fired two rounds directly into the man's buttocks. One bullet entered near the man's rectum, traveled through his stomach, into his chest, and exited through his throat, severing everything as it went through. The man dropped to the floor, dead instantly.

Ribindi smiled with pride as his plan had come to fruition better than he had imagined. He got to his feet and searched the last dead Italian for the keys to the storage locker. He knew it would not be long before one of the crew mustered the courage to peek into the hold. The story, as he told it later, was that obviously these men could not resist temptation. They had been fighting over the 'special' cargo, when he was fortunate to be in the position to kill off the last one before he stole it. A blessed turn for the rest of us, he added, because if any of the shipment had been tarnished or taken, al Zawahiri would have had them all killed.

"I am now in charge of the shipment, as well as the ship," he told them, and gave them orders to clean up the mess and dispose of the bodies overboard. There would be no funeral for the likes of these infidels. There would also be no report to al Zawahiri at this time. Ribindi would report the entire matter when the ship reached its destination safely, with all the cargo intact.

Since they all answered to the same boss, ultimately, they didn't argue with his directives, especially since they were so close to the destination. They all knew the delivery of the cargo was the main objective, and as long as that occurred, there would be no problem with the buyers or al Zawahiri over the shootings. After the massacre was cleaned up and the bodies disposed of, the crew vacated the hold, leaving Ribindi to his devices.

He never anticipated the work would be so easy. Based upon information from the pilot, they were approximately six hours from the rendezvous point. Taking his time, he rolled his steamer trunk down to the room where the heroin was stored and locked the door behind him. No one else had the key, so he was completely alone, unhurried, and able to go about his business in a most precise manner. Inside the locker he donned his respirator, facemask and rubber gloves. The bags of heroin were stacked on four pallets, with approximately 165 one kilogram packages per pallet. It took some doing to un-stack each pallet so that he could access all of the bags, but by late afternoon he had injected approximately 10 ml of the ricin into each one. As he worked, he carefully replaced the syringes back into the molded slot from which each had originated in the trunk, working methodically so that none were skipped over or misplaced.

Satisfied that his work was complete, he closed the trunk, and rolled it back out into the main cargo hold. He removed all of the protective clothing he had been wearing, his face mask and gloves, and, along with the trunk, took everything up to the stern of the ship. There he stripped naked and cast the whole lot overboard. He was sure the trunk would float about for a while but would sink in time. He walked below and got into the shower, washing from head to toe with the strong bar soap that the crew used. Under normal conditions he would never consider using that soap, or any soap for that matter, he hated the smell; it reminded him of Americans. But today was different. He had to be certain that none of the ricin came in contact with his skin. Allah was not ready to receive him, yet.

After dressing, Ribindi returned to his berth and knelt on his hands and knees for prayer. He told his god that the first part of the mission had been completed. He prayed for the grace and courage to carry out the rest of the plan successfully, and he prayed for Allah to allow him to come to paradise soon. During his prayer, he sensed a change in the steady drone of the ship's engines. They were slowing down. The rendezvous point must be near, he thought, and he would be transferring to the Gallierga ship soon. He rose and put his filthy belongings into his duffel bag, making certain that his weapon, his papers, and the cash that al Zawahiri had given him were in a place where he could recover them quickly. Then he slung the duffel over his shoulder and went topside. On deck, he held his head high into the warm winds coming off the South Atlantic as he searched the horizon for the silhouette of the next ship he would be boarding. His jihad was in progress, he had performed well. Allah would bless him.

13

Cortez

On the morning of her date with Marty, Valisé awoke at 6:00 a.m. She loved the early morning; it was, she felt, the only time she had to enjoy serenity. She used the quiet period to watch the sun as it rose over the mountain behind the house and sent blazing light onto Sir Francis Drake Channel. But Wednesday was also the day that the diminutive gardener, Mr. Cortez, came to tidy up the grounds. So she had only an hour or so to relish the view before he would invade her space. She sat on the deck sipping Puerto Rican coffee and watched the world come alive around her. It seemed only a moment had passed before the gardener's old Toyota pickup truck rumbled up the driveway.

Cortez was a curious man. Not a West Indian, but a Latino, perhaps seventy four or five years old. A natural choice for an employee, it would seem, since Perez, the owner, wanted someone he could trust tending to the grounds. The truth was, however, Cortez had been a long time employee of Perez and of Gallierga before him. He was a hired hand for the Cartel for years before Valisé was born.

When she was four years old and too young to remember him, Gallierga farmed Cortez out to the Perez family. He served them well for many years and was later given a retirement in the Virgin Islands, caring for the Perez properties on St. John and St. Thomas. He of course heard from Randall that Valisé would be at the Hill House for a few days, and in the short time before her arrival he recalled memories of the child called 'Miss Vali'.

As he walked along the path below the veranda, he looked up at her and said, "Good morning, Miss Vali," in Spanish. His familiarity in using her nickname set her back slightly.

"Have we met before?" she asked in return.

"Sí, when you were very young, just after you were born, when I was employed by Señor Emilé, and I worked with your mother…" he gasped, and cut himself short.

"My mother? You worked with my mother? How could you have worked with my mother?"

"It was a long time ago, perhaps I am mistaken. So sorry, I have to get after the hibiscus, the damn iguana are eating them all."

"Wait!" she ordered, but it was too late; he disappeared around the corner of the house. Clearly the old man had mistakenly overstepped a boundary. She would find another opportunity to get him to continue. The familiar feeling of dread began to well up in her and she shook slightly, trying to squelch it. There was no time for this now. She had to get ready for her date and she had yet to call Emilé with a report on Conrad – something she did not want to do, but she couldn't put it off any longer.

When she called and told him that Conrad consented to stay on with the company, she left out the part about his request that she look after his daughters in the event something untimely happened to him. Gallierga was clearly pleased with the news and immediately began to tell her about the forthcoming operation and what was expected of Conrad. In fact, he seemed very anxious to get Conrad moving almost immediately.

"Valisé," he said firmly, "we have a limited amount of time. Conrad must be prepared to fly to Isla La Tortuga, for a pickup on Thursday the 15th. It will be a large load; he might need to make two trips. He will be taking the cargo to Montserrat and then on to the U.S., perhaps Miami."

She was surprised at the new plan. "Miami? He has never flown directly into the United States; he's always been an intermediate courier."

"He is aware of the special requirements of his new position. Although in truth, this one job will be slightly different than what we discussed. I'm sure you can clear it with him. He'll be fine."

Emilé didn't wait for her to respond, he simply got right to the details. Sutton would get a complete instruction packet via Randall very soon, but basically, the plan was for Orestes to meet him at Isla de la Tortuga, where the cargo would be loaded. He would then fly two shipments to Montserrat, where everything would be loaded onto a larger aircraft, flown to an intermediate fuel stop, and then ferried to an exact delivery location in the United States. The total load would be 660 kilos, or approximately 1,400 lbs. There would also be a passenger.

"A passenger? Have you discussed this with Conrad?"

"Not yet." Gallierga replied. "But the profits are terrific, Vali, and we will plan very carefully.."

"I will talk to him," she said curtly, "but I think it will be too much for him to digest at this stage. I don't think he was planning on such an elaborate scheme so soon."

"He is an employee, Vali, and very well paid. He will do as you ask, if you *ask* him with the correct approach."

Valisé knew what this meant. And as she got into the Jeep to visit Sutton again, she felt a deep sense of foreboding, an intuition perhaps, that this project of Emilé's had crossed the line of what was prudent. But ever the good company girl, she drove on down the road to Enighed, to Sutton's house.

"Miss Valisé, you have returned so soon. It's a lucky day for me," Sutton said with a smile when she appeared at his door.

"Yes, I just spoke with my uncle. He asked that I come talk to you about an assignment." The look on Sutton's face turned serious, not in any way unpleasant, but focused.

"Please, come in," he said, and beckoning her to a cushioned wicker chair.

She waited for him to sit opposite her before beginning. "It seems that a transaction has developed rather quickly, much more quickly than we had anticipated, and we are in need of transport right away." Sutton followed her face without expression as she explained the mission particulars, the multiple stops involved, and the matter of the passenger. When she addressed the size of the load, he moved slightly betraying his surprise.

"I have not been able ta get the new aircraft big enough for that amount of cargo," he said calmly. "It maybe will require two trips. And I have worries about flying directly into the United States."

"We share your concerns," she said warmly, wanting him to feel that they were in this together. "And so my uncle has assured me the logistics will include a location for entry most likely to allow you to go undetected."

"I don't have concerns about the entry, I have worries about the landing. The Americans like ta control airspace. An aircraft does not show up at an airport without having been someplace else, you need a flight plan, and ta talk with air traffic control." He looked down at his hand pensively, with an air of confidence, but concern.

"About de passenger," he continued, "I will do as your uncle asks. But the passenger will not be allowed a weapon of any kind on the aircraft, and if we have any issues at all with the authorities, he must be prepared ta go through evasive maneuvers, and know that maybe he will not get ta his destination."

"My uncle has made the customer well aware of the risks, and that your primary assignment is the delivery of the cargo, not the wellbeing of the passenger. This is apparently a very lucrative venture, otherwise Emilé would not place your service at such risk. I'm certain he will reward your extra efforts accordingly."

"As you see fit Miss. I will begin ta get ready right now. Ask your uncle ta provide me with the mission packet as soon as possible."

"Randall will have it for you very soon." Sutton smiled formally and she stood to leave. "Good luck to you then," she said. "I expect that I will be back in my office by the time you return, but I look forward to seeing you again at our plantation during your next visit, and perhaps then we will have time to talk of more pleasant things."

"I hope so," he said, "I would like that."

Valisé smiled warmly as she turned to the screen door and passed through it without saying anything further. She knew the assignment she had just given this loyal employee would take him into danger from which he might not return. She knew he would never allow himself or the passenger to be captured by U.S. authorities. Sutton was well aware that death was preferable to capture; as a more gruesome death after capture would be inevitable.

Sutton immediately got out his weight and balance charts to calculate the limitations of the Cessna 310. The truth of the matter, he found, was that the aircraft would indeed carry the weight; the problem would be the limited room for fuel, just three hours-worth. He would need a larger plane or he would need to make two trips. Therefore he would need to know where his flight would originate and his exact destination. In addition, any intermediate fuel stops would need to be airports with fairly long runways, due to the hot, humid, and thin air of the Caribbean. He calculated that the fully loaded aircraft would require at least 4,000 feet of runway to safely lift off, limiting him to paved airstrips. There would be no slipping into a little grass strip or a hard sand beach. This, in itself, increased the risks many fold. The risks would not decrease with a larger aircraft, but he would then be assured of carrying it all in one trip.

A larger issue loomed at the other end of the journey. He would have to find an airport where DEA had no outpost, and where a flight plan would not be required. Or, he would have to figure out a way to migrate into the system without having to pass through customs. There was one thing that would help: Americans value freedom. The aviation laws guarantee it. They are able to buy an airplane, fill it with fuel, take off into the wild blue yonder and fly around, for the most part, unrestricted. What they can't do is fly near a busy centralized airport or over a metropolitan area without telling an air traffic controller who they are, where they came from, where they are going, and where they intend to land. They must have permission to fly through that airspace, which requires establishing contact with air traffic control.

Sutton decided upon a strategy. He would cross the coast of the U.S. low to the water, below DEA and air traffic radar. He would have a small county or municipal airport, a few miles inland, in his sights. This type of airport doesn't normally have a staffed air traffic control tower. He would then pass low over the airport and punch up through the radar blanket, simulating a takeoff from there. He would set his transponder to 1200, the normal VFR frequency, so when radar picked him up, he would look like any citizen out for a ride in his airplane. While climbing out, he would contact ATC and file a flight plan en route, for whatever destination Gallierga had decided upon. The flight plan would give him credentials upon landing and he wouldn't be bothered by customs or DEA because his flight would appear to have originated within U.S. borders. 'Right under their noses,' he decided, 'is the best place ta hide.'

Satisfied, for the time being, that he had a working strategy, Sutton began a checklist of things which had to be completed prior to departure. The call to leave could come at any moment. He stood up to go to his study when the house phone rang. It was Randall.

"Conrad, I got a package from boss Emilé, it just come ta me on the ferry, should I bring it down ta you?"

"Yah man, I be here," Sutton replied. He thought of how Señor Gallierga was so incredibly presumptuous: he obviously sent the mission package before Valisé had gotten his agreement to do the job.

Although, Sutton also realized that Gallierga's confidence was based upon many years of hearing people say 'yes'.

When Randall arrived with the instructions, he said little, but Sutton knew he was dying to know the details. That, of course, wouldn't do. Randall was too innocent to be involved in this dirty business, and although he was into the SFC up to his eyeballs, he had no idea the entire program was funded by Sutton's weekly trips to the north coast of South America. Randall was just naïve enough to believe the car rental business was paying for it all.

"Señor Gallierga wants ta invest in the car business," Sutton said casually. Randall simply stared, cocking his head like the RCA dog. "He's talking about expansion ta St. Thomas and the other islands, maybe build the air charter business, too." Randall nodded blankly and left without any further discussion.

While driving back to the Hill House, Valisé thought pleasantly about her forthcoming day with Peter Smith, a relief from the disturbing morning. She was reminded of how Randall had clearly mistaken Smith for being gay, which didn't surprise her. To the West Indians, two good-looking American men on vacation together *must* be gay, and Marty was definitely good-looking. In fact, Marty was becoming more than just good looking. Valisé sensed a pull, a connection, and noticed subtle signs in her body. There were vibrations and nervousness, and an aura about him that stayed with her after they parted. It was a schoolgirl feeling, like she was going on a date for the first time. She had none of her usual inclination to simply discard him, as she did with other men. This might be, she thought, because she had seen him at his weakest, overcome by exhaustion and taken to near unconsciousness by the stings from a jellyfish. But whatever the reason, she was now thinking of finding a need to stay on the island longer.

She finished the drive back to the Hill House in a dream state, smitten. All of her senses were alive and pulsing with the sugary thoughts of new romance. She was at once both enamored and aroused. Sexual energy twitched at the base of her back. As she rounded the final turn towards the villa, the breadth of the Caribbean came into her view and as she saw the emerald green islands contrasting against the deep blue of the sea, she felt as though she might, just might, bring him there tonight.

But as she slowed the Jeep to a halt, her intoxication was jarred sober by the sight of old man Cortez stepping out from the shadows under the veranda. Her mental love affair quickly morphed into the cold dread that accompanied any thoughts of her past. She looked at the old man with eyes that spoke of irritation as he disturbed her dream. He sensed her displeasure. He had been thinking of her while she was gone, how foolish he was to have gotten himself into such a pickle. As she set the parking brake of the Jeep with brusque ratcheting clicks, the old man spoke.

"I'm very sorry, Señorita Valisé. My name is Cortez. Please don't be upset with my presence. I finished my work just now. I fear that I have dishonored you. I fear that I have betrayed the trust of your…your…uncle. If he finds out that I have spoken to you, he will…."

"Never mind, Mr. Cortez," she enjoined. "I will say nothing to him. That is, I will say nothing to him as long as you finish your story from before. You were talking about my mother; that you worked with my mother, how could you have worked *with* my mother?"

The little old man stood before her and shook. His face had grown pale in the middle of a blistering sunny day. She could see that he had trouble separating his lips as the dryness of his mouth had gummed them shut. She recognized this fear. It was the fear of death. She'd seen it many times on the faces of those who served her uncle. His wrinkled and craggy hand shook as he raised it to cover his eyes and forehead. He made sounds as if he were going to weep. Valisé felt as if she could wrap her arms around this pitiful old man and assure him it would be all right and that he would not be injured, that she wouldn't let anything happen to him. But she stopped herself knowing that this was the first time she had ever… *EVER*…had the opportunity to hear something truthful about her past and she mustn't let the man get away from his dilemma. The only way he could escape death from betrayal would be to betray further.

"I can't, Miss Vali, he will kill me." He looked at her with the kind of sincerity that only mortal fear can portray.

She knew she had him. "You must tell me I'm afraid, or yes, he surely will." His eyes now spoke of his spiteful recognition of the strength of the Gallierga will. Then he sighed in resignation at knowing his choices were few.

Valisé spoke again, in a duplicitous way, reminiscent of Emilé. "Mr. Cortez, I do not desire to see you hurt in any way, in fact, I will protect you from harm. I will make certain that any information you give me will not be traced back to you. I'm trusting in you Señor, I need to know about my past. You must trust that I will protect you."

The color began to return to Cortez' face as he accepted her sincerity.

He raised his hand and scratched the part of his hair with the nail of his middle finger, trying to decide where to begin. "There are no witnesses still alive, except of course, for me."

"I understand."

"And, I'm not sure of all the circumstances. Much of what I will tell you, I heard from others."

"And all of these others are dead?" she asked.

"Yes."

She put her arm inside his, led him to the veranda and said. "Tell me everything."

Cortez began his story. He told her that one of the reasons his life was spared was that he was actually a distant relative of Emilé, a second cousin. He was spared because he was orphaned as a very young child and raised for a time by Emilé's parents in Cartageña. So he had known Emilé for most of his life. He was never invited into the family business ventures, but Emilé's own mother made him promise to always look after Cortez. This, he believed, was why he ended up with such a good position with Perez, here, in the Virgin Islands.

He told Valisé that as a young man, Emilé courted and married a fine beautiful woman from Medellín, named L'Aquila, whom he loved and treated with reverence. She scorned his dirty business, however; all the things he could buy brought her no satisfaction and no esteem for him. They soon drifted apart or, better said, he drifted away from her. He found comfort in the arms of a servant girl, Maria De Soto; an intelligent and beautiful woman, a woman who rivaled even Emilé's wife in her radiance. People in the village considered her to be the most beautiful woman for many kilometers. Unfortunately, L'Aquila discovered Emilé and the servant in the midst of lovemaking in one of the estate out-buildings. She threatened him in the only way that mattered to him. She told him that unless he fired Maria, she would refuse to yield a son that he wanted so badly. She spat on the servant, called her horrible names, kicked and beat her. Emilé felt powerless. L'Aquila took a pair of shears and began to cut Maria's long golden auburn hair. As a servant, Maria was unable to defend herself.

Some said that Emilé and Maria were deeply in love, which would explain what happened next. When his wife began to cut the woman's hair, Emilé could stand it no longer. He grabbed L'Aquila by her own hair and dragged her out into the courtyard. He screamed at her and beat her, telling her that if she told anyone of the servant, he would kill her.

At this point, the old man stumbled in his recount of the story. "The beating was witnessed by several other people in the employ of…of…your Unc…er…Emilé," he said, and then continued.

L'Aquila scoffed at him as he hit her, told him he was of no worth, that it didn't matter if he killed her, he would never have the respect of anyone, he was just a worthless pig. He became so enraged that he dragged her to a nearby horse trough, and while she kicked and scratched at him, threw her in and held her head under the water until she drowned.

Valisé shuddered at the visual. Corteź told her that he was summoned to help remove L'Aquila's lifeless body from the water trough. He and several others buried her, at Gallierga's direction, on a hillside far away from the main house. He said he remembered to this day that very spot and he would never go near it again.

Gallierga went into seclusion for a time while Maria was returned to health. The disappearance of L'Aquila was covered up; buried, like her body, by the awesome power of Emilé Gallierga. Several months later, Maria gave birth to a child. That child was Emilé's daughter. Corteź looked up from his hands, which he had been wringing nervously during the time he told the story, and stared Valisé in the face.

"That child, Miss Vali, is you."

She was staggered. The anger welled up in her so fiercely her entire body began to tremble. Yet she kept it barely visible to Corteź. He knew however, that the revelation had hit her deeply. He also knew that she was too proud, too well trained, too much a Gallierga, to demonstrate it.

"Emilé is my father?" She whispered the question after what seemed to the old man to be an eternity.

"Yes. It is so."

"And what became of my mother?"

"She disappeared; perhaps a year after you were born. She was unable to produce a son. No one knows where she went. It is believed she is dead. There were some who thought Emilé was incapable of having another child, a son. After your mother disappeared, well, there were many women. None gave birth to a son. None gave birth at all. Some believed that God had taken away his seed."

She nodded, staring blankly at the space between where they stood. "So why was I raised as his niece, why not as his daughter?"

"He raised you as his own," Cortéz said. "Perhaps he wanted to spare you the shame of what happened before you were born."

"He is a murderer." She always knew that, of course, but it never struck her so closely. "He killed his wife to be with my mother, and then when he found she could not provide a son, he killed her too. He has always owned me, the servant's daughter, but not as his daughter, as another servant."

Cortéz knew that great anger and hatred would follow. "I am so sorry that you made me tell you these things, Miss Vali. We all loved you so when you were young. I would get reports from time to time telling me of how you were growing up, what a wonderful woman you had become. Of course, you wouldn't remember me; you were so young when I was sent away. Miss Vali, I beg you, if he learns of this he will kill me."

She collected herself. "It's alright, Mr. Cortéz. As I promised, I will protect you. Emilé will never know of this conversation. I will take it to my death. Thank you for your honesty. The story has cut me deeply, but in the end, it will help."

The old man turned from her, made his way down the steps of the veranda and walked toward his old truck with his head down. Valisé staggered into the house, went to the kitchen, and then opened the cookie Jar in which Randall had left a little something for her upon her arrival. She removed the bag inside, pulled a spoon from the drawer and, after dumping a pile of white rocks on the granite counter-top, mashed them into fine powder with the back of the spoon.

14

You Never Know

The new mission parameters were sending Becker, Christian and Keeler in different directions. Marty was committed to the date with Valisé; John Christian needed to keep tabs on Conrad and Jared Sutton; and Keeler needed to arrange for the boat for Marty, but above all else he needed to be ready to hop into his airplane at a moment's notice in the event Sutton took off again.

While driving Marty to the harbor to meet Valisé, Christian swung by Sutton's house first, to make sure he was still there. Satisfied after seeing his Toyota parked in the driveway, they drove back to town and parked in the lot by the docks. Christian went over to Sutton's and rented another car which, as Keeler had said, was now needed. Marty made his way down to the boat to meet the charter captain. He was about thirty minutes early for the sail, allowing plenty of time to check out the crew and make sure the boat was properly stocked for the outing. The captain stood waiting for him on the deck of a dark green and mahogany single mast schooner. It was a forty-foot charter, usually rented bareboat, without crew, to parties of six to eight, but this was the only boat that Keeler could find on such short notice. It was staffed by a captain and two mates, one of whom doubled as a waiter to the passengers. The other mate was CIA out of the Tortola station, but no one knew this, save Keeler.

Marty figured his little cruise had set the taxpayers back three or four grand, but a part of him felt pretty good at the moment. Not in his wildest dreams could he have imagined this scenario. Looking at the whole situation, his spirits were dampened by the realization that he was in the middle of a very delicate and dangerous business. But the reality check was needed; he could not forget that Valisé was a target; that if his cover was blown, the mission was blown and he could easily wind up at the bottom of Sir Francis Drake channel that afternoon. He could not allow himself to forget.

Marty and the captain reviewed the route they would sail. They would cross the channel to the north of Cruz Bay and circle clock-wise around Tortola, returning back up the channel in the afternoon as the sun went down in the west. The entire trip would be around forty nautical miles and the forecast for steady winds promised a good sail. The captain knew of a quiet bay on the northeast end of Tortola, accessible only by boat, where they could stop midday for a snorkel and lunch. Marty took a tour of the boat, making mental notes about the location of the safety devices, as well as where the snorkel gear was stowed. He checked the head and the galley, the wine and liquor stock, and the menu planned for lunch. He made certain that there was fresh mango juice and rum for the afternoon as Valisé had requested.

By the time he finished the pre-sail check, it was well past the time Valisé was to meet him. It was close to thirty minutes past, which was beyond fashionably late, going straight on to rudely late. Surely she would not be rude. He was certain she had a cell phone, but had neglected to get her number. He decided to wait a few more minutes and, if she didn't show, he would drive to the Hill House to look for her. He couldn't believe that she would stand him up; there must be a problem of some sort. He decided to wait for her at the top of the docks, by the parking area.

As he walked up the steps, he saw Randall across the square hanging around JJ's just as he was the day before, so it could not have been Randall interfering with the plans. Impatience turned to worry, and Marty decided to drive to the Hill House. With only one route from there to the docks, he couldn't possibly miss her if she were on her way. As he pulled out onto the Annaberg Road, he felt an interruption in their connection. Something had slipped, or the good karma he felt from her was altered. He pushed harder on the gas, more than common sense dictated.

The Annaberg Road cannot be safely negotiated at more than 30 miles per hour. While pushing the limits of this reality he arrived in one piece at the Road House, took the turn and sped up the Hill House Road. Coming to the top he saw her car parked in front of the house, but relief soon turned into apprehension as it occurred to him that she was probably all right and might have simply stood him up. Taking the steps two at a time and then reaching the veranda, he saw the screen was closed but the inside door to the house was open. He knocked. No answer. He called her name. No answer. "Christ," he said out loud, "I can't just barge in there, what if she's in the shower?" He listened carefully, knocked again and called her name. Nothing. Then he heard it, a soft sound; a moan. He pulled the screen door open and stepped quickly through the foyer and into the tiled salon that opened onto the veranda. Valisé was sprawled on the floor; leaning against the wicker couch, head drooped, froth coming from her mouth. He ran to her and got down on his knees, grabbing her by the shoulders. "Anna Maria," he yelled at her, "Anna Maria, what's wrong with you?"

She groaned and looked at him with bleary eyes; there was mucous coming from her nose, her face was deep red. Her gaze foggy, she mumbled, "Is it time already?" Her head slumped to her chest again, a metallic cough convulsed from her, as she choked and gagged.

"Anna Maria, what the hell...?" She didn't answer. He looked around the room, then in the kitchen, for anything that could clue him in. On the counter he saw it, an empty baggie, the remnants of a large pile of snow white powder, and a rolled-up bill. "Shit," he said, as he put two and two together.

Knowing he had to keep her respiration up and her heart beating, he slapped her face sharply and called her name. She awoke briefly and mumbled something unintelligible. He called her name again and put his ear next to her mouth. She mumbled, "He killed her."

"Anna Maria...wake up...stay with me," he said, yelling. Then he picked her up and carried her through the house looking for the shower. Passing by the back window, he saw the pool. He turned and took her out to the garden, walked down the pool steps and right into the water. The sudden rush of the cool water startled her, and she began to scream and thrash at him. At least she was awake and breathing, he thought, but then she fell off again. It occurred to Marty that getting her heart pumping faster might just pump more blood and therefore more cocaine to her brain. It might have been be frying her at that moment, but there was no choice, her body had to work it off. He dipped her head down into the water and tried to wash out her nostrils. She choked, throwing up mucous. He stuck his fingers in her mouth to clear it out, she gagged and threw up what little was left in her stomach. As her vomit hit the water, he saw streaks of red interlaced in the yellow.

"FUCK!" he yelled, dipped her head in the water again, and she choked when he pulled her out. He yelled her name and she awoke briefly and struggled with him insanely.

"Good, you get mad at me, woman, just stay with me." And then she fell off. He continued dipping her and yelling at her until she stopped falling off completely but, as that phase led to the next, she began to shiver violently. Her body temperature had dropped and her organs were reacting to the loss of heat. He carried her out of the water and into the house and to her bedroom on the upper floor. She was soaked and shaking. He stripped her clothes and laid her in the bed and covered her up, then sat in a chair next to the bed watching as eventually her shivering subsided and her breathing slowed. Marty believed the worst was over. At one point though, her breath was erratic, then nearly stopped. But as it did she gasped for air, stirred and began breathing slowly and steadily again. He felt fairly certain she was there to stay.

As the hours went by, Marty watched her, staring for long periods without interruption. He saw the color return to her face and her breathing get deeper. He saw her facial features transform from trauma to deep sleep. She stirred occasionally and smacked her lips and once even gave up a little snore. He smiled. When he felt free to, he found himself thankful that she was alive.

He looked around her room. Clearly the last time she was there, she had been in frenzy. Perfume bottles and knick-knacks were scattered on the floor, along with her clothes and her jewelry, and whatever else that had been in her suitcase. When he felt safe to leave her, he went down stairs, straightened up the mess she had made, and put most of the leftover drug in the toilet, keeping a small sample to be analyzed, though he was certain it was cocaine. It tasted like the stuff he had tried a couple of times in college. He went back upstairs and straightened her room, putting things back in order. He figured she would probably sleep quite a while, maybe even through the night, so he figured it'd be prudent to get his car out of the yard. He checked her pulse and her breathing and decided to make a run for it. He left the house and drove his car down to the Road House and parked it there. He quickly grabbed some clean shorts and a shirt and then sprinted back up the hill where he found her sleeping just as he had left her.

While he changed, he watched her sleep. He felt the need to make contact with Keeler or Christian somehow. His cell phone had been saturated in the pool. He removed the battery and tried to dry it out, but didn't hold out much hope. Yet he didn't want to leave her again, even for a second, for fear she would wake and he wouldn't be there. The numbers were in the memory of his cell phone, so the house phone was of no use and in any event, it might be tapped. He decided updating them would have to wait. Thinking about the status of the operation, he remembered that he and Valisé *were* the main event and their status was okay at the moment, under the circumstances. The operation was moving forward, he was in control, and a report to Keeler would have no bearing anyway, except to make them both feel better.

Marty sat down and thought back about her words. "He killed her," Valisé had said. Who killed who? Then he thought about the file. The only male it mentioned was Emilé Gallierga; no brother, husband or boyfriend. Keeler had said there was some confusion as to whether Gallierga was her uncle or her father. Regardless, the killer must have been someone that she couldn't lash out at in revenge. It must have been someone whom Valisé was powerless against. In her world, that would be very few people. Okay, Marty thought, suppose that Gallierga is the *he*; who is the *her*? Men sometimes kill their wife or mistress, they rarely kill their sister, or their sister in law. It would have been someone Valise cared deeply about, otherwise, she wouldn't have been pissed enough to binge on cocaine, on her own product. It was someone close to her. Was this an attempted suicide? That didn't line up, Marty thought, stockbrokers kill themselves; cartel bosses kill the other guy.

As he sat on the blanket chest at the foot of the bed, Marty watched her sleeping peacefully, even innocently, and for the moment detached from the questions swirling around her. He felt uneasy, exposed; a sudden concern for her safety jumped to the forefront. She had become precious; she was also the target of his assignment. If something should befall her now, after having saved her life, it would be a great loss to him in both ways.

She couldn't be discovered in this condition. If Randall were to check on her, he'd need to report everything to Gallierga. Marty might then have to neutralize him, creating further problems. Her vulnerability became his vulnerability. The urgency was real; he had to get her out of there.

"The boat!" he said aloud, and then he popped the back cover off his cell phone and reinserted the battery. While silently begging as he pressed the power button, the light came on, and the memory worked. He wrote down Keeler's cell number and went downstairs to use the house phone; it was risky, but he had no choice. He saw her cell phone on the kitchen counter; the screen read '6 Missed Calls'. "Shit," he said, then went to the house phone in the foyer and dialed Keeler's cell.

Keeler saw the incoming number and recognized the local area code; it had to be Marty.

"Speak," he said quickly after accepting the call.

Marty decided to be cryptic. "Jump from the rocks at Coral Bay," he said, hoping Keeler would get the idea, then ended the call.

Valisé would have to be woken soon, for if this escape were to work he'd need her on her feet and cooperating. Considering her mental state, he figured the odds of her going along with him were no better than fifty-fifty.

"Close enough," he said as he went up the stairs. She had rolled over onto her side in his absence. He kneeled on the floor next to the bed and wrapped his hand around the wrist lying next to her face; he squeezed her arm to wake her. Her eyes opened slightly and she pulled his arm under her, wrapping her own arms around it, like a child who wakens to find her favorite teddy bear nearby.

"It's you," she said weakly, and started to drift off again.

Marty kept his wits. "We're even," he said.

Her eyes opened again, wider this time, and her pupils darted around the room; to his face, to the ceiling, to the bedspread. After realizing she was lying naked in bed, she handled it coolly and said nothing, but looked at him intently, trying to put some order into what had happened.

"You can't stay here, they will be looking for you." He tried to smile.

"How do you know?" she asked.

"I know," he said. "We'll be leaving soon. I'm pretty sure Randall will be here any minute."

This thought brought a wounded expression to her face, as did the realization that *Peter Smith* knew more about her than she imagined. 'I've been foolish,' she thought. And then she imagined the mother she never knew. She thought again about how she had been duped her entire life by Emilé, that fucker, who had murdered her mother and raised her to become a servant in her mother's place. She tried to sit up, but fell sideways on the bed and retched in a dry heave. Tears welled in her eyes. Marty brought her some water, which she tried to drink but couldn't without choking, her throat was in such bad shape. When her breathing slowed again, he tried to get her to understand, "You cannot stay here."

"Where will I go? Can I shower?"

"You can try, but be quick. I'll put some things in your overnight bag." She swung her legs over the side of the bed and tried to stand. As she did, the sheet slipped, exposing her nakedness. She started to fall and he caught her. She swore at the embarrassment and the nausea eating at her insides. He sat her on the bed, grabbed a sweater and shorts from the closet and wrestled them onto her.

"You have to trust me," he said. "It's your only choice right now."

She relented and laid back on the bed, breathing heavily, retching from time to time. He grabbed some of her things, her cell phone, went down to the kitchen and found a bottle of water and loaf of bread and put them in the Jeep. In a drawer, he found a piece of paper and a pen and wrote a note: *Randall, went boating, be back Tuesday. Ciao. Valisé.* He wrote it in his best cursive and hoped that Randall didn't know her handwriting. He put the note and the pencil on the counter and went back upstairs to fetch her, then carried her downstairs and out the front door. The cool evening air hit her and she began to shiver. He put her in the passenger side of the Jeep and went back into the house, turned off most of the lights, straightened things up a little, and locked the door on his way out.

At the bottom of Hill House Road, he took a right on the Annaberg Road, heading east toward Coral Bay and Hurricane Hole. The sun was setting low in the sky, casting shadows, so he switched on the headlights. As they rounded the next bend, driving out of sight, Randall turned off the road behind them, heading to the Hill House.

15

Isla Tortuga

"Jump from the rocks at Coral Bay."

Keeler recognized the voice, but he had to replay the words in his mind several times to make sense of them. Marty had been unaccounted for since early in the day. The CIA agent on the boat had called and told him that Marty had been there, but then left. Keeler called the CIA mate back and told him to sail the boat to the other side of the island to Coral Bay, then dock and wait for further instructions. He was tempted to have Christian get on the boat as well, but decided to have him drive a car to Coral Bay, keeping him independent of any danger that might threaten the boat en route. Keeler himself was tied to something else; he was sitting in the airplane he'd flown into St. Thomas from Guantanamo Bay. He couldn't leave Sutton without a tail. So, until the boat arrived at Coral Bay, Christian and the agent would have to keep things moving in the right direction alone.

Christian was staked out at Sutton's house at the time, watching his subject prepare to depart on what would obviously be an overnight stay. When Keeler called him about Coral Bay, Christian told him that Sutton had just that minute left the house, loaded his small Air Force duffel into his car, and driven away in a hurry. Keeler immediately went into motion. He called the tower at the St. Thomas Airport and told the controller it was likely he would be departing at within the next hour or so, and pre-arranged a designated radio frequency which would be kept open indefinitely and reserved for his purpose alone. He would fit into any departure traffic as he saw necessary, and the tower would accommodate him and not alert other aircraft in departure or approach. Keeler would then be able to depart directly behind Sutton and there would be no discussion of his presence. With this arrangement in place, he'd be able to tail Sutton without his knowledge. He asked the controller for a read-back of all flight plans pending for departure from the airport within the next three hours. The controller gave him seven registration numbers for aircraft departing. Sutton's tail number was not among them.

Keeler prepared himself for what might soon take place. He figured that Sutton would be taking off 'VFR'; he would squawk 1200 on his transponder until outside the airport traffic control area, then he would turn off the signal and slip down to the surface of the ocean. If Sutton repeated this pattern again that night, it would validate the hypothesis about his flights. As Keeler waited on the tarmac, he performed a pre-flight check on his complex aircraft in the diminishing daylight so that when Sutton arrived all he would need to do would be to fire up the big turbo-prop engines and pull out behind him. After take-off he would then fly above and slightly behind long enough for him to level out and settle on a direct course. He felt fairly confident that once Sutton had done that, the heading would likely indicate his destination, and an educated guess of that was all Keeler was looking for on this trip.

Keeler had already programmed his GPS computer to take the guesswork out of what he was trying to do. He had input the latitude and longitude coordinates for thirty destinations south of St. Thomas, all within the five or six hundred mile fuel range of Sutton's plane. Once he determined Sutton's course, he could plug the information into the computer and it would give him the destination that Sutton was most likely targeting.

As Keeler double-checked the inputs to the GPS computer, he saw Sutton walking toward the Cessna 310 with his duffel in his hands. Clearly, he planned to be away for at least a one-night stay. He sat and watched in the near darkness as Sutton did a careful pre-flight on the Cessna 310, got in and fired up the engines. On the ground control frequency, Sutton called up: "Ground control, this is Cessna Charlie Sierra Three Three November, VFR ta the southwest, ready for takeoff." After receiving clearance to taxi, the Cessna began to roll toward the departure end of the runway. As soon as Sutton pulled away and Keeler's plane was no longer visible to him, Keeler ignited the turbines in the Heron and called the tower on his designated frequency.

"Tower, Navy Four-Three Tango Papa is in taxi toward the active and will follow Charlie Sierra Three-Three November on takeoff," Keeler said.

"Roger Four-Three Tango Papa, clear to taxi."

Keeler inquired if Sutton had filed a flight plan of any kind, and received a 'negative' in response.

As Sutton lifted off, Keeler watched the navigation lights on the tips of his wings to see what direction he turned on climb out, and then rolled the Heron down the runway behind him. As Sutton banked left out of the departure pattern and leveled off at 2,000 feet, Keeler continued to climb, then leveled off a few hundred meters above and behind him. He was completely invisible to Sutton, but the reverse was not the case. The blip for Sutton's plane was chirping loudly on the panel in front of Keeler, and he adjusted the aspect ratio so that he could assign a signature for the blip, which would discriminate Sutton from anything else which might come within the scope of his look-down radar.

After take-off, Sutton established a southwest heading of 224 degrees, holding it for about twenty minutes until St. Croix passed on the left side of the airplane. He then turned sharply south, to a heading of 182 degrees and as suspected, dropped the Cessna down to just above the surface of the ocean. Keeler tracked him unwaveringly for a full hour. During this time he plugged various 'what ifs' into his GPS computer and was able to determine, with a fair amount of certainty, that Sutton was on track for an archipelago about 100 nautical miles east-north-east of Caracas Venezuela. The exact island plotted by the computer was Isla Tortuga, but it could also have been the one of the neighboring islands of Los Roques or Isla Marguerita, if Sutton varied his course east or west by a few degrees.

'Good enough for now.' Keeler thought. He disconnected the autopilot and pulled up on the nose of the Heron, then added power and executed a perfect rollover 180-degree turn in order to return to St. Thomas. He put the throttles on the Allison engines further forward and trimmed the aircraft for 75 percent power cruise, which got him about 315 knots of airspeed. Within forty-five minutes after leaving Sutton, he was back at Charlotte Amalie airport and taxing to his parking spot.

In the waters to the north of Venezuela al Zawahiri's transport scheme unfolded. The *Dover Mist* rendezvoused with Gallierga's group as planned. From there it was a short cruise to Isla Tortuga, where the goods were offloaded in preparation for Sutton's arrival. Ribindi disembarked there as well of course, and aided in the transfer of the cargo. The combined weight of the heroin, Ribindi and Sutton were less than the maximum weight the Cessna 310 could carry, but this would not allow enough fuel to travel more than a couple of hundred miles. So Sutton would have two make two trips, and even then he would be able to carry only enough fuel to get each load to an intermediate fuel stop, which would then serve as a staging area for combining the loads into a larger aircraft. The intermediate stop was Montserrat, the same island Sutton always flew into with his cocaine hauls. It was seen as the best choice, because Gallierga had facilities for storage and fuel, and political protection there.

Montserrat is a small island which was made even smaller by the eruption of one of its volcanos in 1995; the only such eruption in Montserrat in recorded history. It all but wiped out the southern half of the island, including the capitol, Plymouth, and made the airport unsuitable for commercial traffic. The population dipped from about 40,000 in 1990 to just under 10,000 in 2010. And because the British government, of which Montserrat is a possession, has been unwilling to invest the billions required to rebuild the island to something approaching what it once was, the population continues to dwindle. There exists no real economy anymore, as tourism had always been its chief business. The airport, or what once was the airport, lies in the southern *exclusion zone* where the volcano caused massive devastation. It is closed and abandoned, so there is simply no one there to worry about, but 4,000 feet of the runway remains usable. Several years ago, Gallierga's people commandeered a small airport outbuilding, brought in electric generators and set up a facility for cutting and repackaging their product. The local police force, appointed by the governor and comprised of four of the very few men on the island with a high school diploma, was in Gallierga's pocket. No one was allowed into the exclusion zone, the massive lava flow area, as it was claimed to be too dangerous as yet for inhabitants.

All of the incoming and outgoing flights were done at night, when planes were under cover of darkness. The cocaine distribution facility operated regularly and quietly. The stop seemed to be a natural for the heroin trip as well, except that the larger aircraft would be needed for the final import into the United States. But Sutton felt confident that the partial runway would be long enough.

Isla Tortuga, one of many uninhabited atolls in the Caribbean, is near enough to Colombia for Gallierga's people to properly set up the first stage of the heroin transit, and close enough to Montserrat, about 400 nautical miles, for Sutton to make two trips with limited fuel. It has a few shelters, built by naturalists over the years, for use during tours and studies by various universities and nature groups. The long beaches are pure virgin white sand and the tide runs up flat and long. When the tide goes out, the beaches become open stretches of packed sand, acceptable for landing an aircraft, but difficult to approach by boat. Although actually a part of Venezuela, there are no authorities on the island, no human inhabitants. Sailboats sometimes scatter across its long shallow and vast cays, in order to take advantage of huge crescent shaped reefs, excellent for snorkeling and shallow reef scuba diving. The geography also made it an excellent choice to stage the load from the Dover Mist. Gallierga's people commandeered one of the naturalist huts for a few days in order to store and protect the second half of the shipment, until it could be picked up by Sutton on return from his first trip to Montserrat.

When Sutton made his approach that night, he did so under the guidance of two high-powered battery lights placed on the beach by the Gallierga crew. He made a low pass over the beach first, allowing his landing lights to illuminate the proposed landing area, not completely trusting the landing party's word that the beach was acceptable for touchdown. Once he confirmed with his own eyes that it was, he circled around at very low altitude and executed a perfect wheel landing on the firm packed sand. Using the elevator controls, he held the nose wheel off the surface of the beach until the last possible moment, so that it wouldn't dig into the sand, bury the nose, and flip the plane over. Even with his expert understanding of the variables, and his deft touch on the controls, landing on a beach in a nose-wheel aircraft is risky. In fact, Sutton had thought earlier that day, the likelihood of discovery by authorities was greatly overshadowed by the risk of failure of the mission due to the complexity of the transport process.

As he rolled the 310 to a stop in front of the battery spotlights, Sutton pulled the fuel mixture knobs out to the stops and let the engines burn themselves out of fuel. He did a last check on the fuel gauges and sat there performing some calculations under the dome light in the cockpit. He used his slide rule to recheck the weight and balance of the aircraft based on the cargo he anticipated loading. He computed the winds aloft and their effect on ground speed and the time to destination; and he calculated the amount of 'runway' he would need based upon the weight, outside air temperature, relative humidity and the wind direction. Working fastidiously, he was aware that someone had already opened the rear cargo hatch and began to load product into the aircraft. The man, new to Sutton, began to stack blocks of 10 kilogram packages, wrapped in black plastic, onto the floor of the aircraft. Sutton turned, looked him very directly in the eye and said: "Do not load it yet." The man looked confused, so Sutton asked "Tu hablas englais?" The man shook his head and pointed to a large dark figure approaching. It was Orestes,

"Buenos noches, my friend. I know you are in much hurry, so we will make this quick. What is the maximum you can carry this trip?" he asked. Sutton couldn't answer just yet.

"Hello, Señor Orestes," Sutton said with a managed smile. "Where is the passenger?"

Orestes waved Ribindi over to the aircraft. Sutton looked him up and down with a discerning eye. Ribindi thought, 'No one but Allah has the right to pass judgment on me,' and turned to walk away. Sutton was only trying to get a good idea of the man's weight.

"The passenger plus three hundred thirty kilograms is the maximum," he told Orestes.

With that, Orestes gave quick orders in Spanish to the workers loading the plane. "Each package is exactly ten kilograms. We will load thirty-three packages," he assured Sutton.

Orestes knew from years of loading for Sutton that he was very fussy about weight. He had at times questioned how much the plane could carry. As far as Orestes was concerned, if they couldn't load the plane more than half full, why did it have all that room? Sutton was politely impatient with him at first, but at one point asked him, "Would you rather have the thing reach the destination, or have it ta be scattered across the ocean?" Orestes questioned no further.

After Gallierga's crew had loaded the plane and filled the tanks from portable fuel drums, they agreed on an approximate time to meet on the following night and shook hands. Sutton motioned Ribindi into the right seat and made sure he was strapped in correctly. As he drew near the man to show him how to fasten his seatbelt, the putrid smell of Ribindi's clothing took the breath out of his lungs and nearly made him retch. As soon as the engines were running, Sutton immediately turned the air-conditioning vents to blow fresh air directly at his face. Ribindi was too focused on his own issues to be insulted. He squirmed in his seat, concerned about the reliability of the small plane, and looked over his shoulder at the cargo to make sure it was secured and safe.

Sutton turned the airplane around, ran the engines up to take off speed and let off the brakes. The airplane, now approximately 1,200 pounds heavier, trundled down the beach, slowly at first, until enough airflow over the elevator allowed Sutton to pull back on the controls and take some pressure off the nose-wheel. Finally reaching rotation speed of about 55 knots, Sutton was able to pull the aircraft off the beach. Free of the friction from the packed sand, it gained speed quickly, and within just a few minutes they were cruising at 75 percent power, about 205 knots. Sutton set the autopilot to a heading of 060, directly to Montserrat, leaving him free to focus all of his attention on the radar altimeter. In the darkness, Ribindi could not tell at first how very close they were to the surface of the ocean. At some point, Sutton heard him mumbling an unintelligible group of expressions. He assumed he was praying, then smirked at the realization that Ribindi must have figured out the altimeter. Otherwise, the two men didn't speak for the entire two hour flight.

When Keeler shut down the engines on his own aircraft back on St. Thomas, he called Captain James and asked to meet him at the Coast Guard office immediately. He was sure that James had a solid working knowledge of the islands of the Lesser Antilles, the geographical chain comprising all Caribbean islands, large and small. The Antilles form a line beginning at Puerto Rico and stretching clockwise in a horseshoe-shaped chain all the way to Aruba, off the coast of Venezuela. Keeler knew James would be able to talk about most of the other islands, and give him some insight into what Sutton's strategy might be. He would have to query James without giving him a complete briefing of the operation, because he simply was not yet in a need to know position. He also called John Christian for an update on Marty's situation. Christian reported he'd arrived at Coral Bay at about the same time as Marty and the Gallierga woman, and they were trying to stay out of sight until the boat arrives. He reported that Marty had told him little about what had transpired, only that the woman had nearly died from a drug over-dose.

"Marty also told me," Christian said reluctantly, "'she knows I know.'"

"She knows he knows *what?*" Keeler almost yelled into the cell phone.

"Not sure," Christian replied. "But those were his exact words, '*she knows I know.*'"

The admiral didn't know what to think of that and he didn't have time at the moment to consider all the possibilities. "Why hasn't he been answering his cell phone?" Keeler asked.

"It got wet…doesn't work."

"Well, as soon as the boat gets there, dismiss the crew. Don't let them see the woman. Tell them to drive your car back to Cruz Bay and park it in the lot by the docks. The second mate is CIA, but dismiss him too for appearances then have him come back to rejoin you. Get her on board and below, out of sight. Then shove off as quickly as possible. Do you know how to sail?"

"We'll be all right." Christian replied.

"Okay, there ought to be charts on board. Make sure you have full tanks and leave Coral Bay under power, being careful of the reef. Don't try to raise the sails. On the charts, you'll see another bay, very protected, about two miles north of Coral Bay. It's called Hurricane Hole. It's accessible only by sea. Anchor there for the night and I'll have one of Captain James's people bring me out in the morning."

"Roger, what's the name of the boat, Admiral?"

"The *Lemon Drop,* and tell Becker I want to talk to him as soon as you anchor, away from the woman. Tell him to call my cell. I don't care what time it is. I want you there for the call, too."

"Roger" he said again. "Uh, Admiral?"

"Go ahead."

"Well, sir…" Christian was not sure how to put it. "I think he's falling for her."

"What? How can that be? He's only known her for a couple of days."

"Yes sir, but he saved her life…and things happen like that. Who knows what's gone on, and, I gotta tell ya… she's beautiful."

"Shit."

"You know Admiral, he's a warrior, and he's smart, but he's still a kid in some ways."

"I know. I know. Maybe I shouldn't have…well…I don't know. What's your take on her?"

"I think she's pretty sick, too sick to be faking. When he picked her up to put her in the back seat of the car, she wouldn't let go of him, begged him not to leave; wouldn't let go of his neck until he told her he would stay there, next to her. I don't think she knew where she was or that I was there."

"John, these people are smart." Keeler said evenly. "They have deep intelligence assets and they are not reluctant to bring the battle to us. She could be leading him right where they want him, and we're handcuffed to him."

"Yes sir, I understand that, but if she wanted to eliminate him, why didn't she get on the boat this morning? What she *did* do was to get herself all screwed up and literally fall into our hands. That doesn't make any sense. But more than that sir, none of the intelligence describes her as an operative. She doesn't look...well, she doesn't look...rugged...if you know what I mean."

Keeler chewed on Christian's words. "Yeah, she won't look rugged until she runs a stiletto up under his ribs and severs his aorta."

"I get it, sir. It's just my gut feeling that she's not that kind of killer."

"So you're thinking that we're right where we want to be? I told Becker to get inside her head, and that's where he is?"

"I can't say that much, but maybe DEA had it right, maybe she's just here on vacation," Christian said. "Anyway, she's got some issues. And if he's gotten into her head, the problem is, she's in his head, too." Looking up, he thought he saw the running lights of a sail boat pulling into the harbor.

"The question is: how far?"

"Roger, sir, I agree. I'll have him call you when we get situated at Hurricane Hole." With that, he made his way to the dock.

After the call to Christian, Keeler met Captain James at the office and, having changed his mind, provided him with a detailed account of what was transpiring. His help would be essential as the operation began to get more complex and, though Keeler had reservations about broadening the circle, James had a need to know. He told him they needed a boat in the morning, something fast and sea-worthy but unmarked. Maybe, he was thinking, DEA might have something confiscated that they could use. He also asked James to go with him to the Lemon Drop, in plain clothes, undercover. Keeler thought his request would either make his day or make him shit his pants. James took it all in stride, told him he knew of a boat that fit the bill, and he would have his night crew prepare it to cruise before first light. They parted ways and decided to meet at Wharf 14 at 0400 hours. James left the office, returning to his home and his bed. Keeler found a pillow and blanket in the dry stores area and went to sleep on an old couch in James's office.

Sutton uttered a sigh of relief when he saw on the GPS that he was within ten nautical miles of Montserrat, causing Ribindi to stir. Two hours had passed in close quarters and Sutton was thankful for the lack of conversation. He now had a decision to make, one that had more significance than he realized. He had to decide whether to return to St. Thomas that evening, or sleep in the filthy old airport building at Montserrat. Except for the quick turnaround in Tortuga, he had been flying for six straight hours and he was simply exhausted, but the trip to St. Thomas was only another forty-five minutes. Since he would not be returning to Isla Tortuga until after dark the following evening, he would have too much time on Montserrat, with no shower, bed, or other comforts of home. He needed solid, undisturbed sleep before the next trip and he knew that would be difficult anywhere but at home in his own bed. Also, if he stayed here, he would be stuck with Ribindi, an unpleasant thought indeed. That made his decision an easy one. He'd unload, turn Ribindi over to Gallierga's people, refuel, and take off again for St. Thomas. Since it was about 0130 hours, that would put him on the ground there at 0300, where he would have to wait for the 0600 ferry to St. John, but he'd be home, in his own bed by 0700, and he could sleep all day. This thought made him smile.

Within two miles of the runway in Montserrat, Sutton reached for his radio button. It was tuned to 121.22 MHz. When he clicked the button twice, two small runway end identifier lights lit up. He was then able to get oriented to the runway, fly a low pattern to the touchdown point, and float in for a landing. There were no other lights on the island, at least not any that he could see. As he was gliding toward the touchdown point, his landing lights illuminated the black lava that had engulfed much of the approach end of the runway and, further on, he could see the stretch of the runway that had barely been damaged at all by the eruption. He aimed his descent to meet the tarmac just beyond the flow. After touchdown and roll out, he was greeted by four of Gallierga's men; the same ones that always greeted him here. With the engines idling, they opened the cargo door and began to unload. Ribindi quickly unbuckled his seatbelt, threw open the door and hopped out onto the wing.

"Watch out for the propeller," Sutton yelled over the noise, "I come back tomorrow night."

Ribindi nodded to him, jumped off the wing, and walked to the storage building, watching as the product was handled. With the plane unloaded and refueled, Sutton took off again, He flew the thirty miles or so to the neighboring island of St. Kitts at low altitude. When he was in close proximity, he climbed to 1,500 feet, set his transponder to 1200, and headed for home; a long night, a half ton of drugs, and one smelly Arab behind him.

16

Come on Down to My Boat Baby

From the backseat of the Jeep, with Valisé curled into a fetal position next to him and her head on his lap, Marty saw the boat pull into the harbor as well. That is, against the darkness, he saw a running light on top of a mast coming into the harbor, and he assumed, he *hoped*, it was the *Lemon Drop*.

She was still very sick, occasionally gagging and coughing, and sobbing apparently, either from the pain caused by the remnants of the drug in her system, or from the anguish of whatever it was that brought her to put it there. He wanted to try to talk to her, to attempt to pry from her what had happened, but he wasn't sure which he wanted more: to help her feel better, or to question about the overdose. When she started to cry, he rubbed her head gently to remind her that he was there. Once, when he rubbed her so, she closed her arms around his thigh as if it were a pillow and said, "Thank you," weakly.

Marty was anxious to venture down to the dock to see if that was indeed his boat and if so, to get her on board as soon as possible. If anyone on this small island recognized him or the Jeep, even at this late hour, word could travel back rapidly and the wrong people might find out. As the *Lemon Drop* was pulling into a slip, Christian walked up to the Jeep from behind and squatted outside the door. "I talked to Keeler. I'm going to send the crew away and then we'll get her on board."

"Where are we going?" Marty asked.

"I'll explain later, not far. Keeler's going to join us in the morning."

"All right," Marty said. "Give me a sign when it's clear."

"Just wait for me here, I'll come get you." Christian left.

Marty began to review what had transpired, and disliked the circumstances. A relaxing day of playful intrigue with an incredible woman on a boat in a beautiful setting had turned real sour, real fast. It was his original intent, he assured himself, to eventually be in the position he was now in. But he thought it might have happened in such a way that there would be no fear, no concern for safety, no paranoid slipping away from shapeless enemies or undefined dangers. Valisé Gallierga, no, Anna Maria Santiago, he liked her alias much more, she would fall for him, he imagined, and they would figure it out together. She would help him do his job and he would help her leave hers. She would come over to the good side, maybe be on both sides for a while, but she would eventually come all the way over and they would be understood and accepted in the dark professional community he inhabited. It could be a great love story, albeit a secret one, acknowledged by those who did know about it as something rare in a world where loyalty is transient.

He was certain this wonderful creature was put on earth to be with him, and he had somehow correctly followed the thread of fate that brought him to this island to find her. It wouldn't matter that she might resist. He was, at this moment, so sure, so positive; she wouldn't be able to refuse him. His passion and will about what was right was so strong, she couldn't fail to believe it; she would eventually see it, she had to. And he was confident, in spite of her past, that there was good inside of her. In the preceding hours, as she gasped for the breath of life in a grave place where no façade could be maintained, she was simply too transparent to be inherently evil, too warm-spirited to be a genuine part of the dark world she came from, and too needy to be authentically cold-blooded. He could tell by the way she wrapped her arms around his leg, the way she needed his company and his touch as she struggled to stay alive. He could tell by the way her hair fell on her shoulders, and the way her smile broke across her face when they first met. He could tell by the hurt in her cough and the weakness of her groans as she lay earlier in the day, in spasms, semi-conscious, near death. These were not the sights and sounds of a killer, of a 'Valisé Gallierga'; these belonged to an Anna Maria Santiago: a wonderfully complex woman; but consumed with such hatred at the time that she tried to either escape it, or bowl it over, with a massive dose of cocaine.

He realized he must somehow venture into the soul of this woman; open and consume all of the files that describe her being; help her to sort through them, the good and the bad; strengthen and support and reconstruct the former; and expunge the latter. In a perfect world, the by-product of this would be the success of the mission, an elegant accomplishment, born out of happenstance. The poetry of his conclusion, just this very minute, brought warmth over him and he nodded in silent approval of himself and the delicious logic. Marty was so deep in thought he failed to see Christian walking up behind them again.

"We're good to go." Christian whispered when he reached the Jeep.

Marty shook himself from that place far away, "All right, you go down first, we'll follow," he said.

"Do you need help?"

"Nah, I'm good. Probably best that I just carry her down there. I don't want her to see you yet."

Christian nodded and turned back to the boat. Marty gave him a few paces before he tried to rouse Valisé enough to get her head off his lap and adjust his position so he could pick her up. She was fully asleep. As he cradled her, she stirred briefly and looked at him. She didn't resist and managed to wrap her arms around his neck.

Thankfully, the docks were dark and deserted. Marty took great care with his steps as he walked along the floating deck. He felt the uncertainty of his footing and decided he'd made a mistake not going down there to check it out beforehand. There was a small battery lantern hanging from the lower beam of the mainsail to indicate where they should come aboard. On deck, Christian motioned toward the steps to the cabin below. Downstairs there was a galley followed by a short hallway leading to the head and two small berths. Marty made his way to the forward-most room, being careful not to bump her head on the walls or door openings as he carried her. He laid her down gently on the bunk. She wouldn't let go of his neck right away, so he pulled her arms from around him, his face was very close to her as he spoke. "It's fine. We're fine. You're safe here. We'll be sailing soon and I'll be right down the hallway. Go to sleep now. I'll be back in a little while. I'm not leaving you."

She looked at him blankly, with eyes half open. He could see that the whites of her eyes were bloodshot with a yellowish tint. He felt a chill run through his body as he surveyed the faraway look on her face. He worried that some part of her was permanently damaged from the overdose, wishing she would say something, anything, to indicate she was aware of who she was. He rubbed her cheek gently with the ends of his fingers.

Sensing his touch, she seemed to reconnect, "Okay...por favor...just take me away from here." She watched him dazedly as he nodded and smiled at her, then closed her eyes again and was quickly asleep.

Marty heard the engine start and felt the transmission engage the propeller underneath as he left her. The boat jarred slightly as it bumped into motion, putting a twisted look on his face as he realized that Christian must be driving. Either the man had talents of which he wasn't aware or they were in for a very interesting cruise. He pulled the door to her cabin shut behind him and made his way back up on deck. At the tiller stood the second mate from earlier in the day. He nodded as Marty passed and went about the business of steering the boat away from the slip. Marty looked quizzically at Christian, who then tipped his head sideways at the mate and said, "CIA".

They made their way up to the bow, where no one could hear them.

"Where are we going?" Marty asked.

"To Hurricane Hole, it's a couple miles north. It's a sheltered bay, accessible only by boat. We'll anchor there for the night. Keeler will be out to meet us in the morning."

"Then what?"

"I don't know," Christian answered with a shrug. "I guess it depends upon her. Is she conscious?"

"Barely," Marty said looking down at the deck. "She's in and out."

"What happened?"

Marty relayed the entire story, being careful not to leave out any details so Christian wouldn't be blindsided later. He spoke evenly, trying not to betray that the mission, for him, had taken a personal turn.

"There was something in her file," Christian said after Marty finished, "that talked about her being the daughter of Gallierga. Maybe he did something awful to her."

"Maybe," Marty allowed. "But she said, 'He killed *her*.'"

"Keeler mentioned that she's the illegitimate daughter of a servant woman Gallierga was diddling. Maybe he killed the mother and she just now found out about it." Christian pondered the idea matter-of-factly.

Marty hissed, out loud, mistakenly, at the brutality of it. The slip didn't escape Christian, but he pretended not to notice.

While they were talking, the CIA agent piloted the boat around a peninsula into Hurricane Hole. There was only the sliver of a moon, low in the sky, but it was clear with bright stars, making the bare outline of the shore visible. They could see the parking lights of two other boats moored a comfortable distance away. The agent was steering the boat slowly into the bay, using charts for guidance through the channel and the depth finder and radar to stay clear of obstructions below the surface. Reef, he knew, was the main concern, and so as the bottom began to slope up from thirty feet, he pulled the engine throttle back to idle, cut the screw to neutral and dropped the anchor from the bow. There was no tidal current to speak of and no swells made it past the mouth of the channel, so once the boat found its resting place in what little current there was, he dropped the stern anchor as well. He checked the radar again briefly to be certain that both anchors had dug in and the boat was stationary and then he cut the ignition to the engine. All went silent. Since Hurricane Hole is located in the heart of a U.S. National Park, there are no roads leading in, and no houses in the jungle covered mountains which surround the bay. As Marty looked along the shoreline he didn't see any lights. It was a calm night with just a trace of a breeze, and as the boat came to stillness all that he felt was a very soft roll from bow to stern as slow loping swells made their way by.

The silence was stark; Christian broke it by speaking softly. "It's about 2330 hours. The Admiral will be here early in the morning. We should get some sleep. Are you going to try to talk with her tonight?

"Yeah, if she's awake. I'll see how it goes."

"Okay, I'll go talk to our CIA friend, give him the first watch and then bunk down in the rear berth. You can sleep in the other bed in her berth. He and I will rotate watch at two hour intervals. If you can talk with her, do that and then get some sleep yourself. If not, I wouldn't mind it if you rotated into a watch shift. We all need to be sharp for tomorrow."

Marty nodded then slipped down the galley stairs and walked quietly to the door where Valisé slept. He opened it slowly and noticed it had grown stuffy in the cabin since the boat had stopped moving. He pulled off his shirt, sat down on the bunk opposite hers and reached for the portal type window to make sure it was fully open. He felt as if he needed to wash off the day and contemplated going back out on deck and jumping into the warm sea to wash it off before going to sleep. Then he heard her stir and looked intently at her figure in the darkness. She was lying on her side and as his eyes moved along the outline to her shoulders he was able to make out that her head was propped up on one arm. She had been watching him. He wondered for how long. Though they couldn't see each other's eyes, they were both conscious of the other in the dark.

"You're awake," he said, to break the silence.

"You saved my life?"

"Yes, I think so. I told you we're even now, remember?" He smiled but she couldn't see it.

"I...I don't know...I remember you holding me in the pool...your finger in my nose...I'm so ashamed...so weak." Her voice conveyed contempt.

He made a move to sit closer but she said, "No, lay down with me...please?"

Marty stretched himself out slowly and put his arm under her head to support it. She moved closer and her breath fell on his chest. Her shape fit with him perfectly and it seemed familiar when her chest expanded as she breathed; natural against him. It was as if they had been lying together like that for longer than just a few minutes. She ran her arm around his neck and pulled her face into it and her body closer and tighter to him. He ran his arm up her back and welcomed her there, though he also felt awkward at being amorous. He was surprised to sense that she was interested in his touch in her condition, in her mental state. Maybe she didn't want sex, she just wanted him. The intensity in her breathing betrayed that she felt him growing hard against her leg. He couldn't help it, he didn't want it happen, but there was no stopping it. When she moved into his growing erection, it removed any doubt about how she felt.

Everything about her had him aroused; the day had been full of urgency and pressure and through it they had come to know each other well in mere hours. He decided that if she felt his desire for her, felt every nerve of his energy, it would be good medicine for both of them. She was in touch with this and wanted to run with it, to have the reassurance of his strength, feel the fullness of his arousal and the electricity pulsing from that part of his body. It would be a feeling she could carry with her into the coming hours and days, give her security, knowing that part of him had flourished only for her. It would bond her to him, bring her home. Nothing in her other life mattered at this moment, because she had found the perfect man, for this moment. His lips were on her cheek now and he began to devour her openly. She welcomed his desire and returned it desperately. Their mouths met and were a perfect match.

The movements of their bodies and hands grew fuller and evolved into a rhythm that seemed organic. There was no careful exploration, no hesitation, no awkward second-guessing. Both of them came to breathe harder as their excitement gained an unconscious momentum, leading and then pushing. She rubbed against him, her thin cotton shorts were little separation, and opened herself to him as best she could, availing herself of his fullness. Pleasure shot through her belly as she found him with each pass. He held it for her there; purposefully, strongly. She became wet, feeling the sweet eruption build with each movement, with each gentle bump against her clitoris; with each press it grew in intensity. As she came to orgasm he held her tightly, prolonging the release, letting her feel his sincerity, his authentic focus on only her. She held herself to him and trembled. He took over the movements for her. He held her cheek with his hand as he gently bumped her again and again, locking her in orgasm.

He did not orgasm himself. The beauty of hers and being the reason for her having it was all he coveted at the moment. He held her firmly for several minutes. Slowly their breathing softened and their arms relaxed, though they remained softly molded together. The silence was beautiful, but Marty had the need to speak.

"I want to help you," he said finally. "I want to help you so that I can have you, all of you. If you go back to where you came from it won't be possible; *we* won't be possible."

"I want you," she replied, "I have never wanted like this before. This is right."

"I know." He paused and nodded. "It's right." Then he kissed her again.

After their lips parted she deflated slightly and said, "But I don't know how to do this." Marty was confused and she sensed it. "I mean, I don't know how to continue from here, how to be a normal person."

He couldn't have imagined a more perfect opening. "There's a world where what we want is a real possibility," he said. "It won't be easy to get there Anna, but we can do it."

She pulled herself closer to him and said nothing, digesting the warmth of his optimism. Marty pondered where to go from there; if he should begin the process of exposing everything on both sides and then getting her pledge to join him, or wait until the morning when Keeler would be there to help. There were many things he had to know; and many difficult questions he had to ask. Since believing in her had become natural to him, he decided to start immediately, by telling her who he really was, how he knew about her and what the operation was about. He thought this would build a strong layer of trust before he went into the details of what would be required from her, which might be best left for Keeler to articulate.

"I came to St. John on a mission for the U.S. Government." he began. "We were here at first to investigate the SFC, the Society to Free the Caribe. Have you heard of it?" She nodded her head. "When I met you in the bar that night, I didn't know who you were. I had been investigating Sutton and the car agency." She tensed slightly, thinking of Conrad, and she began to see where this was headed. "After you rescued me on the beach that day, I had a meeting with my superior, a man you will meet in the morning. He's a good man. He will help you. He gave me a file on you at the meeting and my heart sank. My desire for you is real; I need you to know that." Marty didn't sense any skepticism, so he continued.

"The people I work for have discovered that someone in your company has a connection to al Qaeda. That's become my assignment now, to find out all I can about your…uh…uncle and…"

"Wait," she said brusquely and pushed away from him, then struggled to find the switch for the small table lamp next to the bunk. In doing so she knocked over the lamp in the darkness and Marty sat up to help her and get the light working. "He's not my uncle," she said after settling rigidly on the edge of the bed, now in the light. The steely look on her face shocked him, he had never seen this from her in the little time that he knew her. In a more controlled but monotone voice she went into the details of her heritage as told to her by Cortez, the gardener. She spoke slow and methodically, accurately. Through it all she displayed little emotion, completely unlike the person who had an orgasm in his arms just a few minutes earlier. When she came to the end of the story and began to sum it up, she turned her attention to Emilé. "He had an affair with my mother. A servant. She was his concubine. She became pregnant with me and he killed her after I was born. He's a murderer, a murdering pig, and he has lied about it all my life, because he is ashamed of me." She paused as if gathering herself for the final march to the finish and then started forward again. "My life is a lie. My life is born of a murderer's blood; his blood; from his seed. If I am to live freely, he must die. It's the only way I can cleanse myself now. I will do whatever is needed to make it so."

Marty said nothing for a time. She had morphed into a different person altogether. He tried to pull her close and rub her back gently, but she remained tense and detached. He kissed her cheek and forehead until she softened. She began to respond again to his touch. He kissed her long and gently and wrapped his arms around her delicate frame and pulled her close again, as if to convince her, silently, that the person she had just become was not authentic. After she softened again, Marty returned to the details, at least as much of the details as were needed to prepare her for Keeler. He was afraid it might be too much to digest, but necessity pushed him on.

"When Admiral Keeler gets here tomorrow morning, I'll fill him in." He said finally. "He'll ask you to help us. Will you?"

"Will you help me?" she asked in return.

"Yes," he said cautiously, "I will help. My government will do whatever it can to keep you safe. But you will have to go back to him for a while. Do you think you can do that?"

"Yes," she answered immediately, stoically, knowing inside that no fear inside her could derail her pursuit of revenge on Emilé.

"When it gets complicated and dangerous, I'll be there. I'll pull you out. And when we finish with this you will have a new life."

"When we finish with this he must be dead," she said, "or I will have *no* life, I will be dead."

He nodded slowly in agreement, digesting the finality of it. He knew that he had just made an agreement to help her kill her father. He pulled her close and she responded to him, she was back. "I'm with you," he said.

They talked no more, but turned off the light again and lay there in each other's arms. Her fatigue had caught up with her again and soon

Marty felt her breathing become regular, then heavier. He carefully untangled her arms from around his neck and tried to rise slowly without waking her. She stirred and whispered, "Please stay with me."

"I have to go up and relieve the watch. I'll return as soon as I can." She looked up at his silhouette in the dark briefly, then closed her eyes and returned to sleep.

Topside, Marty found Christian sitting with his back to the side of the cabin where it rose out of the deck. He wasn't asleep, but looked as though he was ready to nod off. Marty sat next to him and pulled a wrinkled pack of cigarettes from his hip pocket and lit one. He held out the pack and offered up one to Christian, who declined.

"She's in," Marty said after he took a drag.

"Already?" Christian had heard the muffled rumblings from below. He couldn't help but hear, and had drawn his own conclusion. "I don't buy it. It's too easy. How could she be turned so quickly?"

"It wasn't as quick as it seems," Marty replied, "She's been through a lot. Of course, I've been with her all day; I've seen everything, her expressions, her emotions. You haven't. But the clincher for me is that she wants, *needs*, to kill her father."

Christian didn't say anything right away, just sat there and pondered. "So Gallierga is the *he*..." he said finally.

Marty nodded.

"And who did he kill?" Christian asked.

"It's as we suspected, Gallierga had an affair with her mother, and then murdered her after Valisé was born."

"Why did it take so long for her to find out?"

"I'm not sure." Marty wondered the same thing, and told him the story of the gardener, Cortez.

"Maybe he had her convinced from childhood that her parents were traitors to the Cartel or something. Who knows what kind of sick world they live in?"

They sat in silence again until another thought distracted Marty. "Wait a second, how did the Admiral come up with the place where we're staying?"

"It was probably a rental agency."

Marty shook his head as if baffled by the coincidence, but then returned to task. "We have to get her back to the Hill House soon. They'll be looking for her."

"She'll have to regain her composure first. And we need to turn her into a double in one day. It won't be easy."

"She's motivated," Marty added. "She'll be all right. There's a side of her that's tough."

Christian looked at Marty and tilted his head slightly, "You've gotten to know her pretty well, then."

"Yeah," he said simply, "pretty well."

Again there was silence as they each decided whether there was anything to gain by this line of talk.

"I have to get some sleep," Christian said finally, and he stood up. "You should too. I'm going to get CIA up here for a turn at watch. It's about three hours to sunrise. We should wake her early and brief her on Keeler. But we shouldn't ask for any more information before he gets here. We need to let him lead this now. He's the expert on this stuff and we don't want her to have to repeat it. Save her energy, she's going to need it."

17

Thrashing

Valisé was running frantically on a path through the jungle. Branches and thorns tore her clothes and gashed her forehead and slashed her arms and legs. She was bleeding everywhere and the sting from the poison in the thorns made her weak. IT was behind her, somewhere in the dark. Each bend she took in the path separated her from it, but only briefly. It was fast; flying wildly back and forth across her trail, smelling her fresh scent, smelling the fresh blood from her wounds. Every turn she took confused it, but only for a moment, then it quickly picked up her scent again. It was too dark to see but she could hear the beating of its wings and the screeches it made, excited over her smell. Her aroma was too much. She radiated the sweet smell of human fear, the rank odor of perspiration, of bleeding virginity, of salty tears, of grimy jungle dirt on her hands and knees. She gasped and screamed in fear as she heard it behind her, closing in. It heard her too, and knew it would have her soon. She ran into a low branch in the dark, falling, as the searing pain from the gash on her head knocked her senseless.

In a flash, it was on top of her, pecking gashes in her shoulders and chest, its claws digging into her stomach to gain leverage. Its beak sliced into her neck and breasts, dripping and slurping blood as it pecked her again and again. It tore at her clothes as she struggled with her hands and arms over her face. And then she felt it, the worst of it. She felt its burning member enter her, pound inside her, taking away what little breath she had left. Faster now and harder, pounding away at her until the pain was so great she could feel no more, pounding and pounding, she couldn't scream.

Then it stopped. She opened her eyes to see it over her, staring at her coldly: cold black eyes that were the eyes of death itself. Its long, horrid raven's beak and the black hackles on its neck smeared with the scarlet of her blood. Then the face softened. It changed. The beak grew small and the feathers faded. The face filled out and took on human form, a form of something familiar. She closed her eyes at the sight and then reopened them at the sound of a laugh; a familiar laugh from a familiar face. It was the face of Emilé Gallierga.

She tried to scream again, but this time Marty was there to hold her and let her know that it was only a nightmare. He wrapped his arms around her as she thrashed and held her as she wept hysterically. Christian appeared at the door with his pistol drawn, prepared for whatever he might find. The CIA agent was circling the deck of the boat, looking for a trespasser on board. She settled down as Marty held her tight. Christian went back to his berth without saying anything. On his way he thought that perhaps Marty's intuition was right; she's authentically fucked up.

Keeler and James entered the protected bay as the sun was rising to their right. Marty had called Keeler, as directed, about an hour earlier. He briefed the Admiral on the events of the previous day, explaining in depth the status of Valisé, and his belief that he had turned her. He wasn't sure if this was the way Keeler had wanted it, because she was going to be high maintenance given her mental state. But she was there and she wanted to defect. They had achieved the best case scenario.

Keeler immediately told him that she had to be ready to return to the Hill House within a short time, perhaps as soon as that night. And she must appear normal. He'd need to get right to it with her, there would be no time for gentle understanding, although he felt confident that he could talk with her in such a way as to make her feel comfortable. The key would be, he told Marty, her complete commitment to do whatever was necessary to get the information they needed. Marty reported that she was all in, but there would be a string attached. The operation would eventually have to result in the death of Gallierga.

"We can't kill a foreign national," Keeler said. "

"Well, then she probably won't do it," Marty said, and silence followed.

"Lookit," Keeler said eventually, "the operation has broadened in scope. Washington is, at best, indifferent about what happens to Gallierga in the end. He's an important focus, but only for the moment."

"Admiral, I'm just reporting what I know. She's convinced that if her father isn't killed, she will be. She's not going to jump ship and then have to run for her life until one day she slips up and they catch her and carve her up. Our guys upstairs are going to have to understand that killing Gallierga is the means to an end."

Keeler was beginning to think that Marty was bargaining for her; representing her interests. But he realized also there had to be something in it for her. It became a question of whether they could move forward without her information. In the limited amount of time he had, he decided they couldn't.

"Tell her whatever she wants to hear for now," he replied. "We'll see what we can do about Gallierga; I suppose the world would be a better place without him. But I can't imagine how we're going to get to him without a mission into Colombia. And I can tell you, we have no authority to do anything like that."

"So, I should tell her we have a deal?"

"Deputy," Keeler barked, "just get her up and ready to talk. I'll address it with her."

In his heart, Marty was reluctant to push her so hard so soon, but he knew Keeler was right; they had no time for making nice.

The galley on board the Lemon Drop was fairly well stocked with supplies. Christian managed to get some coffee going and pull some fruit together for a decent breakfast, including the mango juice, and some bread and cheese. He plopped it all out on the galley table for anyone who wanted some. When Keeler stepped on board, Marty had Valisé up and sitting at the table with her head propped by one arm, sipping on some coffee. She still didn't feel well, but she'd come a long way in twelve hours and seemed willing to try her best. Keeler walked into the galley and didn't bother to exchange any pleasantries. He identified himself, sat down on a stool that folded out of the wall and began to talk.

"We only have a few hours," he began. "I have to understand the details of your situation, develop a strategy, and then return you to Cruz Bay. You have to go right back into your life, as if none of this ever happened. Do you think you can do that?"

"I can," she said, "I'm not sure I *will*. Are you going to help me?"

"I'll get to that. We intercepted a telephone conversation between Emilé Gallierga and a known al Qaeda operative in Saudi Arabia. We have no interest in your involvement in the cocaine business, except to the extent that it will shed light on your father's dealings with al Qaeda. Do you understand this?"

"Yes."

"We believe your business is involved in producing income for al Qaeda. Our only interest is following the money stream to its recipients."

"I know nothing of this except that he is under contract to transport heroin for an Arab producer," she replied.

Keeler continued as if she had said nothing. "We will expect you to return to St. John and eventually to Colombia as if nothing has changed. You will be in constant contact with us, through Becker here, providing information about dates and times of the transport and the destination. You will assist in any way that we require. At the completion of this operation, we will extract you from Colombia, provide you with new identity and employment and establish a new life for you. Your service for us will terminate as soon as we have recovered all the information that we may find useful. Do you understand?"

"Yes."

"Do you agree to this?"

"No," she said. Keeler turned to Marty with a look of impatience. "I will not do this," she continued, "unless Emilé Gallierga is dead before I am brought out of Colombia."

"You're free to kill him," Keeler replied. "He is of no interest to us."

She shook her head in disbelief that Keeler could be so naïve. "I can't kill him," she said mockingly, "the chances of success for me, acting alone, are slim. Killing him would be your job and therefore, if you choose to accept, the cost of my cooperation. If he were to live, he would hunt me down with the energy of a blood-hound, and then he would kill me swiftly, or, maybe not so swiftly; maybe tortuously, slowly and with great pleasure. You could provide no protection sufficient to prevent this. The only security I would have would be his death."

Keeler watched carefully as she spoke and was impressed by her strength. She was unlike any woman he had seen before: her cool appraisal of the way Gallierga would treat her was born of experience in these matters. She did not express fear, not outwardly. She simply stated the facts as she saw them, and the way she spoke made it clear that this was not a negotiation. Her intense beauty and street smarts lent her an undeniable charisma that had probably in itself caused many men to simply give her what she wanted. But for Keeler, she was powerful, at that moment, simply because she was right about how it would go down, and she knew it. Her beauty was compelling, but that was not what pushed him. Keeler then looked at Marty as he came to fully appreciate the sexual gauze in which the previous two days had been wrapped. He knew that Marty had already heard the siren's song. This suggested his regard for her welfare would be more developed, especially if there had been sex, and Keeler was convinced that there had; he could almost smell it. The others waited in silence as he chewed on her demand.

Valisé was offering to join the battle, asking nothing more than security in exchange. If he accepted the offer, he also accepted the responsibility for her life as a fellow soldier; no less to her than to any other brother in war. This drew a defining element into the mission, and thus into his approach; she would need to be protected both during the mission and *after* it was accomplished.

Keeler's pay grade meant that he had to make decisions as events unfold, when the objectives are still moving targets. He didn't get paid to take things back to the office and carefully decide on the correct action. And so he arrived at the current decision as he had so many before, with speed, trepidation and uncertainty of the outcome. Like all those times before, his manner didn't show it.

He shifted his attention evenly between Valisé and Marty and finally spoke. "After we reach the point where our intelligence needs for this operation are met, we will do whatever is necessary to neutralize the threat posed to you by Gallierga." His next glance at her questioned whether this amount of commitment would suffice. "Agreed?" he asked.

"Agreed." She said.

18

Cake and Eat It Too

"She have left the island." Randall explained. "I find the note yesterday afternoon. She say she be back today. I figure you know that. I go up there to check on her and see how she doin. I find the note that she say she sailing. I figure you know that."

"Do you know who she left with?" Gallierga barked.

"No sir, I maybe could find out. I maybe could check at the pier. I think maybe that would be the sailboat she take sometimes before, the one that take maybe six people, the tourist one. They go to the British islands, and they stay out maybe two, three nights."

"You do that, Randall. Find out if anyone saw her leave. I've been trying to call her since last night, and I get no answer."

"The phones they do not work over there. They have no towers."

"Call me as soon as you find anything. I don't like it when you don't know *exactly* where she is."

"Yah sir...." Randall replied, but Gallierga had clicked off before he could get it out. He needed her to find Sutton. Several phone calls to his house had gone unanswered. He knew that Sutton had left Montserrat after dropping the first shipment, and he knew that the plan was to complete the second leg of the transit that evening but there were some questions that were unanswered, a condition he hated. He needed control. He wanted to discuss exactly where Sutton would enter the U.S. and when it would happen; he'd be flying in there with seventy million dollars in heroin and carrying a passenger of unknown Arab descent. He'd need to make progress reports to both the buyers and the sellers, and he'd need to coordinate the actual delivery and pickup point and time. All the time while Gallierga was frantically calling Valisé and barking at Randall, wanting answers, Sutton was sleeping in his bed, like a baby.

Gallierga's concern for his exposure with regard to the passenger was well-founded. If either Sutton or the Arab were captured, the U.S.

government would have good cause to devote more immediate attention toward him, and it would not be the type of attention he was accustomed to from the bumbling DEA. The Americans would eventually trace Sutton's plane and connections back to the Virgin Islands and the car rental company, and eventually, after they put enough resources into it, back to him. If smuggling an Arab became part of the equation, the U.S. would pursue him with a completely different energy.

His phone rang. The caller ID told him it was Valisé.

"Where have you been?" He asked, with a mixture of the usual paternal sweetness and a hint of irritation.

"I've had a simply spectacular time sailing. Don't tell me you were worried?"

"Yes, Vali, I always worry about you. Also, the special shipment is in progress and I can't seem to raise Sutton."

"Did you call Randall?"

"Yes, I did. But I don't want him talking to Sutton about the shipment. He went up to the Hill House and found your note. Why didn't you tell anyone you were going?"

"Because, Uncle, every time I tell someone I'm going somewhere, you send others with me. I needed time alone, which I just enjoyed. We're back in Cruz Bay now."

"Who did you go with?"

This would be her first test. "I went with the same captain and crew as last time. Six tourists and I. It was wonderful. My, there's poor Randall now, he looks upset; you have him in a tizzy."

"You see him there now?"

"Yes, I'm at my Jeep and he's walking over. Now, what do you want me to do? Shall I go locate Conrad? Are you sure he's on the island?"

"Yes," he answered. "He completed the first half of the transport from Isla la Tortuga to Montserrat last night; he'll be doing the second half tonight." She made mental notes. "And I need to talk to him," Gallierga continued. "I need to know his plans for entry to the U.S. and the time frame; our customers want a report and there's scheduling to be done."

"Okay, Uncle, Randall and I will drive to his house and see if he's there. Perhaps he is sleeping. Why are you handling this yourself, why isn't Orestes making the arrangements as usual?"

"Because of the special nature of this transport and the amount of money involved, I need to be the one."

"Okay, I'll call you from Sutton's, ciao," she said and clicked off.

Valisé and Randall got into the Jeep and headed toward Sutton's house. Randall didn't ask about where she'd been, he knew that she must have told Gallierga on the phone. He also didn't tell her that, at Gallierga s request, he visited the two charter boat companies she had used before. Neither had a charter sail in progress, nor did either have a record of her on board at any time in the past few days.

They arrived at Sutton's to find him reading an aviation chart on his front porch. Valisé asked Randall to stay in the Jeep and walked up to the porch alone. She smiled genuinely at Sutton and said a pleasant hello, but got right to the business at hand. "Emilé needs to talk to you, he's been trying to reach you. He needs a progress report and a schedule."

"Yes," he agreed with a smile.

"Let me ring him up on my cell phone to make it easy," she said, "and then you can be on your way."

"That's fine, I forgot that I shut the phone off in order ta sleep," he said casually.

"I told him that you probably did just that, and he understands, but he's getting some pressure from other elements of the plan."

"Yes Miss Valisé, call him now."

She selected the speed dial on her cell phone and waited for Emilé to answer. "Uncle? I have him here, hang on."

Sutton took the phone from her, "Hello Señor, I apologize for not being with the phone before. I just got back on the island about sunrise, and I needed solid rest for the trip tonight. ...Yah Señor, I be leaving later for the second trip. I have ta pick up the other plane tomorrow, the big one. ...Yah sir, thank you for the help on that. I think it be the day after tomorrow, at night. I go ta Montserrat and I pick up the whole thing, and the Arab, and we fly north. ...Yah sir, I have to refuel in the Bahamas, then I fly to south Georgia, just north of Jacksonville, and enter there. ...Yah sir, that is pretty far north, but I think safer. I will have ta refuel again in Georgia or maybe north Florida, but there is many small airports, and it will be okay. ...No, we cannot fly directly into Miami, we must find a small commuter airport outside, one without a tower or air traffic control. I think that if all goes good, we will be in the Miami area about midday Saturday. This all depends that we don't get no bad weather though. ...Yah sir, as soon as I get the name of the final airport and the exact time I call you, or I let Orestes know. ...Yah sir, good luck ta you too. It all be good."

Sutton handed the cell phone to Valisé and smiled briefly, now a touch nervous about the fact that the plan was still vague. She thanked him for tending immediately to her uncle's need for information, wished him good luck, and said goodbye. He stopped her just as she was taking her first step off the porch.

"Ah, Miss Valisé, I almost forgot. Remember the other thing we talked about before, the account?" She stared blankly for a moment, and then nodded in recognition of the "other thing." He handed her a small slip of paper. "The password."

She slipped it into her pocket. "That reminds me Señor Sutton, where are you stopping for fuel in the Bahamas?"

"Cat Island," Sutton replied. "It be about the only place with gas there that is not a big airport. The big airplane, the new one you know? It needs the jet fuel."

"It's a jet?" she asked, a little surprised.

Sutton chuckled, "Nah, Miss Valisé, it not be a jet; it have jet powered engines, but it is a turboprop airplane, a King Air."

"Oh," she said, "how nice. Well, good luck and see you soon."

As she and Randall pulled out of the drive, she thought for sure this was the last time she would see Conrad. Then she thought about her promise to him, knowing that now, with the change in her loyalties, she would never be able to see it through. In a fleeting moment of guilt, she imagined it would be a good thing if somehow Sutton could be saved when she was extracted from this mess. Then she put the thought out of her mind as quickly as she let it in. Saving Sutton would not be possible.

During the ride back to Cruz Bay, Randall said, "Miss Vali, you be awful quiet today, is you all right?"

He broke her thoughts; she had forgotten he was even in the car. "God yes Randall. I had a wonderful time on the boat. I'm just tired; I'm looking forward to a good night sleep in a real bed."

"Tell me what boat that you go on? I ask down at the charter office and they tell me that you not go on any of the boats there. Who you go with?"

She felt a tinge of fear. "Randall, were you checking up on me? You're as silly as my uncle."

"He tell me to do that."

"He did? You can't tell him then, he would be so upset."

"What I can not tell him?"

"You have to promise me first," she said, "that you won't tell him. I would never forgive you."

"Yah, it be okay Miss Vali, if you tell me you was okay, and that you was safe, I no tell de boss."

"Well, I had a wonderful time, and as you can see I am safe, and, hmmm, on second thought I think it would be best if you didn't know where I went and who I was with. That way, you won't have to lie if he asks you."

She thought this lighthearted confusion might hold him off, but she also knew that when Emilé did ask him, as he surely would, Randall would not have an answer. He would demand to know where she was and he would be relentless. She was going to have to think of something specific to tell Emilé, and quickly.

"Whatever you think, Miss Vali. I just want you safe, that's all."

"I know, Randall, you are a wonderful friend." They pulled up at the curb across from JJ's saloon; Valisé assumed this would be where Randall wanted to get dropped off.

"So, my flight leaves tomorrow at 3:30. I'm going to take the Caneel Bay boat back to Charlotte Amalie and a taxi from there to the airport. Would you mind meeting me at the hotel and returning the car for me?" Valisé asked him before he got out.

"Yah, for very sure Miss Vali. But the Sutton sisters, they would like ta see you before you go, maybe for a drink tonight?"

"Agh, Randall, I'm so exhausted. Let me see how I feel after I get back and get a shower. Maybe, but if not, tell them we can meet for breakfast tomorrow morning before I leave; maybe the brunch at Caneel Bay? I'll call you later."

Randall nodded as he stepped out of the Jeep. "Ok, I tell them. Bye."

After Randall walked off, she looked at the slip of paper Sutton had given her. On it was the name of the Bank, the account number and the password, which she read to herself aloud: *'rooster in the yard'*. She mouthed the words again. Her mind went to the rooster she had seen in Conrad's yard, flurrying about when she pulled up in the Jeep. Surely not something I'll forget, she thought, then tore the paper in two, so that the bank name and account number were on one half, and the password was on the other. She refolded the half with the bank information and tucked it into her purse. The password half she crumpled up and threw onto the floor. Then she ground the Jeep into first gear and pulled away.

On the Annaberg Road, she realized that she wasn't lying about her fatigue. Her head was heavy and her eyelids wanted to close. She found herself fighting off a nod. As she pulled up to the Hill House, the sun was setting to the left, so the house and the veranda were in the shadow of the mountain behind, but the twin vistas of Pillsbury sound and Sir Francis Drake Channel remained awash in sunlight below. The contrast was almost surreal. The beauty was lost on her, as all she could think of was summoning the energy to climb the stairs to the bed and falling into it. The shower would wait, as would the report to Marty, or so she thought. She walked through the tiled foyer, completely self-absorbed, in a near slumber state, when she heard a hesitant, "Hello," from the rattan chair by the large window. Marty's presence caused her to gasp involuntarily. "God," she said, "I guess we're way past the point where you still knock."

"Sorry," he said genuinely, but with a little desperation. He stood up to greet her. "I wouldn't have done this to you, but the timing is critical; Keeler is waiting for information."

"Shit, Martin, I don't know if I can think clearly, I'm so wasted." He steered her over to the chair and sat her down, then pulled the ottoman up close and sat in front of her. He gently pulled her thong sandals off and rubbed her feet. "I made you some coffee, let me get a cup."

"No, no more coffee, I think that's part of the problem."

"Okay, then just relax." She softened a little as the foot rub displaced some of the stress. "Just tell me everything that happened today, try not to leave anything out. Then you can go upstairs and sleep all you want, I won't have to bother you with this stuff again until after you've rested."

"Will you come with me?" she asked.

"No, I can't, I have to get your report to the Admiral. But I'll be back tonight and slip in beside you as soon as I can." She smiled at the thought. She told him everything that happened since she got off the boat. Marty stopped her in places to get details, and to ask her to elaborate on related points. He was most interested in the details of Sutton's flight that night, and the Isla Tortuga and Montserrat waypoints. He showed little interest in the cargo itself, except to the extent that it reflected upon where Sutton was going. The fact that Valisé knew it was heroin was evidence enough that the cargo was not homegrown in Colombia, and was therefore, the point of the 'Islamic connection' to which Valisé and Gallierga had referred during their conversations. This set of trips was 'special' and included a passenger, presumably a member of the Islamic group, and this became a focus of his questions. Unfortunately she knew little about the passenger, except they were being paid very well for his ticket. Emilé insisted on accommodating the passenger in spite of her objections, and the Arab was now waiting in Montserrat for Sutton's return. It sounded like he would be in Montserrat until at least Thursday night, two nights from the present, because Sutton could not move the shipment further north until he had an aircraft capable of carrying the all the cargo and the Islamic man.

When she told Marty that Conrad was planning to take off again later that evening, he checked his watch and reached for his cell phone. Then stopped, apparently deciding it was more important to finish here, and that there was still time to make the call later. She realized Conrad was probably going to be followed on this trip, and that other people were probably waiting to hear from Marty as to his destination and when he would go. Marty had no regard for the impression he gave her, but simply pressed her for more details.

Sutton told Emilé, she said, that the entire route would be completed by sometime Saturday, so it must be that he was planning a layover or two, probably to sleep. It seemed to her that the logical place for this would be Cat Island, since he had to stop there for fuel anyway, and she didn't see how he could possibly continue on to north Florida the same day.

Marty agreed, and moved to his last question. What did Emilé say was the purpose of the passenger? She said he was there, ostensibly, to protect the interests of the seller, to provide a further safeguard of the shipment, and to make sure the transfer to the buyer took place without any problems. She editorialized, telling him this didn't make sense to her, because the safe transport and delivery was what they, that is, her company, was hired to do, and the Islamists were paying handsomely for this. Why would they pay so much and then make the job more difficult? Surely they understand the risks involved in transporting one of their operatives across the U.S. border. She was concerned the passenger was possibly as much the point as the shipment itself. The realization worried Marty too. He wanted her as far away from this thing as possible, as soon as possible. If the passenger turns out to be a terrorist, and she or her company helped to smuggle him in, nobody, not even Admiral Keeler, would be able to keep her out of the focus of Homeland Security. She might end up in a detention camp. Or perhaps worse, if the Islamists found a need to dispose of all evidence of this smuggling, well, he shuddered at the thought. The risk for her was much greater than just retaliation from Gallierga. But she didn't understand this, yet.

As he stood to go, she sat there, her palms turned to the ceiling and staring at him blankly, expressing her consternation at his leaving without so much as a comment on her thoughts. He turned around with the intent of leaving but stopped and rubbed his face with both hands as if to wipe away the person he was and refresh himself as the man she knew.

"Valisé," he said, "this is a fact finding mission. It has to be. I can't sit here and speculate with you. There are mission sensitive reasons for that. But the reason that means the most to me is that you don't get implicated in this thing any deeper than you already are. I want to finish my job - our job here - and get you the hell out. I want to find out all I can from you, send it along and speed up the time when they - *we* - don't need you anymore, at least not as Valisé Gallierga. I don't *want* you to know everything. I don't want you to be here in this thing with me. I want you somewhere safe where we're not talking about heroin shipments and Islamists. The more you know, the more you are involved, the slimmer the chances are of my being there with you."

Her eyes welled up as his words sank in. She realized in that moment, he wanted the same thing as her. He wanted her as someone other than Valisé Gallierga. And no man, no person at all, had ever wanted her that way. She rose from the chair and went to him. They kissed a strong and desperate kiss. When their lips parted she looked up at him and said, "Please just hurry back."

He released his embrace and left the house, jogging the half mile down the hill to the Road House. It was dark and Christian wasn't there. Marty assumed that he was at Sutton's house. He went to the front porch and prepared to call Keeler.

At this time, Keeler was already in his airplane waiting for Sutton to arrive. He had received a call from Christian earlier that Sutton was on his way out again. When his cell phone rang in his hand he answered "Go ahead" as usual. Marty relayed the details of what transpired between Valisé, Gallierga and Sutton, and that there might be a problem with her cover story. While they talked, Keeler watched in the dark as Sutton appeared, walked across the tarmac and untied the Cessna 310 in preparation for departure. Armed with the new information, they saw no advantage in following Sutton out again that night, as he would be simply taking the same trip as the night prior. Keeler decided it would be best to find out where Sutton was getting the larger aircraft from and follow him from that point forward.

But Keeler wasn't sure what to do with the information. The intelligence had come to them easily, actually falling right in their laps. He needed to make a report to Andrews, and get further orders. At this point they would either be fully involved in an interdiction, or they would be pulled off. He would wait to be certain that Sutton took off from Charlotte Amalie as expected and then go back to the office and call National Security Advisor Andrews.

Valisé had misjudged Randall's fear of Gallierga's reprisal, for soon after she dropped him off at JJ's late that afternoon, he thought better of just letting the charter boat thing go and called Gallierga on his cell phone. "Yah sir, she did not want to tell me where that she was," he told the boss. "She say that if I not know then I not have ta lie ta you."

"She said for you to lie to me?" Gallierga was incredulous.

"Nah sir. She did not want me ta lie, but she did not want ta tell you either. So I have ta call you. She might be mad at me but I have ta call you."

"You did the right thing, Randall."

"Like I say, the charter companies not know anything about her on the boat. I don't know where she go. But funny thing though, the American boys in de Road House? You know de ones I mean?"

"Yes, what about them?"

"They not there all that time either, all the time I go up ta de Hill House ta see if she come back, each time they not at the Road House…and Anya…Conrad's daughter? You know who I mean?"

"Yes," Gallierga answered.

"Anya say she see Miss Vali with one of the American boys at de pier this afternoon, before I get there. Yah sir, but Miss Vali, she not tell me that. There is some funny business goin on there I think."

"Randall, you've done very well. This is why Señor Pereź and I value you so much. You always do right by us. I'll take it from here. Excellent report, Randall, excellent."

"Thank yah sir," said Randall and Gallierga clicked off.

Excellent report indeed, Gallierga thought, as he gripped the phone, surveying the possibilities. He decided to call Pablo Pereź to see if he had any details about the 'couple' staying in the Road House.

After a short but courteous conversation, Pereź told him no, that he knew only that they were a couple, a nephew of a Congressman and his friend. But regardless, he would call around and find out what he could. "Is there a problem?" Pereź asked. Gallierga told him he didn't think so, it was probably just the concerns of an overzealous uncle. They exchanged pleasantries for a moment and Pereź hung up.

He made an inquiry and then called Gallierga back. "They are a writer, a Peter Smith, and his book agent from New York. My broker didn't know the agent's name," Pereź reported. "And Smith is the nephew of U.S. Senator Robert Benson, chairman of the Senate Foreign Relations Committee. So they seem well connected enough."

Gallierga was fighting the urge to explode as his suspicious mind quickly strung together the possibilities in this revelation. "Did he do any background on these people at all?" he asked, trying to say it calmly.

"No, he didn't have any reason to, I imagine." Pereź replied. "Why, Emilé? Why are you so distraught? Have these men caused Valisé a problem? If so, I will…."

Gallierga cut him off. "The problem, Pablo, is that your Robert Benson likely sits next to someone from Senate intelligence or CIA at lunch, who likely sits next to someone else from DEA at dinner, who likely sits at a fancy American bar in the afternoon for cocktails with someone from the Justice department. And they know each other's connections, just as you and I do. And when it comes time to put agents in places to spy on others, they talk to each other and they help each other with plans, just as you and I do. And I wonder just how much of a coincidence it is that these 'American boys' are staying on St. John."

"But they were there before Vali went for vacation, how could they have known she was coming?" Pereź protested.

Gallierga ignored his question, because Pablo wasn't aware of the role of Sutton, and he had no need to know now either.

"Is there anyone else there, besides Randall, who is under your, uh, our employ?" Gallierga asked.

"There's the old gardener, you know, Pedro Corteź, the one who used to work for you. He takes care of my properties. You remember him, don't you?"

Pablo was so naive, Gallierga thought to himself, impatient with the whole mess. He decided the man had already heard too much. He didn't want to give him anything more from which to draw a picture.

"Yes Pablo, I remember him," Gallierga said, "and thank you, I'm sure everything is fine, you've been a great help. I need to run now…thanks again…ciao, my friend."

As the conversation ended Gallierga built a house of horrors in his head. Immediate action was required. He called his 'crew', his black operations people: the ones who gathered information and were well paid to take care of nasty business when needed. He told his contact there that he wanted information on a writer from New York: a Peter Smith. All that was known of him is that he was an author in his late twenties, he might have passed through U.S. Customs in St. Thomas in the past week or so, he might have flown there via a U.S. airline, and he was said to be the nephew of U.S. Senator Robert Benson. He wanted answers to several questions: Does he exist? Who is he? Is there a history of him? How many books has he written? Is he in any way associated with a U.S. Government agency? If so, what agency? And, just to be prepared for the worst, he also requested that a 'specialist' -

an assassin - depart for St. Thomas, U.S.V.I. immediately, and to wait there for further orders.

After Marty left, Valisé remained ill at ease and wondered, as exhausted as she was, if she would be able to sleep. Knowing she might need help, she took a long hot bath with some ginger leaves, readied herself for sleep with a cup of tea on the night stand, and finally reopened the book she'd been reading on the plane several days ago. She hoped to escape, drift off and recharge for what would be a long and stressful day when she woke up. Her respite was short-lived when, on the nightstand, her cell phone jingled. She let it ring once, then twice, afraid to see who it was. She knew she had to react, and when she saw Gallierga's number showing on the display, the dread that she had pushed away returned like a cold wind. She cleared her throat and set herself up to answer in her normally cheerful and relaxed voice.

"Hi Uncle, not to worry, I'm here."

"Hello, my love," he said, equally fraudulent. "Some things have developed. I've decided I need you to stay there a few more days, until Sutton returns from Montserrat to pick up the larger aircraft and departs again. Do you mind?"

"Do I mind, Uncle? I wouldn't mind if I didn't return until next year," she chuckled. "No I don't mind at all. Why though? Do you have concerns about him?"

"Not any real concerns, love," Gallierga was being extra syrupy, "but since he has been so difficult to reach, I would feel much better if you were there to monitor him and help me reach him if needed. And I want to know the minute he takes off in the larger aircraft."

"Where is the big plane?" she asked.

"I don't know." Gallierga said, lying. Sutton rented the larger plane right after he received the packet from Randall. Gallierga had helped him with the arrangements; it was awaiting him, parked on the tarmac at San Juan International airport.

"So I should contact him after tonight's trip to Montserrat, then? I don't want to miss him if he leaves the island. Or maybe I'll wait until afternoon tomorrow, let him sleep some during the day."

"That's a good idea." Gallierga said. "He'll need it."

"What kind of airplane did he buy?"

"I'm not sure. One that's big enough I assume."

"Okay, well, I'll call you as soon as I speak with him again."

"That's good my love, sleep well tonight. Ciao."

Valisé knew Emilé never assumed anything. He was paranoid, a micro-manager, the very reason Orestes never negotiated with suppliers or vendors, and why he was relegated on this transaction as the ground crew foreman at Isla Tortuga. It was also why Emilé required real time information on any and all details in this deal, there was simply no one he would trust. He could recite the specifications on any airplane that was ever used for smuggling drugs; exactly how much it could carry and for what distance. With seventy-five million dollars at risk and the company take from that at twenty-one million dollars, Emilé was not sitting in Colombia guessing details. He was being vague because he sensed that something was out of place on her end. And he was keeping her in St. John because if he had to take action, he would want her in a place where no one in Colombia would witness it. He would want it to be another tragic boating accident.

She debated calling Marty with her suspicions. He told her to call if she sensed anything was wrong. Keeler also told her that she should err on the side of caution. Hearing the words echo in her head, she entered Marty's number and he answered on the first ring. She told him that Emilé had called and asked her to stay in St. John a while longer. This was strange, she thought, and he was acting out of character, being vague with her. Now she was worried that he knew something was wrong and he'd send someone after her. Marty was on his way to meet Keeler at that moment and told her he'd add this to his report. "You should try to stay calm," he said, trying to reassure her, "nothing can happen tonight."

After Sutton departed for Isla Tortuga, Keeler went back to the station and called NSA Andrews. The boss was in a rough mood, as he had to excuse himself from a diplomatic dinner in order to take the call. The Admiral gave him all the details, concluding with, "So I need some direction here, Sir. I don't believe we should let this proceed past Cat Island. Sutton could slip across the border anywhere after that and we don't know anything about the passenger."

"I agree," Andrews said with resignation.

"If we go to Cat Island, it might get dirty," Keeler continued. "Events might dictate our actions instead of the reverse, which doesn't worry me in itself, but once I start this thing in motion, there might not be an end until everybody on one side or the other is dead."

"I understand," said Andrews. "If that happens just make sure it's the other side. I want the Arab dead before he's another terrorist on American soil. Do we know if there's anything else on board that aircraft?"

"No sir, well, we know the plane will be full of heroin."

"So the Arab is in this hemisphere probably as the result of the cell calls CIA picked up between Riyadh and Gallierga. We know the intent is to fly him into Miami. Could it be that Gallierga has moved up a step? Maybe he's found it more profitable to move terrorists than to peddle cocaine. Maybe his payment for smuggling the Arab *is* the heroin. What else is the Arab carrying? We don't know."

"Yessir, that's correct."

Andrews continued speculating. "Do we know where the bigger aircraft is? No. Do we know how many of Gallierga's people are on Montserrat? No. Can we invade Montserrat, a British Colony, by the way, with force sufficient to assure our success? No. Can we call the British Prime Minister and ask him to go through channels and assist us? No, it would take too long and he'd want to see evidence that we don't have. Finally, can we call the Montserrat police department and tip them off? Sure, and read in the morning paper about how they busted up an intermediate stop for cocaine transport and that's all. The Arab gets in another way. Montserrat is nothing. No, we have to act alone, quietly, at least for now. I say, proceed to Cat Island and take custody of the Arab. We want him alive, of course, unless there's no choice."

"Yessir".

"What weaponry do you have available, Admiral?"

"We all have our side arms of course. And James has a fairly good weapons vault, a lot of guns, but nothing silenced, which is really what we need."

"Use whatever assets you can find. Do you want CIA presence?"

"Honestly sir, I have one agent here, I called him in three days ago. He's fine and I'll keep him with me until we leave. When we get to Cat Island it'll be only Sutton and the Arab to deal with, as far as I know. So I'd prefer to keep our numbers small."

"I understand. Nardacci won't, though."

"Yessir, well, that's your territory."

Andrews chuckled. "Yes, that's my territory. I don't want that Arab to leave Cat Island out of our control. If we can't have him our way, then I don't want him leaving at all. As a secondary objective, I would prefer the heroin not leave there either. How many kilos?"

"Six hundred and forty."

Andrews did the math. "That's nearly three quarters of a ton."

"Yessir."

"Splash it in the ocean. I don't want it. I don't want Sutton around either. There can't be any witnesses."

"Yessir." Keeler knew what Andrews meant by that.

"An unfriendly agent is trying to get across our borders, probably with malicious intent, so we have clear and present danger status. We capture and sequester him somewhere with our best interrogators and if no one finds out about it; he gets us to Zawahiri, I'd bet on it."

"Yessir."

"When are you going?"

"I'm thinking tomorrow, sir. I want to be out well in advance of the target."

"Good luck."

"Thank you, sir."

"I want reports, Admiral."

"Yessir."

Andrews clicked off and it was done, the decision made, no more guesswork for Keeler. Within moments Marty knocked on the office door, which was open. Keeler looked at him and said, "We have our orders."

"Sir?"

"We're going to Cat Island in the Bahamas, leaving here tomorrow at 1900 hours, just after sunset; you, me and Christian. I have to do some research on the island and its airport. There are a lot of small out-of-the-way airstrips in the Bahamas, but most of them don't have fuel tanks. Presumably, Sutton chose Cat Island because there is fuel available."

189

Marty listened as Keeler briefed him on the objectives, taking the Arab prisoner alive and splashing the heroin. The National Security Advisor wanted no publicity of any kind. Dealing with Sutton would not be optional; he was not a target of interest, but Keeler didn't see any way of sparing the man's life given what he knew. His airplane would probably be destroyed when the heroin went down anyway, so that part of the objective would take care of itself.

He made it sound simple. They only needed to wait for Sutton to arrive, take over his aircraft and grab the Arab. Knowing what kind of airplane Sutton was going to be flying for the second leg of the operation would be beneficial, Keeler figured, as when they arrived on Cat Island they wouldn't want to waste time trying to figure out which airplane was his.

"I have some news about that, sir."

"Tell me," Keeler said.

"Yessir. Valisé tried to get Gallierga to tell her what kind of airplane Sutton would be picking up tomorrow and where it was located. He told her he didn't know. But she also overheard Sutton talking to him on the phone about the larger plane. It's a King Air. So she knows Gallierga lied to her, and reasons that he did so because he suspects something. He also asked her to stay on the island for a few days longer, ostensibly to make sure Sutton gets off on time and to act as a messenger if needed. She's sure his request is a setup so that he can have her eliminated here, away from Colombia where her murder might get a little messy. She's scared."

"Probably for good reason." Keeler said.

"But the interesting thing is, sir," Marty continued, "his exact words to her were, 'I want to know the minute that Sutton takes off in the bigger plane'. So the other plane must be here, otherwise how could she know the minute he takes off in it?"

"Good point. We can check the airport tower logs to see if an aircraft of that type has landed lately."

Both men sat in silence mulling over the elephant in the room, until Keeler spoke again. "As for her being scared, I was thinking we should bring her with us to the Bahamas. We're probably nearing the end game anyway. When we catch the Arab, Gallierga's surely going to figure out that she helped us. She won't be able to go back. We can get her to a safe house and let DEA interview her. They can decide if there's enough to put together another operation."

"And *our* other operation sir?" Marty asked. Keeler knew what he meant.

"What would you have us do? Fly into Colombia under the radar and assassinate him without any evidence that he's a threat? That's something a love-sick puppy would imagine, Becker."

Marty said nothing. Keeler could see that he was seething.

Keeler looked Marty straight in the eyes and continued. "I gotta tell you, if this goes off okay, you got lucky, *we* got lucky. But it isn't over yet, it's far from over. You need to understand that if it comes down to a choice between her and the mission, she's just like anybody else, and the mission comes first. Can you make that choice?"

Marty felt like he was back home, getting a lecture from his father. "I'll do what I have to do, sir."

"Bullshit. You'll do just what I would do; you'll try to figure out a way to have both. In the heat of battle things will start happening very quickly and you won't be able to control the outcome. It might come down to the split second when you realize it's not possible to help her and accomplish the mission at the same time. Then you'll have to make a choice that you don't want to make."

Neither man said anything for a few seconds. Marty glared at Keeler. He didn't like having his nose rubbed in his dilemma. He knew the man spoke the truth, which made him frustrated and bitter. Keeler didn't care and broke the silence. "Check in with Christian in the morning, but unless you hear differently, bring her to the airport at 1500 hours. Go back to the house now and prepare her to leave. Prepare yourself, too."

19

Ok Corral

In an old storage building at Montserrat Airport, Ribindi sat with his back to the steel wall, keeping watch over the 330 kilos of heroin, the first half of the shipment that had been stacked there since he arrived. He slept fitfully the night prior, so much of the day he spent napping, knowing he'd need to be alert in the days ahead. Word came through that he'd be there for at least two more nights, which put him in a foul mood. There were bunks in one of the storage rooms, but they were all in use by the Gallierga crew and they wouldn't have given him one if there was a spare; he smelled awful and no one wanted him around. There was running water in the storage building, but the sewer had clogged months earlier, so bowel movements were done outside, without actual toilet paper. Although he'd washed thoroughly and changed clothes after injecting the ricin into the heroin, the clothes he put back on were not clean, so his odor became worse as another day of sweat built up in his pants and shirt. Because of this, and because of his naturally foul mood, he was an outcast.

The boredom of the place was unbearable. Ribindi was allowed to spend only short times out of the building, as Gallierga's men would not take the chance that he would be spotted from the air above or by anyone who might happen to breach the line of the exclusion zone. But he wouldn't go out and let the heroin out of his sight for more than a few minutes regardless. He was awake at the crack of dawn that morning, not because there was important work to do, but so he could watch the sun come up and determine where he was relative to Mecca, allowing him to find his Kiblah and thus pray properly at the appropriate times. One of Gallierga's men brought him bread and dried beef and some water after he prayed the first time. He would not touch the beef.

Though nasty and abusive to the outside world, Ribindi was softened internally by the spiritualism of his role. From that perspective, his mission was simple and relatively short in duration. He needed only to accompany the heroin to the drop off point in Miami and ascertain that it got directly into the hands of the buyers, then his service in the current program would be complete. He would melt into the population there and try to find some of his brothers to give him shelter. In time, he would reconnect with al Zawahiri for further orders. He'd pray to remain in Miami, perhaps to watch as his deed came to have an effect on the Americans. Very few others had been able to witness their jihad. He may turn out to be one of the lucky ones, but it would be bittersweet. The true martyrs in his army had gone on to join Allah in the afterlife. They had died in the act of war. Those still alive didn't receive honor from Allah, they weren't graced with hordes of virgins, as they hadn't made the ultimate sacrifice. He knew that if he remained in this world, his name would never be connected with a perfect act of war. He would be anonymous. Allah would know; al Zawahiri would know; and perhaps a few others. He prayed for Allah to reserve a special place for him when he finally ascended to the afterlife. Allah, he believed, would not forget.

Ribindi found himself with the urge to have another bowel movement; the second of the morning. He cursed the water the Latinos had brought him. He'd heard of this; the water in this part of the world was ridden with germs that brought on the diarrhea. He cursed aloud as he squatted outside the building and endured the pain as liquid spat from his rectum. He also endured the indignity of sitting among the piles of manure from the other men who had come to this spot to defecate, some were fresh, some not. He noticed that none of the other piles were like his and wondered how long it took to become accustomed to the bad water. He tore a few pages from the book that was left there to be used as toilet paper. After cleaning himself as best he could, he didn't bother to look at what he had left behind: the spots of blood on the watery puddle, the smear of blood on the pages that he had used to wipe. If he had, his spirits might have lifted. He might have realized his journey to Allah would commence much sooner than he anticipated.

Late that night, Gallierga received a return phone call from the researcher in his black operations crew. It was well after Valisé was told to stay in St. John and well after the assassin had been dispatched to St. Thomas. The intelligence provided by his network was usually very good, not surprising, as it came from an informer in the National Security Administration with direct computer access to nearly all Federal personnel records, including the Social Security Administration, the Internal Revenue Service, the Justice Department, Customs and the State Department personnel files. This last group included not only State Department employees, but files on anyone currently being investigated for breaking international law, as well as anyone convicted of felonies involving international terrorism. The informer was known to Gallierga by the name Fabio.

When Fabio researched Peter Smith, comparing the passport number documented when he passed through customs at Charlotte Amalie to the Social Security Administration database, something very interesting surfaced. He found the Social Security file: 071-91-1164; Peter Michael Smith; Date of Birth: 11/12/1944; Deceased: 5/18/2001; Death certificate number NY55228701.

Peter Michael Smith, the one who passed through Charlotte Amalie Customs on July 7, 2013, just six days prior, and was now staying at the Road House, was sixty-nine years old, and, he was dead.

By the time Gallierga received this information, Sutton had departed Charlotte Amalie to pick up the second load from Isla Tortuga and fly it to Montserrat. He decided against trying to stop Sutton en route because of the new development. Alerting him to something amiss might cause him to abort the mission, which was not acceptable. Sutton must proceed through the stages of the delivery undeterred. Since Gallierga wasn't aware of any exact plans 'Peter Smith' had made to disrupt the operation, it was not yet time to alter anything. It would be better, he thought, to simply neutralize any potential disruption than to delay the shipment and give Smith and his group, whoever they might be, time to organize further.

Turning his attention to Valisé, he assumed that she had become involved with or was a target of Smith and his group, unwittingly or otherwise, and she now posed a clear security threat. How much of a threat depended upon her intent. If she was betraying him, then she could be providing reams of important details about the company and this operation. If the other side had obtained information from her due to her stupidity and innocence, it wasn't likely they had a complete story. Had she betrayed him? He must decide. If she was only a foolish young woman, perhaps lonely, perhaps fallen prey to the guile of a smart and handsome man, perhaps even being a little boastful about her role and her power, maybe she could be spared.

He made a mental list of her transgressions. She had disappeared from St. John for two days without telling anyone where she was going or even checking in. Indeed, she made him call countless times before answering her phone, and then made him seem foolish for being concerned. She was seen on the docks with one of the men from the Road House: an American agent. She had clearly been with this man for the two days and made no attempt to hide it from anyone, except, of course, Emilé himself. And then she lied to him about the boat she was on. She treated him as if he was stupid and paranoid, after she flaunted her independence and importance. The 'old man' was supposed to understand and accept this. As if that weren't enough, she tried slyly to coerce Randall into concealing what she'd done. She was acting big and powerful, as if she could mock his authority by convincing a trusted worker to lie to him. He had heard of this before. When a woman got a little power, she tried to flaunt it. He had heard of this, but never would have thought Valisé capable of it. With all the information and analysis, he landed on the truth: she had betrayed him.

He looked at his watch: it was after 1:00 a.m. in St. John. He would wait until morning, when the mechanic he had dispatched to St. Thomas would be position. Then he would call him with the order to kill Valisé, if it turned out to be necessary. But he would reach out to Jared Sutton for his first line of defense.

While Gallierga finalized his plans, Marty returned to Valisé at the Hill House as he promised. He stopped by the Road House to check in with Christian, but found it vacant and all of Christian's belongings gone. His own duffel sat where he had left it, so he gathered his things and threw them into it. He would be leaving tomorrow anyway; there was no sense in coming back here in the morning. He pulled his 9mm from under the mattress, checked to see that it was fully loaded and that he had a spare clip. He screwed the silencer onto the barrel and slipped the pistol into his holster. Then he went out the side door, locked it behind him, and walked up the drive, leaving his rental car parked in the Road House driveway, just in case Randall were to come by.

The Hill House was dark except for a small light she had left on at the bottom of the stairs. He kicked off his sneakers, dropped his pack on the floor, turned off the light, and made his way up the stairs quietly in bare feet. There was another crescent moon tonight, slightly larger than the one the previous night at Hurricane Hole and the sky was full of stars. The huge window-wall in the bedroom overlooking Pillsbury Sound was fully open and a warm fresh breeze filtered in. The moon and the stars cast the slightest light into the bedroom. As his eyes adjusted, he was able to make out her figure in the bed, sleeping peacefully, beautifully. He pulled his shirt off, pulled the 9mm from the holster and set it quietly on the glass top of the rattan chest of drawers. Then he unbuttoned his pants and let them fall to the floor. He quietly made his way to the master bath, closed the door and started the shower. As the hot water poured over him, he realized that he hadn't had a good shower in several days. He reached for a bottle of shampoo and found that it was some designer specialty with a sweet floral smell, but he wasn't fussy at that point. He lathered his hair up, scrubbed his body, and then sat down on the floor of the shower, letting the water pound on his head and shoulders.

The heat relaxed him and he began to feel better, almost human again. As he stood up, he took one last rinse with his hand to make sure all of the soap was off his body. He stepped from the shower and dried off. Looking in the mirror he took her brush from the countertop and brushed his hair back. Her toothbrush and paste lay by the sink and, feeling sure she wouldn't mind, he brushed away the day and the too many cigarettes he had smoked amidst the tension. He clicked off the bathroom light and made his way back to her in the near darkness. Still slightly wet from the shower, he walked over to the open door to the balcony and let the Caribbean breeze dry him off. From the angle where she lay, Valisé could not see the ocean below, only the room opening up against the star lit sky. She watched his silhouette against the dim light from the night sky. She marveled at the incredible figure of this man; this *Marty* who had saved her life, who had given her a new life; who had excited her with his scent and his strength and his gentle power and passion; who had brought her from the darkness of her old life to the anticipation of a new life; this Marty, she thought, whom she was coming to love.

Marty looked out at the sea below, feeling the peaceful quiet of the world in front of him, so different from the terror that people bring to it. He promised himself that they would return here sometime, when there was no urgency, no mission, no fears, no Gallierga...

"How did it go?" she asked.

Startled from his wandering thoughts, he turned and saw her shape and then her eyes glistening in the dim light. He walked over to the bed and slid in under the light sheet in which she was wrapped. "Shhhh…" he said. "Not tonight."

She slid over to greet him with her nakedness. The sense of familiarity mixed with wonder returned, stronger this time, for at the moment there was nothing to be concerned about; no one up on deck who might hear; no horrible nightmare to run from. She found his lips and devoured them. He cradled her body as she gave herself to him completely, wrapping her arms around his chiseled back and shoulders. She held onto him as a child would, earnestly, trustingly, with complete abandon. As they kissed, he slid his thigh between her legs and she straddled it tightly. With his hand, he grasped nearly an entire cheek of her buttocks and pulled her into him. She exhaled at the pressure of his leg against her spot. He could feel her wetness and heat as he moved his leg there, that wonderland where he hoped to spend years; that spectacular path to her soul, one now forbidden to all, perhaps, except him.

When he entered her, the fit was perfect. She took all of him, and he reached her deepest regions softly, carefully, and gently. No woman had ever given him an erection such as this. It was more than an erection; it was the outlet for his soul. For the moment, their worlds contained only this union. Outside the bubble they were in, nothing else existed.

They made love for a long time. He brought her to orgasm and held her there, each time repeating it quickly yet softly, wanting her to know that he was doing this for her; that his pleasure came from hers; that her smell and feel and taste and sounds were all that he ever wanted and that there could not be a more perfect woman for him. The union of their sexuality was unique to him, it wouldn't, couldn't, be repeated by anyone.

In time their passion converted from explosive energy to tender afterglow, they were connected spiritually. Their eyes grew heavy and their breathing slowed as they listened to their noises, fighting off the sleep that would bring tomorrow all too soon. In a dream-like slumber, they heard the call of a rooster. It was the first sign that a new day approached, a dreadful sound, unlike the friendly cock-a-doodle-doo of a barnyard fowl. The first was off in the distance, answered shortly afterward by a second, with a different pitch and volume. They fell off to sleep against the sound of the faraway cacophony. The sleep would hold off the approach of day, and yet bring it to them quicker. They eventually succumbed against the backdrop of one last screech from a rooster in the yard, out there somewhere.

After a couple hours of pure tranquility Marty felt it, an intuition, a prickly sense in the middle of his semi-consciousness. Something wasn't right. His eyes opened wide as his brain tried to process the stimulus that stirred it. Valisé was still in his arms, peacefully asleep. The sky had lightened just slightly outside the glass wall and an early morning breeze freshened the room. He didn't hear anything out of the ordinary. He had only a sense, possibly a smell. Maybe it was the lack of sound now that the roosters were quiet just before daybreak. He lay there in stillness, all his senses acutely aware of his surroundings. And then he heard it, the dullest of scrapes, like a shoe or hoof on a gravel path. It was not a sound uniquely human, but it wasn't an inanimate either. Some creature had made it. He thought of the wild donkeys, which, he was told, populate the remote areas of the island, and then listened again for more sounds that might explain what he sensed. He heard nothing else. A donkey crossing the drive would not be careful of the sound it made. Donkeys, on that island, had no natural enemies except for man. There would be more steps and therefore, more sounds.

He made a move to get up and Valisé woke with a start. He put his finger to her mouth to shush her and whispered "get dressed."

He made sure his feet didn't bump the floor as he sat up and then stood to put his pants on. He also pulled on the tee shirt he was wearing the night before and picked up the 9mm. He slipped the second clip of ammunition into his back pocket and carefully walked to the glass wall with the gun drawn, hoping not to make the floor creak under his weight. He slowly and carefully stuck his head into the opening, just enough to get a full view of the drive and the parking area in front of the house. There was no one there, but as he looked further down the driveway in the predawn light, he saw a car parked in the distance, a small white Toyota sedan, like the ones that most natives drove. The car was situated to be out of sight from ground level, but from this elevation he could see the roof and hood through the trees. He couldn't tell if there was anyone in the car, so he was careful not to expose more of himself than necessary, knowing his silhouette might be visible to someone sitting there. There was no panic in Marty's demeanor, merely directed urgency. The training he had received in the Georgia swamp was serving him well.

As he turned from the glass to see how Valisé was coming, he saw a spit of white light from the top of the stairs outside the bedroom door; it was accompanied by a metallic thump and a burning sensation across the top of his left shoulder. He immediately dropped to his knees, pointed the pistol, and fired two quick shots into the middle of the dark silhouette from where the white spit had originated. The silhouette fell to the floor with a thump, bringing down with it a tall and slender plant stand. The glass top shattered as it hit the tiled hall floor and Marty realized the silencer on his pistol didn't mean much anymore. He remained completely still but looked at Valisé who was alarmed, though surprisingly composed. He figured that whoever he just killed was not alone, and waited for someone else to follow from behind. He crouched in complete silence, and motioned for Valisé to slide off the bed and onto the floor. The sting in his shoulder was severe, but he didn't think he had lost any mobility in it. A quick pat of the area revealed a gash, bleeding, but not badly. He'd only been grazed.

Satisfied after a few moments of silence, he motioned for her to join him by the door, and told to her wait while he went out to the body lying on the hall floor. He stayed low, and as he got to the body, he felt the neck. No pulse. In the dim light he saw the face. The pictures Keeler provided were good enough. He reached over and grabbed the dead man's gun and motioned Valisé to come out next to him. When she arrived, he handed her the gun, and showed her the safety. It was a 9mm Beretta with a silencer. A much better gun than his own, actually, but not previously owned by a better marksman.

She looked down at the body on the floor in front of them. It was a West Indian man, a native; he seemed tall and large, but not stocky, and he was well groomed. She looked closer but didn't recognize the face and gave Marty a quizzical look. He knew she would be saddened for Conrad. Valisé was not put off by death, even as close as it was in front of her now. Death had been a part of her life. When Marty whispered to her, "Jared Sutton," she sighed and, putting two and two together, they both realized that he was there to kill her, likely sent by Gallierga.

Marty knew there had to be others with him and, in fact, there were. And in fact, in the wee hours of the night prior, Gallierga had called Jared Sutton at home, woke him from his alcohol induced slumber, and proceeded to tell him that his niece, his own niece, his own flesh and blood, who he had nurtured and loved and provided for all her life, had become an agent for the American DEA. He told the young Sutton that he had just learned she was planning to inform the DEA about his father's missions between Colombia and the islands, that she had to be intercepted immediately, and there was no one else for him to turn to. Valisé was no longer his flesh and blood; she was planning to betray them, and she must be eliminated. He told Jared that since they both had a deep interest in preventing her from such treason, it was up to him to stop her; it was what his father would want him to do, were he in a place where he could be contacted. The young Sutton was so moved by the thought that the great Gallierga would turn to him in a time of such crisis, that he sprang into action.

So Jared's last words just prior to entering the Hill house that morning were in a whisper to Randall, directing him to remain outside and shoot anyone other than him that walked out the door. Randall was equipped with a snub nose .38 special, a crude and noisy weapon, notoriously inaccurate from further away than ten feet.

As they made their way quietly down the stairs, Marty saw that the sun was coming up and it was getting brighter outside, an advantage because anyone on the outside trying to look in was less able to see into the relative darkness of the house. Marty slipped into his sneakers at the bottom of the stairs where he had left them. They carefully walked through the foyer against the wall. There was no one else to be seen, either inside or outside the house but, again, he couldn't imagine that Jared was alone. He also considered that there might be someone waiting in the car down the road. Rather than walk out the main door, he guided Valisé to one of the sliding glass doors facing the ocean. From there, they could follow the veranda to the back of the house and into the yard through the pool area, providing an element of surprise to anyone expecting them to exit out the front door. As they inched their way along the veranda, Marty scanned the area, looking for anyone guarding the perimeter.

Near the front door, Randall grew impatient. Standing against a wall adjacent to the veranda with his gun drawn and his back to the pool area, he'd heard the crash of the plant stand and waited in silence for an impossibly long time. As Marty and Valisé approached from the rear his back came into view. Marty motioned for to her get down behind the stone wall that surrounded the pool. Standing fully abreast with his feet braced and the gun supported by both hands, he pointed it directly at Randall, shooting range style; the most stable position from which to fire, and therefore the most accurate. Randall's upper back was clearly in his sights, about fifty feet away.

Marty yelled, "Don't move."

Randall spun around and saw the gun pointed at him. He dropped to one knee and started pulling the trigger of the .38 wildly. The unsilenced gun exploded against the serenity of the morning and the recoil had Randall's hand bouncing uncontrollably. He really had no chance. The bullets missed Marty by feet, and he didn't want to shoot the man, but with shots being fired at him like that he had to respond, and calmly pulled off two quick, silent shots. The first hit Randall in the neck, just below the right ear. As he reared back from the impact of the first, the second hit him directly in the center of the chest. He was dead before his body thumped to the ground.

Valisé choked at the sight of Randall lying there, a pool of blood beginning to form underneath him. Marty knew this wouldn't be easy for her. She genuinely cared for the big man and ran to him from behind the wall, kneeling by his side.

"Randall, why were you here?" She cradled his lifeless face in her hands.

Marty knelt beside her. He put his arm around her for support but, as sorry as he was for her, he was sure it wasn't over yet. There was still the matter of the car down the drive. He tugged her gently, nudging her to come with him.

He stood her up and held her shoulders firmly in his strong hands. "Listen, our lives are at stake here. Sometimes we can't make sense out of what other people do, remember that. Now, we have to get out of here. We have to get to St. Thomas. Please, pull yourself together and look forward, not back. Go upstairs and get your things, I have to check out the car they came in. Grab my duffel on your way out. Carry the gun with you and don't hesitate to use it."

She managed to rub her face and nod her head, and then she stumbled off toward the door to the house. By the time she reached the stairs to the veranda, she had regained her composure. Marty ran in a low crouch down to the edge of the forest toward the driveway, being careful to not be seen from the parked car. As Valisé went through the door to the house, Marty heard the engine start, then heard it screaming under full throttle as the car barreled up the driveway toward him. Still out of sight, he ran back to the stone wall and knelt behind it, steadying his gun at the opening in the trees where the car would soon appear. When the Toyota burst out of the opening he saw the driver was a woman. As it came closer, he realized it was Anya Sutton, Yendi was next to her, leaning out the window with a gun pointed in his general direction.

"Christ," he said to himself, "I can't kill these women." Anya drove the Toyota up on the grass in front of the stone wall. Marty had his gun pointed directly at her head from about twenty feet away but hesitated just long enough. Both women had their guns out the window and began firing at him. He ducked down behind the stone wall to avoid the volley of bullets spraying at him. They both had MAC 10 machine pistols, spitting out rounds at a terrifying rate. Marty was pinned down behind the wall. In the mayhem, he swore at himself. The car came to a stop, and the twins opened their doors and got out, continuing to fire wildly from behind the open doors. He managed to stick his gun up above the wall and pull off a burst of quick shots in the face of the screaming fire ricocheting off the wall. One of his shots hit Yendi in the chest, knocked the gun from her hand and spun her around before she fell to the ground. Anya stopped for a split second as Yendi fell. Marty couldn't see the result of his shots, but heard the diminished gunfire and took the opportunity to poke his head up slightly over the wall. Enraged, she began firing again.

Anya crouched behind the trunk of the Toyota. The MAC 10 ran through rounds so quickly, Marty hoped that when she stopped to reload, if she in fact was carrying another magazine, he would have a chance to jump up and pull off a couple of shots. He would soon be low on shells himself: the Glock had a twelve shot clip, and by his count he'd used nine. He had three left before he would need to change to the other clip in his pocket, but he had only fifteen rounds total. When he heard a break in the spray of bullets coming at him, he figured that Anya was reloading and seized the moment. Crouching low, he moved to another spot behind the wall, about twenty feet away, stood, and prepared to fire. Anya was not there; she had either ducked down behind the car or changed spots as well. He quickly pulled the other clip from his pocket and ejected the empty one from his gun. Just as he did she appeared over the back of the Toyota with a smile on her face. She knew she had him. But in the split-second before she could squeeze off the volley that would be Marty's death sentence, he heard a dull thump come from the direction of the house. Anya's head kicked sideways unnaturally. Blood and bits of hair burst from her skull. He looked toward the house and saw Valisé standing there, in a perfect target stance with the gun still pointed in Anya's direction. She looked at Marty and said, "Now you owe me again."

Marty went to see if either Anya or Yendi had a pulse and found nothing. Neither he nor Valisé spoke as they surveyed the carnage until Marty broke the silence. "Grab the luggage and put it in the car." She gave a questioning look but did as he directed. Marty moved the two bodies away from the car and climbed into the driver's side. Miraculously, through the entire foray, the engine remained running. This, Marty realized, was probably because most of the shots were fired *from* the car, not toward it; added testimony to that fact that he had put himself in a very difficult spot. He backed off the grass and they sped down the driveway.

"Fuck," Marty yelled, as they drove down the twisting road. He looked at her and shouted, "NEVER hesitate." She knew he was talking to himself.

Marty slowed as they neared the end of the Hill House Road. He thought it would be best if they stayed in the Toyota, at least until they approached Cruz Bay. But he was trying to decide the best direction in which to drive. It would be quickest to head directly for town on the Annaberg Road, but if someone were looking for them, they would be most likely watching that route. If they took the back way; driving toward the Annaberg Plantation and then cutting over to Centerline Road and coming into Cruz Bay from that direction, it was much longer. He figured after all the ruckus, they needed to get into town quickly, blend into the tourist crowd and get aboard a ferry as soon as possible. He decided to take the direct route to Cruz Bay. They would stop short at Caneel Bay, ditch the car and walk along the shore on the footpath into town. This trip, of course, would definitely take longer, but they would not be visible on the road in Cruz Bay. The difficulty would be trying to get onto the ferry at the docks without being recognized. Surely, within a couple of hours, Jared and his sisters would be missed and if any other members of the SFC knew about the hit attempt, they would be off to the Hill House to look for them. After the bodies were discovered, Valisé would become hot property. Keeler was not expecting them in St. Thomas until 1500 hours - seven hours away. Once they got situated on the shoreline, Marty would call Keeler and get orders.

As he turned left on the Annaberg Road, he was careful to drive off slowly, normally. He tried to slow the effect of adrenalin pumping into his system. About a mile down the road, Valisé recognized the pickup truck approaching them from the opposite direction. As it passed, she saw that it was old man Cortez. He was probably on his way to the Hill House to do the gardening. She told Marty about it, and she felt certain the old man did not notice that it was her in the Toyota.

Cortez was indeed on his way to the Hill House to do some cleanup tasks. Pulling into the driveway he noticed Marty's car at the Road House, as it had been on and off for the previous week. His little pickup truck revved and groaned its way up the road. When he arrived, he didn't notice the carnage in the side yard at first. He simply parked in front as always, got out of the truck and walked to the garden storage room built into the house under the veranda. He took out a bamboo rake and hedge clippers, put them in the wheelbarrow and wheeled it around the back of the house. He entered the garden pool area from the same direction that Marty and Valisé had used to sneak up behind Randall less than an hour before, parked the wheelbarrow near the pool, and began raking the grassy area just opposite where Randall lay dead. He made a couple of small piles of fern leaves and walked back to the wheelbarrow to retrieve it. When he looked up, he saw the body lying over by the house. He just stared, stunned. Finally, he walked over and bent down; he recognized that it was Randall. "Sweet Jesus and Maria," he said.

He reached to feel for a pulse and found nothing. Then he stood erect again and looked around the grounds. He saw the bodies of Anya and Yendi lying on the other side of the short stone wall. In his surprise and disbelief he set forth with a string of profanity, conveying only to himself his sense of disbelief at the death around him. As he started to make his way over to the sisters, Randall's cell phone rang in the pocket of his sport jacket. The gardener hurriedly managed to get the cell phone out. The incoming caller ID said 'EMIL'. He knew who that would be and debated for a few precious seconds as to whether he should answer it. Reluctantly, he answered. "Señor Emilé?"

"Who is this?" Gallierga replied.

"Señor, it is Cortez. I am at the Hill House. Randall is dead. I just get here this minute. Randall is dead, shot two times. The Señorita Sutton, Anya, she is dead too, and her sister…shot many times…it looks like war here. Randall is on the ground at my feet, what could have…."

Gallierga cut him off. "Cortez, calm yourself, it's all right. Do you see the Sutton man, Jared?"

"No Señor, he is not here….not on the outside. Is he supposed to be? I have not been on the inside." The old man was frantic.

"Okay, Señor Cortez, relax. Please go into the house and see if Valisé is all right. Stay on the line with me as you walk."

"Sí Señor." Cortez said gravely, then walked up the stairs to the veranda and made his way into the house.

"There is no one on the first floor Señor, should I go up the stairs?" Cortez was frightened out of his wits, unaccustomed to such terror.

"Yes, good…if she is not there, please check on the second floor."

As Cortez climbed the stairs and approached the master bedroom, he saw Jared's body lying by the door, a huge pool of purple blood had coagulated beneath him. "Ay Dios Mio." He said into the phone reflexively, and then bent down to see the man's face closer.

"It's Jared Sutton Señor. The last one here, it's Jared."

"Poor man," Gallierga said dramatically. "Poor Sutton. He will not have seen his children alive one last time. And thank God, if you'll allow me, Cortez, that Valisé is not among them."

"Sí Señor, amen for that."

Gallierga instructed Cortez not to call the police, but to leave immediately, someone else would find them. There must have been some treachery going on, he told Cortez, and we mustn't allow Valisé to become involved in it. He asked Cortez to see if she had left anything in the house, clothing, toiletries, anything like that. Cortez checked around and reported no, she seemed to have taken all of her belongings.

When Gallierga hung up, he immediately called the mechanic, who was staying in a bungalow on Lindbergh Bay, very near the airport in St. Thomas. "Are you in position?"

"Sí."

"Do you have email at your position?"

"Sí."

"A photo will arrive in a moment. She is traveling under the name Anna Maria Santiago. She will be with an American; an American agent. They are likely to be on their way to St. Thomas from St. John right now. Look for them either at the ferry docks in Red Hook or in Cruz Bay. Neither is to leave St. Thomas."

"They won't."

20

Paradise Lost

Sutton was completely exhausted when he saw the GPS indicating he was just a few miles out. For two consecutive nights he had flown the stressful trip first between St. Thomas and Isla Tortuga and then on to Montserrat. The deep skill he had accumulated from years of flying at low level over the ocean was being tested. The principal battlegrounds in his struggle against fatigue were his neck, arms and hands. At thirty to forty feet above the surface of the ocean, there was simply no opportunity for complete rest. His eyes began to tire after about an hour into the flight. His neck would soon stiffen from holding his head in one constant position. He had to guide the control yoke very steadily, making only tiny corrections, so his hands and arms would begin to ache with layers of intensity. Sometimes his muscles became so fatigued that an involuntary twitch developed, remedied by continually switching hands on the control yoke. It was a battle against the ceiling of discovery above and the floor of death below. One trip per week was generally manageable, as he benefited from days of rest between trips. But Sutton was not getting any younger. He had recently celebrated his sixty-third birthday. Every year he noticed that some of the things he did in the prior year he could not now manage as well for the same length of time.

He set the main wheels down first, then the nose wheel, as his Cessna 310 settled onto the old runway in Montserrat. The plane hit with a rougher than normal thump and screech. Once he was safely rolling out after landing, he was able to stretch body parts as needed. Doing so he found that his buttocks and the back of his legs had been without circulation for so long it was painful to move. But the relief was enormous. When he opened the door, he swung his legs out to stand on the wing-walk of the airplane with some difficulty. And when he finally managed to get to the ground, he paid no attention to one of Gallierga's people who was chirping in his ear. He had all he could do to keep his balance, never mind carry on a conversation.

During the long flight he had debated as to whether he should return to St. John to his own bed again, or find a place to bunk down at the airport. Standing there wobbling next to the plane, he settled on the latter. He was simply too spent to fly any longer that night. So he informed the Gallierga captain that he needed to sleep, undisturbed.

"Have your men take out all their bed things from the bunk room. No one be going back in there until I am finished," he said sharply. "I don't want ta have ta call Señor Orestes and complain about the accommodations."

The Captain objected but grudgingly accepted Sutton's demands. He ordered his men to go into the bunk room and remove their belongings. Much moaning followed, but after a short time the room was cleared out.

Had Sutton decided not to stay on Montserrat that night, had he decided to take his chances with the fatigue and return to St. John, it was likely that he'd have caught wind of Jared and his daughters preparing for the ambush at the Hill House and intervened. But that didn't happen.

Stumbling toward the old airport storage building, he stopped to urinate at the designated spot downwind from the building, and then made his way inside in hopes of finding a reasonably comfortable and clean place to sleep. The captain and his crew carried the cargo in from the plane and stacked it adjacent to the pallets that were placed there the previous night. Sutton walked right past the heroin and Ribindi, who was counting packages as they were brought in, and closed the door to the bunkroom behind him. The air in the room was wretched, owing to one tiny window open to the outdoors, and also to the fact that so many filthy and smelly workers had been sleeping there for so many days. There was no maid service.

He would not sleep on any of the bunks, the odor repulsed him. In his knapsack, Sutton carried an inflatable mattress and blanket for just such an occasion, and his airplane was always stocked with a pillow and clean clothes. He turned up the wick on the kerosene lamp and looked around for the best spot for the mattress. His nose began to adjust to the smell, but he realized he'd probably have to discard his things after this mission, as everything would pick up the smell of the hellhole. In retrospect, Sutton had spent nights in much worse conditions. The base camp in Vietnam from which they flew operations was not much above the level of the rice patties surrounding it. During the rainy season, water would overflow the patties and flood into the camp, washing under the tent platforms they used as barracks. The latrine would overflow as there was no lower ground for the sewage to move to, and garbage from the camp kitchen could sometimes be seen floating around as well. Sutton reminded himself that in comparison, the bunk room at Montserrat was an upscale accommodation. He kicked a wooden chair out of the way and made his bed for the night.

In the other room, Ribindi was finishing his count of the packages and decided to ask Sutton when they would be leaving. After confirming that the quantity was correct, that there were indeed six hundred and forty one-kilogram bags of heroin, he walked up to the bunk room door. He didn't knock, but turned the handle and walked in. Sutton was not yet asleep and was in no mood for a visitor, especially such filth as this one. "What do you want?" Sutton growled.

"When are we leaving?"

"We will leave when I have rested," Sutton replied nastily.

"But you have to go retrieve another airplane?"

"Yah,"

"And when will that be?"

"Tomorrow,"

"What time tomorrow?"

"Listen ta me," Sutton spit out, "you are on my schedule. I am not on yours. When I have got enough sleep that I know I can fly the next leg, we will go. The sooner you let me sleep, the sooner that will be. Now get out of here and let me be. You smell."

Ribindi left and shut the door, smiling to himself. If it weren't for the fact that Sutton was the pilot, he would slit his throat right now and piss all over him as he bled to death. Ironic that Sutton's thoughts were very similar, he might just push 'that piece of shit outta the airplane' on the way to Cat Island. The flight to the Bahamas in the next day or so was setting up to be an interesting time for the two of them.

Ribindi didn't feel well. The diarrhea hadn't gone away and every time he drank any amount of water or ate the tiniest bit of food, he had to run to the crap spot and empty his bowels. His stomach was sore and his rectum had begun to bleed from the irritation. He was sure the water they'd given him was tainted and he told them so. They laughed at him. They told him they had brought the water in themselves. He watched them drink and not get sick, which pissed him off. It also confused him. Could there be something else wrong? Maybe he had the flu or maybe he had gotten food poisoning on the Dover Mist and it was just now taking hold. Or maybe some of the poison from the mission had found its way into him; that what he was feeling was what his enemy would soon feel. Maybe, praise Allah, he was being summoned after all.

When Sutton woke the next morning, his neck was stiff from the hard floor of the bunk room. During the night, the air had leaked out of his mattress. He was so exhausted that he slept completely through the deflation and the eventual landing on the floor. It was daylight outside. He looked at his watch. It was past 10:00 a.m.; he had been sleeping for nearly eight hours. This disturbed him, with such a full day ahead. He got up slowly, rolled the mattress up and put the rest of his things in his knapsack. He changed into the clean clothes and went outside to find some water to wash his face and brush his teeth. Ribindi was still guarding the heroin and looking very pale. It reminded Sutton of malaria symptoms from Vietnam: the man was sweating, glassy-eyed, smelling of fever, with his arms wrapped around his gut. He walked over and stood in front of him, not too close. "I am going ta get the other plane, I will be back just after dark. Be ready ta leave as soon as that."

Ribindi nodded his head wearily. It was clear to Sutton that he had not slept in quite some time. He was beginning to regret having Ribindi on the airplane and decided that he would have to ride in the back. The other plane, the King Air, was a fairly roomy aircraft, made for eight to ten passengers comfortably, so there would be plenty of room to stretch out. So much the better, as the further away this man was, the less chance he would have of catching whatever illness he was incubating.

Sutton went outside and pulled the airplane over to top off the fuel tanks. He had some serious doubts about the wisdom of taking off from this island during the daytime, especially since it was so late in the morning. But he would fly low until he was in the close proximity of St. Kitts, about twenty miles away, and then punch up into the radar as if he had just taken off from one of the airports there. Then, as he had done the last time, he would turn on his transponder, squawk 1200 and fly at a normal VFR altitude. He sought out the captain of the Gallierga crew and told him to contact Orestes, now in Colombia, to report the Arab's condition. "The man is very sick and should be in a hospital." Sutton told him. "But I am okay with still taking him tonight, except Mr. Emilé should know about this." The captain assured Sutton he would make the call and wished him good luck.

Feeling as refreshed as could be under the conditions, Sutton climbed into the airplane, did his run-up at the departure end of the runway and took off. He stayed low and took the shortest route out to sea. After about fifteen minutes, aimed in the direction of St. Kitts, he was able to pull the airplane up off the deck and climb out as if he had just taken off from the Basseterre Airport. He had almost forgotten what it was like to fly at normal altitude. There were several boats out on the seas that morning and he was sure he raised some eyebrows with his low level flight, but he didn't get close enough to allow his registrations numbers to be read.

It was approximately 1200 hours, or 12 noon, on Wednesday, the 18th of July. Sutton was oblivious to the fact that death had come that morning to all the people in the world he cared for. He had no real interests of his own. The happiness of his children came first, then the betterment of his people. His children were now gone. Had he known this, it was likely he would have little reason to remain living; he might have decided to fly the airplane into the surface of the ocean.

In his ignorance, the mission remained foremost in his mind. He was going over the details of the plan as he flew. The King Air that Gallierga had helped him lease was waiting for pickup at the San Juan International Airport on the north coast of Puerto Rico. Being so late in the morning, he decided to fly directly to San Juan, take possession of the King Air, and return directly from there to Montserrat that evening after dark. While in San Juan, he would take a room at an airport hotel, get a shower and some room service. He'd need to check in via radio with Anya at the office as he flew near to St. John, to let her know his schedule.

The flight that evening would be around 1400 nautical miles, comprised of two legs: San Juan to Montserrat, Montserrat to Cat Island. The longest leg, to Cat Island, was nearly eleven hundred nautical miles and it could not be flown in a straight line. Because of his low altitude, he would have to thread his way through the southern Bahama Islands, adding at least another one hundred nautical miles to the leg. So his time at the yoke of the King Air would be approximately four and one-half hours; another grueling task at forty feet above the surface of the ocean. The advantage to the King Air, a multi-million dollar airplane, was that the radar altimeter was linked to the auto-pilot. It also had a redundant radar altimeter, for safety purposes. The fact that this airplane had the convenience of automatic altitude control was a real luxury for Sutton, though he was reluctant to completely trust the safety of the mission to electronics. He had seen such things fail before. But he should be able to relax his concentration occasionally, affording him some relief.

One of the issues facing Sutton was that the shipping lanes serving Central and South America, Cuba and the Hispaniola islands, all lay in his flight path. Some of the largest shipping vessels sit as high as one hundred and sixty feet above the surface of the ocean. All of them have powerful navigation lights which signal their presence to other ships, but he'd be traveling at 300 mph and he'd come up on them very quickly at that speed. He'd need to keep careful vigil over his path as well as his altitude. The trip would be difficult, more like a combat mission than anything he'd flown in many years. His powers of concentration would have to be fully engaged and tuned in.

Passing over the U.S.V.I. at 10,000 feet en route to San Juan, he flew above Pillsbury Sound between St. Thomas and St. John. It was a crystal clear summer morning, and the visibility was nearly perfect. He could see the ferry steaming from Red Hook to Cruz Bay, along with other boats; most of them pleasure craft, cruising around the islands. At that altitude, they were specks of white in an unending background of azure sea. He could see the town of Cruz Bay to his left and, scattered in the rain forest on the mountainous terrain, he could see the residences of the rich and famous cut into the hills. He knew the island and the terrain so well he could name the owners of almost all the houses. He'd delivered cars to most of them over the years, and Cruz Bay being such a small and close knit community of natives, almost everyone knew someone else who worked at one of the houses. He could see the Hill House, a spec on the mountainside, and was reminded of his trust in Miss Valisé. He hoped she would do everything he asked should something befall him on this most dangerous of missions. He was sure she would. He didn't realize on this beautiful morning, as he glanced out the window and down at the Hill House, that the bodies of his children were lying there, still, spiritless, baking in the sun. He clicked the radio talk button on the steering yoke and spoke into his mouthpiece, "Sutton air one ta Sutton base…over."

He repeated the query three times before he saw the island of Puerto Rico coming up in the near distance. There was no answer.

After Marty and Valisé pulled into the parking lot for the Caneel Bay Hotel, they sat in the Jeep for a moment while Marty called Keeler.

"Go ahead," the admiral answered.

"We've had some trouble," Marty began.

"Tell me."

"We were ambushed by Jared Sutton, his sisters and Randall. They're all dead."

"What?" Keeler asked incredulously.

"Yes, sir. It was just after sunrise. Jared was in the house. Randall was outside waiting in ambush, and the twins were waiting at the end of the driveway. The shit hit the fan and they're all dead. I'll give you the details later, but right now we need to get off this island, we can't wait until later. When the bodies are discovered, we're going to be real hot property. We shouldn't try to get on the ferry. Any ideas?"

"I'll come pick you up with one of James's boats. How far are you from Coral Bay?" Keeler asked.

"We're in the Caneel Bay lot, so it'll be a half-hour or so."

"Get there as soon as you can. I'll be in a marked CG craft."

"Roger, sir." Marty clicked off.

"We're going to meet him at Coral Bay." Marty said as he started the Toyota again and pulled out of the parking spot. Valisé said nothing in return, realizing that her future had just taken a turn. As was her practice, she successfully prevented emotion from showing on her face. But, inside, the relief had nearly taken her breath away. The events of the last hour made her return to Colombia unlikely. Emilé's orders, unsuccessful as they were, had released her. She wouldn't be going back to face him alone. She had friends now, of sorts, and was leaving the island with them.

Marty pulled out onto the bumpy road in silence. It occurred to him that Keeler's idea of meeting at Coral Bay was a good one. It was a long drive, thirty minutes or so, and a longer boat ride back to St. Thomas, but they would be able to board the boat normally from the docks and without much fanfare as they loaded. There was no way word of what occurred at the Hill House had reached there yet, even if Cortez the gardener had discovered the bodies a few minutes after he passed them on the road.

It also occurred to him that he was somehow behaving rationally and calmly after having killed three people and watching as Valisé killed another. Perhaps it hadn't sunk in just yet; it might after the adrenaline was gone, or maybe it would come back to him in a nightmare. Maybe he would recall the look in Anya's eyes and the expression on her face as the bullet struck her in the side of the head and exited the other side in a red spray. He might reconcile the horrible visual by knowing if Valisé hadn't killed Anya at that instant, he would be dead instead. Perhaps he could always use the idea of self-defense to counteract the guilt. Perhaps Valisé could also, if needed. But at the moment, his only emotion was the security that came from knowing she would be under his watch until she was out of danger, or until they were also both dead.

Back on the Annaberg Road, they had to retrace their recent drive, passing by the road to the Hill House en route to Coral Bay. As they approached the turn to the Hill House, they both stiffened, seeing the tail end of a Jeep turn right and enter. Marty slowed the car quickly to make certain that whoever was going up there would not be able to see them pass. He then pressed his foot deeply into the accelerator, figuring that every minute between now and the time they would get on the boat could make a difference between surviving and not. As it turned out, Keeler and James would already be at the docks, waiting for them as they arrived.

After parking the car, Marty and Valisé calmly pulled their bags from the trunk and made their way to the docks as if this was a normal departure. There was no one around to take notice of them except for a man and his wife on a nearby yacht. The fact that they were boarding a Coast Guard cruiser raised the casual interest of the couple, but no captain pays much attention to the Coast Guard unless he needs help.

After Marty and Valisé were boarded, Keeler cast the dock lines back into the boat and stepped on board over the gunwale. James engaged the transmission and they were off. As they cruised slowly departing the bay, Keeler turned to Marty. "So tell me," he said.

Marty took a deep breath and began with the point where Jared was in the hall outside the bedroom. When he mentioned that they were lying in bed when he felt a strange sense that someone was in the house, Keeler turned his head toward Valisé, then back to Marty again. Marty showed him the wound on his shoulder. The bleeding had stopped and, since the bullet had not penetrated any bone, aside from the fact that the pain was intense, it was not an issue at the moment. Marty then detailed the rest of the events, concluding with his thoughts on the aftermath. "I believe we were able to complete our response to the attack without any immediate knowledge by the local authorities. As we were leaving, we passed the caretaker on his way in to the Hill House. It's likely he found the bodies a short time later."

Valisé and Marty waited while Keeler digested the details. There were so many sides to their situation, he knew what he wanted to say but struggled for the right way to say it. Looking through the cabin window at the ocean passing by, he finally spoke. "Look," he said with an impatient air, "I don't have the time or convenience to be sensitive about your feelings, so I'm going to be really fuckin blunt here. The fact that you two are involved with each other doesn't mean a hill of fuckin beans to me, except that your relationship could poison this mission. If that happens, if you fuck this up, I'll shoot both of you myself." His impatience was replaced by irritation. "Having said that," he cleared his throat, "it's probable that if you had not been there, Becker, Miss Gallierga would be dead. Sutton didn't come to the Hill House this morning looking for you. He came there to kill whoever he found there. If she was alone, he would have shot her," Keeler pointed at Valisé, "without a second thought."

Keeler turned away from them and shook his head, partly in disbelief, party in disgust. "Sutton and the others were a hit squad, not a very good one apparently, but a hit squad nonetheless. They were probably sent there by, well, let me see now, hmmm, oh yeah, it must be Gallierga." He frowned. "And as soon as he finds out this hit was not successful, he will send another team. In fact, there are probably others waiting for you, check that, *us*, as we make our way to the airport in St. Thomas." There was silence for a few seconds as Keeler pondered the realization. "Honestly?" Keeler continued, "the mission would be in better shape if the hit squad was successful. You two are now a liability."

Marty sat up with a 'wait just a second' air. "*Honestly* Admiral? If Valisé wasn't here, we wouldn't even know about the Arab; we wouldn't know that they are stopping at Cat Island. We'd still be chasing the SFC around St. John, while the guy slipped into the country and did whatever he's planning to do. With due respect, sir, what you just said is a crock of shit."

Keeler let slip a hint of a smile at Marty's willingness to meet the challenge, but then returned to topic. "Becker, how we got here isn't important. We got here, how we got here. The mission doesn't owe anybody anything. If we fail, nobody's going to say 'it's okay fellas, we understand, you did the best you could.' There is no room for failure here. The only good thing we can say is that the longer Gallierga is in the dark about what happened, the better chance he won't have time to change the plan for Cat Island. If he does that, we're screwed."

Valisé re-crossed her legs where she was sitting and spoke up. "He won't change anything," she said. "He won't tell Conrad that his family is dead, because he knows it would cause him to abort the delivery. There's too much money riding on this sale for him to stop it."

"How much money?" Keeler asked.

"His cut is twenty-one million."

Keeler nodded. "Let's hope you're right. But he could still contact Sutton and warn him about you, or us, if he knows about us. I have to assume he does. He could tell Sutton not to use Cat Island; tell him to go somewhere else."

She smiled coolly and said, "Emilé doesn't know that Conrad is going to Cat Island. Sutton didn't tell *him* that he was going there; he told *me* that he was going there." She paused for a moment to let them grasp the idea. "And he wouldn't tell Conrad anything that might make him nervous. He can't afford to. If Conrad knew any of this, he wouldn't fly. Emilé is pinched."

Keeler nodded again as she finished.

Becker smirked. "Some liability, huh?"

Christian was waiting for them at the Coast Guard slip in Charlotte Amalie when they pulled in. Standing in the bow of the boat Marty saw him there, pacing, as they approached. He seemed agitated. There were two Coast Guard staffers waiting as well, and after James eased the boat into a slip, Christian helped pull out the dock lines and tied it down. Keeler was first to step off, Marty and Valisé followed. Christian saw Valisé and waited until he was clustered with Keeler and Marty. "What the hell is going on?"

"Not here," Keeler said and nodded toward the CG office. They all followed. Inside, Keeler asked Captain James to join them and closed the door. He gave Christian and James the highlights of the day's events and told them they would be departing for Cat Island as soon as he could fuel the plane and do a pre-flight check. He told James to call the duty officer in Cruz Bay to see if anything unusual had occurred that day. James called on a land line and the officer reported that everything was normal, there had been no activity. The island seemed quiet. "Good," Keeler said, "now I need to see your munitions stores."

After visualizing the worst scenario they might confront, he made a mental list of weapons that could be of use and recited it to James. "We'll need an M240B; a tripod-mounted machine gun." James nodded, no problem. He asked if he had a hand-held nautical GPS they could take and a shoulder mounted AT-4 grenade launcher. James eyes got a little wider at that request but, again, he nodded yes.

Christian had been waiting for an opening to speak, didn't see one forthcoming, so he interrupted. "Admiral, a DEA agent came by before you got here. He said there's a guy on the island that we should know about."

"Go on," Keeler replied.

"Early this morning they spotted a guy at the Red Hook ferry dock, named Lorenzo Encarnación. He's a Colombian national." Christian glanced briefly at Valisé and handed Keeler a photo of the man. "DEA says he's a certified bad guy. He's not a mule or anything, more likely a black ops guy."

Keeler looked at the photo and handed it to Valisé. "Recognize him?"

She looked carefully and then shook her head. "No."

Continue," Keeler said to Christian.

"Anyway, they don't have any probable cause, so they can't detain him. But they put a tail on him and sent the photo and his vitals over to customs to see if he's here under a visa or other legit pass through. Customs came back with an affirmative, he has a visa, and he passed the check point in Charlotte Amalie yesterday. His visa expires in twelve days. So he's here on borrowed time."

"He isn't going to need twelve days to do what he's here for," Keeler retorted and glanced at Valisé.

"Anyway, it seems the guy is real slippery," Christian continued.

"Ah, shit," Keeler said, "don't tell me those jackasses lost him."

"Yep, the way they tell it is that he somehow picked up the tail and then vanished."

"He picked up the tail because those DEA guys have crew cuts and strut around with their chests puffed out like a bird in heat. My mother could figure them out."

"Yessir." Christian fought off a smile. "Well, he's here and they don't know why. They can't find him right now, but they said he was very interested in who was getting off the ferry at Red Hook."

Keeler looked at Valisé again. "*We* know who he's looking for. Let's get the plane loaded, we gotta get off of this island." Keeler stood up. "Captain James, can we get into the munitions stores now? We need that gear."

21

Foutons Le Camp

Lorenzo Encarnación, the assassin, found it very easy to slip the DEA tail at the ferry docks at Red Hook in St. Thomas. All he had to do was look like a passenger. He wasn't wanted for breaking any U.S. laws. His only minor concern that morning stemmed from passing through customs the day prior. He was on record now and he did notice the DEA agent shadowing him, changing locations occasionally, but hanging around. After watching two ferries arrive in St. Thomas without Valisé on board, he decided to get onto the 8:00 a.m. boat returning to St. John. There was a crowd of passengers shuffling like cattle over the wide gangway to the boat. When the agent tailing him changed locations again, Lorenzo simply melted into the crowd and got onto the boat. As they pulled away from the docks, he looked back to see the agent leaning against a lamp post looking left and right, trying to find his mark.

In Cruz Bay, Encarnación waited near the docks, hoping to see her in the departing crowd. He had no success. He knew that the next ferry would return and reload in an hour, so he'd be able to continue on to the Hill House and search for her, with enough time to return before the next departure. There were two car rental agencies with dockside rental counters. One was Sutton's company, whose kiosk was not manned that day; the other was Surf Jeep Rentals. Within ten minutes he had taken a Jeep for a four hour rental and was driving slowly up the Annaberg Road looking carefully inside each car as it passed, making certain he looked at both the driver and the passenger if there was one. If he had thought to pull into the parking lot at Caneel Bay as he drove past the long entrance road, he would have seen Marty and Valisé sitting in the Toyota sedan. If he had seen them, their departure from St. John that day would have been very different indeed. But they saw the tail end of his Jeep instead, when he turned up the road to the Hill House, as they hurried to meet Keeler at Coral bay.

The mechanic drove up the Hill House road a short distance, pulled off to the side, turned off the Jeep, and doubled back to the

Road House where Marty's rental car was still parked. He looked inside the house and surmised that whoever was staying there had left for good. He then set out quickly up the Hill House Road. En route, he heard Cortez's truck roaring down the drive, and slid into the underbrush at the side of the driveway. Cortez passed by him unaware, and swerved wildly around the Jeep parked a short distance past. Cortez wanted out of there and had no interest in anything else. After the old man drove by, Encarnación continued up to the Hill House.

Though he did not know the Sutton sisters, from Gallierga's description he was able to recognize Randall, who had not been dead for very long. The mechanic moved quickly into the house, through the first floor and up the stairs to the hall, where he found Jared Sutton as well. He was able to deduce what had happened in short order. He hurried out of the house, ran back to his Jeep and drove calmly but speedily back to Cruz Bay. Mindful that his target could still be on the island and planning to get on the next ferry, he waited by the docks patiently, out of sight. He wondered if the old man was going to report the murders.

The St. John Police station sits directly across from the parking lot for the docks. He kept his eye on the police cars out front and the small collection of officers milling around talking, directing traffic here and there; in general, not doing much of anything at all. Apparently, no report had been called in. About half an hour had passed since he saw the old man. When the next boat arrived, Marty and Valisé, of course, were nowhere to be seen. As Encarnación made his way up to the gate for boarding, he stopped at the public phone by the ticket kiosk. He put in a quarter and dialed the emergency police number shown on the phone placard. When the police dispatcher answered he spoke in a monotone voice, "There has been a murder at the Hill House on the Annaberg Road." He saw no reason that the police couldn't help corral his subject.

Back in Red Hook, he surveyed the docks before getting off the boat, then disembarked carefully using the full cover of the crowd. In the lot, he slipped into a taxi quietly, showed the driver a fifty dollar bill and told him to get to the airport fast; he was late for his flight. The cab sped off in a cloud of smoke and dust. During the ride Encarnación grew peeved that his best chance for locating Valisé had already passed. He looked at the crowded streets of Charlotte Amalie as they drove through. St. Thomas is a very busy place and the airport would be no different. She would be difficult to find. Another concern was that the American authorities knew he was there and he would have to dodge that faction as well. They could detain him if they wanted, despite the fact that he had a legitimate visa. If they detained and then released him, the time lost would cause him to miss his objective and that wouldn't play well back in Colombia.

The ability to think like a victim separated Encarnación from others who sometimes failed in his line of work. His sense of how people do things had usually served to put him in the vicinity of where a victim *should* be. In this case, he reasoned that Valisé and her man did not have plans to leave early this morning. If they had, they wouldn't have been surprised in bed. And, they must be secret lovers, which would explain why Jared's ambush did not work. He was expecting to find her alone. The file described her not as an operative, but as a business agent. She didn't kill four armed people by herself. No, Encarnación decided, they were lovers, sleeping in, surprised by the ambush, but able to prevail because the American agent was a capable killer. They were not planning to depart first thing in the morning, so they would not have tickets purchased in advance for a scheduled flight. It was likely, he thought, that they were going to be extracted by someone else. He decided to go to the Fixed Base Operation at Charlotte Amalie airport first, where private aircraft are parked and serviced. If he was unsuccessful there, he would circulate through the public airport terminal as a last ditch effort. If unsuccessful there, he would return to Red Hook and wait again by the ferry. If they escaped his grasp through all his searching, well…there's a first time for everything.

There are two fixed base operators at the Cyril E. King Airport in St. Thomas. Nearly a hundred private and commercial aircraft, ranging in size from single engine trainers to large corporate jets, are scattered across the taxi area which fronts the two businesses. Three oval WWII style aircraft hangers sit between the offices of the two operators. The shared hangars house larger corporate aircraft and private jets owned by the island's wealthiest residents. Keeler's Heron 12-D was temporarily housed here in a secured section, parked next to a U.S. Coast guard helicopter and a DEA pursuit aircraft. The huge door to the hangar was left open all day as planes were brought in and out and readied for use. Two airport workers had finished pre-flight on the Heron, preparing it ready for departure. They were now using a small tug to pull the plane through the door, to a spot where a fuel tanker was waiting to top off the tanks.

Keeler used a computer in the office to access the automated flight control systems he would be passing through en route. He filed a flight clearance order which informed air traffic control of nothing about where he was going. This clearance would make him immune to contact except for the necessity of keeping him separated from other aircraft. ATC would steer all other aircraft around him. On his transponder throughout the flight, he would squawk the code 3313, signifying his status on radar screens as untouchable. This would guarantee a direct route to Cat Island.

Marty, Valisé and Christian were waiting tensely inside the lobby at the smaller of the two FBO stations. Keeler was outside with the ground crew, watching them preflight the airplane, actually doing some of it himself. The Heron, though a relatively simple airplane, still contains complex flight control systems. The control surfaces, elevator, rudder, ailerons and flaps, as well as the landing gear, are all electrically or hydraulically operated. There are no simple cables controlling these while in flight. Complex systems invite failure. As a seasoned and skilled pilot, Keeler knew this all too well and would take nothing for granted. If something on the plane needed repair, he wanted to know about it and calculate the relative risk to the flight and the mission, although under the current circumstances, there would have to be something vitally wrong in order to generate a 'no-go' decision.

While he examined the airframe, James and another officer pulled up in a van and began loading the guns and munitions that Keeler had selected. After the tanker had finished filling the fuel tanks, Keeler dismissed the ground crew before they completed their part of the checkout. He'd take care of the rest. When James finished unloading, he went through the list with Keeler to ensure it was complete. There was no small talk, each man was operating under a sense of mission priority, and spoke only about those things relevant to the task at hand.

Captain James found that his role was nearly completed. This business was about to leave his island and he had mixed emotions. For Keeler, the real mission was just beginning. He had to get to Cat Island and he had no idea what might be waiting there when they arrived. The two men shook hands and parted without ceremony. Keeler patted him on the shoulder, thanked him for his assistance, and told him he'd be in touch. James got into the van and drove away.

Inside the FBO, Marty was pacing back and forth while keeping an eye on Keeler through the plate glass window. He also scanned the surrounding area for anything that might be out of the ordinary. He knew that there was no possibility of being stopped by local authorities at this stage, but was anxious to get Valisé into the air and away from any additional threat posed by Gallierga. Those last few minutes before boarding the plane were passing very slowly for him.

Keeler finally walked up to the front door of the lobby, stuck his head inside the door and said, "Now." Marty moved to the side while Christian and Valisé stood, letting her go first through the door behind Keeler. He kept her in front of himself and Christian, but slightly behind Keeler as they walked the short distance to the plane. All three men were on high alert, turning their heads from side to side as the group entered the open area of the tarmac. A stiff island trade wind was blowing, causing their ears to miss sounds. A jumbo jet had just began its take off roll at the departure end of the runway, which was perhaps a quarter mile away, and the noise from the jet engines spooling up to full power was so loud it made it impossible to hear anything but the piercing whine of the engines and the whoosh of the strong wind. The air stair to the plane was already lowered, and Keeler picked up the pace as he led them straight for it. Marty noticed it had become very hot outside. The mid-afternoon sun burned brightly as they walked and the heat reflecting off the tarmac was almost stifling. The heat combined with the overwhelming noise of the jet engines left Marty with an uneasy feeling, eerily similar to the one he had at the Hill House when Jared's presence outside the bedroom had awoken him. He didn't like it.

Marty's sixth sense would soon become something he would trust without question. At that moment, downwind, about 200 meters away, Encarnación aimed a 7.62 mm Kalashnikov M76 sniper rifle at them. Inside the high-powered scope, the crosshairs were bouncing around Valisé's back and head as he moved the nose of the gun to keep pace with her movement. He was leaning against the corner of the last hangar, supporting the barrel of the gun against the edge of the building. On the end of the barrel was a 350 mm silencer attachment, which gave the entire apparatus an awkward length, but which also assured that the noise emitted from a shot would be no louder than the sound of a rubber mallet striking a brick wall. He chose this downwind location carefully to add to the inaudibility. The 'poomp' sound of the rifle wouldn't carry 200 meters up-wind.

The wind itself, however, was giving him fits. From that distance the slightest movement of the barrel translated into feet of error at the target location. He was also aware that at that distance the heat rising up from the pavement would carry the projectile off line to some degree. He would have adjust his aim into the wind and low by a few inches to accommodate the deflection. Aiming for a body hit would carry the highest percentages, he decided, so he held the crosshairs slightly low and left of her waist and squeezed the trigger smoothly.

Marty heard nothing, but knew what happened from what he saw. The impact spun her around awkwardly and she reached for her thigh as if reacting to a bee sting. He looked down and saw the hole torn in the side of her shorts and the blood spatter where the bullet had exited. He immediately reacted, pulling his weapon and jumping on top of her to shield her. Encarnación, meanwhile, correctly perceiving he hadn't delivered a lethal shot, and trying to re-sight after the recoil, had squeezed off another round as she fell. This one missed entirely; the puff of dust and the sound of the ricochet on the pavement giving Keeler and Christian a general idea of the direction from which the shot had been fired. Christian looked up and saw the barrel of the gun move away from the corner of the hangar after Encarnación saw that his second attempt had also failed, and pulled back from his position. Escape and regroup was now his objective. He knew the longer he could delay the takeoff, the better his chance of getting another shot at her.

Christian was up and running toward his location. Keeler checked with Marty and Valisé, who was screaming. The heat of the projectile passing through the fleshy part of her thigh had cauterized the nerves on the way through and the pain had yet to set in. She felt only the pressure of the impact and the initial sting as the bullet broke her skin. Her upper leg began to bleed profusely, and Marty realized he had to stuff something in there to stop it. Keeler gave him the all clear sign, so he picked her up and carried her to the airplane. Once they were inside, Keeler also took up the chase.

The area behind the hangars was like a junk yard. It was a place where airport equipment is kept that is either unwanted or unusable, but not quite decrepit enough to completely discard. Tropical weeds had grown around some of it. Christian turned the corner of the hangar and stopped, knowing he'd be an easy mark for the shooter if he pursued him into the open yard. When Keeler followed a few seconds later, he chose to go directly through the hangar, thinking that there must be a man door out the back. As he ran through, he caused some surprise and commotion for the workers inside, but he knew this was no time to be concerned about appearances. He had to cover Christian's back and the quickest way to catch up would be straight through the hangar instead of around it.

At the back of the hangar, Keeler found the man-door and opened it just a crack in order to look outside without putting his head out first. Christian was in his line of sight, crouched behind an old airplane tug that was rusting away in the weeds. There was no sign of the shooter. He whistled to get Christian's attention and signaled for him to stay where he was.

Encarnación hid behind a large clump of tall tropical grass that had sprouted up in the sandy soil. He watched undetected as Christian came around the back corner of the building. This was working out well so far. He had drawn one of the American agents away from the airplane and knew that another would be close behind. He saw the man door move slightly and figured that must be the other one. If he could get them both together, either pinned down or dead, he could make his way back around to the front of the hangar and finish the job on Valisé. He knew the third agent would not leave her side, but also wouldn't take off without the others.

He watched in silence as Keeler slowly and carefully came out through the door, his gun leading the way, and patiently resisted the temptation to pick him off as he walked. The angle from where he was sitting was not advantageous at the moment. If he shot Keeler from this location, Christian would know where the shot came from, which would prevent him from doubling back to the airplane around the opposite side of the hangar. He had to wait until Keeler was behind cover, hopefully next to his partner. Then he could fire a few covering shots in order to keep the two of them pinned down long enough to make his move back to the plane. He'd have to take his chances with Valisé's escort when he got there. Of course, because he'd be leaving these two alive, he'd also have to take his chances dealing with them again after he was finished. He watched as Keeler broke into a running crouch to get to Christian's location. 'Wonderful,' he thought. Then he got up and broke into a dead run toward the opposite corner of the hangar. The whistling wind kept the small noise he made inaudible to them. He found cover again behind rusting portable airliner stairs, and saw that from there he had a good angle to break for the plane, so the immediate objective was to keep his pursuers fearful of moving.

Keeler crouched next to Christian. "We don't even know if the fucker is still back here."

"I know, but we have to pursue him, we'd be sitting ducks out on the runway. Is she hit bad?"

"I'm not sure, she took one in the leg, which could be a problem if it got bone. Becker carried her into the plane."

"We gotta get this guy."

"We better split up," Keeler said, "provide each other cover and leapfrog across here until we flush him out. I'll go first."

Christian nodded his head, Keeler peered over the tug, preparing to make the first move. As soon as he did, the mechanic pulled off two quick rounds, both ricocheting off the tug. When Keeler fell back to the ground behind the machine, Encarnación made his move. He threw his rifle into the weeds, un-holstered the Walther 9mm pistol he was carrying, and took off in a dead run for the airplane.

Marty wasn't expecting the assassin to appear, but was splitting his attention between Valisé and being on the lookout for Keeler and Christian. She was losing a lot of blood even though it was just a flesh wound. The bullet didn't hit bone, but tore a hole in the meaty part of her thigh, especially large at the exit point. When he got her on board, Marty took a clean shirt from his knapsack and ripped it in two, stuffing half of it into both sides of the wound, and using the other half to wrap around her upper thigh, tying it to cut off circulation. He felt fairly sure this would stop the bleeding, but her pain level was skyrocketing and she'd need a doctor soon. She was lying in the aisle between seats, moaning and crying. Marty tried his best to make her comfortable, but there was nothing he could do for the pain. He stood up to look for a first aid kit, then checked out the window and caught sight of the mechanic, running full speed toward them.

"Shit," he said, putting it all together. Where the hell were Keeler and Christian?

Marty pulled his gun from his shoulder holster, repositioned himself so he was kneeling and facing the opening in the airplane from an angle, and had the Glock aimed with two hands directly at the center of the door. Valisé was lying on the floor behind him. Encarnación slowed as he reached the air stair door and crept up the steps. As he came through the door, there was no hesitation this time. Marty immediately fired a shot into the center of Encarnación's chest. The bullet exploded through his sternum, tore into his heart, then flattened out and lodged in his backbone, leaving no exit wound. He was dead instantly and fell against the back of the co-pilot seat. A small stream of blood flowed onto the carpet. Marty dropped his head in relief then turned to Valisé and saw the anguish on her face. She groaned at him, "Martin…when will this end?"

Keeler and Christian, still believing they were pinned down, heard the pop of Marty's pistol. They knew that it came from the direction of the plane. Without saying a word, Christian was up and running; Keeler followed on his heels. John reached the plane first and leapt over the first four stairs and then caved in to the relief of seeing Encarnación lying slumped on the floor and Marty kneeling, tending to the wound on Valisé's leg.

She was a mess of blood. Keeler knew they had to get into the air quickly and put St. Thomas behind them, but he wondered how far she could go without medical attention. He could see from the pastiness in her face that she wasn't in great shape, but her eyes were open and clear. As he approached, she held her hand up in protest, "It's okay…I'm okay, let's just get the fuck out of here."

Keeler looked at Marty, "Where is she hit?"

"At the top of her thigh; I stuffed some of my shirt in there and put a tourniquet around it. I don't think the bullet hit bone, she was weight bearing coming in here. She's lost blood, though it's slowing down. There's a pretty good size hole at the exit wound."

"A hole?" Valisé asked, "You mean there's a hole in my fucking leg? …SHIT," she started to rev up. "FUCKIN SON OF A BITCH!" She yelled, struggling, trying to get up on her elbows, "THAT COCKSUCKER SHOT A HOLE IN MY LEG?" The pain of movement forced her head to fall back onto the carpeted floor with a thump, "Fuck it hurts."

Keeler thought she was plenty alert. "Becker," he said out of the side of his mouth, "there's a med kit in the storage compartment over the top of the last seat, get it. Valisé?" he said as he turned to her, "honey, we're going to get out of here right now. It's going to take a few minutes to get airborne. Then we'll get you fixed up, okay?"

"All right," she said with a scowl, "but this fucking thing hurts. That son of a bitch. I can't believe it…I'm gonna fuckin kill that fuckin bastard. Shit…hurry up. And don't call me honey, you asshole."

Keeler didn't say anything more to her. He turned to Christian and told him he was going to taxi over to the side of the hangar. "You drag the body out and leave it there in the brush." He said. "I'll call James later and tell him where it is."

Marty came back with the med kit. Keeler told him there should be a vial of morphine in it. "Give her five milliliters, and there's some bottled water in the mini fridge, that'll settle her down." Marty went to work.

Keeler sat down behind the control yoke, flipped some switches, turned the key and pressed the spool-up button for the left engine, then the right. Both turbines whined and came to speed. He released the parking brake and started to move the plane forward. Christian remembered to hit the switch to raise the air stair just in time. As they rolled about as far as Keeler could take them without going off the pavement, John lowered the air stair door again and pushed the body out. Encarnación's lifeless corpse tumbled down the stairs and John followed. When he got to the ground he grabbed the body by the ankles, pulled it to a cluster of pampas grass and managed to drag it into the middle. Lorenzo Encarnación lay in a heap in an airplane junk yard, shot and disposed of in the same way he had disposed of others so many times before. 'What a way to go,' Christian thought to himself as he turned from the body and jumped back on the plane. Nobody felt sorry about it.

When Keeler finally pulled the airplane off the ground, he called James on the sat cell. "Encarnación's body is behind the hangar in the weeds," he said over the drone of the engines.

"Another body sir?"

"Yeah, he clipped her with a rifle from long range, but we got him, it wasn't pretty." Keeler felt a twinge of empathy for James, remaining behind to clean up their mess. "Just call it in anonymously to the St. Thomas police, so you don't have to deal with it."

"Is she dead?"

"No, she got it in the leg. If we can get her a doc, she should be okay."

"Ay sir, I'll call it in."

As they climbed through 8,000 feet, Keeler turned the cabin pressurization system on and leaned out the jet fuel mixture on the big turbine engines. He needed to be thinking about fuel economy, as there was a long journey ahead of them. Cat Island was some 950 nautical miles away, and he was flying right into the teeth of a stiff head wind. He calculated their time to destination at four and a half hours. He leveled the airplane out at 18,000 feet, set the altitude hold and set the autopilot to maintain the course plotted out by the GPS. With these systems engaged, the plane was flying itself.

He looked back and motioned for John to come to the cockpit. Christian sat in the right seat, while Keeler explained their course, altitude, air speed, and the power settings. The man did have approximately fifty hours piloting a single engine aircraft, so he was fairly fluent in the science of flying, but he had never been pilot in command of an aircraft this complex. Keeler felt confident, however, that he could safely leave the controls in Christian's hands temporarily.

As he turned to make his way back to where Valisé lay on the floor, he saw that she had settled down when the morphine took effect, but she shook intermittently, was restless, and beads of sweat had formed on her forehead and upper lip. Keeler gave her the once over and said, "She's lost some blood, she might be in shock, I don't know for sure. That's all I can think of, the wound isn't that bad." He looked down at the bloody wrapping around her thigh. "We really ought to roll her over onto her stomach and put a better dressing on the wound, get some antiseptic in there."

"Is John flying the plane?" Marty asked skeptically.

"John is watching the plane fly, he's fine. Now help me roll her over. Then put a new tourniquet on her, at the very top of her leg, so we can work on wounds and she won't bleed out."

Marty pulled off her waist belt, a thin designer leather strap, thinking it would work better than the one he used earlier. They struggled in the tight aisle to get her onto her stomach. Marty used his jackknife to slice her shorts and expose the wound, then wrapped the belt around her thigh and pulled it tight. They worked to turn her again, on to her side, so that both the entry and the exit wounds were exposed.

"Jesus, the thing made a mess on the way out, huh?" Keeler said. He worked quickly to remove the piece of shirt that Marty had stuffed in there, and poured nearly an entire bottle of antiseptic on it. He used whatever materials he could find in the meds kit to clean the wounds. He coated the area with Betadine solution, packed the wound with gauze, soaked everything with saline, and wrapped her leg a final time with heavy gauze dressing. When he finished, he told Marty to get some blankets out of the storage cupboard as the morphine had slowed her pulse, dropping her temperature.

"That will have to do." Keeler said. "We can't get to a doctor until tomorrow, and then only if everything goes right."

"Man," Marty said, "where'd you learn how to do this?"

"Field dressing, Becker, one of the benefits of battle experience, now you have it." They moved her over on to her back and Marty placed a rolled-up blanket under her head. Keeler stepped over her and made his way back up to the pilot seat. "About four hours to Cat Island. Get some rest, you'll need it."

22

Get a Grip

It was Wednesday evening at approximately 7:00 p.m. Gallierga felt as though he was isolated on a deserted island. For the last twenty-four hours he hadn't heard much, and what he did hear wasn't very good. He'd had no report from the mechanic and couldn't reach him on his cell phone. Valisé was likely either dead at his hand or now sharing secrets with the U.S. government. Sutton didn't have a cell phone and several calls to his house went unanswered, not that Gallierga would have told him anything about the day's events, but talking to him would at least provide assurance that the shipment was proceeding. He called Orestes in Isla Tortuga the previous night, but it was too late, Sutton had already come and gone. After a few hours, late in the night, Gallierga tried to reach the crew in Montserrat without success and kept trying throughout the morning. Finally, a call to the cellular company on neighboring St. Kitts disclosed that the cell tower serving Monserrat was out of service. Then he called the leasing company in San Juan that afternoon to see if Sutton had taken delivery of the King Air, found that he had, but Sutton had already left after signing the contract and told them that he would be returning for the aircraft later that evening. Sutton left no contact number, they were sure he'd be taking off after their offices were closed. The rental agent agreed, however, to leave a note in the plane instructing him to call Emilé.

So he knew only that Conrad had been to Montserrat with the second load from Isla Tortuga; that he must have stayed there over the night and then departed to pick up the King Air in the morning. Anxious to grasp at any piece of information, he decided to go online to see if any news websites were reporting any murders on St. John. The search engine quickly brought him to the San Juan Chronicle:

Reuters

ST. JOHN, USVI. Thurs. In the aftermath of what appears to have been a gangland war shootout, the bodies of four USVI residents were found ridden with bullets on the small island of St. John. Three of the victims were related: Jared Sutton, 31, and his sisters Anya Sutton and Yendi Sutton, both 28, and another man, Randall Stevens, 37, were discovered at approximately 1:00 p.m. local time on Wednesday after police received an anonymous tip. The bodies were strewn about the grounds of an exclusive hillside retreat overlooking Pillsbury Sound. Police have yet to identify any specific motive in the murders, but a source close to the investigation says that an unidentified woman from Medellín, Colombia, SA is believed to have been staying at the villa at the time of the shootings. The source says her whereabouts is unknown and investigators suspect she might have already left the island and returned to Colombia. She is wanted for questioning. The U.S. government has no recognized extradition treaty with Colombia.

In what police believe is a related shooting, the body of an unidentified man who sources believe to be a Colombian national, was found at approximately 5:00 p.m. Wednesday behind an airport hangar at The Cyril E. King International Airport in St. Thomas, USVI. The man is believed to have been killed by a gun fired at close range. Sources didn't disclose the time of death, but say that the man's body had been there only a short time. No other details of the shooting are available, and a murder weapon has not been found. There have been no arrests in connection with the murders.

Gallierga was shell shocked. If the 'Colombian National' was Encarnación, not only had he failed in his mission, but he was dead, and that meant that his last line of defense against Valisé defecting to the Americans had vanished.

He wondered how he got to this point. Valisé was only going on a short vacation. Was she really more paranoid of being involved with the Arab heroin traders than he thought? She was hesitant about it, that he knew. But she never really seemed overly distraught. He went over everything he knew about the events since she left, trying to determine what had caused her to change her position so radically. Then he remembered Cortez.

Did she speak with him? Did he tell her? If so, it could be that she had run away. Perhaps she called on the Americans? No, how could she have done that? Perhaps it was just a coincidence that they were there. But still, she was with them, or with one of them. She must be with him now. She escaped from the Hill House; Jared and the others are dead; Encarnación is dead. She is gone.

Gallierga was depressed; helpless. Psychosis overcame reason as he started to feel victimized. Back and forth he went, stewing about all that he had done for her- made her one of the most powerful women in all of South America, and at a very young age. After the wonderful life he had crafted for her, he was betrayed.

Maybe if she would listen to him, he softened, she would see; he could make her see that what she was doing was wrong; that the world they were building together could be so grand. They would have enormous power and wealth. How could she be happy on the other side? She couldn't. They had fooled her. He would tell her he was sorry about all of the things he kept from her, and then he would make it right for her. Just as he had in the past, when she was struggling with her dolls or her horses or college or anything, he had always made it right for her. He loved her.

They might have brainwashed her, told her anything and made her believe it. They have their ways, he knew that; he'd heard of their ways. If she wouldn't listen, if they had brainwashed her and she insisted on betraying him, then he would find her and kill her. With his own bare hands, he would kill her. 'I'll show you what happens when you betray me,' he said to himself, he said to her.

"Corteź," he said out loud. He had to find out about Corteź. He had to find out what she was told. It was late in the day, he thought, Corteź must be in his little house on the island, eating his little peasant dinner. Or maybe he was sitting in his old chair, nodding as he listed to Caribe music on the radio. Everything was fine in *his* world; Gallierga thought, his simple little world. If he had told her, did he know what damage he caused?

Gallierga's thoughts drifted back to Valisé's mother, Maria; back to when he was young and virile and able to steal the heart of any woman he desired. Now they just wanted to be paid; short term, long term. It was all the same. They just wanted the money. But when he was young, they wanted him. They wanted his power. They wanted to tame his power and have it all for themselves. His power blinded them. His power melted them in his presence.

He thought of how beautiful her mother had been. It was no coincidence the beauty had multiplied in Valisé. She had her mother's beauty; more than her mother's beauty, she had his beauty too. She had his brains and his drive and his will. That was what made her truly beautiful.

He had great enduring sex with her mother. She loved him deeply. She inspired him to hours of lovemaking. She had ways to make him feel powerful, strong, yet peaceful. He would go to his house and lay in bed at night next to the witch that was his wife and crave Maria. He would slip out from the bedroom in the wee hours and meet her in the garden. They would go to the shed down by the carriage house and have sex until the sky would lighten. Then they would go back; back to reality. And she would fix breakfast for the house and the rest of the servants and she would serve it to him. As she put his eggs in front of him he could smell her again, as he had smelled her all that night. He always wanted to have her again, as he had her just hours before. He never tired of her. She was a good woman, he thought, and he smiled. The smile didn't last long as he remembered the day he sent the order to have her killed. She bore no son.

"*Corteź*," he said aloud again. He had to find out if Corteź told her. If he did, she would be gone. He would never get her back. He'd have no choice but to hunt her down and kill her. This time he'd have to do it himself, to make certain it was done, without question.

He picked up his phone and called Pereź. "Pablo?" Gallierga asked when the man answered, "have you heard of the problem on the island?"

"Yes, I'm afraid I have, the police contacted my rental agent, who then contacted me." Pereź paused and asked, "Have you heard from her?"

"Not since late last night. That is why I am calling. I spoke with Corteź earlier today. He spoke with her a few days ago. I need to talk to him." Gallierga's tone of voice left no room for negotiation on the request.

"He is a harmless old man, Emilé. He has no part in this."

"That might be true. It's something I have to research. He knows her past and she has disappeared. I need the number, Pablo."

Pereź complied, reluctantly. After he hung up from the short conversation, he realized that in addition to all the mess he had to deal with at the Hill House, he would probably need to look for a new gardener as well.

Gallierga dialed Corteź's phone number. The old man answered in a tired raspy voice, it was after 9:00 p.m., very close to his bedtime, and it had been an exhausting day. When Gallierga identified himself, the old man's hands began to shake. He had spent the day fearing the worst, trying to come up with an explanation, knowing this moment would come. He knew in the small breadth of his understanding that he was damned. If he didn't tell the truth and Gallierga discovered that he was lying, he would surely die. He knew also that if he told him the truth, he would surely die. It would not come in the open. It would come quietly, when no one was watching, or maybe when someone *was* watching. But it would come. He knew that the torture of waiting might very well kill him before the hit man could.

He had been on the fringes of Gallierga's brutal world for many years, but it had been a long time since the darkness was so close. Corteź was compelled now, for fear of what would happen to the rest of his meager life, to tell the monster that he had betrayed him.

So he broke down and told the story of his lapse that morning; that he slipped and was then forced to divulge the entire history of where she came from, who her mother was, and, who her father was. He told Gallierga of how she threatened him; forced him to tell. He begged for mercy. When Corteź finished the story and was reduced to sobbing at the other end of the line, Gallierga said nothing of comfort; he said nothing to fear, he simply hung up. The truth was, the future of old man Cortez was not foremost on his mind at the moment.

Gallierga retired slowly to the mahogany paneled study in his Medellín home. He remembered how he had stood there with her a few days previously, how he had suggested, almost demanded, that she take time off and go to her favorite place. Go to St. John. She should go, he remembered saying convincingly, because it would be good for her. A simple trip turned out to be so complex. Now he was faced with crisis, without any good options. Al Zawahiri was expecting not only a progress report, but a firm date, time, and place where the passenger and the goods would be delivered. The Arab had met his end of the bargain, he had deposited $13 million, which included one half of the agreed fee and $five million dollars for the passenger. Now al Zawahiri would be more aggressive. He had paid half of the transit expense. The pressure would be on Gallierga to complete the task; the customer was empowered and would soon become impatient.

He had to talk to Sutton. He had to find out where he was stopping in the Bahamas. He dialed the number of the crew chief in Montserrat again, hoping that the call would finally go through. It was now 9:30 p.m. eastern time and he was uplifted when the crew chief answered.

"This is Gallierga." he said energetically.

"Señor Gallierga, good evening, sir. Are you well?"

"I'm fine," Gallierga said. "Is the plane there yet?"

"Sí, Señor. He just arrived, say, thirty minutes ago. We are loading the goods now. I tried to call you earlier today, but the Arab...well...the Arab is very sick. He has been for two days, he can barely walk."

"He's sick?" Gallierga demanded. "Sick from what?"

"Who knows? He smells worse than a pig...he can't eat."

"I don't care about him," Gallierga answered, "I want to talk to the pilot, get him for me."

"Sí Señor." Gallierga heard the phone crackle as the crew chief went to find Sutton. He was still impatient, but feeling less agitated.

"Hello Señor Gallierga, this is Sutton."

"Conrad, I'm glad to finally have found you. I was worried, but no matter. You have the King Air, I take it?"

"Yah Señor, it's a good plane."

"Good. We need to make sure that we have a direct line of communication as you move forward. Tell the crew chief that you are taking his cell phone with you. I need to be able to reach you anytime between now and Saturday."

"Yahman, I can do that."

"Good, now tell me Conrad, where are you stopping for fuel in the Bahamas?"

"I am sorry Señor, didn't Miss Valisé tell you? I am stopping at Cat Island. It is the only place where they have jet fuel with no customs. It's a private airport."

"Valisé knows that you are going to Cat Island?"

"Yah, sir."

"Have you spoken with her today?"

"No, the funny thing too is that I want her ta go by the car office and tell my daughter Anya what the schedule is, I am not able ta reach anyone there earlier. Can you ask her ta do that for me?"

"Well...yes, but what is the schedule?" Gallierga asked.

"We be leaving here pretty soon, maybe about an hour or so. Then we fly ta Cat Island, which is maybe five...five and a half hours. Then we fuel up there, and I maybe have ta wait till the morning for that. But that be okay because the next leg is up the east coast of the U.S., up to Georgia, then we land again. Maybe 8 hours flying there, and I have ta do that at night. So I need ta rest in Cat Island. So I think we stay in Cat until tomorrow, Thursday night, then we leave for the U.S. right after dark. We be in the Miami area Saturday morning, latest."

"We can count on that?"

"Yah, sir, unless we get bad weather. Señor Gallierga, is Miss Valisé okay? How come you have not talked with her lately?"

"She's been busy," Gallierga said. "How is the passenger? The crew chief said he was sick."

"Yah, sir, he's in pretty bad shape."

"Well, don't get too close to him, I don't want you getting sick."

"No worries. I'm fine."

"I'm sure you are, Conrad, you have my complete trust. Call me from Cat Island, okay?"

"Yah, I'll call you then."

Gallierga clicked off. All hope was gone. She flat lied to him about knowing where Sutton was stopping for fuel, which meant she didn't want him to interfere with the plan. The U.S. agents must be en route to Cat Island. Gallierga knew now that he couldn't combat this alone. He called Pereź back.

"Pablo? Emilé again." He didn't bother with any niceties.

"Yes." Pereź answered. He didn't bother with any either.

"I need your brother's help. I need an aircraft with a pilot and four quality soldiers; but I want them out of uniform." Pereź's brother, a General in the Colombian Army, would provide military assistance, for a price. He had employed the mercenaries under Pereź's control several times over the years, but it was becoming more difficult these days. The Pereź brothers had to make certain that the fighters chosen for the work were not loyalists, but rather gunmen without honor willing to do the Cartel's dirty work for a fee, and willing to keep it secret. These men were a dying breed, as the Colombian government made headway in the fight against corruption.

"When?" Pereź asked.

"In the morning; sooner if possible."

"What is this about?"

"Pablo, you know better than to ask that. It's not something you can know about. But it *is* something that must be done. The aircraft has to be fast and able to travel a long distance; to the Bahamas."

"Where will you leave from?"

"From here, from Medellín."

"All right, let me call him, I'll call you back." Pereź clicked off.

Gallierga had a plan. If he was somehow wrong about Valisé, if she was not traveling there with American agents, if Sutton was not threatened, there would be no harm done. It would be just a long ride in an airplane. He would explain to Sutton that he had received some incorrect information; and that he traveled there to offer protection, as insurance. He might not even tell Sutton that he was there. However, if the Americans intended to intercept his shipment, they would have to contend with soldiers of the Colombian Army, and of course, they would have to contend with Gallierga himself. If Valisé was there, as he suspected, he would find her and kill her and be done with it.

Gallierga's phone rang. "He will have a plane ready and equipped within four hours. Meet your pilot at the departure area at the airport at 0200 hours. His name is Captain Ramirez. Wait for him inside, an exit visa will not be required. He will escort you. The General asked that I be your contact for payment on this excursion. This will not be inexpensive, Emilé."

"How much?" Gallierga asked.

Pereź hesitated, which caused Gallierga to wonder where the number was coming from. "Five hundred million pesos, or two hundred and fifty thousand American dollars. They would prefer dollars, of course."

"Of course." Gallierga replied with sarcasm, but he actually felt it was a bargain, a small price to pay to exact the revenge burning in his heart. "It's agreed. Make certain they are well equipped with weapons."

23

Too Late Now

Before leaving San Juan in the King Air, Sutton filed an IFR flight plan from his hotel room. This would provide for air traffic control from St. Kitts, adjacent to Montserrat, to Cat Island, Bahamas. It gave him legitimacy in the air if he decided against trying to make the first leg of the run at low level. He listed Cat Island as a fuel stop of one hour. The second leg of the plan was from Cat Island to Orlando, Florida. He could activate the flight plan after takeoff, if he chose to do so. Any activated leg would remain in the ATC system for thirty days. Of course, even if he did activate the first leg, he would not activate the second. Then after Cat Island, he would not be in the system, and the second leg would be erased after twenty-four hours.

As he began his pre-takeoff run-up on the runway in Montserrat, he checked the systems in the big Beechcraft King Air. Everything was operating properly, and the plane idled smoothly, ready to depart. He had been debating the wisdom of activating the flight plan since he left San Juan some three hours earlier. On the one hand, the flight plan would allow him to make better time to his first stop. He could bring the big cruiser up to 22,000 feet, take advantage of better fuel economy; and most importantly, he would not have to worry about the hazards and physical strain of flying so close to the ocean surface. The King Air behaved very nicely at low level on the first leg from San Juan to Montserrat, but as usual, it was very draining. On the other hand, if he activated the flight plan, the air traffic control system would know where he was. He would need to be in contact with them throughout the flight; follow their orders for altitude and course; and close out the flight plan upon landing at Cat Island. He would be betting *against* a British customs agent or a DEA agent somehow receiving notice of his flight plan and expecting him to report upon landing.

Before pushing both throttles for the big turbines forward to the stops, he made one more review in his mind about the pros and cons of filing the flight plan. He looked at his watch; it was 2215 hours, or

10:15 p.m. eastern time. The risk, he decided, boiled down to two things: did customs or DEA have a night shift on duty at Cat Island and would they bother waiting for him when his flight plan indicated a fuel stop only? He decided the boldness of the flight plan would work in his favor. It would be unlikely that an agent would pay special attention to a flight plan. It was too obvious, too honest, and too open. Who would file a flight plan to smuggle drugs? He again confirmed to himself that sometimes it's best to hide in plain sight.

Sutton stood on the brake pedals as he pushed the throttles forward. The big Allison turbines cranked up to 100 percent power. The tips of the propellers, turning faster than the speed of sound, created a powerful racket as they worked to pick the big airplane off the ground. The airplane was big and heavy, and the shortened runway at Montserrat presented a takeoff challenge in this configuration. Sutton figured he had about 3,500 feet of usable runaway to become airborne, and he had to make a left turn immediately after rotating off the tarmac in order to stay below the radar until he reached the shore of St. Kitts. The mountainous terrain meant he had to thread his way out to the open ocean. The air was humid and warm this night, making the job more difficult, as the wings wouldn't generate as much lift.

The maneuvers he faced were not different from what he'd always done on his way into Colombia, but the King Air was simply not as nimble as his Cessna 310. He knew the next ten minutes would be challenging, requiring his undivided attention and all his considerable piloting skills. Rotation off the ground would need to happen very quickly. The stall warning buzzer would be screaming, he knew. But as soon as possible, he would get the wings flying, pull up the landing gear to reduce drag, gain airspeed, and make the required left turn. He needed to achieve 65 knots in 3,300 feet of runway. Taking off with 20 percent flaps would increase lift and decrease his stall speed, but it would also increase drag. As soon as the wheels left the ground and he passed 75 knots, he would be able to retract the flaps; but he had to time it perfectly. If he retracted the flaps too soon, the airplane would sink back toward the ground with very little margin of altitude. If he retracted the flaps too late, the increased drag would prevent him from gaining enough airspeed to make the quick sharp left turn, and he'd fly into the built up lava flow that was still present on the rest of the runway. Thirty feet of altitude is simply not much room for a sharp turn in an aircraft with a 50-foot wingspan.

When the airplane was loaded, crew members carried Ribindi from the storage building on a makeshift stretcher. By this point, he had no control of his bowels and was bleeding from his rectum. His pants and robe were stained with blood and urine, and the top of his shirt was a smear of vomit that convulsed from his mouth periodically. One of the more compassionate crew members had given the man sips of water, as it seemed he was suffering from fever. His body couldn't absorb anything and his brain was overheating. He mumbled nonsense and struggled against their efforts. He smelled of death.

Sutton leased the aircraft in cargo configuration so all of the seats had been removed except for the pilot and co-pilot seats and two jump seats aft. The cargo took up a good portion of the bay area. It was originally planned for Ribindi to sit in the co-pilot seat next to Sutton, but at this point the man couldn't remain upright. The crew laid him down in the cargo bay, still strapped to the stretcher, and wedged a bottle of water under his shoulder so that Sutton could reach back and give him a drink when he was able to. Ribindi was a distraction Sutton did not need. He considered leaving the smelly and dying Arab behind, but knew the contract called for him to be delivered. He also knew, however, that Ribindi would never see Miami alive. He'd seen enough death in his time to recognize the last stages of life and the curtain was definitely being lowered on this man. Sutton wouldn't let Ribindi's condition take his mind off the task at hand. If the man died in flight, he would simply become one more piece of dead cargo, to be unloaded by someone else.

When Sutton released the brakes under full engine power, the King Air rolled down the runway smoothly. As it accelerated, he watched the airspeed indicator climbing quickly toward 65 knots. When he reached that threshold, using about 2,500 feet of runway, he pulled back on the control yoke, only to feel the controls still mushy and hear the stall warning horn start to scream. With the weight inside and the warm air temperature outside, the plane was not yet at the airspeed where it would fly. He could see the end of the usable runway some 500 feet away in his lights, the wall of lava looming large. He'd passed the point of a 'no-go' decision, there was no turning back. As the airspeed indicator passed 70 knots, he pulled back gently on the yoke once again. The stall horn screamed again, but the airplane lifted off the pavement sloppily, just as the shallow edge of dried lava overflow passed under the wheels. He quickly threw the switch for gear up and reduced flaps to 10 percent. The plane sank slightly in the moist air, but the reduced drag helped him to gain airspeed rapidly and achieve enough altitude to barely prevent the belly from scraping against an outcropping of lava. It had been close to disaster, he knew, and it wasn't over yet. In the near distance stood a ledge of built up lava and beyond that the steep side of the surrounding mountains. He began his left turn gently, watching to be sure the left wingtip did not hit the lava as he banked. The airspeed passed 120 knots at this point and as he slid by the huge ledge of lava, he knew it was unlikely the plane would sink back to earth. Deep into the left turn, he rolled out to straight and level and held the relatively comfortable altitude of forty feet.

When St. Kitts came into view, the airport beacon for Bradford airport in his sights, Sutton felt relief. The short trip from Montserrat at just forty feet above sea level water wasn't difficult, especially after the nerve-wracking departure. But he was glad that he decided to file the flight plan. The thought of a grueling five and a half hours at this configuration wasn't pleasant. He'd have done it if absolutely necessary, but the risk assessment was a push. Hopefully, by the time he arrived in Cat Island, the customs agent would be at home in bed.

He was traveling at 275 knots, nearly 320 miles per hour, just above the surface of the ocean. He could see the familiar lights of St. Kitts, dotting the scattered homes and resorts facing the Caribbean to the southwest. It was a windy night owing to a cold front moving into the area, and the ocean below was rougher than when he flew in earlier. He'd have to fly directly into this front, but as soon as he was able to imitate climb out from the Bradford Airport, he would be facing it at 22,000 feet, and the worst part would be the decrease in ground speed as the headwinds would be in the 75 knot range. A small price to pay, he thought, for being able to turn on the autopilot and cruise along relatively relaxed.

He headed directly for the airport beacon. When his GPS indicated he was one mile from the center of the airport, he made a turn to line up with the path of aircraft normally departing and climbing out, and then pulled back on the control yoke and trimmed the aircraft for a perfect 500 feet per minute climb. As the King Air climbed through two thousand feet, he radioed air traffic control and activated his flight plan. He had a friendly and efficient chat with the controller and was then handed off to another controller who assigned him an altitude of flight level 20, or 20,000 feet, and a way-point heading which would bring him very close to the incoming traffic pattern for Cat Island. Based upon the groundspeed of 230 knots displayed on the GPS, touchdown at Cat Island would occur in approximately five hours, twenty minutes. This was a long trip for any pilot, especially since he had no co-pilot to relieve him from time to time, but he had done it many times before and under worse conditions than this. The Beechcraft had a very comfortable pilot seat and under autopilot, the airplane would fly itself.

Once he had the plane correctly set up on the assigned altitude and heading, he engaged the autopilot and leaned out the big turbines for maximum fuel efficiency at 70 percent power. All systems looked normal. After a sigh of relief he thought about the dying man in the back. He felt obligated to find out if there was anything he could do for him. After another thorough check of the instruments, Sutton unbuckled his seat belt and stood up in a crouch to take the few steps to where Ribindi lay in the throes of death. He switched on the cabin light and saw the man was obviously dehydrated with a parched mouth and a swollen tongue. He found the water bottle tucked next to him on the stretcher where the crew had left it. Sutton was reluctant, knowing he would have to lift the man's head in order to help him to drink. He decided it must be done. He'd wash his hands in the small lavatory at the back of the plane when he finished.

Ribindi drank the water ravenously, but couldn't hold it down. A soon as he swallowed, he vomited spastically. It all came back up, along with blood and black bile. Sutton was repulsed. He couldn't imagine what disease would torture someone to this form of death.

When Ribindi settled down, he looked at Sutton through glassy eyes, began an evil laugh and said, "Don't you see, black man? Allah is bringing you with me. Don't you see? It's here...it's right here...you will have it too...you will be with me SOON."

Sutton fell away from him, partly in revulsion, partly in fear. He looked at his hands and quickly walked to the rear of the airplane to wash thoroughly. As he passed by on the way back to his seat, Ribindi opened his eyes and laughed again. It was then that Sutton made up his mind. When it was time to descend into Cat Island, he'd slow the airplane enough to open the cargo door and throw the animal out. He'd probably be dead by then anyway.

Returning to his seat, he checked the instruments. His eyes moved to the darkness outside the windscreen. There was nothing to see.

"What did he mean?" he asked aloud, facing the blackness. "It's right here...*what* is right here?"

"Never mind this," he answered himself. It was only a dying man's crazy riddle. What Sutton could not get past though, was that Ribindi had said it with such emphasis, such clarity; a completely unnerving statement from a man who hadn't spoken an intelligible word for two days.

24

Sister Morphine

In the skies over the south Atlantic, no one in Keeler's plane knew that they were ahead of Sutton in the trip to Cat Island by approximately three hours. As he flew, Keeler reached out to NSA Andrews via sat phone and asked him to arrange access to air traffic control records. He needed to find out if any flight records existed for Sutton's flight into Montserrat or into Cat Island. Likewise, Andrews wanted information about current events, and Keeler gave him an earful. He was anxious, of course, that events were moving so quickly and again offered to send assistance in the form of CIA backup. Keeler felt he already had adequate firepower, and since they were headed for a British possession, it would be less likely to create a ruckus if he kept his number small. He knew it might get a little noisy when Sutton's plane was forced into the sea, but he planned to pull the Arab off the island without alerting local authorities in any way.

Andrews provided him with a direct hook up to Air Traffic Control. Keeler called and requested a read-back of any flight plans filed from Montserrat or St. Kitts into Cat Island within the last five hours. This was almost too easy. There was a King Air, N3343A, which activated a flight plan from St. Kitts at 2015 hours. The flight was en route and squawking 2312 on the transponder at flight level 20. His specific destination was the airport at New Bight, Cat Island, a Unicom airport, meaning there was no control tower or approach control. There was fuel available, but not at this time of day. Keeler checked the airport guide, which indicated fuel available from 0600 to 1800 hours only, so the pumps were closed. A curious piece of information, as the flight plan listed the waypoint as a fuel stop only. A second leg for the same flight plan was filed, the controller told him, from Cat Island to Orlando, Florida. Estimated departure time was listed at 0500 hours, or one hour after arrival at Cat Island. The controller wondered how he was going to take off again if he didn't refuel, which couldn't happen until 0600 when the pumps opened. Keeler didn't comment on the anomaly and switched off the conversation with the controller.

It had to be Sutton. He had actually filed a flight plan. With his arrival at Cat Island estimated to be 4:00 a.m., Keeler did some mental gymnastics. He looked at his watch; it was 2350 hours and they were about two hours out. Doing the math, he calculated that Sutton had departed Montserrat about an hour ago, and computed that they would arrive about three hours in advance, which was perfect. That would give them time to find Valisé a safer and more comfortable spot to wait this out; or maybe even find her a doctor. Most important, they'd be there sufficiently ahead of him to get set up and be in position upon his arrival. Keeler didn't anticipate much trouble. The three of them could certainly handle and overpower Sutton. The Arab shouldn't be much of an issue either, although being a fanatic, he might do something unpredictable. The most advantageous aspect of it, he knew, was that Sutton had no knowledge that they'd be waiting for him. If they allowed him to fly in quietly and park, plenty of opportunities would arise where they could take control of the plane and apprehend the Arab. Christian and Becker were specifically trained in this type of operation. He felt confident.

In the back of the Heron, Marty watched as Valisé slept. He felt the need to sleep as well; it had been a long and difficult day and it wasn't over, but the jarring of the aircraft would wake him again almost as soon as he began to doze.

He had killed four human beings that day, and then wondered how many people in the world had killed another human, even just one human. He had killed four. Marty could justify his actions; he was protected by the law. He had defended himself and his country. It was murder, he thought to himself, but it was righteous murder. God was on his side. He almost laughed. The other side has a god too.

Then he looked at Valisé again, lying there badly wounded but in relative calm under the influence of the morphine. When this was over, he thought, they wouldn't be able to simply melt back into the world, go to work in the morning and then meet for dinner later and tell each other of their day. They wouldn't be able to do anything normal, not ever, unless they killed her father first. But even then, Marty wondered, even if the beast was dead and she was loose of his tentacles, would they then be free? Once you've killed a human being, can you ever again be truly free?

'Very nice to meet you Mr. Becker, and what do you do for a living might I ask?'

'I'm a spy, and, well, sometimes I kill people. My girlfriend does too, but only when it's for a good reason, that's the thing. Trust me, we're spies, we know the difference.'

"What a fucked up deal," he said aloud.

Valisé stirred. He held a bottle of water near her lips. She was groggy, obviously feeling a lot of pain again, with tears in her eyes. "Martin...it hurts so bad...every time the plane bumps. That dirty son of a bitch Emilé. I'm going to fucking kill him with my own hands...I'm going to make him suffer like this...."

"I know, and I'll help you," he said. "I'm gonna go check with the Admiral, see if I can give you more pain medicine." She nodded as he gave her a sip from the bottle. Marty went to the front of the plane. The Admiral was watching the instruments and making notes on a pad clipped to the top of his leg. Christian was asleep in the co-pilot seat, but woke up when Marty bumped him as he squatted between the seats. "How's it going up here?" he asked.

"We're about three hundred and seventy nautical miles out, which puts us there in about an hour and twenty minutes. How's the patient?"

"She's hurting, swearing like a project chick, the morphine must have worn off."

"She's got spirit."

"Yessir and the bleeding stopped, so your field dressing is sparing the carpet. Should I give her more morphine?" Marty asked.

Keeler took a moment to finish what he was writing on his knee pad, then gave Marty his full attention. "Well," he said, "we're walking a fine line here. If we knock her out too much, she might be more difficult to handle when we have to move quickly. I don't know, I was hoping to find a doc when we land." He was actually waiting on a call back from Andrews, who was looking for a CIA or DEA doctor in the Bahamas. "Give her just two more drops on her tongue. She'll probably wake up again about the time we land. Be careful now, just two. After she's out, come back up here so I can brief you guys."

Marty went back and prepared the morphine as Keeler had told him. He realized that what he held in the dropper would kill her if he gave her too much. 'Poison,' he thought. Good only in small doses. When he got back to her he was holding the dropper up so the liquid wouldn't spill out. She looked at him. "What's that?"

"Stick out your tongue," he answered. "Remember that day on the beach when I got stung by the jellyfish? What was in that lotion that you put on me?"

"Aloe, and bean oil, coca paste...cocaine...in paste form. Well, it was mostly cocaine."

"Yeah, well, it really worked," he said as she stuck out her tongue reluctantly. She winced from the awful taste.

"It's liquid morphine," he said. "In a couple of minutes you'll be out again for a little while."

"Martin...listen...I have to talk to you about Emilé. I was...uh...I thought...uh...he's not..." the morphine was kicking in quicker than he imagined. Valisé felt numbness in her tongue and at the back of her throat. She swallowed hard to fight it, but her speech was slurred, and she couldn't focus. Her eyes turned glassy. "If..." and that was the last thing she said as her eyes closed and she slipped away.

Marty put the morphine back and moved up front again. "Man," he said, "that stuff works fast."

"Yeah," Keeler nodded, "now you know what Mick Jagger was talking about."

"Sir?" Marty asked. He and Christian looked at him quizzically.

"You know, Sister Morphine?" Keeler looked at them and saw no understanding.

"Never mind...before your time. Anyway, listen up." He held an aeronautical chart out so they could see it, folded so that just the portion that contained Cat Island was face up.

"Cat Island has two airports. This one on the north end," he placed his pointer on it, "is run by the government, it's like a county airport in the states. It has a British customs office with all the bells and whistles. This one at New Bight, on the south end of the island, is private. No Fixed Base Operation and no customs. Sutton listed it as a fuel stop on his flight plan."

"He filed a flight plan?" Christian asked, surprised.

"Yeah, pretty ballsy, huh? He did that so he'd look legit. And it would've worked if we hadn't been on his tail already. Of course, he doesn't know about us, at least we're going to assume that. When he shows up, he should be completely in the dark."

"We think it's just him and the Arab, right sir?" Christian asked.

"That's what she said." He nodded his head back at Valisé. "I find it hard to imagine that he would have anyone else along, not with all that weight. The only wild card we face is the possibility that Gallierga has people on Cat Island. If that's the case, it could get a little robust."

'Robust,' Marty thought, 'is another way of saying we're fucked'.

Keeler continued, "I'm fairly certain that Sutton is planning on staying the day at Cat. He's going to have to get fuel, which is only available from 6:00 a.m. to 6:00 p.m. Since he's scheduled to arrive at 0400 hours, he'll have to wait for the pumps to open. By then it will be daylight."

"So we'll be sitting there waiting for him sir?"

Keeler nodded. "The second half of his flight plan lists Orlando as his destination. There's no way he's planning on landing there during the daytime with a ton of heroin and a terrorist on board. My bet is he's planning to use his standard MO. Take off again from Cat, fly at low altitude to somewhere on the Florida coast and go in under the radar. He'd have to wait for cover of darkness to do that. And he'd need to rest, so I think we have him in Cat for the whole day."

Becker and Christian nodded their understanding.

"Andrews…." Keeler sighed as he began again. "Andrews wants us to capture the Arab without any noise. No one can know."

"Why sir?" Becker asked.

"Well," Keeler said after again debating the 'need to know' status of the two of them, and then affirming it. "At the detention camp in Gitmo, where we used to incarcerate all the terrorist POWs, the press, the Red Cross, the Geneva Convention people and even American civil rights activists are bird-dogging our interrogation methods. We have to be humane to them now. It didn't take long for the terrorists to figure this out, so they keep their mouths shut. They know we aren't going to pull their toenails out anymore. Our interrogation methods are not effective. When the Secret Service has a chance to catch somebody outside the watch, they want to take advantage of it. Their ultimate objective is to get to a new al Qaeda leader named al Zawahiri, and they figure the guy with Sutton can lead us to him - if they can get him to talk."

"What about Sutton?" Marty asked.

Keeler looked first at Christian and then at Marty. "NSA doesn't want anything to do with the heroin; he wants us to splash it."

"And we just let Sutton go?" Christian asked. "And what about the whole Gallierga operation? We have the chance to put a big crunch on that."

"We don't care about Gallierga. If we can get the Arab out of this secretly, we might throw DEA some intelligence for a mop-up operation. But we don't want the heroin bust to hit the news. We don't want to risk someone learning we have a terrorist. And as for Sutton," he continued, "he's a witness; we have to splash him too."

Marty nearly opened his mouth and let his brain flow out. The contradiction stung his mind. 'Now let me get this straight,' he wanted to say. 'Our mission is to capture a foreign national so that we can interrogate him outside the rules of the Geneva Convention and international law. In order to do this, we have to kill an American citizen, a decorated war hero who has the right to a fair trial. And since all of this has to remain secret, we can't expose a massive drug ring that would be crippled by what we know; a drug smuggling operation, by the way, that supplies America with the crap people suck up their noses and turns them into vegetables. And you want me to believe we're doing all of this in the name of what? Freedom?' He somehow managed to hold his tongue, but failed to block the twisted expression on his face.

The Admiral saw his anguish and sliced through the confusion without hesitation. "Welcome to the world of black operations, Becker, nothing makes sense here. Get used to it, or look for another place to draw a paycheck."

The plan for the interdiction was simple. They would land the plane ahead of Sutton and find a quiet corner of the ramp to park and wait. Upon his arrival, they would sit in the dark and watch his moves. If he parked his plane, they would know his plan was as Keeler guessed: he'd be there until the next evening. If Sutton had made some special arrangements to refuel and depart immediately, they would react immediately, too. Their ace in the hole was that, no matter when

Sutton left, either directly after refueling or later that night, he would not know of their presence until it was too late. After he started his engines and was prepared to taxi for takeoff, they would rush the aircraft and gain entry in any way necessary. They'd apprehend the Arab and remove him from the plane. Sutton would be told in no uncertain terms to take off immediately and not contact anyone. If he was not off the ground within two minutes, they'd tell him he and his aircraft would be destroyed where it sat.

They'd take the Arab back to the Heron, shackle him, and take off immediately behind Sutton. Then they'd follow him for a few miles out to sea. At the appropriate time, they'd pull in just above him, open the cargo door in the rear of the plane and shoot him down. Since Keeler himself would have to be at the controls of the Heron, Marty and John would do the shooting. It would be important to concentrate their firing pattern on one engine and on the wing just behind where the engine was attached. If they hit the engine, fire would spread to the fuel bladder behind it, quickly causing an explosion, separating the wing from the rest of the airframe. The plane and Sutton would then auger into the surface of the ocean, and sink quickly to the bottom.

25

Incoming

The highest ranking general in the Colombian military has privileges. He has a tenuous relationship with the civil authorities, the politicians, the President and the governors of the provinces, or, more precisely, they put up with him. The President, who is elected, purportedly by a popular vote, is not the commander in chief of the armed forces. The general has a constituency of his own in his army and he's a force to be reckoned with. If the President disagrees with him, he disagrees with the army as well, which might shorten his term of office suddenly and not by due process of law.

Pablo Corteź' brother was this general. When General Armando Corteź wanted a crew of soldiers assembled and a jet to provide transport for a drug lord, it happened; and no one dared to question him. It's all about autocracy and greed in a country of widespread poverty. It's all about the money.

The Colombian Air Force has a modest number of military fighting aircraft. There are a few surplus American F-14 fighter jets which are, by today's standard, obsolete. And since the Colombian government refuses to sign an extradition treaty with the U.S. and refuses to cooperate completely with anti-drug smuggling efforts, the U.S. has cut-off sales of military components almost entirely. The French, however, have not. And when the Colombian Treasury can afford it, the air force has purchased Mirage 2000 fighter jets from France, at $65 million per copy. The air force owns a total of four of these beauties. The reality is, there's not much use for them: it's mostly for show, for national pride. On the other hand, the government needs diplomatic and official transport and, since the Gulfstream series of jets are classified by the U.S. as 'civil' aircraft, the Colombian government has been allowed to purchase as many of these as desired, at the relatively meager price of $45 million each. The air force has three, all of them built and assembled in Savannah, Georgia, all of them with sophisticated options and very comfortable furnishings.

That night, high over the south Caribbean, Emilé Gallierga sat proudly in the right seat, the co-pilot seat, of a Colombian Air Force Gulfstream V. In the back of the jet were four mercenaries, on an 'extra' mission for the General. The extra mission tonight was paying them each one thousand American dollars, a month's salary, by Colombian military pay standards.

They were traveling at 35,000 feet, where the air is thin and aircraft move very fast. The Gulfstream was zipping along at a crisp 450 knots, nearly 525 miles per hour. This would get them to Cat Island in about three hours. They hadn't filed a flight plan. They were, after all, the Colombian military. If the plane was traveling on official government or military business, there would be a diplomatic pouch or official visit notification attached to the flight, and the Bahamian government would receive a courtesy call. There would be no courtesy call tonight, so the landing that night in Cat Island would be tantamount to a small invasion.

Gallierga wore expedition clothing: khaki pants and a finely knit dark green cotton shirt. His shoes were ankle-high leather military boots. His image was straight out of an Orvis catalog, like a gentleman on bivouac. But he was not feeling like a gentleman that night. He was in a foul mood, consternated over the things that could go wrong and holding out more than just a little fear of reprisal from the Arabs should he not deliver on his end of the deal. He had driven a hard bargain, and if he didn't meet his obligations, al Zawahiri wouldn't be interested in excuses. Gallierga was aware of the differences in objectives between himself and his partners on this venture. The Arabs simply didn't care about details. They weren't after profit for profit's sake. They needed profit to fund terrorist operations. They had a higher calling and they would not waste time with him.

There was also the matter of the passenger, the very sick passenger. Gallierga strongly suspected that delivery of the passenger was as important as the delivery of the heroin. He wondered if there was some diabolical plot this man was supposed to carry out that would now be foiled because of his illness. Gallierga put himself in the shoes of the customer. He figured *he'd* be extremely upset if it cost *him* five million dollars to ferry what turned out to be a worthless passenger into the U.S. And to hear Sutton tell it, the Arab might not live long enough to set foot on American soil. Gallierga didn't know that, at this point, al Zawahiri really couldn't care less about Ribindi.

He considered calling al Zawahiri with a report, then decided to wait. Technically, he had no obligation to assure the passenger's health. His only responsibility was to deliver him to Miami. Then he thought about Sutton, considering whether he should alert him not to land at Cat Island. Or perhaps he should just go there as quickly as possible and make sure Conrad passed through the fuel stop safely. If he believed Cat was unsafe for some reason, he'd refuse to travel further, thinking the situation too hot to continue. What would happen then? Could he land at an alternate airport? Maybe, but he had chosen the airport at Cat Island for a reason; most likely because he judged it quietest. At this point he might not have enough fuel to redirect to an alternate anyway. The worst possible scenario, he thought, would be for Conrad to somehow gain knowledge of his family having been slaughtered in St. John after he left. He might see it on a television news report or on the front page of a newspaper in a hotel lobby. All things considered, he confirmed, it would be best to let Conrad continue as planned.

But he desperately needed to arrive at Cat Island before Valisé and the American agents, although he knew he might already be too late. He also knew that the speed of the Gulfstream would put him there some two hours in advance of Conrad, allowing enough time to secure the airport for his arrival. If things didn't go well he would have no choice but to contact Conrad via cell phone and call him off. Gallierga thought a remote possibility remained that the Americans hadn't landed yet. In which case, he would let Sutton continue unaware of his presence. The situation was fluid at best. Gallierga was certain of only one thing, every minute spent in the air was one minute not spent protecting the shipment. He needed to be in Cat Island quickly. He turned to the pilot abruptly and asked, "How fast are we going?"

The pilot checked the GPS readout. "Our ground speed is four hundred ten knots...we have some headwind"

"We must go faster," Gallierga said sternly.

"I'm at seventy-eight percent power now, we will gain only another fifty knots by going to maximum power and we will use twice the amount of fuel."

"I don't care how much fuel we use. Do you have enough to get there at full power?"

"Yes, but, operational regulations require that..."

"I don't care about your regulations, go to full power."

"Sí, Señor."

"How long is it until we land?" Gallierga asked as the pilot was advancing the throttles on the two Rolls Royce jet engines. Gallierga felt the aircraft respond, the jet noise increased in pitch. The pilot then moved to re-trim the control surfaces, as the increase in throttle at the previous trim put the plane into shallow climb. He didn't answer Gallierga immediately.

"How long until we land?" he asked again, louder and more sternly.

The pilot, nervous at his insistence, reset the GPS to display time to destination. The computer recalculated based on the new groundspeed. The pilot read it from the display, "One hour, nine minutes, Señor".

"Good," Gallierga checked his watch. One hour and nine minutes would put him there at 2:20 a.m.

At 20,000 feet, Sutton was plugging along, relatively speaking. His course from Montserrat to Cat Island was on a northwesterly heading, putting him right into the teeth of the winds aloft, which reduced his groundspeed in the big twin to around 220 miles per hour. His travel time would be closer to six and a half hours, instead of the five and a half he originally projected. A more grueling job than anticipated.

In the hours of boredom during the flight, Sutton had plenty of time to think about the Arab's words. While in Vietnam, he had seen several men in the final throes of death. He had seen some be placid to the end, and some delirious from pain and medication. The onset of death can bring about great lucidity, he knew. He couldn't remember a time when delirium or hallucinations had come without the help of pain medication. It was usually morphine that brought on the craziness, but, Ribindi hadn't taken morphine that Sutton knew of. He thought again about what he said: *Don't you see black man? Allah is bringing you with me. Don't you see? It's here...it's right here...you will have it too...you will be with me soon.* Sutton remembered the look in his eyes as he spoke.

There was no craziness, no drug-induced lunacy; there were only the eyes of a fanatic, a believer, a man clearly in the throes of a horribly painful and undignified death who could think of just one thing, his god. He remembered the look; he remembered also his mouth clearly as it formed each word. The movie replayed in his head. He needed to replay it; he needed to be able to make sense of it. He needed to be sure that there was nothing in the Arab's rants he should take stock of. The replay shifted to slow motion as Sutton looked through the windshield into the dark night. The Arab's face was red and yellow against the blackness. *'It's...right...here,'* it said to Sutton slowly, each time the eyes would look to the left, and then return to his own confused face. *'You...will...be...with...me...soon.'* And then the laugh would come; a laugh at his ignorance and fear; the laugh of a fanatic hiding a sick truth.

Sutton shook the image from his mind. He checked the autopilot and the gauges, then got out of his seat and moved back toward Ribindi, who lain there in silence since his earlier outburst. His eyes were closed and his chest heaved slowly with each breath, but he was still alive. Sutton pulled his switchblade from his pocket and pushed the button. The shiny blade sprang and locked open. He took the bottle of water and dumped some on the Arab's face. Some of it went into his nose, causing him to retch and cough and spit out bile. Sutton put the point of the blade to the man's face and sliced a small gash in his cheek. "Tell me what it is that you know."

Instead of laughing Ribindi looked at him and shook his head slowly side to side. He spoke weakly as blood trickled to the floor. "It doesn't matter. I am going to Allah. He has blessed my work, he has decided. I am going."

"What have you done?" Sutton yelled, and moved the knife close to Ribindi's throat.

"Cut me...send me sooner...it doesn't matter, black man!" Ribindi screamed, and then recited a Muslim chant with his eyes closed, a prayer that Sutton couldn't understand. He went on with his mix of screaming and chanting which caused Sutton to become incensed. He was just about to plunge the knife into Ribindi's chest and silence the madness forever when the man gave out one last scream and then became silent, mouth wide open in mid-scream, watery yellow eyes looking up at the ceiling of the aircraft. His head fell to the side as he passed out. Sutton looked at his chest; he couldn't bring himself to touch him to check for a pulse, but he saw his chest heave slightly as before. Unfortunately, the filthy pig was still alive.

He sat there staring at the man for a few seconds, convinced that there was something deeply amiss. The Arab had done something;

something that Allah had praised him for; something heroic. He could hear ATC calling on the radio speaker up in the cockpit. "King Air three three four three alpha…Nassau Control."

Sutton left the Arab and for a moment pushed aside his thoughts of whatever evil the man was up to, put his headset back on, and pressed the talk switch on the control wheel. "Nassau Control, King Air three three four three alpha, go ahead," he answered.

"Three three four three alpha, turn to heading three five zero, descend to nine thousand, contact Nassau Approach on one-two-two-point-three-five for landing clearance to New Bight."

Being sixty miles out of Cat Island, Air Traffic Control was handing him over to Approach Control for landing. It was too late to dispose of Ribindi as he had hoped. He'd now too be busy descending into New Bight and landing the airplane. If he woke up later and refused to tell him what he had done, Sutton decided, he would kill him and dispose of the body somewhere on the ground.

The New Bight airport is a quiet place late at night and, as in this case, early in the morning. He had been there twice previously on trips north so he was familiar with the layout. There is no Fixed Base Operation there, only a small shack with an office for the day attendant and the fuel tank farm. The tanks hold both 100 octane aviation fuel and jet fuel. The runway itself is owned by a wealthy American manufacturer who built an enormous estate facing the Caribbean. He built the runway in order to accommodate his own jet and those of his visitors. He sold fuel to help defray the cost of the operation. The 6,000 foot runway is just long enough to land larger private aircraft, and it isn't unusual to see several corporate jets and a King Air or two sitting on the ramp when the owners fly in for a few days of vacation.

Sutton decided to park among the other aircraft and walk the short distance to town to find a room for the day. His presence wouldn't attract attention, he was sure, as nothing attracted attention there. Unlike other islands in the Bahamas chain, Cat has hilly areas and relatively dense vegetation. With this picture in mind, Sutton felt confident that if need be, he could get rid of Ribindi's body just off the airport grounds and it wouldn't be discovered until long after he departed.

He contacted Nassau Approach control as directed. The controller gave him instructions for approach to the airport, just as he had done for Gallierga's group about two hours prior and, shortly after that, to Keeler as well. Sutton would be the last to arrive. He landed the King Air perfectly, without any knowledge that he was being carefully watched from two other aircraft on the ramp, shut down, and sitting in the dark.

From Gallierga's vantage point, he'd seen Keeler and the others land in the Heron. He had no knowledge that it was them, but he began to suspect so when no one deplaned after a half hour parked on the ramp. They were quite a distance away, perhaps 300 feet, and his view was partly obscured by other aircraft parked between them. Keeler left the cabin light on briefly after landing, but there was no way Gallierga could recognize anyone inside the aircraft and within a few seconds the lights were shut down. Since he had no idea of what kind of plane the Americans were flying, Gallierga simply could not be sure, and the possibility remained that the Heron was just another private twin; perhaps a single pilot flying in to pick up his employer early in the morning and now resting in the rear of the aircraft as he waited.

Sutton rolled out on the runway and turned onto the taxiway. From their distance and in the dark, neither Gallierga nor Keeler could be certain that the plane was a King Air. But as the blades of the big turbines spun at partial throttle and Sutton taxied onto the ramp, the familiar shape was silhouetted against the early morning sky. It was him.

The other aircraft parked on the ramp were loosely scattered across the three acres making up the tarmac parking area. Since there was no attendant on duty, there were no instructions on where to park or how to line up. Most pilots were simply careful to make sure they didn't block any aircraft in, or block the taxi route to the fuel island. Aside from the three planes that had just arrived, there were four other large turboprop aircraft, three jets, and a dozen or so single engine airplanes parked in a line to the left and tied down to the ground with ropes. When Sutton came to a stop, he pulled behind a Cessna Citation jet, obscuring Gallierga's view. Inside the Gulfstream, Gallierga swore quietly at the misfortune. Sutton really could have just as easily pulled further past the jet and turned the nose to face the runway, which would have given Gallierga a full and unobstructed view.

Keeler, on the other hand, had a perfect line of sight and the three men sat and watched quietly in the dark, waiting for Sutton to make a move. They had prepared themselves during the wait: their handguns had silencers attached and their faces were covered in shoe black.

Gallierga had one goal: do whatever necessary to remove the threat of the Americans interfering in his shipment. He would follow Sutton as well, shadowing him for protection, but wouldn't make his presence known if no threat appeared. If Sutton left the King Air, he would take two soldiers with him and follow closely behind. The others would remain to keep watch over the shipment and make certain no one went near the airplane. Gallierga did not like the idea of leaving the shipment himself, but he, of course, could not be in two places at once. He decided that he'd have to trust the Colombian soldiers to keep an eye on Sutton's plane.

Sutton gathered his belongings and made sure the cargo doors were locked from inside the plane before he lowered the air-stair door. He took one last look at Ribindi before pressing the button for the door, thinking he'd surely be dead before he returned. When the stair went down, Keeler and Christian slipped quietly out of the cargo door on the Heron. Sutton walked down the stairs, not being particularly quiet, and closed the door with a key switch. Keeler whispered to Christian that he was alone and then slipped off between airplanes to keep his target in sight and follow at a safe distance. He noted that it was strange that Sutton locked the door from the outside. Gallierga couldn't see Sutton from his location, but when he saw Keeler get out of the Heron and slip off discreetly, he and two of his mercenaries did the same.

26

Hours of Boredom, Moments of Terror

Sutton knew where to go to sleep: at an inn where he had stayed on a previous trip. There was a light left on in the foyer regardless of the time of day. After several turns on the manual doorbell, a sleepy but friendly proprietor opened the door and welcomed him. He made small talk as he assigned Sutton a room. "Were you in that last plane that flew in?"

Sutton looked at him quizzically. "There was more than one plane this late?" He asked.

"Oh yes," the innkeeper said. "We hear them all you know. Gotten sort of used to it; fly right over the top of the inn when they land. We don't often hear a lot of bigger ones this late, or early, depending on how you look at it. Gotten so I can tell the jets and the turbines from the piston engines, yep, I can tell singles and twins. And the really big turbo props, probably like the one you flew in. They make a sound almost like an airliner."

"How many of them came in this morning?"

"Well, there were three. This first was a jet, no doubt about it, then a turbo prop, almost one right after the other, then another turbo prop just a little while ago. I expected we'd see a few more people looking for a room, in fact, told my wife she better start figuring on a bigger breakfast."

"I am in room four, that right?" Sutton interrupted as he looked at his key.

"Yes sir, number four, that's right, and breakfast will be served in about...well gosh...about two hours now, right up until 10 a.m., and I think she's got...Helen," he yelled to the woman in the back, "you got blueberry pancakes this morning? Yup, that's what she got."

"I won't be having no breakfast thank you, but can I have a call ta wake me up?"

"Well we don't have any phones you know, most people don't like em in the rooms, they kinda like to get away here. But we can knock on the door for you. What time would you like?"

"Four in the afternoon, that be good."

"Four it is Mister, uh…" he looked at the register, "Sutton…and you sleep well now. I know you must be tired flyin all night and all. Keep the shades down, and the ceiling fan on so that hot sun won't even bother you. It's so dark in these rooms…they were designed that way ya know."

Sutton backed out of the room as the man continued with his chatter. He must have been used to it, because as Sutton opened the door to number four a little way down the hall, the innkeeper stopped himself in the middle of his next story and concluded with, "Good night." As he closed the door behind him, he thought it curious there was no activity at the airport given all the arrivals. He concluded that perhaps the innkeeper was a little loony and probably got his times mixed up.

Keeler found a place in the dark to wait during Sutton's rest time. Outside the inn, near the small freshwater chlorine pool the innkeeper kept for his guests, he watched as a light went on in a room on the first floor. It had to be Sutton, he figured, as no one else would be up at this early. The light remained on for only a few minutes, which made perfect sense, as tired as he must be. Keeler wasn't aware though, that as he sat there and watched, a few meters behind him at the edge of a line of palm trees, Gallierga and two of his henchmen were observing him through infrared night vision goggles. Gallierga realized this was the perfect opportunity to take Keeler out; sneak up behind him and run a knife into his heart from behind, silently; twist it in as he sat there and hold his mouth closed until he bled out. He slid his knife from the sheath on his leg, showing it to one of the henchman, pointing the tip at Keeler, making a twisting motion with it, directing the thug to advance on the Admiral and complete the deed. The thug took the blade from Gallierga and rose silently, preparing to advance as directed. But before he could move a step, Keeler also rose from his crouch and moved toward the road again. Gallierga quickly grabbed the leg of his henchman, and motioned for him to wait.

In the Heron, Marty was at Valisé's side as soon as Keeler left. She remained in a dream state of morphine intoxication. He wondered how long it would last as he looked at the sat-phone Keeler had left behind, begging for it to ring. Andrews would presumably call with news of a doctor for her. He hated to leave her, or the phone, but they needed to go to the King Air and determine the status of the Arab. For all they knew, he was just a phantom; no one had seen this man in the flesh. A phantom terrorist would certainly mean a happier ending for Sutton. But surely her information was correct and Sutton's hours were numbered. He wondered how she would feel when she learned of it, imagining she was fond of the man.

As he and Christian readied themselves to depart the Heron, the phone buzzed. "Becker here," he answered.

"Becker, this is NSA Andrews. Where is Admiral Keeler?"

"Out on a surveillance, sir. He left word that you would be calling."

"CIA found a doctor for you. His name is Posada. He'll be there at 0430, look for him."

Marty looked at his watch; it was 0415. "Yes sir. Where will I find him?"

"He'll be waiting by the fuel tanks. Do you know where that is?"

"No problem, sir, I'll find it."

"Good luck," Andrews clicked off.

Marty turned off the phone. "We have to split up. Andrews has a doctor coming in fifteen minutes. You go to the King Air and I'll meet the doc." Christian agreed and they made preparations to leave.

Christian had been thinking about the Arab for some time. He couldn't just pick the lock and barge into the airplane. Surely the guy was armed.

Earlier, when they were in the meds cabinet, he had seen a stethoscope. He went back there and grabbed it, putting it around his neck. He stuck his pistol in the back of his pants and gently lowered the air stair door. They stepped quietly down the stairs and onto the tarmac. It felt good to be out of the closeness of the airplane, they each took a deep breath of the clean night air before moving on. They raised the air stairs and went their separate ways. The Colombian guards watched them deplane, uncertain of what to do or how to reach Gallierga; they decided to do nothing at present but pay careful attention to where the two Americans were going.

When he arrived at Sutton's plane, Christian saw no sign of activity through the wind screen or portal-shaped windows. There were no lights on. The Arab must be asleep. He sat under the belly of the aircraft in the darkness and considered his options. He thought it strange the Arab hadn't left the plane for some fresh air when they landed. It must be very stuffy in there at present. It wasn't a hot night, about 70 degrees, he estimated, but with no circulation the air must be lousy. He pulled out his pencil flashlight and shined it down the belly of the plane. Near the mid-section, there were four post-card sized vent scoops. These would be sealed when the plane was in flight and pressurized, but were usually left open on the ground while parked or taxiing. He quietly duck-walked over to one and put his ear up close.

He heard nothing at first and shook his head at the apparent futility of this approach. A few seconds passed when he heard a faint sound, a low groan followed by a weak cough. He put the stethoscope to his ears and rested the drum on the airplane vent. He held it perfectly still, hearing nothing for a time, then heard it again, not any clearer this time but magnified in volume by the scope. While he listened carefully for several minutes, the groans would stop and start, often followed by coughs. At one point, he heard a retching sound, as if the man were vomiting, then a pitiful whining, like a chant. And once the chant contained a group of unintelligible words, louder, followed by more coughing and moaning. He began to understand why Sutton left the plane alone. Whoever was making those noises was very sick.

Marty got to the fuel tanks a few minutes early, so he slipped into the shadows and waited in silence. Shortly thereafter, he heard the sound of footsteps, and in the light of the outdoor lamp of the airport office he could see a man with an old-fashioned doctor's bag. Marty stepped out and walked toward him. The man had long shiny black hair tied back in a ponytail, and a full beard. He wore a stylish Hawaiian shirt, khaki shorts and leather sandals. He stood much shorter than Marty, about five-foot-eight. Marty bent down at the head slightly when he approached the man.

"I'm Posada," the man said softly. "Are you Admiral Keeler?"

Marty almost chuckled. "No, I'm Becker. Are you the doctor?"

"I'm a Physician's Assistant."

Marty looked at him without saying anything, but the silence conveyed his skepticism.

"I did two tours as a medic in Afghanistan with the Secret Service. Believe me, I'm the one you want. Where's the wounded man?"

"Woman, in the airplane." Marty nodded his head in the direction of the Heron and led the way.

Back at the King Air, Christian worked at picking the lock on the cargo door. Eventually, he felt the tumblers line up and, with one last twist, was able to pull the latch open. When he opened the door, the stench nearly knocked him over. The lack of ventilation had caused the man's odor to build up and combined with the humidity, the contrast with the outside took Christian's breath away. He took his shirt off, tied it around his mouth and moved into the airplane on his hands and knees. He crawled up to the cargo and lifted the blue tarp cover. Underneath he saw the kilos of white powder stacked neatly in rows. 'Probably a hundred million sitting there,' he thought. He held his penlight in his mouth as he crawled past it and then saw the Arab lying there, tied to the stretcher, moaning incomprehensible Arabic words, clearly very ill.

Hiding in the bushes at the inn, Keeler figured Sutton was surely sound asleep at that point and there was no need for him to sit and watch the window to a dark room. He slipped back to the road and turned in the direction of the airport. Gallierga decided to stay put, and after giving Keeler a few minutes to be well in front, he sent the two guards back to the Gulfstream and took a room at the inn. Like Keeler, he had been able to judge from the action of the lights approximately what room Sutton was in. The innkeeper gave Gallierga a room directly across the hall. He lay down and set the alarm on his watch for 0700.

By the time Keeler arrived at the plane, Marty had returned with Posada and just as he started to close the door, Christian arrived as well. Posada went directly to work on Valisé, while Christian briefed Keeler and Marty on the Arab.

"I left the cargo door open," he began, "because we might want to go back there sooner than planned. There's a huge stack of drugs, in packages. I didn't taste it, but it must be the heroin. The guy is sick as hell and the airplane smells like death inside; he might not be around much longer. If he's going to be of any use to us, we gotta get him out of here and to a hospital. He's mumbling crazy Arabic, so I can't understand what he's saying. It's sort of like a chant. Maybe it's a prayer."

Posada overheard part of the report as he unwrapped Valisé's dressing. "I'm fluent in Farsi and Arabic. Tell me a little about what's going on here and as soon as I finish with her, we can go look at him…if you want."

Keeler nodded and walked over to Posada. "How's she look?"

"Who did the field dressing?" he asked back.

"I did."

"Nice job. She'll be fine. The bone is intact, but she's got muscle damage. It'll be a while before she's frolicking in the waves again. If I stitch it up now, the healing process will begin and she'll probably be up on crutches in a few days. But I'm no plastic surgeon; considering where it is, well, she might be pissed at the scar. You know how women are about their legs…."

"Just sew it up," Valisé interrupted. The pain of Posada removing the dressing and cleaning the wound had shot through the lingering effects of the morphine. "I don't want a staph infection. Get the fucking thing closed off and then give me some more of those drugs. The pig had someone shoot his own daughter. I'm gonna fucking kill him."

Posada looked at Keeler for direction, who in turn looked at Marty. "Sew her up," he said. "You have anything for the pain that's better than morphine?"

"Dilaudid. If we're going to stitch, I have to inject some to knock her out. She'll come around in a couple of hours. You might have to go back to the morphine or maybe some oxycodone afterwards, the pain will be fierce. How much time do we have?"

"Not much," Keeler said. "I need you to get to the Arab before daylight and before he gets any worse."

"Well, I gotta finish her first. I can't go see him and then come back to her. Who knows what he's got. I don't want to bring it back." He looked at Christian. "Did you touch him?"

"Hell no," Christian said, then thought to himself, 'Shit, I was close, though.'

Posada took a good look at the three of them. "You guys are filthy, clear out of here, except you Becker, go to the sink and wash up thoroughly. Then help me get the IV in her and turn her so I can get a good angle at her wound, then you get out of here too." He looked at

Keeler, "I'll need forty-five minutes. Go get some fresh air and leave the door open, it stinks in here." Keeler nodded and he and Christian left.

Posada worked expertly, applying dozens of stitches, the exit wound taking most of them. The entry side of the wound was coagulating and had stopped bleeding. He just threw a few stitches across the opening to pull it together. The exit wound was a mess, however. The skin was shredded. He tried to realign the muscle strands as he put them back in place. He sewed her as best he could and redressed the surface with meters of bandage wrap. He finished in just about forty-five minutes, as estimated.

By the time they were headed back to the King Air it was almost 0600 and the sun was beginning to peek over the horizon. In the Gulfstream, two of the guards and the pilot were asleep while one of them kept vigil, watching the comings and goings at the Heron. He watched as Keeler, Christian and Posada approached the King Air. Marty stayed behind to keep an eye on Valisé. He sat close to her in one of the passenger seats and closed his eyes. With a few moments of respite from the worry, he fell off to sleep. When the others reached the cargo door, Posada stopped them. "Now lookit, I don't know how much I'm going to be able to do for this guy. What's the deal here?"

"The objective is," Keeler answered, "to get him well enough to travel to a hospital and nurse him back to health. We want him for interrogation. We think he might have ties to al Qaeda leadership."

"I've seen hundreds of these guys over there." Posada said. "Our guys, they always thought *this one* will get us to the top." Posada shook his head with the memory. "I hope this one does."

Christian crawled in first, followed by the doc and then Keeler. When they got to Ribindi, his breathing was choppy and his head rolled slowly side to side. Posada pulled a small miner's light from his bag and put it on his head. The change in light caused the Arab to open his eyes, and then be blinded by the relatively bright light. He hollered sharply, almost gleefully. The brightness from Posada's light combined with his beard and dark complexion, mixed with the delirium from sickness and oncoming death, led Ribindi to imagine that the doc was someone or something other than what he was.

"What is your name?" Posada asked him in Arabic.

"My sweet God...I am Ribindi...I knew you were sending for me. I knew that the greatness of my deed would bring me to you. Who else has done such a vast killing? Who else will eliminate as many of them as I did? When the poison got to me too, I knew it was you. Praise God," he said in ending, and closed his eyes from the exhaustion of talking.

Posada turned to Keeler, in a whisper. "He's dying, hallucinating. He thinks I'm Allah, come to greet him and welcome him to paradise. He's done something big though. He's talking about it."

"Find out," Said Keeler. "What's he talking about?"

"Tell me about it," Posada said. "How did you do it? Tell me so I might ordain your martyrdom."

"You saw me, didn't you God? I put it in there, the poison from the bean plant, so much of it, tens of thousands it will kill, a million it could kill."

"Where did you put it?" Posada asked, wondering how long this man would continue to believe the ruse.

Ribindi was gasping his last breaths. "It's in there...in each of the packages...as he said you wanted it..."

"As who said?" Posada asked. The man was beginning to fade. His brain was starving for oxygen and the muscles in his heart, lacking fluid and glucose, were beginning to fail. He was near the final stage of gruesome death, beyond pain at this point. Posada knew he would be going fast, but not what the cause was. "As who said?" Posada yelled at him, and then slapped his face to try to bring him back long enough to get an answer. "As who said?" he slapped him again.

"Zawahiri" the dying man mumbled, and then let out a paroxysmal and convulsive squeal. His body went into a spastic flick for a few seconds and then his breathing stopped. He continued to twitch with the aftershock, but he was dead.

Posada looked at Keeler. "This guy put a bunch of poison in something. He said, 'The poison from the bean plant...it's in there...in each of the packages.' He said it will kill tens of thousands, maybe a million...said Zawahiri told him it was what Allah wanted."

"Poison from the bean plant?" Christian asked.

Posada nodded. "Could be ricin. They make it from the castor bean plant."

"What did he die of, Doc?" Keeler asked.

"Christ, who knows. He said the poison got to him, too."

"Can you tell if he was poisoned?"

"No, not for sure. Not without an autopsy. He's got symptoms of it. His pupils are dilated, but that could have been from the light. He's clearly been losing blood through his bowels; there's probably a couple of pints of it on the floor. And he's been vomiting for quite a while." Posada pulled up Ribindi's shirt; his abdomen was distended, and there were no marks on his flesh. He looked at his hands, no markings there either. His skin was hanging off his bones. "Well…he must have lost a lot of weight quickly…the blood he's been losing through his rectum…yes…could definitely be symptomatic of poisoning. It could be a lot of other things, too." Posada looked around the airplane. He saw the stacks of heroin kilos covered with a tarp. "What's in there?"

Christian reached over and pulled the blue tarp back enough to expose the white sacks.

"Holy shit." Posada said. "Must be the *packages.*"

The realization hit Keeler like a hammer. "How can we tell if there's ricin in there?"

"Can't, not here. We'd need a lab, not only that, but a quarantine lab. If it's in that stuff, you'd have to be very careful handling it. Just a speck of it will kill you." He looked back at Ribindi and nodded his head. "As you can see."

Christian dropped the tarp and moved away from the stack.

The three men squatted between Ribindi and the heroin and contemplated the gravity of the intended plot. The Arab was dead. There would be no interrogation. They would have to wait for another chance to get to al Zawahiri and that was a loss. But a more pressing task was now in front of them.

Keeler said calmly, "Let's get out of the plane. Open the air stair door. I don't want us to crawl past the stacks again." Out on the tarmac, Keeler turned to Posada. "Doc, you've been a great help. I'm not sure where we would have been without your talents. But it's going to get pretty dicey around here in an hour or so. You should bug out."

"I'll give you my cell number. If you need help, just call."

Keeler and Christian went back to the plane to get Marty. They wanted every bit of muscle to restrain Sutton. By this time it was nearly

0700 hours, the sun was shining brightly and the day on Cat Island had begun. Keeler stopped by the airport office, checked in with the attendant, flipped him a hundred dollar bill and pointed to the Heron. "We'll be departing shortly, so put in two hundred and fifty gallons, right away, okay?"

The attendant had a frustrated look on his face. "De pumper truck is down, so ya have ta bring it over here to de main pump. I have no tug either."

"All right, give me the hundred," Keeler said, ever the accountant. "I'll taxi over just before we go. But be right ready for us and I'll give it back to you." The attendant begrudgingly handed back the bill and nodded.

They walked down the road, trying desperately not to look conspicuous. When they reached the inn, Keeler pointed to Sutton's window and told John and Marty to wait for his signal. It was then 0720.

He went in the front door and quickly took stock of the cozy lobby. The innkeeper was not around, so he took the master key from the rack behind the desk and stepped quietly down the corridor that led to the rooms facing the pool. Counting windows on the outside earlier, he believed Sutton was in the third room on the left. He was unaware that behind the door across the hall, Gallierga sat listening for any activity outside. When Keeler opened the door to Sutton's room, and stepped inside, Gallierga waited. As soon as he heard the door close, he slipped out into the hall, walked directly out of the inn and turned left toward the road. Marty and Christian, who were waiting on the other side of the inn by the pool, didn't see him leave.

It was dark inside Sutton's room; Keeler stood silently and allowed his eyes to adjust. When he was acclimated, he walked over to the bed and held the barrel of his 9mm directly against Sutton's temple. He awoke with a start. "Don't move, Mr. Sutton. Don't get up until I tell you to or I will scatter your brains all over the bed. Do you understand?"

Sutton nodded carefully.

"When I tell you, get up slowly and put your pants and shirt on, we are leaving. I will have my gun pointed at you all times. If you try to escape or do anything but walk calmly, I will kill you."

Sutton nodded again, thinking his kidnapper was an American agent of some sort and the jig was up.

"Good, now get up." Keeler backed away slightly to give him room, never taking the 9mm off of him. He went over to the window and raised the shade all the way up, then partway down, signaling the others to come in. Sutton stood slowly and dressed, he was tying his shoes as the others arrived. Keeler waved the barrel of the gun for him to move out. Christian put his hand on Sutton's shoulder as if they were old friends when they walked through the lobby and out the door. Keeler walked behind, carrying Sutton's overnight bag, using it to shield the gun from sight.

They walked down the road without incident while Sutton began to consider his options. "Where we goin?" he asked, his eyes darting side to side, though his head remained still, as he looked for anything that might avail him a means of escape.

"Shut up and keep walking," Keeler replied, having already reassessed the objective, now that the Arab was dead. The most that could be done would be to send the tainted heroin off to oblivion. Sutton would be doing the delivery.

With the airport in sight, about a quarter mile away, they directed Sutton left onto a footpath through a treed area, a shortcut to the tarmac, where the planes and airport service building sat in the distance. A few steps in, Gallierga and two of his guards waited behind a hedgerow of flowered evergreens a short distance off the path. When Gallierga whispered a count of three, they opened fire, taking care not to hit Sutton. From the distance, the accuracy of their silenced pistols was less than dependable. Shots flew everywhere. Sutton ducked to the ground, while Keeler, Marty and Christian dove for shelter in the surrounding trees. The ambush had worked well. Since Keeler was the only one whose weapon was drawn, only he was able to return fire immediately. But then he took a flesh wound in the left arm, just before he found cover behind a tree. Marty escaped the barrage unharmed, while Christian took a bullet in the side, just above his left hip. Within seconds he was in tremendous pain and losing a large quantity of blood. Still, he managed to drag himself behind a tree and returned fire, but he couldn't be effective. When he looked down at the blood pouring from the hole in his side, he knew it wasn't good.

Sutton's first reaction, though he was confused and uncertain in the mayhem, was to stay low and escape from his captors. Moving from them he saw an opening for his escape. He glanced at the shooters and was shocked to see Gallierga among them, yelling for him to get to the plane. 'You don't have ta tell me twice,' he thought as he broke into a run, leaving the fray to get the King Air fired up and rolling.

Gallierga managed to slip away under the covering fire of his guards and ran full speed toward the Gulfstream. The pilot and the remaining guards were waiting for him. He told them to follow in the jet after he took off in the King Air with Sutton. He ran from the jet, but he had one more stop to make, one more piece of business to attend to. He bolted for the Heron; pulled open the cargo door, jumped inside and found Valisé where she had been laying, in and out of consciousness, for nearly eighteen hours. He leaned over and picked her up off the floor. She groaned with pain and tried lamely to resist, but it was of no use. "You're coming with me, you ungrateful piece of shit. I will need you." He threw her over his shoulder and ran to the King Air, where Sutton already had the propellers turning.

Gallierga was slightly shocked to see the Arab laying inside, dead. He put Valisé down in the jump seat which folded out from the wall and dragged the dead body out the door, letting it fall to the ground. Then he closed the door and sat in the copilot seat. Sutton let off the brakes and they began to move. Valisé was slumped in the seat still drugged, but in terrible pain.

Back on the footpath, Marty, Christian and Keeler were hopelessly pinned down. Keeler's pain was starting to increase to the point where he wasn't able to move his arm to reload his pistol. Christian wasn't returning fire either, as he was in the beginning stages of shock. Marty was the only effective shooter in the group, but the two guards had put themselves in such a good position of cover that he couldn't get a clear shot at either of them. He and Keeler were wasting ammunition, returning fire at a clump of trees, with no real hope of hitting anyone. They knew that Sutton and who he assumed was Gallierga were getting away in the King Air; they could hear the propeller tips of the big turbines spool up in preparation to taxiing. Marty worried about Valisé as well; he knew she was alone and he became desperate. Suddenly, from behind the guards, he heard the sound of a pistol, and saw the plume of fire from a gun tip in the darkened midst of the stand of trees. Within seconds, the shooting from the guard's location stopped and Posada ran out of the cover, yelling at them not to shoot.

"Where the hell did you come from?" Keeler asked, not really caring at the moment.

"I found some better pain meds for her and I found some information on ricin. I was coming back to talk to you about it. I see you've been busy."

"We have to pick up Christian and get to the plane fast. I think he's hurt pretty bad."

Marty jumped up and moved to where Christian lay bleeding and unconscious. He and Posada picked him up by the knees and armpits and carried him to the plane. The jarring brought Christian out of his unconsciousness. Posada saw that he was shot in the stomach, "Ah fuck, it's a gut wound," he said under his breath.

When they got to the Heron and climbed inside, they saw the bloodstained carpet where Valisé had lain. Marty turned to Keeler. "They took her."

In the distance, the King Air was lifting off the end of the runway and the Gulfstream was beginning its take-off roll right behind. They saw the dead Arab lying in the middle of the tarmac and heard sirens in the distance. Someone had seen the skirmish and called the Bahamian police.

Keeler's status in the U.S. Navy would have no value now. "We gotta get the fuck out of here," he said.

"Go ahead and get the engines started," Posada said. "I have to run back to the woods for my bag."

"You coming with us?" Keeler asked.

"Yeah" he said, nodding at Christian, "it's the only chance he's got."

"Well, run like hell. Those sirens aren't a welcoming committee."

Posada ran for his bag and was back at the plane within three minutes. Keeler had already begun to taxi as he was approaching, so he ran along the side of the plane, threw his bag in and jumped in after it. They taxied recklessly to the departure end of the runway. Keeler told Marty to sit in the left seat. "Have any time in this type?" he asked him.

"Only a few hours in single engine," Marty answered, "but I'm a quick study."

"Then quick study yourself onto that control wheel. My right arm is useless…you steer, I'll throttle. Just do as I tell you and we'll be fine."

"Yessir," Marty answered, focused on the task at hand, but overwhelmed with worry. He wondered if Valisé was still alive.

27

Mad Dogs

Fuel was becoming an issue for everyone, as the fracas at Cat Island had prevented all three planes from filling up. The Colombian jet was probably least in need, in principal. Climbing out from the New Bight airport behind Sutton, the junta pilot calculated his fuel range at about three hours, plus reserves. This would get him back to Colombia easily, provided he was able to ascend to high altitude where the air was thin and the jet engines would be efficient. But now, while following Sutton at low speed and low altitude, the Gulfstream was being flown in a configuration for which it was never designed and was burning fuel at a prodigious rate. Of more concern to the pilot was the fact that he took off and left two Colombian soldiers behind. It wasn't concern for their welfare, but the knowledge that when he returned to Colombia without them there would be anger and blame. He assumed that something bad had happened, otherwise they would have escaped. Back in Bogotá someone would take the fall for this, and, it wouldn't be Gallierga. All of this made him nervous about plunging any further into places unknown. If the $45 million worth of airplane he was flying ran out of fuel and ended up at the bottom of the ocean, he knew he might as well go down with it, because the welcoming party he would face back in Colombia would provide a less pleasant way to die.

Keeler had about two and a half hours of fuel remaining – not a lot considering the expanse of ocean he might need to traverse. He watched from the runway as Sutton took off and banked his plane to the southeast, staying low over the ocean. This surely was a variation from plan, as it was the opposite direction from the U.S. Sutton was probably following Gallierga's orders, whose best move, Keeler figured, would be to turn tail and head back to Colombia, although that would certainly necessitate a fuel stop. Keeler estimated that Sutton had two hours of fuel at best. Less at a low altitude.

Cruising at just 3,000 feet, Sutton was also working to calculate his range. He stayed at relatively low altitude until a plan was formulated and was therefore suffering the twin problems of lower airspeed and higher fuel burn. He estimated a total flying time of 2 hours, 15 minutes. At a ground speed of 240 knots, they had a range of approximately 540 miles, not nearly enough to return to Colombia without stopping, regardless of the altitude he chose. Gallierga wanted the jet to remain with them as an 'escort'. This would give them clear passage through ATC, but it would not exempt them from inspection and seizure if a customs official became suspicious of their purposes. Therefore, Sutton was not free to land at an international airport and tell the attendant to 'fill it up.' He needed an airport that was out of the mainstream, but with a runway long enough to accommodate the Gulfstream as well. Sutton and Gallierga assumed that the two guards left behind had neutralized the Americans. They had no idea that Keeler was behind them and he was equipped with look down radar in the nose cone of the Heron.

Keeler, who was actually only ten nautical miles behind, brought the Heron up to 10,000 feet and engaged the radar. On the screen he saw two blips, heading southeast, and moving in conjunction at the same pace. The King Air was quick, nearly as quick as the Heron and Sutton was moving very fast for his altitude, being pushed by the Gulfstream close behind. Keeler had some ground to make up and would have to put the throttles to the stops in order to catch them. Then they would be in a dogfight of sorts - two against one. Not very good numbers.

The other dilemma was that if he went to full power he would have to land for fuel soon also. Even if he caught them before they landed, he would have little time to linger and try to shoot down the King Air. If he wasn't able to overtake quickly, or they landed before he caught up, he might be so low on fuel he'd have to land behind them. That wasn't a good scenario either, knowing that Gallierga had the better numbers and they weren't all shot up.

As he watched, the first blip - Sutton, turned abruptly to a more southerly heading of 160 degrees. The Gulfstream followed, indicating that someone had made a decision. Keeler plugged the new course information into his computer and saw that they were headed directly for another island in the Bahamas chain, Great Inagua. He knew the place, the southernmost island in the Bahamas, about 80 miles north of Haiti and 120 miles northeast of Guantanamo Bay, Cuba. He also knew that the main airport in Inagua, Mathew Town, is long enough for the

Gulfstream; it had the jet fuel they needed, and it was the least attended of all public airport facilities in the Bahamas.

Keeler looked at his fuel flow meters and his tank level gauges. The big Allison turbines were devouring fuel fiercely, at the rate of 140 gallons per hour. He would make it as far as Mathew Town surely, but he'd have to get fuel there. If Sutton were to pass by instead of landing, Keeler would have to land anyway. He would be down to less than an hour of fuel.

"Okay," he said to Marty, "you're going to turn the control wheel to the right until we get to a heading of one six zero." Marty did as he was told and started to roll the plane back level at 155, so he wouldn't overshoot the desired course.

"That's pretty good," Keeler said, moderately impressed.

"Now, see these two blips on the screen?" Keeler pointed. "Sutton and the Gulfstream." Marty nodded.

"Make sure you acknowledge me with a positive *YES*, so that there's no confusion about whether you hear me or not, okay?"

"Yes." Marty answered firmly.

Keeler filled Marty in on his assumptions of where Sutton was headed and what might be necessary fuel-wise.

"If he flies past Great Inagua, we have to land, or within a short time we'll have to ditch."

"Yessir."

"And that would fuck up our day pretty good."

"Yessir."

"But we can't allow him to continue on without us, because if Posada is right and that heroin is laced with ricin, a lot of people are going to die. We can't let that happen."

Marty began to see where Keeler was headed. "Yessir," he said reluctantly.

"When we approach Inagua, we're going to descend and get closer to him. If he keeps going, we're going to shoot him down, somehow, before we run out of fuel."

"What about the Gulfstream?" Marty asked.

"We'll hope they don't see us; that we can come in from behind and get it done before the dicks in the Gulfstream have a chance to respond."

Marty knew there was a fifty-fifty chance that Valisé was on the King Air. He couldn't come up with the odds that she was still alive. But if she was dead, he figured she'd have been left behind on the tarmac, with the Arab.

"And the woman?" Marty asked.

"She's secondary."

Marty shook his head. "I don't buy it, sir. If you were on one of those planes, we'd be busting ass to get you off alive. It'd be the same with any of us. We owe her."

Keeler said nothing for a moment. He knew, of course, that Marty was right. He also knew that it didn't matter; she had become expendable. "In this business, Becker," Keeler said finally, "there always comes a time when nobody owes you squat."

In the King Air, Sutton watched his instruments as they sped toward the fuel stop. There had been no discussion about a plan with Gallierga, who was sitting in the co-pilot seat next to him. There was only his order to find fuel and return to Colombia. When he asked why Valisé had been there on Cat Island, and was now with them in the plane, badly injured, Gallierga was duplicitous. "She was captured by the Americans." He didn't add that she was one of them now, that she had actually been captured *by him*, that *he* needed a hostage. Gallierga believed, wrongly, that the Americans would not shoot them down if she was on board. But it wouldn't do to discuss any of this. One question would lead to another, which would lead Sutton to wonder about what had occurred back home that led to her capture and where his children fit into it all. That wouldn't do. He would not be a willing servant if he had unanswered questions about that. What Gallierga needed now was only six more hours from him at the controls, flying south. After they returned safely to Colombia, he would deal with Sutton. Gallierga had already decided however, their long-term engagement would come to an end after only a few more hours. In the detached atmosphere, Sutton did his job: he directed his skill toward getting the airplane somewhere relatively obscure in order to fill the tanks.

As Keeler would speculate, the Matthews Town airport in Great Inagua, Bahamas, would be Sutton's best choice for fuel. Even though it is an 'airport of entry', there aren't many tourists arriving there. Most enter at either Nassau or Freeport to the north. So it's a quiet airport, relatively speaking, usually just one airliner lands each day. At times, the terminal isn't even staffed. Jet fuel is dispensed by tanker truck and those in need of fuel call in ahead so that an attendant from town would be sent out to do the pumping. Sutton had been there several times in the past on charter flights. After rechecking his calculations and the heading required, he told Gallierga of his intention and set the King Air on course.

Valisé was awake in the back, and, though she was suffering mightily from pain, had her wits about her. She possessed only a cloudy memory of what happened on Cat Island, but was conscious when the Arab's body was dragged off the plane and dumped onto the tarmac. From this she deduced that things weren't going smoothly for Emilé, which brought a smile to her face in spite of the pain. But while wondering how Emilé had gotten to Cat Island she realized that he couldn't have been traveling alone; there must be another plane with his minions in it somewhere. Also, thinking about Marty, knowing that Emile had captured her, she was sickened. Something bad must have happened. Marty and the others must have been either badly hurt or killed.

But her instinct for survival forced her to return to the situation at hand. She sat slumped in the jump seat, looking at the back of Emilé's head in the co-pilot's seat in the front of the plane, her own head bobbing weakly with the motion of the aircraft. She thought about how much she hated the shape of his head, of how badly she wanted to smash it, end his violent and twisted existence. There needed to be a plan for this. The risks were small and she had little to lose. If Marty were gone, she wouldn't want to live anyway. If Emilé was aware of all the details of her involvement, she would soon be dead regardless. She wondered, in this vein, why she remained alive. He had tried to kill her twice already. When she was lying unconscious in the other plane, why hadn't he just finished the job there? If the circumstances were reversed, she would have taken his life in a second, without any remorse, except that she might have wanted him to suffer before the final breath left him. She felt satisfaction at this thought, but again wondered why she was still breathing.

The plane zipped along for nearly an hour as Valisé sat in her dream state of revenge. She took stock of her injuries. When she tried to move her toes on her wounded leg, she felt sure they moved, but the pain was overwhelming. Walking was probably out of the question. Then as hatred-induced endorphins were released in her blood the pain was all but washed away. She scoffed at the memory of the doctor earlier, saying that she would need plastic surgery, as if any of that could matter again. If she could kill Emilé and somehow survive, she would never have any plastic surgery. She would forever keep the scar as a symbol of his anguish, not cover it up to relieve her own.

Valisé then thought of the only possible explanation for why she remained alive: Emilé must have needed her for something. He had to believe she would shield him. She was a hostage. This energized her, for if he needed a hostage, it meant there was someone out there to fear. But she was on borrowed time. When Emilé was secure - no matter where they were headed - as soon as he returned to his sphere of influence, she would be disposed of. There was now urgent clarity of purpose.

Matthews Town airport is lightly attended: only a clerk at the terminal desk, two baggage handlers who also serve as maintenance workers, and one customs security officer. The Airport Facility Directory, the pilot's bible, directs unscheduled aircraft on approach to radio in to the customs office for entry into the country. Those in need of fuel only are directed to radio ahead on a different frequency to request the fuel truck from town. They are not required to contact customs first. It was 9:45 a.m. and the airport was beginning to heat up in the summer sun. Only the terminal clerk was in attendance, as the baggage handlers were not scheduled to report for work until later in the afternoon. When Sutton saw the green island of Inagua materialize on the horizon, he dialed in the Unicom frequency for fuel, as specified in the directory, and said over the radio "Matthews Town fuel, King Air N3318A is sixty miles inbound, in need of fuel."

A voice came over his headset, deeply steeped in a Caribbean accent, and Sutton was charmed momentarily by the warm sound of his own culture. "Yah, King Air tree-tree-one-eight, the truck be out there just in time for ya. How much fuel ya be needing?"

"Six hundred fifty gallons," he replied.

"Six-fifty, roger, we have that, it be there."

"Thank you, fuel man, three-three-one-eight out."

Sensing that they were about to land, and not in Colombia, Valisé believed that she must do something immediately. She looked around the cabin carefully for some kind of weapon, something she could use to inflict a crippling wound; something that would incapacitate him with one penetrating blow. She thought of her handbag, left sitting in Keeler's plane, a hefty steel fingernail file was inside it; stout enough, she was sure, that with the force of her weight she could drive it into the base of his neck, dig deep into his spinal cord and pith him like a laboratory frog. The electrical pulses in his brain would be cut off from the rest of his body. His diaphragm would stop expanding so there would be no fresh air pulled into his lungs. Then she could watch him die slowly, without motion, except for involuntary twitches in his legs. His brain would be conscious, but he would have no control over anything. This would drive the him insane, silently.

She could find nothing within reach to serve the purpose. But the adrenaline that was now driving her thoughts and soon, her actions, embellished too greatly her estimate of the chance for success. She had a visual of her thumbnails, long and sharp and sturdy, plunging deeply into his eye sockets, all the way into the milky gray of his brain; blinding him at the very least. It would cripple him with pain and confusion, long enough for her to get her hands around his neck and choke the life from him. She was strong, she knew it. She looked down at her two thumbs. If she could just get him close enough, thrust them at him, hit her targets and drive the little spears home, she could succeed.

The pilot of the Gulfstream had been in official contact with ATC throughout the flight to Inagua. He told Nassau control he was Colombian Air Force; that the aircraft he was shadowing was Colombian Diplomatic and that all communications should pass through him. He also requested that conflicting traffic be directed around them; in effect, clearing the way for their route. He knew that it was of very little importance at this point, that he'd already broken several international rules of diplomatic transport. But he had only one objective in sight: to get the King Air on the ground in Colombia. All other issues would be resolved by someone else. He had kept the Gulfstream throttled back to 55 percent power as they progressed, so that the much quicker jet would not over-run Sutton in the King Air. Then, when the island of Inagua came into view some 60 miles in the distance, the Colombian pilot pushed the throttles forward to 70 percent power, quickly caught and passed the King Air, and headed toward final for Runway 210 at Matthews Town airport. The pilot planned to be on the ground waiting for the King Air when it touched down, allowing the two remaining guards to make certain nothing would interrupt Sutton's refuel. He would then direct them to take off immediately again while he added a few hundred gallons to the Gulfstream tanks.

Keeler had been in contact with Air Traffic Control also, except that he did not bother with Nassau control; he dialed up Miami. This gave him the ability to ask for and receive discretionary clearance anywhere he wanted based upon his security code. He requested that Miami Control send this out in an advisory to several southern Air Traffic Control stations in the Bahamas and Caribbean, advising that he was official U.S. Military cleared, which forbid them to contact him. Thus, the Colombian pilot would not hear any 'chatter' over the Nassau ATC frequency, tipping him off to their presence.

Keeler saw an alignment change in the two blips on his radar screen. Although he had been running his engines at nearly 100 percent for the previous hour Keeler was able to close the distance between himself and Sutton by only a few miles. He knew there was no chance of overtaking them now as they prepared for landing at Matthews Town. From five miles behind them he watched as the Gulfstream increased speed significantly while Sutton's plane turned in preparation for a long final approach to runway 210. He and Marty watched this develop for a few minutes and confirmed that landing was in fact Sutton's intent. Then with his good hand, Keeler reached down to the roller ball control and moved the cursor on the radar screen to draw a box around the two blips and the yellow outline of Great Inagua. He then clicked the zoom button and after just a second of the hourglass 'think' symbol, the new screen showed a larger outline of runway 210 with dimensions and specifications appearing next to it and the two blips lined up on approach. The Gulfstream was nearly touching the end of the runway, while the King Air was still on long final approach, about three miles out.

Keeler knew his fuel supply would soon be critical. He could not count on being able to refuel the Heron. Landing behind Sutton now would turn them into sitting ducks for the Colombian soldiers in the Gulfstream, but stopping the heroin from getting back to Colombia was the essential objective. Keeler decided they had to take the maximum aggressive action. If this meant engaging the Colombian crew in a fire-fight, so be it. Political ramifications became secondary.

"Looks like you're going to get your chance," Keeler said, tipping his head in Marty's direction as he put the Heron into a shallow descent.

Marty had spent the previous hour reviewing in his mind the sequence of events at Cat Island and possible scenarios, trying to figure out something - anything - that would allow them to stop Sutton's progress and do it without having to shoot him down. When it became clear that they now had no choice but to land behind Sutton, Marty knew he might get a chance before Keeler said it, and he quickly came up with a strategy.

"Admiral, I'd like to speak freely."

"Go ahead." Keeler said.

"The way I see it," Marty began, "our mission is to both destroy the weapon, that is, the heroin, and to bring her back alive. These aren't mutually exclusive objectives now that they're landing in Inagua. If they *weren't* stopping and we were able to shoot the plane down before we ran out of fuel, then I agree, that's what we'd have to do. But that's not the case. Also, she will be a valuable informer for DEA and Customs when we get her back, just as the Arab would have been to CIA and Homeland Security. It's the same kind of asset sir, in two different wars. Now that we know they're landing, we have to try to bring her out."

"Tell me what you're thinking."

"Well sir, the Gulfstream is on the ground now, right?"

"Yes,"

"And the Colombians are likely setting up for suppressing fire, if necessary, while the King Air refuels."

"Likely," Keeler allowed.

"If that's so, they won't shoot at us when we touch down; they'll wait until we roll out, to identify us as an actual threat and, if so, let us get close enough to make sure they hit us. Also sir, they don't want to hit us on the runway and disable the plane in the middle of it, blocking their takeoff."

This was good thinking, Keeler knew, but he wondered if the Colombians were smart enough to not hem themselves in. They might very well get trigger happy and fuck themselves. "As far as we know," Keeler said, "they aren't even aware we're behind them. They were long gone before we took off."

"Even better," Marty said, "but let's assume they are expecting us."

"Okay, go ahead."

"We try to time our landing for when the King Air is in the process of fueling. They'd be most vulnerable then, because it would take longer to get the plane unhooked from the tanker and ready to fly. Also, there will be big pressure to fill the tanks to the top. They must be heading back to Colombia, don't you think?"

"I do."

"Okay, so as soon as we hit the ground, I open the cargo door and we deploy the grenade launcher that James gave us, launch one right at the Gulfstream."

"Nope," Keeler said shaking his head, "the problem is, you can't fire it from inside the airplane, the weapon has a back blast, and it'd kill everyone in here. So I'll have to stop the plane on the runway, you guys jump out and shoot."

Marty smiled, "They won't be expecting that."

"No, I don't imagine they will, but you might be shooting at your girlfriend," Keeler answered. "What if she's in the Gulfstream?"

"It's an educated guess that she's not, sir. I figure, dead or alive, she must be in the King Air with Sutton and Gallierga. Otherwise, there would have been no reason for Sutton to waste time dumping the Arab's body out of the airplane back on Cat Island. He did it, or Gallierga did it, in order to make room for Valisé."

"It's no more than a coin-toss," Keeler said.

"Yessir, but it's a chance we have to take. The Gulfstream has to be destroyed anyway, at this point, in order for us to get to the heroin."

Keeler nodded in agreement.

In the King Air, Sutton was on final for landing at Matthews Town. He had the plane perfectly trimmed out for a descending glide that would touch the plane down in the middle of the runway and allow him to roll out briefly, and taxi directly to the fuel truck. Gallierga was busy trying to spot the Gulfstream in the distance and looking for any other suspicious aircraft on the ramp. He then saw the jet parked away from the small terminal building and what he thought was the fuel truck nearby.

"I have to piss," Valisé yelled. The sudden loud voice from behind startled them, broke their concentration. Gallierga ignored her at first.

"I have to piss," she yelled again. "If you don't help me to get to the bathroom, I'm going to do it right here."

"Hold onto it, you wretch," he yelled back. "We'll be landing soon, you can do it then."

"Fuck you. You lying fucking pig…you fucking coward. I'm letting it go right here," She knew this would be more than he could sit for.

Gallierga stood up and walked unsteadily toward the back where she sat. Valisé had her good leg cocked directly beneath the jump seat. Her left foot was flat on the floor, putting her in position to thrust herself at him with all available leverage. At her sides, she clenched her fists and extended her thumbs, resting them on the seat where he couldn't see them. As Gallierga approached he saw her watching him intently, staring directly in his eyes. It was an unfamiliar look. He had never before seen her take dead aim.

When he came to within three feet she made her move. Knowing it would be her only chance, she sprang upward on her good leg and lunged at him, bringing her hands to his face with thumbs extended, heading directly at his eyes. But she wasn't nearly as quick as she had imagined, and her thumbs never reached his eyes; he saw them coming, which caused him to flinch and spoil her line. One of her nails impaled his face and dug a nasty gash in his cheek, but there was no debilitating wound to the brain. When all of her directed weight in a forward motion didn't meet any resistance, she lost her balance and fell. He pulled her up from the floor, threw her back to her seat, gripping her hard by the neck, and shook her violently.

"Why did you do this to me?" he screamed into her face. "I gave you life. I gave you everything. But it wasn't enough…you had to have it your way…you wanted my business your way. I will kill you… you fucking putan cunt." He hit her with the palm of his hand; the impact blurred her vision. Blood streamed from her nose. She thought he was going to kill her right then and there.

Sutton heard the impact of the first blow and her yelp right after it. He turned and saw Gallierga raise his hand back in a fist to strike her with greater force; Sutton could never stand the sight of a man hitting a woman. It repulsed him. He turned the control wheel sharply to the right, causing the plane to jerk abruptly. Gallierga stumbled and lost and his grip on Valisé. She fell into a heap next to the jump seat.

Gallierga regained his balance and yelled, "What was that?"

"Turbulence off the ocean." Sutton answered. "I need your help up here."

Gallierga looked at Valisé. He spat out the blood that ran into his mouth, then staggered his way up to the front and sat down. She was spared again, for the moment.

"Tell the pilot on the jet to get the fuel truck over there, I don't wanna park by the terminal," he said to Gallierga, who then got on the radio to the Gulfstream.

The wheels of the King Air met the runway with a thump. Valisé had retained a blurry consciousness, but her right eye was swelling shut and she felt blood run from her nose to the back of her throat. He was going to kill her as soon as they stopped, she was sure. In the time it took for the King Air to roll out after landing and taxi to the fuel truck, she gathered herself for one more assault. With little to lose now, but unable to fight him physically, she changed tactics.

When Sutton cut the fuel switches to the big turbines, all went quiet in the cabin. With all her strength and will she yelled out, spitting blood with her words, "Did he tell you he sent people to kill me, Conrad?" She swallowed hard to clear the blood from her mouth.

"Did he tell you about your beautiful children, Conrad? How he sent them to kill me and they died trying? Did he tell you about Jared and Anya and Yendi? They're all dead, Conrad, he sent them to kill me but they're all dead."

Gallierga shook his head with a pitiful look. "She's insane, Conrad. She's damaged in the head; that's why she went to the Americans. She sold us out. She's insane…look at her…she's crazy. There's nothing wrong with your children, my friend, they are waiting for your return. She's just trying to destroy us. It's all that she wants now."

Sutton, confused, looked back and forth between them; not knowing where this came from; not knowing if it was real. How could it be real? He said nothing, just looked at her slumped there, believing that her insanity would be over with soon. She would suffer no more, he imagined, as he looked back at Gallierga still enraged, knowing he would not be able to stop him again. Then he looked at Valisé once more. She didn't have the strength to say anything further.

They left her alone in the plane, semi-conscious. Gallierga went to check in with the pilot of the Gulfstream and to ensure that the guards were in place. Sutton went to supervise the refueling. He handed the attendant twenty, one-hundred American dollar bills. "Just fill it fast." He said.

The driver ran the large hose out of the truck, and, using a stepladder, climbed up onto the wing and threaded the fill spout to the orifice on the King Air. After climbing back down he started the pump. Fuel streamed into the plane quickly, though not nearly fast enough for Sutton's liking. His anxiety wouldn't subside until they were back in the air, because the chances of them being caught and interdicted once airborne were small. They had a military escort and would soon be flying high over open water, outside of any national airspace.

It seemed to take an eternity. As he waited, Valisé slipped back into his mind. She seemed so earnest and sincere. She must have been hallucinating horrible things from the beatings. But what about her injury, where did the wound come from? His thoughts were interrupted by a disturbance at the Gulfstream. The guards were scrambling, repositioning themselves behind the plane, and then crouching by the wheels, guns drawn and aiming at the far end of the runway. Sutton turned to see the Heron that was parked at the airport in Cat Island slowing in the middle of the runway, 500 meters away.

He watched, mesmerized, as if the action before him was in slow motion. Two men ran from the opposite side of the Heron and crouched by the tail. The propellers were still turning. One man held a tube on his shoulder, aiming it in the direction of the Gulfstream. A billow of smoke puffed from the back of the tube, followed by a pop and a hiss. Sutton was jarred immediately as the side of the Gulfstream exploded in an inferno. A second, larger explosion quickly followed, as the fuel tank in the wing ignited. The shock from the second blast knocked Sutton to the ground and he tried to clear his head from the ringing in his ears. As he stumbled to pick himself, he saw one of the guards burning in flames, running blindly, trying to escape the hell of the fire consuming him.

Sutton and Gallierga had mistakenly thought there were no risks in leaving the King Air door open. The explosion at the Gulfstream rocked the plane violently and served to rouse Valisé from her state of semi-consciousness. Over the ringing in her own ears she vaguely understood that it meant trouble for Emilé, hoped that the root of the trouble was Marty, and she was invigorated. Gathering all her strength and conviction she dragged herself across the floor toward the door. As she reached the threshold she pulled herself over and tumbled down the stairs. Unable to effectively control her fall, she slid and banged her way to the pavement. Any additional pain she felt was offset by the prospect of freedom. The possibility of survival existed once again.

The King Air was parked far enough from the Gulfstream so, that aside from some burning debris which landed on the wings, there was no major damage from the explosion. The fuel attendant, knocked to the ground by the explosion and concussed as well, got up, turned off the fuel pump and stumbled toward the terminal in panic. Sutton, knowing the importance of having full tanks, staggered to restart the fuel pump. He saw that the fill gauge indicated some 375 gallons had been pumped in. 'Enough,' he thought, and quickly disconnected the hose, throwing it to the ground, then secured the fill cap on the wing. He climbed down the ladder, ran up the air stair door and began the process of starting the engines. Suddenly the King Air was rocked again from the concussion of another explosion. The other wing tank on the Gulfstream had finally ruptured from the heat, and the 250 or so gallons of jet fuel, heated to vapor, exploded violently, sending burning shards of aluminum into the air and raining down on everything.

Valisé, now having crawled about thirty feet away from the plane, was low to the ground and thus missed the bulk of the concussion from the latest blast. She curled herself into a fetal position as best she could, hoping the debris flying around her would miss. Gallierga, stunned by the turn of events and badly concussed by the explosions, picked himself up off the tarmac and ran through the acrid black smoke, disoriented. As he approached the King Air he caught view of Valisé balled up on the ground. Although in his stupor he had nearly tripped over the pilot burning and dying back by the Gulfstream, he had recovered enough now to grab Valisé by the hair and drag her back toward the King Air, not in an effort to save her life; but to reserve the pleasure of ending it himself. She dug her fingernails into his hands as he pulled her. The pain made him lose his grip for a moment, but he regained it, grabbing hold of her flailing arms as she reached for any part of him she could injure.

Marty finally reached the scene of the explosions and slowed carefully in order to work his way through the dense smoke. His eyes burned as he coughed and stumbled, trying to find Valisé. By this time he had his shirt off and wrapped it around his face, but it was of little help. Keeler taxied the plane closer to the terminal, but his visibility was near zero also. He couldn't safely advance any further for fear of hitting Marty or another aircraft and his wound made him essentially useless as anything but a taxi driver.

Sutton, knowing there was no time to wait, started to taxi the King Air away with the stair down. He knew his life was now at stake and he needed to get airborne. As the air stair began to scrape along the ground, Gallierga struggled to get Valisé up it and inside the cabin. He yelled to Sutton to get moving as he wrestled with her. Marty heard the engines spool up to taxi speed. The smoke blinded him, and there was little air to breath. From the ear-splitting volume of the propellers he knew that the plane wasn't far away. He could feel the blades impacting the air, almost as if they were pounding on his chest. He turned around confused, the noise so great he could no longer tell direction. He looked for anything to help regain his bearings, but everything was black and gray. Instantly, he saw the wing tip of the King Air, just three inches above his head, and felt the tremendous wind created by the propellers directly to his left. He turned away from the beating blades reflexively, then moved in the direction of where he thought the body of the plane would be, hoping to grab onto something, a door handle, an antenna, anything. It was then that the bottom of the air stair, scraping along the ground, hit him in the legs and knocked him off his feet. The violent suction created by the propellers drew in some clearer air, giving Marty a few feet of visibility. As he fell, he looked up the stairs and saw Gallierga there, struggling with the last effort to get Valisé into the plane.

Lying on the tarmac, Marty pulled his gun from his waist and fired at Gallierga. The bullet caught him in the right shoulder, knocked him off balance, and he rolled down the stairs out of control. After he hit the pavement, Gallierga looked up to see the tail of the King Air disappearing into the smoke. He got to his feet and ran after the plane as it taxied into out of sight. Marty had again lost his reference completely in the black smoke. He could hear the roar of the engines but could not discern the direction in which he should run.

Sutton, meanwhile, looked back in the cabin and saw Valisé lying halfway in the door, but there was no sign of Gallierga. He immediately applied right brake to stop the airplane and turn it sideways, to get out and find Gallierga before taking off. The smoke was so thick Sutton could see nothing through the windscreen. As he set the brake and rose from his seat to pull Valisé inside the plane and go down the stairs, Gallierga, disoriented from the wound; eyes watering and blinded from the smoke and sound, closed in wildly on the airplane, unaware it was at rest broadside in his path.

When he stumbled into the spinning blades of the propeller there was nothing Sutton could do. Blood and chunks of flesh slammed into the fuselage and into the open door the blades carved a path through his body.

"What was that?" Valisé yelled, after feeling the shudder and thump and seeing the scarlet chunks spray onto her through the door.

"I think it was your uncle," he yelled over the noise.

Her smile didn't show through the swelling of her face.

Sutton realized that all that he could possibly do was to get airborne. He pulled Valisé into all the way into the plane quickly and flipped the switch to raise the air stair. He looked at the mess of her face, her bloody swollen lips and eyes, and felt no sympathy for Gallierga.

"You have to wait!" she yelled. "Marty is out there!"

"I cannot do that," Sutton yelled in answer, "you be living still, that have ta be good enough," and he sat down at his seat and quickly applied power to the engines to taxi.

Marty finally determined the direction of the King Air as the engines increased in speed. He fired his gun wildly through the smoke in the direction of the sound, but it was hopeless. Sutton had his fuel and was bugging out. Marty felt dreadful, he couldn't believe he'd lost her again. When he finally managed to locate the Heron, he climbed aboard and shook his head as Keeler met him with an inquisitive look. "He got away; I couldn't get there in time. Gallierga bought it though; it's just her and Sutton on the plane."

"Fuck," Keeler yelled.

Posada had been hovering over Christian, trying urgently to stop the bleeding, which had persisted in spite of the yards of bandages he had applied earlier. "Admiral, if we don't find a blood supply soon, he's going to die." They heard sirens in the distance.

"Well, we might have to give him some of ours. Close the door, Sutton is getting away. Becker, I need you up here." Marty thought about Valisé. She was alive, but he was right back where he started.

28

Haitian Remorse

On climb out from takeoff Sutton was confused and near panic, a state not typical for him. He tried to suppress his emotions, get a grip on the situation and assess what course would best put them out of reach of the Americans. They would be following again for sure, and they were well armed. Gallierga was dead. He couldn't continue on to the U.S. He couldn't go home. But his mission was still intact; he had the shipment and the airplane was fully operational.

Orestes became the natural choice. Definite in this decision, Sutton turned the king Air to a course of 190 degrees south, descended to about 50 feet above sea level and set his instruments for navigation to South America. After setting his course, which would take him underneath Cuban and Haitian airspace, he began to revisit the horrible things Valisé had said earlier.

There was such menace in her voice; she seemed desperate to be heard, to be believed. He wondered what had crazed her so, and shook his head as thoughts of her words crawled back into his mind. He tried to remove a visual of his family lying dead, but it persisted. It couldn't be true. It was much too bizarre to be true. He wondered about her condition, lying there in the back of the plane; hoping that he would get some answers to the riddle. But going back to talk with her was impossible at the moment.

Sutton decided to check in at the rental office. That would settle it. Anya would be there for sure and, since everything was in disarray, he should let her know he might be off the island for significantly longer than originally estimated. The King Air was equipped with only standard VHF radio equipment. As good as this setup was, a VHF signal would not reach all the way to St. John, some 600 miles to the southeast. Then he remembered the cell phone, the one that Gallierga made him carry from Montserrat, and wondered if the cell towers in Haiti or Cuba would be strong enough to attract a signal. The phone was in the seat pocket next to his leg. He reached down, found it, switched it on, and waited impatiently as the phone searched for a connection. The signal strength meter finally showed one bar, indicating that, at least signal-wise, a call could be made.

He dialed in the country code, area code, and local number for the office in St. John. The phone rang several times and until he heard the office 'away message', which was strange, he thought, as the office was always staffed at mid-day. He clicked off and dialed in the same set of numbers for his home, thinking that perhaps the girls had left the office unattended briefly and gone home for lunch. The phone rang several times, giving him a wicked sense of foreboding. Then the receiver was picked up at the other end, but the split second of relief he felt was squashed when he heard a strange voice say, "Hallo?"

"Hello?" he returned, "who is this?"

"Ahh… this is Isabella, Mr. Conrad, where has you been?" Isabella lived next door; she wept upon hearing his voice.

"Isabella? What is wrong with ya woman, why are ya there?"

"I can no tell you." She squealed hysterically, "I can no say…is so awful."

"Isabella, stop, calm down woman." She sobbed a few seconds more, trying to get control of herself.

"Tell me, what is wrong?" he demanded.

"Mr. Conrad, I duno how…ahh…they was up there, it is soo bad."

"Who was up there, Isabella? What is so bad?" Sutton felt a nauseous dread begin to build in his stomach and chest. Now afraid of what she might say, he steeled himself. "What is wrong, Isabella? TELL ME!"

"They was up there…at the Hill House…when the gun people come…they is all dead." She squealed and shrieked with the pain of death and with having to be the one to tell him.

"WHO?" he yelled into the cell phone.

"Jared and the twins…they is all dead…they was shot." She cried again hysterically, "Where is you Conrad…when is you comin home?" He let go of the cell phone; throwing it away from himself; as if it was red-hot, as if it contained a filthy disease he did not want to catch. Then he stared out into the expanse of ocean in front of him.

Everything in the world became one-dimensional. There was no depth or detail to the picture in front of his eyes.

As Keeler pulled back on the control yoke and hit the switch to retract the landing gear, his agile mind was racing. He estimated that he had approximately forty minutes of fuel remaining. In that amount of time, he would have to find Sutton and either shoot him down or force him out of the sky and into the ocean. Then he would then have to find an airport and land, or ditch his plane in the ocean as well. It was a stretch, he thought, to imagine complete success with all of it. If he could find Sutton and catch up to him quickly, bringing him down should be doable. But survival afterward posed a second set of problems.

He considered the conditions. There was a life raft and a survival kit in the cargo area. If he performed it perfectly, the Heron could be flown onto water with a lot less risk of death from the impact than if he crash-landed it in the jungle. He could leave the landing gear up, approach the ocean at a very shallow angle, pull the nose up just before contact was made, and hope nothing on the front of the plane dug in to the water and flipped it over. Skip, skip, skip, slide, stop, and then.... sink. The last part was the problem: they would have to open the doors and get out of the rapidly sinking plane very quickly to survive.

In their case, it would be tough to do anything quickly. His shoulder injury was a handicap; he had lost a fair amount of blood and had only one good arm. He might be able to get out and tread water, but he couldn't swim or assist anyone. Christian was unconscious and possibly mortally wounded. That left Marty and Posada to deal with two invalids in a plane crash. The prospect of them handling this was not good.

But thinking about crash landing was getting way ahead of the program. He first had to take care of Sutton and the cargo. Playing bumper-cars in an airplane over the ocean while traveling nearly 300 miles per hour was not on the top of his bucket list. His best chance would be to pull up above Sutton where Marty or Posada could open the cargo door and fire away with the M240B machine gun. He knew that death for Sutton, and the destruction of the heroin, however, would also mean death for Valisé. Again, he was getting ahead of the program. First, he had to find Sutton.

During climb out Keeler trimmed the airplane to execute a rapid climb to 10,000 feet. He engaged the radar, and as they passed through 9,000 he saw it: a familiar blip on the screen. The same signature they had followed into Inagua was now on a course due south, about fifteen miles from their position. He turned the Heron onto the same heading, cut back the power to conserve fuel, and nosed over into a shallow dive. The plane accelerated to almost 400 knots, very close to the maximum design airspeed, though Keeler knew this was no time to be concerned about such things.

In the right seat, Marty had been allowing the Admiral to concentrate on takeoff and the emergency situation they were in, but he couldn't stay silent any longer. "We gotta try to communicate with him, give him a chance to surrender," he said.

"I thought about that," Keeler replied. "There's no way to do it. His radio might be tuned to any of a thousand frequencies."

"Pull up next to him….wave him down. Have Posada open the door and show him the gun."

"We don't have enough fuel," Keeler said, deflecting Marty's attention to their own plight. "We've got maybe forty-five minutes at most."

"Wait, why not at least try? She's on there too…."

Keeler cut him off; there was no way to deter him. "We've been told to destroy both the heroin and Sutton. We can't let any of it survive, Becker. Andrews gave me a direct order."

At that moment, with their eyes glued to the radar screen, they saw Sutton's blip make an abrupt turn to the east. He had clearly changed his mind, decided on a new course to a different destination. The distance to target, according to the radar, was now about ten miles. Keeler turned sharply to the left to follow, surprising Marty and Posada as the plane banked over.

"Now why would he do that?" Keeler asked, mostly of himself. The chart for the area was on a clipboard on the console between them. He reached for it to check what might be Sutton's destination. The only land directly in his path was the island of Haiti.

"Doesn't make sense," Keeler said aloud, "why would he go to Haiti?"

Marty looked at him with a glimmer of hope. "Maybe Gallierga has people there?"

"Maybe," Keeler allowed. They were bearing down on him quickly, now only about three miles to his rear. And at 5,000 feet of altitude, they could see him off in the distance, indeed low to the water and heading directly for the Haitian coast, about ten miles away. His move presented a greater urgency. They could not let him get over land again, for risk of losing him. The western coast of Haiti is very mountainous and filled with virgin jungle. The heroin could survive a plane crash and be recovered. Keeler pushed the throttles to the forward stops, taking the Allison turbines to nearly 100 percent power. All the fuel he saved in the dive from 10,000 feet in the last fifteen minutes was now being chewed up at an extraordinary rate. Posada staggered his way to the cockpit as the plane bounced around from hitting the low-level turbulence at such a high rate of speed. He looked through the windshield over Keeler's shoulder and saw the King Air and the Haitian coast closing fast. Keeler said to him, "Get ready with the gun, and don't miss. That plane has to go down in the water, not over land. I'll try to stay a little above him. You won't have much time."

Posada knew what to do. "Roger," he said, and then moved back to where the gun was set up and opened the cargo door. The wind came screaming into the opening and the Heron rocked violently. Keeler struggled with his good arm to maintain control and keep the plane on path. Posada worked with great difficulty to get stationed behind the M240B, then pull the arming mechanism back and chamber the first round. He fought the bouncing and jostling; making it nearly impossible to steady the gun. As Keeler managed to get the Heron stabilized the gun barrel stopped oscillating and Posada looked over at Christian. He was bleeding profusely again as the wound had re-opened when he was thrown around violently in the mayhem. In the front, Keeler and Marty stared out the windscreen at the King Air while gaining rapidly on the Haitian coast as they bore in. Marty was burning inside.

Sutton was in a state of despair. He looked out toward the coast, wondering how it had come to this. How it could be that all of his children were dead? Gallierga had been so obsessed with finding his daughter guilty of something, of expanding his own power beyond the boundaries of reason. The result was that all the people Sutton had loved were gone. He was disgusted by his own aid to the beast and lost touch with any thread of a reason to remain alive. Despondent to the core, if he had been conscious of his own breath moving into his lungs, he would have tried to stop it purposely, just to put the pain in his soul at rest. The world was closing in around him. His visual field was reduced to just that directly in front: a one-dimensional movie played against a grainy black periphery. The drone of the engines and the whistle of the wind on the airframe faded to the background. The pain of his anguish became a high-pitched hissing envelope, overriding all his senses. It was too strong to repel, even if he had the will. He just wanted it all to stop. He had no fear of physical pain; no thoughts of tomorrow; no wondering about plans; no concern for the moment, the hour, or the day. He was dead inside; murdered by the broken words of a West Indian neighbor; dealt the final and most powerful blow to mortality; brought to a place where the silence of death was preferable to the screaming spasm of life; where the fear of death did not overcome the torture of consciousness.

A gray line of volcanic cliff marked the edge of Haiti: a stark growth rising up from the calm, blue ocean. His plane progressed toward the edge, gaining ground quickly, revealing to him more details of the face of the cliffs. He saw in the stone the answer to his need for serenity, the route to reunion with his children and the relief from the screaming in his spirit. His right hand dropped to the throttles and pushed them all the way forward to the stops. The turbines roared at 100 percent.

In the Heron above, Keeler watched as the King Air stayed at the same altitude, yet increased in speed, momentarily thwarting his attempt to catch up. Trailing by just a few hundred meters, he was nearly in a position where Posada would have a reasonable chance of hitting the plane with a volley of bullets. But then Sutton's lurch of acceleration produced the need for Keeler to do the same, in defiance of the mountains and cliffs looming at eye level two miles dead ahead.

"Don't wait," Keeler yelled to Posada. "As soon as you get a clear shot past the wing, take it."

"BECKER!" Posada yelled frantically above the howling wind coming in the cargo door and the scream of the engines. Keeler looked back to see him with blood up to his wrists, pinching flaps of stomach flesh together, trying to keep Christian's blood from spilling out.

Marty was dumbstruck. He simply stared at Keeler and made no move toward the gun.

"GET BACK THERE, BECKER." Keeler ordered frantically.

Marty looked through the windscreen at the King Air low and away, only minutes from Haiti and closing the distance quickly. He turned back toward Keeler, but didn't look him in the face.

"SHIT, I KNEW YOU'D DO THIS!" Keeler yelled.

Marty's paralysis caused him to stare at the instrument cluster in front of them. "I can't," he said in a surprisingly normal voice, then yelled, "I CAN'T!"

"GET UP AND GET ON THE FUCKIN GUN, BECKER, THIS IS YOUR JOB!"

Marty only stared out front at the King Air, refusing to move. Keeler let loose of the control yoke with his good arm, intending to strike Marty in the face with the back of his hand and knock him from his stupor. But as he did the plane jerked to the left, causing him to miss altogether as he needed to regain control with the yoke. Marty was startled by the outburst and stared at Keeler in confusion, torn by his misunderstanding of right and wrong.

"YOU HAVE TO." Keeler yelled in frustration. "IT'S HUNDREDS OF THOUSANDS OF LIVES."

"DRUG ADDICTS," Marty yelled in return, as if it made a difference, and was then consumed by sadness as he stared through the windscreen, watching Sutton's plane gaining on the coast and the window of opportunity closing rapidly. He moved to get up, stopped, hesitated, then moved again, finally getting to his feet and wobbling back toward the gun.

Marty made a half-hearted attempt to get his bearings and aim the gun through the door. "I CAN'T SHOOT PAST OUR WING," he yelled. "YOU HAVE TO GET MORE ABOVE HIM."

Keeler pulled the plane into a sharp climb, hoping to expose a clear shot. Marty struggled against the sudden change in direction, the noise, the air rushing in the door at 350 miles per hour, and the wrenching in his gut.

"TAKE THE SHOT!" Keeler yelled again, frantic that Sutton would cross the coast, unaware that he intended to fly right into it.

Marty didn't hear the fuel warning sound or see the lights for both the main and auxiliary tanks illuminate on the control panel in Keeler's face. As soon as he had a clear line of sight at the King Air with a margin for error from the wing, he led the target slightly and pulled off a volley of rounds. The noise inside the Heron was ear splitting as the big gun spit out bullets at the rate of about six per second. Marty pulled the trigger in two to three second bursts, being careful not to let the recoil bounce the barrel up to where he would shoot the wing of the Heron before hitting Sutton.

Sutton recognized the effect immediately. He'd heard and felt bullets penetrating an aluminum airframe several times in Vietnam. A few of the rounds perforated the cabin of the King Air first, but caused no debilitating damage. Two shots hit and passed through the left wing, which was now leaking fuel behind the engine, but he paid no attention to it. He was aware that someone was shooting at him and concluded that it must be the Americans, but it didn't matter as he needed to keep flying only a few thousand more feet. He unconsciously pulled back on the control yoke slightly to climb, knowing the only thing between him and the cliffs, whose image now completely filled his windscreen, would be the water below. He watched as the image grew increasingly clearer, huge cracks in the wall of rocks that represented relief from his pain, moving intensely fast toward him.

A second volley of bullets hit the rear of the fuselage and the tail section, damaging one of the hydraulic lines controlling the elevator. Though the hydraulic line that would make the airplane climb remained fully operational, the other line, the opposing hydraulic that made the plane dive, remained only partly functional. A balance couldn't be maintained. The King Air went nose up radically, attempting to climb. The sudden change in the attitude caused the wings to buffet violently as they approached stall in the relative wind. The plane did gain altitude however, quickly enough to fly above and pass by the oncoming wall of stone. But with the elevator in a radical climb position, the wings went into full stall and the airspeed bled off rapidly.

Instinctively, Sutton struggled to keep the wings level and prevent a spin. It was a natural reaction for him, stemming from thousands of hours at the control wheel. The death wish he had just seconds prior was overridden by some deep instinct to get the plane flying again. He tried desperately to bring the nose down and recover. But there was nothing he could do with the elevator stuck in the full climb position. As his forward momentum decayed and the plane sank through the sky just hundreds of feet above the ground, Sutton knew he was headed into the jungle treetops.

After nearly a final half mile of erratic flight, as the airspeed bled off at a rapid rate, the forward center of gravity of the big plane caused it to finally nose over by itself and, instead of crashing into the earth tail first, the King Air slid on its belly into the jungle. Sutton heard and felt the wings snap off tree tops and limbs, each collision bleeding off more speed, down to about 50 mph. He was a bystander now, having no control, even if he wanted it. He looked on as the nose of the plane parted the forest like a plow, until a huge mahogany tree trunk was exposed just feet away directly in his path. Finally, he got his wish. The aluminum of the fuselage in front of him crumpled like so much card-board against the tree. He felt nothing after the initial slam of the impact, but merely melted into the silent blackness of death.

Keeler had a front row seat to Sutton's demise. After Marty shot at and hit the King Air, Keeler pulled up sharply and drove the Heron into a hard left turn to get a better view of the crash that was sure to follow. They watched the King Air nose up and then settle into the jungle, though they couldn't see it hit the tree and come to a stop. Keeler then turned back toward the crash site, pressed his GPS for coordinates and stored them in memory. He flew directly over the scar that was gouged into the woody jungle carpet and could barely make out the fuselage deep within, crumpled against the tree and smoldering. After making one more fly-over, burning one more minute of precious fuel, hoping to see a fiery explosion incinerate what he knew still resided in the back of the King Air, Keeler finally realized the effort was for naught. He then put the Heron into a shallow climb and set his course for Guantanamo Bay, about 80 nautical miles to the southeast.

Marty stared out the cargo door, having no regard for the fact that their fuel situation was perilous, picturing his woman, lying in the back of the plane smoldering in the jungle, barely alive and suffering. He imagined her unable to move from the wreckage, helpless, alone, and awaiting a fiery death as fuel spilled everywhere.

Precious seconds slipped by as they flew further from the crash site. Marty looked at the parachutes hanging on the deployment rack on the far wall, jumped to his feet, then nearly stumbled over Christian while making his way across the cabin to strap one on. Posada watched the action intently, holding his bloody hands on Christian's belly. As Marty made his way back to the cargo door he yelled to Posada, "Which one do I pull? This one?" pointing to the D-ring on the main chute release.

Posada nodded, "Yes, pull it quickly, you don't have much altitude. The smaller one to the left is the reserve."

Keeler, hearing the commotion from behind, turned to see Marty at the door preparing to jump. Knowing there would be no stopping him, he said nothing, but turned again briefly to bring the plane closer to the crash site.

"Send a helicopter," Marty yelled.

"I will. Good luck," Marty put his hand on the D-ring, and jumped through the cargo door into the rushing wind.

Valisé lay In the back of the King Air, gasping for air, trying to gain control over what remained of her consciousness as the plane filled with smoke. She found herself impossibly tangled and bound up by freight netting that had come lose from the wall during all the thrashing in flight and which surely saved her life in the crash. Her first realization was that the plane was no longer airborne. Then she saw Sutton's bloody corpse up in front, smashed into the windscreen and mangled beyond recognition; then she saw light through the portal windows and green leaves pressed up against the glass. Then she smelled jet fuel and heard the pop and hiss as electronics in the cockpit smoldered under battery power. She would finally be free from this living hell if she could just manage to drag herself away from the wreck. She would also be free from it very soon anyway, if she couldn't.

Yelling loudly and fitful with urgency, she untangled herself from the netting, clawed and scratched and pushed herself with her good leg over to the cargo door and pulled the emergency release pin. The door didn't move. She reached up to the red-handled lever and with all her weight pulled downward in one last desperate effort, hoping that she had got it right. The door broke loose from its mounting and fell out into the dense jungle. She pulled herself out behind it then tried to grasp at something as she fell the few feet from the door edge and slammed to the ground. The smell of jet fuel permeated everything around her as she righted herself and crawled, grunting and moaning and sobbing, away from the sizzling heap of aluminum. Through the trees and thickets she crawled, dragging her bad leg behind her, knowing it was a race for her life.

Keeler slowed again to watch where Marty's parachute drifted into the jungle in relation to the hole in the forest canopy where the King Air went down. Through one of the cabin windows Posada watched as well, and yelled, "TWO KILOMETERS SOUTHWEST," when he saw the parachute submerge into the jungle.

"ROGER THAT," Keeler yelled back and then knew he had to forget Marty for now and concentrate on getting home. The GPS readout for distance to the Navy air base at Guantanamo Bay was 76 nautical miles, mostly over water. The electronic fuels quantity gauge showed less than 40 gallons remaining in the reserve tank. This was going to be very close. He knew that the gauges at very low fuel levels were notoriously inaccurate. He prayed the error was in his favor.

Standard procedure in this situation is to climb at a shallow angle, as altitude equals time. The Heron has roughly a 4.5-1 glide ratio, meaning that every foot of altitude lost during a power off decent would produce 4.5 feet of forward glide. If the plane had two miles of altitude and the engines ran out of fuel, there would be nine miles of glide available in any direction. Keeler put the Heron into a gentle climb. Those nine miles might prove invaluable at the end of this short flight. When they climbed through 10,000 feet, Keeler leveled off and set the engines up for maximum fuel efficiency at 65 percent power. He then radioed to the base.

"Guantanamo approach, Navy Charlie Echo 3343 heavy, 80 miles east, inbound for straight-in landing, runway 24".

"Navy 3343, Gitmo approach, negative, runway 6 is the active, call 5 mile right base for landing on 6."

"Negative Gitmo approach, I have wounded on board and fuel is low. This is a may-day call for emergency landing, runway 24."

"Uh...Roger Navy 3343. Emergency landing...Roger...Navy 3343. Squawk 0100 and ident.

"Navy 3343 squawk 0100 and ident, Roger Gitmo tower." Keeler knew that his transponder was now showing 0100 next to his signature on the controller's radar screen. He also knew the controller pressed the emergency alert button at his station and fire trucks and ambulances were now rushing out to standby next to runway 24. Two F-16 fighter jets were also being scrambled and would be flying out on after-burner to greet them.

The controller came back, "Navy 3343 identify yourself and the number of souls on board."

"Roger Gitmo, this is Vice Admiral Allan Keeler, Navy 3343 is inbound with three souls, one critically injured."

"Roger Admiral, let's see if we can't get you in here safe and sound. Please state your emergency status."

"Roger Gitmo, safe and sound would be good, fuel status is critical, anticipate power off landing at or a little short of runway 24. We are level at ten thousand; groundspeed is two-four-five. Fuel supply is estimated at two-two minutes to empty; GPS reads three-five minutes to destination."

"Roger Navy 3345. Look for traffic three-five miles bearing two-seven-zero at six thousand feet and climbing…traffic is your escort."

"Roger, will look for escort traffic. Gitmo Tower, standby for further instructions, do you copy?"

"Roger 3345, will copy, go ahead."

"Gitmo Tower, scramble a helicopter extraction team to the following coordinates, approximately two miles inside Haiti border, approximately 87 miles northeast Gitmo station." Keeler read the GPS coordinates of the King Air crash to the controller. "Team to approach twin engine forced landing site at low level. Extract one to three friendlies. Chief interest is Deputy U.S. Marshal Martin Becker. Do not, repeat, do not allow Becker to remain at the crash site. Do not harm, but otherwise use all necessary force. Do you copy?"

"Roger 3345, copy that. Scramble order sent, all necessary force for extraction, no harm. Navy 3345 contact your escort on one-two-two point six-five, see you on the ground sir, Gitmo tower out."

Marty hung from the trees, swinging from his parachute cords, twenty feet above the floor of the jungle. When he hit the treetops, the limbs and branches that broke his descent also inflicted painful abrasions on his arms and legs. As he hung there in the air, he realized he was fortunate not to have lost an eye or been impaled by the stiff woody vegetation. He took stock of his condition. His pistol remained tucked in the holster under his arm and his buck knife was still strapped to his leg. His challenge now was to unbuckle his harness and find a way to drop to the ground without further injury. He swung himself back and forth, gaining enough momentum to latch onto a large limb to his left, allowing him to unbuckle his harness, get ahold the stalk of the dense tree from which it grew, and climb down.

Once on the ground, he found the going easier than anticipated, because little woody vegetation grew in the dim light of the jungle. The worst obstruction was the gnarly vines growing upward to reach sunlight. But the visibility through the tree stalks was decent, hampered mostly by the relative darkness under the dense cover. As he floated in the parachute before landing, he saw his location relative to the hole the King Air had carved during the crash and saw a trace of smoke rising from the tree tops. The afternoon sun was to his left, the crash site in front of him, an estimated two miles away. He peered up through the trees, trying desperately to confirm his location relative to the position of the sun and head directly to the wreckage as efficiently as possible, to not get turned around. He finally got a glimpse of it, felt fairly positive of the direction he should take and set off quickly through the forest.

Urgency consumed him. His intuition told him she was still breathing: there was no absence of the deep connection he'd felt for the previous six days; no silence in his soul. She was alive, he knew it, felt it. He tried to signal to her subconsciously as he ran through the underbrush; calling upon their spirituality to communicate to her that he was near, on his way. She needed only to hold on a little while longer. "Hold on," he said out loud, trying with all his might to force the communiqué.

Busting through the underbrush frantically, he emerged onto a path, a worn route through the trees leading in the general direction he was headed. He stopped and looked down at the trail, his intensity broken by all kinds of alarms going off in his head. There were tracks there. It was a frequently traveled path; not ancient and overgrown, but freshly renewed. He drew out his 9mm and advanced slowly at first, warily, hoping there was no one ahead of him, no jungle scavengers en route before him rendering his arrival too late.

Then the explosion came, a loud primary boom in the distance that seemed to last for seconds, and then silence again. Marty broke into a dead run, forgetting about the possibility of other travelers on the path. His only hope was that she was somehow clear of it.

Valisé was, in fact, close enough to the heart of the blast that the concussion deflated her lungs, depleting her breath and sending her beleaguered consciousness into blackness once again. She became vaguely aware of hands on her, picking her up. The last thing she sensed before passing out was the intensity of the ringing in her head. All of the pain had left her. It was almost a relief, as the lights went out.

The two Haitian rebels, jungle foot soldiers who had heard the air battle rage and watched from a tree top outpost as the King Air caromed into the jungle, were carrying Valisé back to their ATV. She was their prize, scavenged from near the wreckage, but they dropped her after being knocked down by the blast. They pulled themselves up off the ground, quickly regained their bearings, gripped her once again under the armpits and knees, then made their way to the four wheeler and dumped her into the small trailer attached to the machine, wasting no time being gentle. Marty's parachute, which they also saw as the drama above the jungle unfolded, meant that someone was not far behind. One of the men felt her neck to be certain bringing her back would be worth the effort. He found a pulse. The other hopped into the trailer with her, the first swung his leg over the back of the machine to sit behind the driver. He said to the back of the driver's head, in a Spanish Caribe brogue, "Go to camp...fast." They sped off down the wider path, with Valisé bouncing around roughly on the bed of the trailer.

It took Marty nearly thirty minutes to reach the King Air, or what was left of it. The final leg of his trek was through vegetation, off the worn path by several hundred meters. He had heard the engine of the ATV accelerate away long before he neared the wreckage. The skeleton of the fuselage sat smoldering in small flames, the smell noxious, and the remaining heat on the metal too intense to approach. After a few moments of fitful helplessness he managed to peer into the cabin, now devoid of any recognizable finishes. The jump seat where Valisé once sat was just a bare burned metal frame jutting from the wall; as was the pilot seat, upholstered now by ashes of flesh and smoldering bones. Sutton's bones, he thought. He looked for the spot on the floor where the stacks of heroin once sat. All that remained was a gaping hole, burned through the floor of the fuselage where the pallet was strapped in. The intensity of the inferno was augmented by the ether contained the heroin. The drugs had been completely incinerated, and presumably, Marty thought, the ricin as well.

He searched outside the charred shell for any sign of her; for another pile of burnt flesh and bones, but found nothing. He widened his search, around the periphery of the blackened vegetation and then wider still, into the jungle, carving a perimeter wider and wider until he was circling some fifty meters away, through thorns and vines. Still, there was no sign of her. He went back to the fuselage, now cooled significantly, to look more closely; to be certain there was no remnant of her that he'd missed. His search was disturbed by the sound of helicopter blades; off in the distance at first then growing louder, approaching. He became eager; Keeler had sent help, as he promised. A Blackhawk helicopter appeared and hovered in the air over the crash site while several figures repelled down a rope slung out the door.

He went out into the jungle again, further this time, yelling her name. Then he stumbled upon a piece of white gauze with a blood stain and examined it closely. It was the same material that Keeler had wrapped around her leg in the Heron. Taking a few steps further he walked onto a narrow roadway of mud and compacted sphagnum. He yelled her name louder, trying to overcome the noise of the blades beating in the air and waited for the crew to aid in his pursuit.

The Blackhawk pulled away from the scene, to return later when summoned. As he continued to call her name, the four man unit finally reached him. He saw the tire tracks in the narrow road made by the ATV and the foot prints where it had stopped, where she was loaded. Four Navy Seals emerged from the Jungle and peered at him; the leader held his M-16 across his stomach, slung from his shoulder, but pointed directly at Marty.

"Identify yourself," he barked, looking Marty straight in eyes with deadly seriousness.

"I'm Becker," Marty said with incredulity, as if he could be anyone else.

"Marshall Becker, our orders are to return you to Gitmo immediately. There are unfriendlies here."

"I'm not leaving without her," he said, adamantly, pointing down the narrow path where the tire tracks led.

"We can do this one of two ways, deputy," the leader said firmly. "The first is you can come with us willingly, which is the smart thing to do." He moved his weapon so that it hung down his back and then put one hand on his waist and the other hand on the Taser gun holstered to his belt. The three others with him moved slightly, getting into a more coiled position, ready to move toward Marty instantly. "The second way is, well, it's not what I would choose." The leader concluded.

Marty sat down awkwardly in the damp soil, resigned, consumed by remorse. She was alive, he was sure. But she had slipped away again, taken by another enemy; this time, by an enemy he did not know, and his own people wouldn't let him go any further.

Late afternoon began to close in on the jungle as he sat there for a moment in a despondent fog, wondering if his search would go on and how he would begin it, *if* he could begin it. He couldn't imagine where she would end up now, or if she could survive yet another ordeal of capture. But the connection was still there, she was alive, he felt it. As long as that remained, so would his determination.

The leader of the extraction group spoke into the microphone clipped to the shoulder of his black armored vest, "Echo-Bravo-three-four-four, this is sea dog four, return to the extraction site poste-haste, over." Marty didn't hear the response from the helicopter, only the Seals heard it, in their earpieces. Then within just moments, he could hear the beating blades again in the distance.

29

Slip-sliding Away

With the runway at Guantanamo Bay air base in sight, out of fuel and running out of altitude, Keeler had ridden the Heron in a power off glide for nearly as far as it would go before running into something wet or hard. He managed to keep the plane airborne just long enough to cross over the rocky beach of Cuba and skid it on its belly into the unpaved area at the end of runway 24. A Navy Medevac helicopter had been warmed up directly after the tower received his emergency call from out over the Ocean. And before the Heron hit the ground short of the pavement and skidded to a stop among cactus and rubble, the helicopter was in the air and en-route.

Posada and Keeler managed to drag Christian from the wreckage before a broken and leaking canister of oxygen turned the Heron into a short lived but ferocious incendiary wreck.

The medics were the first on the scene, and given the condition of the airplane, they were amazed to find anyone clear of the disaster, still in one piece, and breathing. But Christian was fading fast. They loaded him into the helicopter and took off immediately for the thirty minute trip to Veterans Hospital in Miami. Keeler and Posada were loaded into an ambulance and taken to the base medical clinic. Marty joined them there after he was extracted from the jungle and returned to base.

Marty and Posada received treatment for their cuts and scrapes, and the relatively minor bullet wound Marty sustained at the Hill House was treated and bandaged, then they both were released. But really having nowhere else to go, they hung around the room where Keeler was hospitalized. Keeler called Will Davis at his office in Washington and briefed him about the mission. He was required to stay in the clinic for one night, in order to ascertain that no infection was growing in his wound, but if all went well, by mid-morning of the next day he and Marty and Posada would be on a Cessna Citation Jet bound for Washington and a personal briefing with National Security Advisor Andrews.

In Keeler's room, Marty was peevish, sulking silently, not saying anything in front of Posada. He and the doc were assigned quarters for the night in a secured wing of the officers housing building, sequestered as a security precaution, and two guards waited outside

Keeler's door to escort them when the time came. They thought all the fuss was excessive, but they also understood the way the Navy thinks. For Andrews, it was better to over-prepare than to be casual and then have to deal with the consequences if something totally unanticipated occurred.

Before they left the clinic, Marty told Posada he would meet him out in the hall, he wanted a moment to talk with Keeler.

"I'm going after her," Marty said after Posada left.

Keeler nodded. "I knew that," he said evenly. "But you couldn't have stayed in Haiti now, not today." He looked at Marty sternly. "You would have screwed the mission, screwed me, and screwed yourself."

"I'm going back," Marty said, "as soon as we finish your paperwork and report bullshit. I don't care about the consequences after that."

"We don't even know that she's there."

"She's in Haiti." Marty pulled the swatch of blood-soaked gauze from his pocket. "I found this in the jungle, away from the wreck." Keeler looked at it and recognized it as the same type of gauze he used to bandage her leg.

"You think she's alive?" Keeler asked, skeptically.

"I know she's alive, Admiral. Some things you just know."

"When we return from Washington," Keeler said, "we'll put something together; maybe a post-op re-con, to establish that the cargo was destroyed. Andrews would approve that."

Marty nodded and changed the subject. "I would like a security clearance to contact the hospital and check on John," he said firmly. He wasn't in the mood to show respect for rank at the moment.

"That isn't going to happen," Keeler said matter-of-factly. "But I'll send word to the FBI security chief to forward updates to you wherever we are."

Marty was astounded at how suddenly he was detached from the proceedings. The wheels of the National Security Administration had kicked in and taken over. He was now a part of the drive train and he would have to adjust to life within it. He spent a restless night in the little apartment with Posada, anxious for some kind of report on his partner and impatient to get through the coming hours and back to Haiti. At 0345 in the morning there was a knock at the door. A female agent in civilian clothes stood outside when Marty opened it.

"Deputy Becker? Sorry to disturb you so late. I'm Agent McGowan, FBI. Admiral Keeler said you would want to know some things right away."

"How is he? Is he okay?" Marty asked.

"May I come in?"

"Oh, sure, of course."

Posada was awake and out of bed also, standing in the door to his room in his skivvies. She noticed him there and he ducked back into his room to find his pants. Marty moved aside to let the agent enter and then stood in his hospital scrubs and tee shirt waiting for her to speak.

"John Doe is out of surgery. He has spleen and liver damage. They removed a bullet from his pelvis. He's critical, but they think he'll make it. They're looking for a liver donor right now."

"Aw, Christ," Marty said. "Did they say anything else? Has he been conscious?"

"I'm sorry, Deputy, that's all they told me."

Marty looked at Posada and then stared away at the floor. He broke his thought after a moment, returning his attention to the agent. "Thank you, agent uh…."

"McGowan," she said.

"McGowan…right…thanks for the report."

"No problem. Just so you know, my boss in Washington told me to keep after the hospital for reports and to deliver them directly to you. So, I guess you must have some pull. I'll probably have more to tell you tomorrow afternoon."

"Thanks, we'll be leaving for Washington ourselves tomorrow, so please forward any new reports through Admiral Keeler, okay?"

"You got it." She turned to leave and stopped just before she opened the door. "Hey, I was just wondering, what did you guys do, save the world or something?" She looked at him and smiled. "I know you can't tell me. All I can say is you guys are pretty hot property right now and a lot of doors are opening. So whatever you did, it must be good, and well…since all of us are working hard to keep things safe, it seems like somebody ought to be saying thank you…and thank God."

Posada said nothing and went back into his room. Marty just nodded as she walked out. 'It had nothing to do with God,' he thought to himself while staring at the closed door after she left. 'God would never have anything to do with any of us.'

Nor had he thought about what they had done as being 'good'. He scoffed quietly to himself, wondering how he could call it *good*, the tradeoff of losing Valisé for the sake of heroin addicts or saving Valisé and forsaking the addicts. A bunch of poisoned drugs never reached the target. So maybe you could say that's a good thing. He shook his head, repulsed by the ambiguity of it all and finding no solace in the deed, given the death he had conveyed to others. He knew he would be trying to reconcile it for a long time to come.

Marty, Posada and Keeler spent the following day traveling to Washington, meeting with NSA Andrews, Chief Marshall Davis, and Deputy Director CIA Nardacci. Marty tried to be patient and give them complete answers to everything asked, but he was aching to get to out of there; to get to Haiti. Posada was booked on a 1645 flight to Miami and then a puddle-jumper back to Cat Island. Marty grew antsy about his own plan. Keeler knew he was distracted and anxious and, as they walked out of the National Security Administration building on Pennsylvania Avenue, he addressed the topic.

"Nardacci told me he dispatched a CIA crew to the crash site to eradicate whatever might be left over," Keeler said as they walked down the long front steps, "but he's not going to pursue her after they've mopped up. Which, if you think about it, is probably a good thing."

Marty scoffed but said nothing until they reached the curb and Keeler raised his arm to wave down a taxi. "I want some time off." He said finally.

"You deserve it, we all deserve it. The standard R&R after what we've been through is thirty days. I took the liberty of talking it over with Davis. He said if you want to get out of Dodge for a while, consider it done."

"Really?" Marty asked skeptically.

"Yeah, even though nobody besides the group we just left knows about the operation and never will, you did the Marshals Service proud; you and Christian. Davis is going to give you guys a choice of assignment when you get back, so you might want to start thinking about that."

"Hopefully John will be around to make the choice." Marty said.

"The doctors say he's got a lot of heart. They think he's going to pull through."

"Yeah, he's tough." Marty nodded pensively, then continued. "I want to stay in SOG. But I got to get something settled first. I'm going to take that leave."

"I already told him that. Your transit paperwork should be waiting for you when you get back to your room. I'm flying back to Gitmo in a new Heron they assigned to me. You can fly right seat if you want, interested?" Keeler looked at him with a mock inquisitive expression, already knowing the answer.

"Yes sir, I am. Then I need a helicopter to Haiti."

"We can probably work something out," Keeler replied. "I told Andrews we need to slip back in to the crash site, take some lab samples, stuff like that. He approved."

"Uh, sir, what are you going to do?"

"He gave me a choice. I can finish my tour in Gitmo, maybe two more years, and then retire...."

"Retire? And do what?" Marty asked cynically.

"Or...he said I could head up another task force he wants to form, under the Homeland Security Act; a rapid response black ops squad outside the charter of any of the current agencies. I told him I'd have to have my pick of the crew. Know anybody who might be available?"

Marty produced as much of a smile as he could muster at the moment and said, "There might be a couple of marshalls and a long-haired CIA doc needing a job in a few weeks. I'll keep you posted."

***

Books by Dwight Mathieu

The Big Hit
No Men of God
Bella
(fall 2014)
The Club
(winter 2014)

www.dmatbooks.com

www.ingramcontent.com/pod-product-compliance
Lightning Source LLC
Chambersburg PA
CBHW021310250626
47155CB00002B/466